SAN LUCCI ISLAND

by

ROSEMARY RE

SAN LUCCI ISLAND

Copyright © 2024 by Rosemary Re

For information contact:

 BRIMINGSTONE
PRESS

Dallas, Texas, USA
www.brimingstone.press

Book and Cover design by *Brimingstone Press*
ISBN: 978-1-953562-07-4
Second Edition: June 2024

10 9 8 7 6 5 4 3 2 1

My novels are filled with travel experiences.

"To never have traveled is like opening a book and reading only the first page."

\-   Rosemary Re

San Lucci Island is the first volume of the saga. *The Vineyard* comes next.

Table of Contents

CHAPTER 1

Heather clicked off the alarm clock and stared at the ceiling. Her beach house was quiet except for the distant shriek of gulls. She reached over the cold sheets to the other side of the empty bed. She lay there, reflectively, as her hand traced her body as it became aware of long forgotten sensations. It had been a long time since experiencing the pleasure of a warm body beside her own. But Heather didn't give it too much thought anymore. It was easy getting out of the habit of making love when there was so much to do, so many plans and goals to be realized. One being the upcoming 10K run she was preparing for. Heather jumped out of bed and pulled on jogging clothes.

Outside, the new sun resembled a big orange beach ball as it rose, chasing away the darkness as it rose higher and higher, illuminating the sky. Heather inhaled the crisp air and slowly let it out through her nostrils. Rubbing her hands together, she stretched her legs. She always began her run in the same way. *Such comfort in habit*, she thought.

"Out for your morning run, Heather?"

Heather turned.

"Hi Clyde, how are you?"

"Kinda cold this morning," Clyde replied. "Better bundle up."

"I will, thanks."

Heather watched as Clyde passed her in his beat-up delivery truck, loaded with *The Seaport Gazette*. No one would have guessed that this newspaper vendor was once a famous author, having written bestsellers that were made into award-wining movies. His pen name was Zack White, with nothing but success in front of him. Yet he cracked one day at a council meeting—right in the middle of it, he began raving and screaming. Some people said it all started the night he came home and found a note from his wife and all her clothes gone. Rumors circulated that she ran off with the cook from Al's Coffee House.

After selling his large Hacienda-style home high in the hills, he disappeared from the public eye for years. The house was turned into a bed and breakfast with a beautiful view of the harbor. Clyde now lived in a small home in *Lower Mountain* and does bank commercials in addition to delivering the paper.

The skies brightened as Heather crossed behind the golf course, the horse stables, and the old Chandler Mansion. The town stirred as the street cleaners and garbage trucks alerted everyone it was a new day.

Heather drew in another deep breath and smiled when the sweet salt air reached her nostrils. She began her ascent up the first hill of the day. She would cover six of these hills in her four-hour run.

Half-way up the last hill, just before her descent, she was blinded by a shiny object in the roadside bushes. The sun was striking the mirror of a woman's compact. Scattered about, she discovered a woman's handkerchiefs with the initials S.L., lipstick, comb, pen but no ID. As Heather walked near the precipice to look over the ravine, she tripped, hurtling twenty feet down the mountainside. She checked herself—every limb was still working—no broken bones. She then realized to her horror that she had landed on something cold, but familiar. A dead woman in her twenties, smartly dressed in evening clothes, with a large shoulder bag dangling across her body...she was attractive, at one time, sans the bruises on her neck and face.

Heather climbed back up the mountain in an incredulous daze, urgently focused on getting back to town to report what she had seen. Off-season on the island, she encountered no one as she ran back.

CHAPTER 2

Heather never planned on making San Lucci her home, but a sad turn of events brought her here. *It was fate*, she thought. She was just a baby when her parents died in an automobile accident, and her grandparents raised her. They had a summer home on San Lucci Island and Heather spent wonderful summers here. When she was ready to start high school, her grandparents moved permanently to San Lucci and Heather graduated from San Lucci High School. When it was time for Heather to go off to college, she chose Casa de Alta Moda, in Rome, the prestigious fashion designing school. Although not wealthy by any means, her grandparents had put aside a sizeable trust fund for Heather's schooling. She dreamed of one day becoming a fashion designer and owning her own chain of boutiques.

She spent three glorious years in school, but it all came to an end when her grandfather died. She returned to San Lucci to comfort her grandmother. She told herself she would return to school after she had settled her grandfather's affairs, but within two months, she had buried her grandmother. The time passed and with it went Heather's desire to return to school, so when her friend Roxanne asked her if she would be willing to manage one of her boutiques on the island, she accepted with enthusiasm. She loved managing the shop and especially dressing the windows. New shipments arrived twice a month and Heather carefully displayed each lovely dress.

Even with the long hours at the store, Heather still had too much time on her hands. The nights were long and lonely, especially in the winter—with no boyfriend. Most of the boys she graduated with had left the island for more lucrative frontiers. Those that stayed were not Heather's type. She didn't frequent the local pubs, even though she was invited by Roxanne who drank the night away at Mickey's Place, Shanty Shack, or P.J.'s, Heather declined, working out at the gym, instead. She was looking forward to the 10K run in March. Perhaps it would relieve some of her sexual stress. Her social life was minimal.

Roxanne lived with Charley, but they had separate lives. They stayed together for economic reasons, since living quarters were expensive and hard to find on San Lucci. Roxanne was saving her money to purchase an expensive condo at Canyon Cove, then it was "goodbye Charley"!

CHAPTER 3

San Lucci was a small, sleepy island in the Atlantic Ocean of about two thousand people, measuring ten miles wide by ten miles long. Everyone knew everyone although sometimes they wished they didn't. A gossipy place, but that was the way the Islanders liked it. Whenever there was a birth, anniversary or death, it was posted on a store window before it appeared in the town paper. Virtually no crime—Islanders left their doors unlocked. The closest civilization "off the rock" known as the real world, was Meadowbrook—thirty-six miles away by water.

San Lucci offered a Mediterranean climate and the ideal setting for the homeless. Wally slept in the storage area of Hal's diner and did odd jobs for Hal. Bobby had his own boat, docked for over twenty years. It had no motor and numerous small holes which Bobby repaired with duct tape. He lived from month-to-month off his welfare money, which he carried in a paper bag. His wardrobe was from the local thrift shop. He wasn't always like this. The Islanders say he was once a highly respected businessman, in Meadowbrook, but suffered a great tragedy when his wife and three sons were killed in a train accident over twenty years ago. He drifted around until he landed on San Lucci Island. This once handsome, self-assured man was now a stooped wino. When he was not on his boat, he was on his favorite bench, sleeping it off.

Such sights were common in San Lucci. Whenever one old

timer died, another one arrived on the next ferry to take his place. The most recent addition was Bandana Luke, so named after the bandana he wore around his neck. He was a quiet, reserved, retired schoolteacher who maintained a low profile like the other drop-ins. He eked out an existence on the island, although no one knew where he slept. He had two pairs of slacks, two shirts and a red bandana, which were always clean. He was seen early in the mornings washing his clothes in the ocean, then laying them on a rock to dry while he bathed himself in the ocean. He attended daily mass at the local Catholic Church, then walked the rest of the day.

"It relaxes me, relieves my stress," he told one of the locals. What sad stories he must carry around with him.

The Islanders formed The Retirement Club. To join, you must donate a bottle of liquor. The members took turns buying the week's supply, then sat on the pier all day drinking and swapping stories. Its members included some very colorful characters.

Tony, an ex-marine, was a big guy with a red nose who suffered from gout. He was the town instigator and council critic. When inebriated, he turned on his Marine Hymn tape and the lyrics of "From the Halls of Montezuma to the Shores of Tripoli" can be heard all over the island. Tony wrote articles which were posted in the town's city hall-where the Islanders gathered for the latest news and gossip. Tony always signed off by "the pin{sic} of Mark Twain..." Tony never learned to spell.

Then there was Mike. He placed himself on the left-hand side of the pier where the dinghies were docked, one hand clutching his bottle, the other a sign reading "Dinghy for sale." A familiar ritual to the Harbor Patrol...they gathered all the boats, returned them to their rightful owners and returned the money to the victims. The only thing that Mike owned was the bottle he carried with him!

The bright green pier was another gathering place for

Islanders and tourists. Nestled between Angie's Fish Market and Chris's Rent-A-Boat was a long row of pay phones. On busy mornings, it resembled the New York Stock Exchange, with each phone occupied.

San Lucci sat nestled in a harbor with mountains hugging it from all sides. The architecture was tile roofing and stucco for the affluent residents, and wood roofing and siding for the least affluent. These wood sided homes were once tents in the 1800's. There was no wrong or right side of the tracks, your financial status was determined by how high in the hills you lived.

The higher you lived on *High Mountain* the more affluent you were. The less affluent lived on the *Lower Mountain.* The poor resided on Rocky Beach in old Quonset huts that were left here from the World War II military base. But this was where the segregation ended. Everyone strolled down Main Street, attended the same church, and ate in the same restaurants. The Islanders were very friendly and greeted each other each time they met, which could be as much as six times a day!

San Lucci was proud of its nice, slow pace. The Islanders were tolerant of its culture of procrastination. They even bragged about it. When Charley and Roxanne's stove went out as Roxanne was cooking her Thanksgiving turkey, she calmly wrapped up the turkey and took it to Wilma's house to cook. The stove didn't get repaired until the following Thanksgiving Day.

"No one rushes here, isn't that great? Don't you just love it?" Charley asked Roxanne with a big grin.

The town boasted of having one dentist, one optometrist, one barber and beauty salon, one supermarket and one hospital with a visiting doctor who came over on Saturday and Thursday of each week. Eye problems had to wait until the last week of each month. Toothaches—they were told to apply aspirin until the dentist returned, any day now. On Fridays, Jack, the local judge, came over. There was no shoemaker, but one wasn't needed as the uniform of the day were shorts, shirt, sandals, or sneakers.

Dress up was to don designer sneakers. You didn't need an extensive wardrobe on San Lucci as there was not much to do here. A night of drinking at the local pubs satisfied your social intercourse. For the Islanders who preferred a classier ambience, with dancing, there was The Lei or Pelican's Beak, near the island's private airport.

A highlight of the island was the big fisherman's derby held once a year in September. The fisherman paid thousands of dollars to compete in this derby. The two-day derby started at Rocky Beach and the Islanders waited, patiently, for the first big catch of the day which was announced by a loud blast of gunfire that ripped throughout the town.

The most popular island tour was Bert's Inland Bus Tours. The three-hour trip covered the island's interior. Bert was a friendly tour guide, and if you could put up with his rambling braggadocio personality, it was quite an adventure.

Bert told how sea lions strolled through the deserted streets during off-season to beg for food from the Islanders. He told about the buffalo that came down from the hills in search of water, during the drought season. His favorite story began with...

"You probably don't know it, but San Lucci was home of the famous buffalo burgers. It started when the movie industry was shooting a movie in the hills of San Lucci and needed buffalo, so they shipped over hundreds of them. When they completed the movie, they left them here to roam the hills. They rapidly multiplied into thousands."

One off-season, twin brothers Rodney and Randy went camping in the interior but didn't tell anyone, so no one missed them when they didn't return after several weeks. They didn't know the area, had no maps, and got lost. When they ran out of their meager rations, they killed a baby buffalo, skinned it and cooked it slowly over the fire. They discovered that the meat was lean and sweet. As soon as they found their way back to town, they opened up the island's first buffalo burger place known as

"Ranrod's Buffalo Restaurant."

Now, about twice a year, the truck rounds up a bunch of buffalo for their trip to Meadowbrook's slaughterhouse. They get shipped back a bit shrunk, of course." Bert got a big laugh here.

Bert was a tour bus driver for eight years. Every year, he said he was leaving, but each season found him right back behind the wheel of his bus. He knew everything there was to know about the island and what he didn't know, he made up.

San Lucci was an expensive place to live and sacrifices had to be made. Most Islanders had more than one job. Where else would you find the president of the local bank extending you a business loan in the mornings and selling you a dress in his clothing store that same evening? Bert doubled as a tour bus driver and a mortician. Sharon worked in a boutique shop and as justice of the peace. That was the only way one survived, living in this paradise. After a few seasons, the Islanders left only to return in a couple of years to try life again. San Lucci hosted some famous locals. Several individuals went over to Meadowbrook where they made a name for themselves, then returned to San Lucci to retire. Old Kurt Fendon was well known for his appliance commercials and was now the town's official greeter. Peter Pierson played the suave playboy, Robert, on the soap opera, "This is My Life." He now owned the local ice cream shop.

CHAPTER 4

"Damn it, Ernest, where are my onions? I told you; I wanted lots of onions," Deputy Sheriff Dan Dawson shouted at his deputy, Ernest Frye. "They were out of onions, because the barge never came in."

Ernest hated the way Dan ordered him around like an errand boy. It was another quiet afternoon in the Sheriff's Department. They didn't expect anything to happen. Nothing ever did. The last big, exciting day was a month ago when Betsy's cat was reported missing. The next day, they found it 'hanging' out in cat's alley, a place where all the strays went, about thirty of them. "The Cat Man", an old hermit, fed them. When they thought they had located Betsy's cat and tried to retrieve it, the other cats panicked, hissed and jumped all over them. By the time they arrived at Betsy's house with what they thought was her cat, they had scratches all over them. Betsy answered the door, holding her cat which had returned during the night!

Deputy Dawson had been with the Sheriff's Department for the past ten years. He was born and raised in San Lucci and attended the local high school. Because of his pugnacious personality, he was not well liked. When classmates teased him about being fat, he told them he was just big boned, but they laughed and made fun of him. He vowed he would get back at them and when he became deputy sheriff, he was true to his word. He was a vindictive man while hiding behind his badge. He scouted around the town and, while off duty, crept up on his former classmates and made their lives a living hell. He instigated fights and when they took the bait, he hauled them off to jail. Referred to as "The Crime Buster", he was eventually transferred off the island, but no one was sorry to see him go.

...

Heather pushed open the glass doors to the Sheriff's Department panting and blurted out such a loud and rapid barrage of words that Dan put up his hand to slow her down.

"Whoa there, Heather, take it easy. What is the problem?"

"I was running in the hills. You see, I'm getting ready for the 10K run in March, and anyway, something caught my eye. I didn't know what it was at first but then it blinded me and then I kept looking and...and I slid and landed right on top of a dead body!" Heather struggled to get the words out.

"Okay, okay," said Dan. "That's enough. Let's back up and fill out this report. Phone number?"

"Oh, is that necessary?" Heather became increasingly aggravated by the deputy's blasé manner.

"Listen, Heather, if you want me to take your story seriously, I suggest you cooperate," Dan said.

Heather never liked Dan but knew if she expected him to listen to her, she had better answer his questions. After completing the two-page report, Dan rose and showed Heather the door.

"I think that's it for now, young lady. We'll take it from here."

"But don't you want me to show you the exact spot?"

"That won't be necessary. I've lived here all my life and know every ridge and gully on San Lucci Island. I'm sure I can find it." Dan slammed the door after her.

Heather stared at the closed door in bewilderment as heat flooded her face and she clenched her teeth.

"That bastard doesn't give a damn. He just wants to get back to his lunch," she yelled back at the door.

Heather watched through the glass door as Dan, with his feet on the desk, leaned back in his chair and calmly ate his lunch. Ernest had a scowl on his face as he looked at Dan after the way he spoke to Heather and asked. "Don't you think we should go up to Fork Road where Heather discovered the body?"

"All in due time. Anyhow what's the rush? The way I see it, a dead body is a dead body no matter how you look at it...how much deader can it get?"

Dan howled at what he considered a witty remark. Ernest looked away in disgust. Dan noticed the way Ernest looked at him and didn't like it.

"Ernest, you're new to San Lucci so I'm gonna excuse you, this time," Dan said in a patronizing tone.

"But, you see, here in San Lucci, we take it easy. No one rushes or gets excited about anything. Know what I mean? Now, I've lived here all my life and that's the way it has always been. See? Now, you come along and want to change things. Tsk, tsk. Now, you expect me to just drop everything I'm doing and run up there?"

Ernest began to speak up and say that Dan wasn't doing anything, but Dan raised his hand to stop him.

"Now Ernest, I know what you're gonna say. You think I'm not doing anything, but you see, you just missed my point. On San Lucci, we've established a certain attitude, a certain kinda way of doing things and we all, yes all of us operate the same way or we just wouldn't be here, now would we?" He paused and observed Ernest's reaction, and satisfied that it was neutral, he continued.

"Okay, as I was saying...if we was to get excited and rush out of here every time something happened, we would be altering our flow, know what I mean?" Dan paused again, then relented. "Okay, get your hat."

CHAPTER 5

The shopkeepers on Main Street scurried about getting their stores ready. It should be a good sales day because today was cruise day—twice a week, the cruise ships came into port for a one day stop-over on their way to the other islands.

The shop owners were switching their signs to read, "half-off today." If only the tourists knew that the items selling for sixty dollars today sold for forty dollars on regular days! That's the way it was on San Lucci. In order to survive, someone had to pay for the barge bringing merchandise over.

The Islanders knew this and took the ferry "off the rock" to Meadowbrook once a month and brought back supplies. The boats' low, moaning horn sent out a proclamation throughout the town. The store owners visualized dollar signs as their eyes resembled vultures descending on their prey.

Charley and Eddie, the local musicians, put out their tip jar. They always made out well when the tip ship (as they called it) came in.

"Hi, neighbor. My name is Charley and I am on the keyboard. And this here is Eddie, on the guitar, and we are The Neighborhood Band. We're all neighbors in this big, old crazy world of ours, so why not turn to the person next to you and say, Hi neighbor."

They began their theme song—*Thirty-six miles across the*

sea—San Lucci Island waits for me—Romance, Romance, Romance—It's the Island of Romance. The Islanders and the tourists drifted in from all over, attracted by the lovely music coming from Main Street. Earl, the town's town guide, was posted at the far end of the pier and greeted the shore boat bringing the tourists over from the ship. They were given the grand San Lucci tour starting on Main Street where TNB had been entertaining passersby for years.

Charley, the younger of the two, played keyboard and sang. He loved the island, and everyone was just great as far as he was concerned. He never complained...he just went with the flow. He had a long gray-white beard and flowing shoulder-length hair, covered by a baseball hat. He wore the same shirt, slacks and sandals almost every day. His demeanor reflected the laid-back persona so prevalent in San Lucci. Looking at him now, you would never guess he once attended a prestigious San Francisco College. Riots were the climate of the day and smoking pot was hip. Charley was expelled. He arrived on San Lucci one balmy weekend and never left. He worked just enough to sustain his modest existence and he still had plenty of time to play his music. As long as he had his six pack and his pot, he was a happy man.

Eddie was the complete opposite. Never married and looked every bit the carefree bachelor with his bright eyes and captivating smile. Six-two, lean and tan, Eddie played racquetball at his private health club in Meadowbrook. His fit body and boyish personality belied his sixty-two years. His shock silver hair and blue eyes enhanced his debonair look. His grand persona attracted the ladies. He dressed in white linen pants, a blue nautical print shirt, white loafers and a white straw hat. His fingers flew across his guitar strings, similar to the style of the great guitarist, the late Joe Pass.

Eddie was the descendant of one of the pioneers of the island and was heir to the Chandler sugar empire. He maintained a residence on *High Mountain*. He traveled eight months out of every year and returned each summer to play with Charley.

The moment Betsy heard the music, she tied her cat named "Dog" to a grocery cart, lifted her skirt and danced. Betsy was a short, fat woman in her late sixties with stringy blonde hair. She always wore a Hawaiian Muumuu with a flower behind one ear. She looked like she could have used a good bath. She shook her hips and flirted with the young men. Occasionally, she would go too far and would start to perform a striptease. That was when she was taken in for her treatment, at the sanitarium, in Meadowbrook. It wasn't that Betsy was clinically crazy, she just went crazy from too much island living!

Maggie also loved to dance to the local music. Maggie, the town's former telephone operator was a small woman with lovely legs. She was once in the dance follies in New York City, back then she moved like a much younger woman. Maggie was now in her seventies and also liked to shake her body around but didn't appear as vulgar as Betsy. The two couldn't stand each other. However, since they worked together at Dominic's Pizza Palace as clean-up crew, they were forced to get along.

Whenever Maggie found herself sharing the Main Street stage with Betsy, she would walk off, telling on-lookers, "She's crazy. It's time to take her to Looney town" (meaning the Mainland).

CHAPTER 6

The aroma of fresh coffee and sausages drifted down Main Street from Al's Coffee House. The counter stools were filled with the regular Islanders—in their special seats—a mixed group, ranging in age from the thirties to the seventies.

Tommy sat hunched over the counter, his fingers grasped his coffee cup, a somber look on his face. He was thinking of Maria. He hadn't stopped thinking of her since she left him for a younger man. They had been together for the past three years and he thought they were happy. Even though they never married, he even raised her two boys and loved them like they were his.

It happened when he returned from his weekly trip to Meadowbrook to play in a tennis tournament. Evidently, the affair had been going on for some time, right under his nose, and he never suspected a thing—as he was so trusting. Tommy was never the same since. He seldom smiled anymore and looked like a lost soul. San Lucci could be a lonely place for someone without a mate, especially during those long, cold winters. God must have had San Lucci on his mind when he said, "It is not good for man to be alone."

"Sherry, can I have more coffee?" Reginald asked, taking a cookie from his bag. Reginald, the town busybody, always brought his own bag of cookies. The Islanders called him cheap, but his response was, "I like my cookies better, that's all!"

Reginald was back in his seat after a two-month stay in

county jail. He had been accused of molesting some local boys but he denied it. He was known, however, for his effeminate behavior. Stories about this circulated around San Lucci. Some were true, some were not. No one cared, though, as long as there was something for the Islanders to talk about. They loved gossip!

"So, tell me Russ, what do you hear from your buddy?" Sherry asked, as she filled Russ's coffee cup.

"Na-n-nothing," Russ stuttered. Russ always stuttered when he was nervous, and Sherry's question made him very nervous. She was referring to Russ's musician friend and partner, Jamaica Benny.

Russ and Jamaica Benny owned The Lei, the local Polynesian club. Jamaica Benny wasn't his real name—no one knew—but he was called that because he was from Jamaica and played the clarinet like the late famous Benny Goodman. Lately, however, the Islanders referred to him by another name. Six months ago, during Super Bowl season, Jamaica Benny started a hundred-dollar pool and got all the Islanders to bet.

The day after the game, Jamaica Benny slipped out of town on the last boat, never to be heard from again. He got away with a couple of grand. Of course, the Islanders jumped on Russ and accused him of being in on the scheme...but he had been taken, also. Rumor had it that Jamaica Benny went back to Jamaica to open a bar and play his music.

"Oh, look everybody, Remo's back."

They all turned.

"Oh, he's so cute," Reginald continued.

Remo was a tall, lean, good-looking man in his thirties. He had blue eyes and long white wavy, flowing shoulder-length hair. He was an artist and painted beautiful murals in town. His one problem was that he loved to play the horses. Whenever he had a little money, he visited the racetracks in Meadowbrook. Unfortunately, he usually lost and borrowed heavily from the Islanders whom he seldom paid back. When the heat got too much for him, he would skip. He returned about every six months and was welcomed back like a prodigal son.

The men were taking their time this morning, nursing their coffee. On cruise ship days, no one was in a rush to leave Al's. There were too many tourists floating all over town today, sitting on their favorite benches! The Islanders had ambivalent feelings towards tourists—they needed them and were happy when they arrived, spreading their money around town, but then complained about them. They were so possessive of their favorite benches that when someone died, they engraved their name on their bench. There was Chick's Bench, April's Bench, and Stanley's Bench.

Some of the men, young and old, liked to sit "on the wall", and watch all the ladies go by. Then the whistling and lewd comments began, much to the ladies' chagrin. Many romances began from this innocent pastime. Some even led to long-time affairs with the ladies cashing in their return boat tickets.

The Islanders thrived on routine. One daily ritual was an afternoon card game, held on the beach from one to five. The usual players were Remo, Tommy, Reginald, Aaron and Ingrid, his Swedish housekeeper.

Another favorite ritual was the "suckers' game." Eddie and Uhrick started it. When they spotted a tourist on a bench, they would sit next to them.

"So, did you drive over, Uhrick, or take the ferry?" Eddie would ask Uhrick.

"Oh, I drove over on the new bridge." Uhrick answered.

"How was it?"

"Oh, it was great. It sure was a lot faster than taking that ferry."

The gullible tourists asked where the bridge was located.

"On the West-end of the Island," Eddie answered.

As the tourists left to investigate, the men would grab their sides laughing, shaking their heads in disbelief that they could

31

fool the tourists into thinking there was a thirty-six-mile bridge connecting San Lucci Island to the Mainland.

...

"Now, you be a good boy till Mother gets back," Harriet told her cat. The single women of San Lucci were so lonely that they took in all kinds of pets. Mabel paraded in town with "Gigi," her pet pig, on a leash. Betsy dressed her cat in clothes, put a ribbon in the cat's hair and called it Dog. She never went anywhere without him. He was the ugliest cat on the island—bald all over. She pushed him around all day long in a shopping cart. Harriet entered Al's and sat down at the counter. Although in her sixties, she loved to flirt with men of all ages. Whenever she entered, the men would bow their heads over their coffee cups. She placed the same order every day, one small coffee and one small water. Harriet was so absentminded that sometimes she called her cab before receiving her order and only realized her mistake after arriving home. She would later return in the same cab, to pick up her meager order.

...

Located outside Al's, at the base of the pier, facing Main Street was Horny Corner. Every night, after seven, the teen-age boys gathered, waiting for Harry, their supplier for anything they needed—liquor, condoms, drugs...even girls. You won't find any teetotalers on San Lucci. Some were such when they arrived, but years on San Lucci proved hard on your spirit, and soon even the strictest teetotalers gave in.

It was reported that over seventy-five percent of the residents were alcoholics. Many a night, Billie, the former sheriff, would give Eddie a ride home after seeing him stumble along Main Street. Yes, the island was tolerant of its drunks.

CHAPTER 7

The island was a seasonal home to many famous movie stars. They brought their yachts, their guests, and even their troubles here.

It was a cold, clear New Year's Eve when The Sabrina, a 150-foot yacht, pulled into the harbor. San Lucci's harbor was aglow with holiday lights from off the boats casting halos in the water. Big Band music rang out from The Venus Ballroom, high on the hill.

Stephen Cross, and his wife Sabrina Sands were ringing in the New Year, along with an entourage of servants and guests. Stephen was in his forties, a successful director and producer, and very much a ladies' man. Sabrina was a well-known movie actress, a lovely lady in her mid-thirties who had become quite insecure about her looks. For years, she relied on diet pills and alcohol. She, too, had had her share of flings.

By eleven in the evening, after celebrating all day, their feelings against each other were acrimoniously unleashed.

"I will not tolerate your sleeping with Jacqueline and making me the laughingstock of Hollywood," Sabrina lashed out at Stephen.

"Well, look who's talking? What about your co-star, Lance? Ha! Didn't think I knew about him, now did you?"

Sabrina's mouth dropped open as Stephen continued.

"I even let you invite him along just to see what you two

34

would be up to right under my nose. Real interesting the way you two have been sneaking around the boat late at night when you thought I was asleep."

Sabrina, mouth agape, tried to counter but was at a loss for words. Stephen smiled, smugly, enjoying the discomfort he was causing her.

"Oh, you bastard, you degenerate, you make me sick," she sputtered out as she stormed out of the cabin.

Stephen calmly fixed himself a tall glass of scotch, sipping it slowly as he flicked off the light.

Sabrina shivered on deck in her skimpy white gown. She was unprepared to spend the night on a deck chair, but she would not stay in the same cabin with Stephen. No, not tonight. She upbraided herself for having invited so many guests—now all six of the yacht's cabins were occupied.

Damn, why did I invite all those leeches? She considered going to Lance's cabin, but they argued earlier in the day and weren't speaking. Sabrina grew jealous when she saw Lance flirting with one of her guests, a silly little blonde. She couldn't even recall her name.

Oh, hell, I'll go apologize. After all, I did start it.

As Sabrina crossed the deck to Lance's cabin, she heard voices. Lance was not alone. As Sabrina drew closer, she recognized the stupid blonde's voice.

"Oh, honey, there, there, oh yes, yes, yes, don't stop, faster, faster, faster! Oh, Oh, Oh!"

Sabrina fell back against the door and the sound startled the occupants.

"Who's there?" Lance called out. Sabrina hurried out of sight just as Lance opened the door to look around.

Sabrina reached in her pocket for the Valium she always carried with her. Her hand shook as she tried to open the top. The bottle slipped out of her hands and rolled to the edge of the deck. Sabrina rushed to retrieve it and slipped on the wet deck.

...

"I bet I can make this skim more times over the water than you."
The young boys challenged each other as they stood by the waters' edge skipping rocks in the ocean.

"Nah, I bet I can," claimed the other.

As they continued down the beach, they suddenly stopped, frozen in their tracks. Washed ashore was the body of a woman in a skimpy white evening gown. Around her neck was a diamond necklace with the initials S.S.

CHAPTER 8

The island was known for its big New Year's Eve gala held at the historic mansion once owned by the late sugar millionaire, Nathan Chandler. It had a theater, museum and art gallery, all located on the ground floor. A gym was on the fourth floor and The Venus Ballroom was on the tenth.

Mr. Chandler founded San Lucci in 1886. Since his death, most of the land had been donated to the island for conservation. Some of the Chandler family still kept residences there. Every New Year's Eve, the island came alive as the big bands arrived on the ferry. The Venus Ballroom held two thousand people and on each New Years Eve it was filled to capacity.

The mansion overlooked the harbor. As the boats swayed in the harbor, the twinkling lights resembled jumping fireflies.

The crisp December night was clear with a half-moon riding high in a deep black sky adorned with diamond stars. The countdown began, "10, 9, 8, 7, 6, 5, 4, 3, 2, 1." Strains of *Auld Lang Syne* and noisemakers carried over the water. No one was aware of the tragedy that took place at that exact moment on The Sabrina.

...

The sun streamed into the cabin where Stephen was sleeping.

"Damn it."

Stephen reached for the drape, pulled it closed, and fell back to sleep.

When he awoke hours later, he heard noises from topside. His guests were moving about. The clock said noon. Through the open door leading to his wife's room, he saw that the bed hadn't been slept in. He let out a sardonic laugh.

Hmm, it seems Madame found another port in the storm last night.

The topside was coming alive with Bloody Mary's and strong black coffee. Lance was on his second Bloody Mary, by the time Stephen appeared.

"Sleeping beauty not up yet?" Stephen glared at Lance.

"What do you mean, Stephen?"

"Oh, please don't play that innocent act. I know what's been going on around here. I know where Sabrina spent the night."

"Stephen, what are you talking about?"

"Sabrina didn't sleep in her room last night and she's not here now. Now if she isn't in your cabin—then tell me where is she? In the ocean?"

Stephen walked away in disgust.

With Stephen's last remark the guests all looked at each other, with concern. They knew Sabrina couldn't swim. Frantic calls for Sabrina rang out throughout the boat. Their cries for Sabrina were picked up by the nearby boats and somebody finally called the harbor patrol.

Lance stormed into Stephen's cabin.

"Stephen, Sabrina is not aboard. We've looked everywhere and she's nowhere to be found."

With a look of concern, Stephen pushed past Lance and ran topside just as the harbor patrol pulled alongside The Sabrina.

...

Stephen sat ashen-faced and visibly shaken. Lance fixed him a drink. He had just returned from town after identifying Sabrina's body. No one spoke. They were waiting for Sheriff Dan Dawson to share the outcome of his investigation.

"Uh huh, just as I thought," Sheriff Dan Dawson quipped as he examined the deck on The Sabrina, from where Sabrina fell to her death.

"See here," he gestured to Stephen to look at where he was pointing.

"Here's the skid marks from your wife's shoes, where she slid across the deck." He then made another discovery as he picked a small item off of the rope rail.

"Hmm, interesting. Well, that explains it!" Dan held up part of a red fingernail.

"Explains what?" Stephen asked, visibly annoyed at Dan for the way he was dragging this out—almost as if he was enjoying seeing him suffer from his loss.

"Well, when your wife was brought in, I went down to the morgue to take a look at her. Whew! Boy did she look terrible! I mean, she was all bloated up and all!"

Looks of shock pockmarked the gathered group. Stephen clenched his fists so hard, his knuckles turned white. *My God, what an insensitive monster*, Stephen thought.

"Well, anyway, what was I saying?" Dan looked at them, coldly.

"Oh yes. I noticed your wife's nail was broken off, and this matches it. It seems to me that she probably grabbed the rope to stop her fall and broke her nail." Dan examined the evidence in his hand, turning it over slowly. He enjoyed making them squirm, especially Stephen. Dan hated these "rich" people coming over to his island and bringing their troubles with them.

"The autopsy showed that even if your wife hadn't fallen overboard, she had enough pills and alcohol in her to kill her. Yep, that's right. We found a bump on her head which probably knocked her unconscious when she hit the water. So, my report reads accidental death by drowning."

Stephen took a long breath. "Then you're saying, the investigation is over, and I can take Sabrina home?"

"Oh, yes sir-ree, you bet you can." *You can't leave too soon for me*, Dan mused, to himself.

Back at the Sheriff's Department, Dan closed the file on Sabrina Sands.

"Well, that's over with. Wish these damn tourists would stay home and die there! Ernest, run over to Hal's and bring me back a hamburger...and don't forget my onions!" He shouted after him.

CHAPTER 9

Three sounds of the boat horn signaled the ferry's departure for Meadowbrook. Paula clutched her tapestry tote to her breast as she scurried to the boat dock. The gangway had been pulled away and the boat began backing out just as Paula arrived. She wasn't concerned—Paula wasn't going anywhere.

Paula was in her fifties, slightly built with champagne, silver-streaked hair. The pain and disappointment of the last twenty-five years had taken its toll on the once beautiful woman. Her drooped shoulders and listless eyes spoke of the sadness she felt.

Paula was a young bride of nineteen when her husband, Neal, brought her here. Those early years were filled with love, happiness and prosperity. Little did Paula realize that five short years would be all they would have.

Though Neal was fifteen years older, he was the perfect mate for the naive Paula. Neal was the successful contractor who had built the expensive condominiums, Canyon Cove, in an exclusive area of the island. The condos sold for one-quarter to one half-million dollars and were purchased as a second home by the affluent from Meadowbook.

One day, shortly after a small earthquake hit the island, Neal was inspecting one condos' balcony when it gave way and he plummeted fifteen feet down to this death, on the rocky beach below. He died instantly.

Neal was loved and respected by all the Islanders for the benevolent charities he began and was missed. His death was especially hard on Paula, who was not a strong woman emotionally and had depended on Neal for everything. She was at a loss in dealing with the considerable estate he left her. Paula was not prepared for what would happen next.

...

Another boat pulled into the harbor. As the passengers disembarked, Paula stretched her neck to observe each person as they passed her. Soon the boat was empty and waited for another group of passengers for the return trip to Meadowbrook and so it went.

An hour passed and the damp ocean night air sent chills throughout Paula's body. She looked forlornly out to sea as she picked up her tapestry tote bag and slowly walked back to the small home she shared with Yvonne, her best friend.

It was a very lonely time for Paula after Neal died. She contemplated leaving San Lucci, but where would she go? This was her home, and Neal was here, buried high on a hill overlooking his beloved island. So, Paula became a recluse, a prisoner in her own home. It was a comfortable life, as she had everything she needed in her beautiful ten-room estate, along with her faithful maid, Eva, who took good care of her.

Paula spent hours sitting in her favorite chair in her bedroom by the window with a panoramic view of the whole harbor. She could hear the low haunting sounds of the boats. This was her refuge from the violent storms that life had dealt her. Yvonne urged her to stop mourning and start living again. Paula finally agreed to accompany her to the exclusive Salmon Club, where the wealthy Islanders belonged.

Dressed conservatively in a spice-brown silk blouse and

cream wool pants, Paula hadn't been there since Neal died. Paula became maudlin as she looked around the familiar room reminiscing about the happy times she spent there with Neal. The sound of a voice brought her attention back.

"Good evening, ladies. My name is Cameron. May I start you lovely ladies with a cocktail this evening?" His voice was throaty.

Paula looked up at the most handsome face she had ever seen. Cameron was tall, in his late twenties with an exquisite body. He had chiseled features with deep-set gray eyes, prominent cheekbones, thick black hair and long sideburns. Their eyes locked and Paula sat speechless as a hot wave surged from the pit of her stomach and reached her face, turning it crimson.

"Why Paula, you're blushing!" Yvonne said. "The waiter asked for your order."

Throughout the evening, Paula was barely aware of what she ate, drank, or Yvonne's endless chatter. She was only concerned with Cameron's darting, salacious looks at her, as he passed among the guests.

"Good night, Mrs. Winchester, Ms. Clawson. So nice to see you again." Victor, the club's manager, unlocked the door and showed them out.

Paula dreamily undressed by the moonlight that streamed into her bedroom. She quivered as she remembered how Cameron would look at her. She easily brought herself to an orgasm. It had been a long time since Paula had had these feelings. She had forgotten what it had felt like. She thought those feelings were gone for good once she buried Neal. Until tonight, she'd never had a desire to touch herself. Cameron had awakened the longing in her!

When Eva announced a visitor the next day, Paula's heart fluttered. *Could it be?* She let the thought linger as she asked Eva who it was.

"A Mr. Wilson, Ms. Paula."

Paula didn't know any Mr. Wilson.

"Show him in, Eva."

When Paula recognized him, she became flustered. In his white cotton shirt and tight-fitting pants, against his tan face, he looked magnificent.

"Oh, I didn't realize it was you. I didn't know your last name..."

"I'm terribly sorry, Mrs. Winchester. I should have given your maid my full name." His deep voice and presence confused her.

Why is he here? Paula wondered.

"But how did you know where I lived?"

"I found your initials embroidered on one of the folds of your fan and asked Victor where you lived, so I could return it."

An awkward silence followed as Paula stared at him and fantasized. *My God, he's so tall and so exquisite-he looks like a Greek God!*

Cameron interrupted her thoughts.

"I beg your pardon, Mrs. Winchester..."

"Oh, please call me Paula."

"Perhaps I overstepped by coming here so boldly without prior notice."

"It's quite all right," said Paula. "It was very nice of you to bring my fan to me, Mr. Wilson."

"My pleasure, Paula, and call me Cameron." He paused, studying Paula's face.

"Well, I'll be leaving." He turned to go, then hesitated.

"Perhaps I could call on you, sometime?"

"Perhaps," Paula did not want to seem too eager but the prospect of seeing him again made her heart skip a beat.

After Cameron left, Paula wondered why he never asked if there was anyone in her life—husband, boyfriend, lover. *Did he just assume I was fair game with no ties to anyone? Hmm, I'm not sure I like this. Now wait, He must had inquired about me, perhaps from Victor. Yes, of course, that's it. Victor told him about me. After all, the whole town knew I never go anywhere and had been alone since Neal died.* Her rational thoughts satisfied her.

Paula was soon involved in a clandestine romance, and her innocent, unsophisticated nature was no match for the worldly-wise Cameron. A more experienced woman would not have been so easily fooled by Cameron's charms; she would had noticed Cameron's changed facial expressions when he was around a woman...love, hatred, indifference. The glacial light in his deep-set gray eyes could turn a suspecting woman cold. But Paula missed all this...she never stood a chance.

When Paula married Neal, she was a virgin. He had been her first and last lover, so it was no surprise that Cameron swept Paula off her feet. The way she felt with him astounded her. She never felt this way with anyone, not even Neal. Cameron taught her more about making love in one short week than all those years with Neal.

Their appetite for each other was insatiable. They made love every night everywhere...in her deck Jacuzzi, overlooking the harbor lights while sipping champagne. They sailed in Paula's sailboat to the other side of the island and made love on the desolate beach.

Cameron cupped her face with his strong hands, kissing each crevice and dimple, slowing moving his hands and lips to her neck, licking it with his long, tongue. He moved his hands alongside her breasts and Paula's body became rigid as he circled her hard protruding nipples with his tongue, sucking them forcefully. She mentally begged him not to stop. He continued, tantalizing her until he heard her groan. He slowly moved down her body, brushing his lips past the top of her pubis, to the inside of her thighs. Paula's body rose to the occasion by arching her body to meet Cameron's lips; wrapping his lips in her dark, curly long hair, he continued to saturate her with his tongue.

After Paula collapsed in complete satisfaction, he mounted her. Anticipating the inevitable, her hips instinctively moved in slow, rhythmic gyrations. When Cameron's corpulent penis penetrated Paula, she yelled out. Never had she had it so good, so big, so hard! In and out, slow at first, then faster and faster. Cameron's endurance was fantastic as Paula reached another orgasm. Roughly turning her over, he entered her once again grabbing her hips in a bestial manner and pushing himself harder into her making her cry out from the painful force. Paula grabbed the bedpost for support as Cameron rode her like a wild stallion out of control. The furious rocking caused Neal's picture, sitting on the nightstand, to topple and fall, shattering the glass. Cameron fell with a shudder and a groan on top of Paula.

It was time. She was ripe now, Cameron decided...and he proposed marriage. They had been, verbally, expressing their love for each other for the past week-so it came as no surprise to Paula.

However, before they could marry, Cameron told her he had some debts to clear up. He confessed that he had been a bit of a rogue prior to coming to San Lucci. He had gambling debts in Las Vegas that he had to take care of. He had absconded when the casino owners started pressing him. Of course, Paula would help him. After all, she was madly in love with him. She gladly gave her savings to Cameron. He kissed her, smiled, and said it wasn't enough. She then sold her jewels, cashed in her stock and gave Cameron the money. When Cameron let out a rueful sigh and said he needed more, she signed over the deeds to her home and Canyon Cove. Paula had nothing more to give Cameron, but herself.

...

"Of all creatures that had feelings and intelligence, women were the most unhappy of all. First, we give up everything we own to a man who becomes the tyrant of our bodies and what's worst, we don't know if he'll be good or bad." - Medea.

Paula had become that woman.

...

The night was damp and the fog was rolling in when Paula walked Cameron to the ferry. He would return when he had settled all his affairs. He gave her a long, hard kiss.

"I will be back shortly, my darling. Wait for me here."

And so, for the past twenty-five years, Paula met each ferry that came in. She knew in her heart that Cameron was not coming back, but she just couldn't sever that small thread of hope. Here she sat, a sorrowful figure, as the fog engulfed her in a veil of white.

CHAPTER 10

San Lucci buzzed with the news. The counter stools at Al's Coffee House were filled with the regulars and everyone had their own version of what happened. Some were convinced it was the blanket of fog that had shrouded the island for the past week. Others argued the captain was drunk. Still others believed it was drugs.

The Seaport Gazette's headlines screamed the news.

"Disaster hits San Lucci as two ferry boats collide, in the fog, just five miles from the town," it declared, "First disaster in the fifty years the ferry had been running. Many lives lost."

The names were listed in alphabetical order. Near the end of the list was the name of one Cameron Wilson.

...

The fog was extremely thick that night when Paula arrived at her usual bench at the ferry dock. She listened to the three horn signals announcing the boat's arrival, but the fog was so dense, she couldn't see the dock. The damp, cold winter night, coupled with the fog, deadened the sounds of his footsteps as he approached her. She strained her neck as she dimly made out a figure approaching her. She studied him carefully.

He was a tall man with fine, chiseled features, high

prominent cheekbones, deep set gray eyes, and thick wavy black hair with long sideburns. Paula clutched her chest as her heartbeat rapidly with the memory of her long-lost love.

Could it be, no, no, my God! What is happening to me? Is this a dream? Has time stood still? How can he look so young when I am so old? These thoughts raced through her mind.

"Mrs. Winchester?" The soft young sound of the stranger's voice brought her back.

"Oh, Mrs. Winchester, please don't be alarmed."

The blood had drained from Paula's face, and she was visibly shaking.

"I am Keith Wilson, Cameron Wilson's son. He told me I could find you here—that you would be waiting here." Paula covered her mouth with her hands as she cried softly, her eyes glistening with tears.

"Please don't be frightened," Keith sat beside Paula and took her hand. It was ice cold, and she was trembling. Paula stared at him, speechless. *He looks just like Cameron when I first met him. It's like I had been in a time capsule for twenty-five years.* She felt weak and dizzy. She was afraid she might faint.

"My father told me about you, Mrs. Winchester. After he left San Lucci, he met and married my mother. Although he had plenty of money when he met her, he liked to live high and after years of drinking and womanizing, he ran through it. When my mother divorced him, he went downhill, rapidly, and became a drunk. Whenever he was sober, which wasn't often, he would visit me and talk about you. He said he'd been a real charlatan with you. I never knew what he meant. Then he would drop his head and cry."

Paula hunched over and cried at the thought of the man whom she'd once loved grieving over her.

"Dad said that he really loved you, in his own selfish way and was sorry for ever having hurt you." Keith paused, waiting for Paula to speak. Paula stared out to sea; tears frozen on her cheeks.

Keith continued.

"Well, the last time I saw Dad, he was real happy. He told me. 'Son, I had finally found my peace. I know what I must do.' That was the last time I saw him," Keith's voice broke, and his own eyes filled with tears.

Paula turned and faced him. "Why was he crying? And where on earth was he headed to?" Paula asked the question that haunted her.

Her perplexed look made Keith realize for the first time that she didn't know about his father's accident.

"Mrs. Winchester," Keith hesitated, gripping her hand firmly, "Dad was on his way here...to be with you!"

Paula's face lit up, in anticipation, waiting for him to continue. Keith forced the words out.

"The ferry accident...a week ago—" His voice trailed off as Paula waved her hand in front of him in an effort to stop him mid-sentence.

"Your Dad...my Cameron...was on that ferry?" Paula's words came out very slowly. She shook her head, not wanting to believe what Keith was telling her. She remembered hearing the town talk about the collision, but she never paid attention to the details, nor did she bother to read the paper.

"Tell me...how it happened," Paula asked, hesitantly.

Keith sighed mournfully as he continued to grasp her hand tightly.

"When the ferries collided, pandemonium broke out on the boat as everyone fought for a life jacket. When the boat lurched forward, it tore a small boy from his mother's arms and the boy fell overboard. Dad jumped right in after him. He lifted the boy up to waiting arms, but no one noticed when Dad quietly slipped away down into the cold, dark, water. You see, Dad never learned how to swim. His body was never recovered."

They sat silently for what seemed like forever, both feeling their own personal loss. Keith broke the silence and took

50

something out of his pocket.

"Oh, I almost forgot. In going through Dad's things, I found this in his suitcase."

Paula stared down at the face of a woman she once knew. A very pretty, young, happy face. The photo was faded, and the corners crimped. She turned it over tearfully and read, "To my darling, Cameron, with all my love, Paula."

"Dad always carried this with him and looked at it often. When he saw me watching, he would smile sadly and put it away. I thought you would like to have it. I'm sure Dad would want you to."

As Paula clutched the photo to her bosom, she remembered slipping it into Cameron's hands twenty-five years ago, just before he boarded that ferry to leave. She stood up, slowly. She felt so old and tired, yet she also felt a tremendous sense of relief, like a large load had been lifted from her body. She looked down at the same handsome face of her lost lover, inherited by his son, and cupped his face in her hands. With tears in her eyes, she smiled at him.

"Thank you, my son. Oh, you could have been my son, you know." Paula embraced him.

"Thank you for ending my vigil," she sighed, "I always knew he would come back to me...one day. Now, I can rest in peace."

Paula walked away into the fog as the last ferry's horn signaled its departure.

CHAPTER 11

Philip's long frail hand separated the drapes as he peered around it. Philip Powers, now in his eighties, was tall and gaunt with sunken cheekbones. His face was pale gray thanks to all his years of self-imposed exile in his Dolly House.

His story began fifty years ago, when he was only sixteen. He heard that gold was being discovered in the hills of San Lucci, so he came in an effort to strike it rich. He prospected and worked at odd jobs for five years, until one day, while digging, he struck one of the richest veins on the island. At twenty-one, Philip was the one of the richest men on San Lucci Island.

He began planning for Dolly, his childhood sweetheart, to join him. He purchased ten acres on *High Mountain* where he built the Dolly House and spared no expense furnishing it. The marble entryway and columns came from Italy. The tapestry and oriental rugs from Bangkok. The intricate parquet spiral staircase, leading to the second floor, had been hand-carved in Spain. The gardens, with its copious flowers and herbs, compared with England's finest. The smallest breeze permeated the town with the sweet aromas of French lavender and rosemary.

This was no ordinary house. It looked like a fortress on the outside, and a palace on the inside. The property line began at the base of the town, one mile up...deer, squirrels and mountain goats could be seen in the brush. The aroma of Eucalyptus Trees was overwhelming. Massive stone walls, and wrought iron gates sent out a foreboding message. For most, it was an honor to be allowed inside its sacred premises. Numerous statues of Greek gods and goddesses graced the circular courtyard. In the center, a fountain of a pair of lovers, with the male statue "urinating" water. An orchestra of chirping from exotic birds could be heard from the bird aviary that sat majestically in the rear grounds. This was an enchanted garden, a majestic jungle and a rainforest, all rolled into one fantastic adventure.

Philip began preparations for his wedding to Dolly. Caterers worked around the clock, to prepare the food, along with the four-inch tier wedding cake. Lobsters were brought in from Maine. The Dolly House was turned into a wedding chapel. The gardeners meticulously tended the grounds and rare orchids were shipped in from Hawaii. The invitations were sent out. All was in order. Philip sent for his bride. The response came in the form of a telegram.

The following day, everything came to a stop. The gates were locked, the drapes were drawn, never to be opened again. A shroud of darkness fell over the Dolly House.

With telegram in hand, Philip walked onto his bedroom balcony and with a booming voice so it carried out to sea, vowed...

"No woman will ever step foot in this house."

Philip crumpled the telegram and threw it over the balcony where the winds carried it all the way down the mountainside. A passerby picked it up and read...

"I can't marry you - stop - I am so sorry - stop - I can't live on San Lucci Island - stop - All my love, Dolly - stop."

Philip honored his vow. From that day on, Philip's prejudice against women bordered on outright misogyny. No woman ever set foot in his home. He had very few visitors. A dismal gloom fell upon the estate, an abandonment, as if Philip had died. In a sense, he did. The servants would see him, with just a candle, walking through the dark rooms late at night. A sad, melancholy, possessed man in search of a companion. A dead man trying to put his soul to rest. The estate turned into a living tomb for Philip.

...

Mario and Louie Farnesi hung their closed sign on their barber shop door and locked up for the night. They were paying their semi-monthly visit to Philip. It was time to give him a haircut, shampoo, manicure and pedicure. Not that he needed it that often; he always requested them to be there every two weeks. They didn't mind, as they were generously paid. They knew he looked forward to their visits, to hearing the latest gossip in town. Philip was lonely and they were his sole link to the outside world.

The Farnesi brothers were born and raised in San Lucci and lived here all their lives. They had a thriving business and enjoyed a comfortable lifestyle. But then, they were the only barbers on the island!

The brothers had very different personalities. Mario, the oldest, was the flamboyant one. He was gregarious and always singing. Everywhere Mario went, he did so with a song. Perhaps because he was named after the late famous singer, Mario Lanza. Of course, his voice was not near that of his namesake, but he kept the women happy, as he sang his happy tunes.

With the likes of "O Sole Mio," "Arrivederci Roma," the bachelor enjoyed serenading the ladies of San Lucci as he strolled through the streets, and they adored him for it.

Louis was just the opposite. A quiet, soft-spoken, family man. They made a nice balance, working side by side in their little barber shop.

It was a bright sunny spring morning when the Islanders woke to see Philip's Coat of Arms flag flying at half-mast. Philip had died quietly in his sleep. He was laid to rest in his tomb beside the bubbling brook, at the far end of the estate. They could still hear Philip's vow through the whistling wind.

"No woman will ever set foot in this house!"

CHAPTER 12

Dominic took a long drag on his Havana cigar and smiled.

"Ah, life is good," he murmured to himself. Dominic adopted a luxurious lifestyle a long time ago.

He leaned back in his big black leather desk chair and surveyed his richly decorated office. It was large enough to accommodate an eight-foot black buffalo leather sofa with accompanying matching leather chairs. Dominic loved the feel, the smell, the look of leather. "It reminds me of a beautiful sexy woman," he told Guido.

Guido, his right-hand man and business partner accused him of making love to his furniture. Dominic didn't care, he loved everything in his life to be of rich quality. His office was paneled in the best mahogany. Ah, Dominic did love his life. "La Dolce Vita," (the beautiful life) as he called it.

Dominic Visconti owned the popular Pizza Palace, located opposite his office. It was also the "front" of other lucrative enterprises he ran. Dominic was one of San Lucci's affluent individuals, owning several pieces of real estate. One was a large, luxury hotel on the highest hill on San Lucci, The Hotel Capri. Dominic lived in the penthouse. Because of its chalky white appearance, the Islanders dubbed it The Milk of Magnesia. The Islanders were fond of nicknames and gave one to everything and everyone.

Dominic was in San Lucci for only two months and the Islanders were happy to have him. He brought prosperity and jobs to their island. Rumors circulated about what his "real business" was and that the Pizza Palace was just a "front," but nobody cared as long as he brought money into their little town.

Dominic favored custom-made suits of the finest imported fabrics. His ties were all made of silk and he always sported a matching handkerchief. He wore only the finest soft Italian leather loafers. On his pinky was a large diamond ring with his initials DV which he never took off.

"It brings me luck," he reasoned.

He stood out among the residents of San Lucci, but he was never really one of them. He took many trips abroad for business and pleasure.

Today he glanced out the window and smiled broadly at his 250-foot yacht, The Regina. Ah! He was so proud of her. Dominic was a true ladies' man, even naming his boat after one of his girlfriends. He loved women, all women, showering them with jewelry and French perfume and the women adored him.

"I feel off balance without my bella donnas," (my beautiful women) he told Guido.

"Oh, damn those kids. I wish they wouldn't get so close to The Regina", he yelled out the window. The children were diving for coins the tourists threw in when their ferry docked...an old island tradition.

"Bastardo, bastardo, no toccare!" (don't touch) Dominic resorted to his native tongue whenever he became upset...it was the only way he could get things out of his system.

Guido heard Dominic yelling and knocked on his door.

"Entrare chiudere la porta." Guido entered and closed the door as Dominic instructed

"Dom, what was it? Those kids getting to you again?"

"Eh, what do you expect? Those poor kids raised without a father and living in Rocky Beach on welfare?" Despite all his exterior roughness, Dominic still had a soft heart when it came to children.

"Guido, we had to talk. We were a couple of kilos short again this month. Salvatore told me he personally weighed all of it, before the pick-up. Now, I have my suspicions. What do you think about that new girl we hired?"

"The one who was a tourist guide for one day?'

"Yeah, that's her. What's her name?"

"Sylvia Lawson."

"Yeah. That's the one. I kinda felt sorry for her, you know. I just wanted to give her a break. So, what do you think, Guido?"

"You did good by her, Dom. You really did. Yeah, I'll talk to her."

"Yeah, you do that Guido, then you do what you gotta do, know what I mean? Hey, I leave it all up to you. Me, I wash my hands of it," Dominic rubbed his hands together and let out a long sigh.

"You know, I was really beginning to like that broad."

...

When Sheriff Dawson looked out the window and saw Guido approaching, he immediately straightened out his uniform and was on his feet ready to greet him as he walked in.

"I understand you found an unidentified woman's body near Fork Road," Guido said.

"Yeah, we did," Dan answered. It didn't take him long to figure out why Guido was interested.

"This is from Dominic. He wants to make sure she gets a nice funeral, flowers, the works—you know. He thinks it's a shame no one claimed her body. He's got a soft heart and doesn't like her leaving like this. If you need more, you call me, caprice?"

When Dan opened the envelope, he found a stack of hundred-dollar bills.

...

"So, you took care of it, Guido?" Dominic asked, gruffly.

"Yeah, yeah, Dom. All taken care of like you ordered. Don'tcha worry."

"Yeah, that's what you said the first time and look how you botched it. She wasn't supposed to be found!" Dominic raised his voice sharply. "That was a messy job."

Guido had Pipe—a local Indian—handle it. Pipe lived in Rocky Beach, wore his long hair in a ponytail and was never without his corn-cob pipe...filled with pot that Dominic supplied as payment for any job Dominic needed done. This time he messed up.

Pipe and Sylvia grew up and attended San Lucci High School together. Then they went their separate ways. Sylvia to the streets and Pipe doing odd jobs for Dominic.

When Pipe invited Sylvia to his place for a night of "fun", she readily accepted. Since her mother died, Sylvia lived from day to day, and from man to man. By the time she arrived at Pipe's hut, he was ready for her. He had prepared two "sweet smelling" corn-cob pipes, poured two shots of whiskey. By midnight, they were both "flying."

"How's about you and me goin' for a little ride?" Pipe slurred his words.

They got into the sleek black Cadillac that Guido let Pipe use whenever he had a "job" to do. Pipe loved driving this car and touching and smelling the rich red leather seats. It was the only time Pipe felt like somebody.

He drove around the mountains wildly, screeching the brakes at every turn and skidding near the edges of the cliffs.

"Stop the car, Pipe. I don't feel so good."

Pipe pulled to the side of the road, his front wheels near-hanging precariously over the ridge. Sylvia stumbled out and immediately went into retching spasms.

Pipe found his perfect opportunity. As Sylvia leaned further over the cliff, Pipe picked up a big rock and aimed it at her skull. The impact forced Sylvia's purse to fly open, spilling the contents all over, as she fell down the mountain. Pipe looked over the ridge and was satisfied that she wouldn't be seen from the road. It would be a long time before she would be discovered as this was an isolated part of the mountains and a long way from town. By the time the tourist season would begin, and the hikers came up here, her body would be decomposed.

...

The deputies watched Guido as he walked out the door, and Ernest spoke first.

"Do you think he had anything to do with it?" They both knew he was referring to Dominic.

"I can't say, Ernest."

"Well, maybe we should at least question him?"

Ernest had transferred to the San Lucci Police Station, a subsidiary of Meadowbrook Police Station, two years ago. He was young, enthusiastic and eager to serve. He was conscientious and honest and never understood Dan's complacency in doing his job.

"Okay Ernest, so we just go running over there, harassing people when we have no evidence," Dan exclaimed, sarcastically.

"But I think we do. I think we have 'probable cause,' because—"

Dan cut him off.

"We ain't got any 'probable cause,'" he spit out sardonically. How he hated it when Ernest sprouted out these legal terms to him!

60

Ernest did not back down this time.

"Well, I always felt we didn't do right by the dead lady."

Dan pulled up his pants, a symbolic gesture of authority—It was a habit of his—whenever he felt insecure—and at that moment Dan felt inferior to Ernest. Ernest represented everything Dan envied. He was highly intelligent, from a wealthy family and had polish. He liked his job, the people, and above all they all liked him. He was always inundated with invitations to their homes while Dan was practically ostracized by the Islanders.

"First of all, Ernest, the 'lady' was no 'lady', she was a prostitute. Secondly," Dan's face turned ashen with indignation towards Ernest. "Her death was reported. Now, if someone knew who done it, they would-a come forward by now, don'tcha think? Besides, who said anything about foul play? The way I see it, she might-a slipped in the dark, fell down that ravine and hit her head. That would account for her death and the bruise on her head."

With another jerk of his pants, Dan stalked off, satisfied with his explanation.

Ernest glared at him with disgust. He concluded that Dan was uncouth, insensitive and a stupid ignoramus, not fit for his office.

"So, how did she get so far inland without a car?" Ernest called out after him.

Dan stopped abruptly, turned around and glared at Ernest.

"Well, maybe she had a fight with one of her customers and he threw her out and she started walking back to town and fell."

Dan leaned in toward Ernest—he was ready to pounce—daring him to say another word.

"Listen to me. As far as I'm concerned, the case is closed. Okay?"

Dominic was one of the few people in town who was nice to him. He welcomed him into his restaurant, and never let him pay for his pizza and beer.

Hell, that asshole was trying to ruin it for me. So, what if he had his own suspicions? He didn't have anything on Dominic anyway, so it was best left alone. A lot easier this way! And with that, Dan marked Sylvia Lawson's file closed.

CHAPTER 13

The church bells chimed eleven as the Islanders hurried by Heather's house to make the eleven o'clock Mass at St. Mary's church. What kind of sermon will the new priest Father Albertelli give this morning, they wondered?

St. Mary's by the Sea Catholic Church had a high turnover of priests. Father Albert, as he was called, was the fifth one in five years! It wasn't that the priests didn't like it here. It was just that things didn't work out for them. Whenever the church needed to remove a priest from the Mainland, they transferred them, here to St. Mary's. Some say it was the church's polite form of ex-communication. The priest usually arrived here with an infamous past, but easily blended in with the tolerant Islanders.

There was Father Ed whose behavior became so bizarre he'd appear at Mass with just his underwear on.

Father Riley loved his drink and finished all the communion wine before Mass.

The Islanders would have lynched Father Calhoun if he hadn't received his orders to leave. He was fond of his altar boys. It was later learned he died from complications of the AIDS virus.

Father Masella became friendly with Dominic, who was active in the church and donated generously to the collection box. When Dominic asked him to keep some of his "merchandise" for him, he couldn't refuse. Dominic used all of the towns' people to do his dirty work. He had such a way with them and was so charitable to all their causes, they could never refuse him.

One day, the Altar Society held a fund-raiser luncheon in the hall of the church. While searching the pantry for sugar, they came across packets of white powder high on a shelf. Just then, luckily for them, the good Father walked in!

Father Albert was a handsome man in his thirties and a wonderful orator. He didn't drink, smoke and seemed just perfect for St. Mary's. They did notice, however, that he did have a lot of company from the Mainland. He told everyone that his "relatives" were visiting. He was seen riding around town in his golf cart with his "women relatives." His "cousin" had been coming over quite a bit lately and staying longer than the rest. She was a tall buxom blonde who wore short, sexy dresses!

...

The church bells rang to signal the end of Mass. Aaron and Ingrid were returning from church. Aaron, forty, lived on San Lucci Island for the past ten years, five of them alone.

One day, a lovely young eighteen-year-old girl arrived. Blonde with blue eyes, she was trim and spoke with a Swedish accent.

"My new housekeeper," Aaron told the Islanders.

However, the Islanders knew she was much more than that.

Ingrid was a beautiful bodacious young lady, and all the

men took notice of her when they saw her in town with Aaron. She was 5 ft to Aaron's 6 ft and his long stride made it difficult to keep up. She literally "ran" after him.

Aaron was very possessive of her and almost never let her out of his sight. The only place he trusted her alone was at St. Mary's, when she volunteered for Father Albert.

One night, Aaron arrived home earlier than expected from his poker game night. When Ingrid heard the key in the lock, her lover grabbed his underwear and ran out the back door.

Aaron ran after him, but it was so dark, he couldn't make him out.

"When I find out who you are, I'm going to cut your balls off," he shouted after him.

...

It was Sunday. Just as the church bells stopped chiming for the Sunday Mass, the patriotic sounds of a trumpet playing, "America, the Beautiful" came drifting down from *High Mountain*.

Henry, the dentist, announced that he was back. Every time Henry returned from Meadowbrook, he sat on the balcony of his large home on *High Mountain* and played his trumpet. His playing could be heard all over town, and the next morning, the Islanders lined up outside his office for treatment.

Homer, the butcher, was his first customer of the day. Homer was out all night, drinking, and returned early in the morning, banging on his door. Hetty, his wife, had locked him out. The local police were called in because he was yelling, kicking the door and making such a ruckus. They found him bleeding at the mouth and missing a front tooth. They were accustomed to Homer's monthly drunken binges—they were as regular as clockwork.

...

The Fourth of July fell on a Tuesday this year which meant extra business for the merchants as the cruise ship would be in, which made everyone happy. The town was preparing all week for the big event. The Islanders were very patriotic and the whole town turned out in costumes with decorated floats to march in the annual parade.

The Master of Ceremonies this year was Jason Thomas, the popular sportscaster from Channel 43. The director of the fanfare was Rita Smith, a local celebrity who recently won the million-dollar lottery. She had become the talk of the town ever since. Rita was also the recreational director of San Lucci Island parks and beaches. As she was seen to be active on San Lucci, people were relieved her winnings had not changed her character one bit.

Riding on one of the floats was the 200 lbs Marcia who wrote for "The Seaport Gazette". In an ironic note, her column was titled: "Successful Diet Tips!"

CHAPTER 14

Dominic stared out his office window and watched the 300-foot yacht, "Buona Fortuna", slowly pull into the harbor. Two flags were flying on the mast head-one the USA's red, white and blue-and the other the green, white and red of Italy.

The town was filling up with Islanders and tourists from the cruise ships for the Fourth of July festivities. The stores were booming in business.

No one noticed the five strangers as they made their way through the town towards Dominic's Pizza Palace. They were expensively dressed in custom-made suits and imported leather shoes. The four men wore three-piece white linen suits, with white-on-white silk shirts, black silk ties held in place with a diamond tie tack. They had white leather loafers, white Panama hats and dark sunglasses.

The older man, in his seventies was the leader of the three younger men, all in their early thirties. The woman, in her late twenties was also in a white suit, white stockings and five-inch white heels. Her wide-brimmed white straw hat and dark sunglasses shaded her lovely face. She was adorned with expensive jewelry and the scent of expensive French perfume lingered in the air as she followed the men. If it weren't for all the festivities in town that day, they would have turned heads. As it were, they were able to move discreetly through the town.

Dominic greeted them with exuberance.

"**Buon Giorno, Buon Giorno**." Dominic embraced the men warmly with a kiss on each cheek. With Regina, he cupped her face with one hand, telling her "**Faccia Bella**" (beautiful face) and with the other, her rounded hard ass.

"Guido, take Gina into the restaurant and get her something to eat. The boys and me need to talk." He patted her ass, as she followed Guido out the door.

When the office door closed behind them, Dominic signalled for his **compagnos** (comrades) to sit.

"**Poss offrirle qualcosa da bere et mangiare?**" They gladly accepted Dominic's kind offer of food and drink.

"**Si, granzi tante**." (yes, many thanks.)

Dominic called into the kitchen and ordered lunch. After everyone had eaten they expressed their thanks to Dominic.

"**E stats un pasto delizioso, ci e piaciuto, grazie**," (it was delicious, thank you.)

They got down to business. Salvatore, the big boss, began.

"Dom, we're planning on expanding the territory, but we need your help."

"How can I help, Sal?"

"These runners you hired from the town are not too reliable, you know what I am talking about, Dom?" Salvatore questioned him with raised eyebrows.

"Si, Si," Dominic was clearly embarrassed with Sal's reference to Sylvia Lawson.

"So, I was thinking. Maybe you could recruit those nice, innocent tourists from the cruise ships to run for us. What do you think, huh?"

"Yeah, sounds good, Sal. Yeah, I will look into it, right away."

Their business was then over. When Salvatore got up to leave, his boys, Johnnie, Vincent and Sammy followed him.

"Dom, it has been good to see you again. I could have called but you never can tell about phones these days, never can tell who is listening in, know what I mean?"

Dominic nodded, in agreement, as Salvatore continued.

"Anyhow, this way, I figure I bring Gina to you. I know how much you two have missed each other, eh?" He grinned and nudged Dominic.

"I will send her in now. Me and the boys will wait in the restaurant until you finish." He winked at Dominic.

"Buon viaggio." Dominic wished him a good journey as he embraced him. Moments later, Regina came in and was immediately pulled into Dominic's arms.

"Bellismo, bellismo, my beautiful one. Oh! How I missed you!"

Dominic unzipped his fly hastily, with one hand, as he caressed Regina's perk breasts with the other. He reached down, lifted her skirt and picked her up, placing her on the edge of his desk. With one rapid sweep, he wiped everything off his desk. The lunch tray clattered as it hit the floor. The four sitting right outside the door heard the loud noise and smiled knowingly at each other.

Dominic ripped Regina's white satin panties off and thrust his penis into Regina's wet, eager vagina and thrust into her for a few strokes, then he withdrew.

"Just an appetizer, my bella mia, my sweet one."

Dominic hadn't seen Regina in weeks and was not going to rush their lovemaking. He intended to enjoy every moment of it. He lifted her off the desk and laid her on the eight-foot black leather buffalo sofa and began to fondle her. He directed her head firmly down on his hard, throbbing organ.

Ah, what bliss, thought Dominic, to have Gina's big red lips around my penis with the sweet smells of her feminine scent and my leather sofa … the combination was more than he could bear and before he could stop himself, he exploded in Gina's mouth.

"Oh, shit!" He yelled out as his semen flowed from Gina's mouth and down the front of his gray silk pants.

"When am I gonna see you again, Dominic?" Regina asked, licking her lips as she stepped into her panties and took out her compact.

"Soon, my sweet thing, soon. **Io amare tu**." In his moment of blissful satisfaction, Dominic surprised himself when he told Regina that he loved her. Regina was also surprised. This was the first time he told her this.

"Io amare Dominic, tu," She repeated it back to him.

After Regina and the others left, Guido came into Dominic's office and saw the mess on the floor.

"So, when you gonna marry her, Dom"? Guido asked while staring at the wet stain on Dominic's fly.

"What are you talking about, Guido? Why should I marry her and ruin a good friendship?" They both laughed. This was always Dominic's answer whenever anyone asked this question. But Dominic was beginning to think seriously about it, not that he'd ever let anyone know. After all, he wasn't getting any younger and Gina was a good woman. He had been with her for ten years, and with lots of other girls too during this time. Yet she understood him. She knew he ran around, but this was expected of a hot-blooded Sicilian. Anyway, he always came back to her. This she knew.

Dominic had fond memories of their long, romantic courtship and when he first saw her.

CHAPTER 15

He was thirty-eight. She was working as a salesgirl in the toy department of Lee's Department Store, in Brooklyn, New York. She was sweet and naive.

Such a fragile girl. She looks so anemic, Dominic thought. She had the helpless look of an orphan. Dominic had an uncontrollable urge to whisk this waif of a child into his waiting limousine and feed her a five-course dinner. I would give her lots of bread to fatten her up and red wine to build her blood, Dominic said to himself.

Povero bambino, poor baby, Dominic thought.

Regina was five-six but looked taller because of her thin body and long, dancers' legs. She looked undernourished but that's what attracted Dominic to her. He had a soft heart for children and poor people. It made him feel good inside to help the underprivileged. In spite of his rough exterior, Dominic was a gentleman.

Regina's long chestnut hair fell forward and covered her face as she reached for the counter to retrieve the red fire engine Dominic pointed to.

Dominic leaned over the counter brushing his lips over

her hair and smiled. Her clean hair smelled like ivory soap. Dominic's manly urge was to bury his head in her hair and kiss each strand.

"For my little Godson," he told her.

A more sophisticated woman would be wearing Chanel No.5, but Regina didn't own any expensive cologne, nor make-up. She wore only lipstick. She had a flawless porcelain skin, and make-up would have ruined this "Madonna." Her clothes were inexpensive but clean. She usually wore a black ribbed turtleneck sweater with a tight black skirt, with a kick pleat in the back. This was her required uniform for work. She had only two sets of clothes, but she switched the parts around to create more outfits. She was good at this, but then she had to be.

Dominic studied her face. *Ah, a face like an angel with long brown eyelashes and big brown velvet eyes.*

Regina had been working at Lee's for about a year, ever since she graduated from high school. She lived with her widowed mother in a cold-water flat, in Brooklyn. It was very modest but clean. Her father died when she was just one month old, and her mother never remarried. Regina always wanted a father. She felt something was missing in her life.

Regina's mother was a strict Catholic and made sure Regina went to Mass every Sunday. She taught her morals and values and would make sure Regina remained a virgin until she married. Regina loved her mother, and they were very close, but she wished she wasn't so strict. Regina didn't have a boyfriend and never dated. The only friend her mother approved of was Angela Brazzi, her best friend. They were inseparable.

Being twenty years older than Regina made it easy for Dominic to work his way into her heart; it filled the void she felt all her life...a missing father.

Dominic moved slowly with his precious find, not wanting to scare her off. Regina, not being wise with the ways of the world, especially men, didn't pay too much attention to

Dominic's frequent visits to the store.

He must be very fond of his Godson, to buy all these gifts for him. How lucky to be so loved, she concluded. Regina was so naive; she didn't realize that Dominic was interested in "her."

When Dominic finally asked her out to dinner, she blushed shyly and said no. How could she? Her mother would be waiting for her. She always knew the exact time Regina arrived home from work. Besides, how could she go out in her uniform? She didn't have anything nice to wear! She didn't have to explain her dilemma to Dominic. He knew.

*Ah, this is a good Catholic girl. She does not know about men. She is a virgin...*the mere thought excited Dominic.

Regina looked forward to Dominic's visits and studied him carefully when he wasn't looking. He wasn't a man most young women would have given a second look to as he was approaching middle age and looked like somebody's father... precisely the attraction for Regina.

Dominic was five-eight with a rotund body. His dark brown hair was thinning on top. He had a large Roman nose and the cutest dimples on his round cheeks, which winked each time he smiled, which was often. To Regina, he seemed kind, sweet and safe. The perfect father figure for this emotionally starved innocent girl.

Dominic understood women. So, when Regina said "no" to his invitation, he didn't feel rejected.

She needs reassurance, she is afraid. She needs to feel safe. After all she's been sheltered all her life, he assured himself.

He wanted her even more and he would have her! Dominic accentuated this resolution with a forceful jut of his chin.

When Dominic didn't return to the store for the next two weeks, Regina began to panic. For the first time in her life, she felt like someone cared for her, other than her mother, and now he was gone.

Oh, he was probably upset when I said "no" to him. I

have lost him, Regina sighed.

Regina was in the stockroom, on the ladder, stocking her shelves when she felt a warm hand gently touch her leg. She reacted with a jolt, then happiness, when she looked down and saw Dominic looking up at her, smiling. He reached up and lowered her down, rubbing his body against hers. So happy was she to see him that, without thinking, she kissed him. A sweet, friendly kiss on the cheek. A kiss to tell him she was grateful he came back.

"So, my little angel missed me, ah?" Dominic's booming, cordial voice revealed his joy at her warm reception.

This time, when he asked her out, she didn't hesitate. Regina told her mother she was going to the movies with Angela.

Their courtship continued for several months. Then one day, Dominic told her not to go to work and to call her mother and tell her she was spending the night with Angela.

She was so excited about spending the whole day and night with Dominic when he told her he had something very special planned. It was a glorious day, right from the start—a day Regina will never forget.

They arrived at their first stop of the day—The Regency, an exclusive hair salon on Fifth Avenue. Dominic introduced Regina to Michael and told him to make her even more beautiful than she already was. As soon as Dominic walked out, attendants flocked around her. While she was being pampered, Dominic made a purchase at an elegant lingerie shop down the street.

Regina stepped out of the salon, manicured, pedicured and with a sophisticated, upswept hair style. She looked ravishing and much older than her years. Dominic was pleased with his "gem." He hired a carriage for a ride through Central Park and then stopped for lunch at an outdoor cafe in the Park. Afterwards, they went to the movies and held hands, like two teenagers. To climax their lovely day, Dominic chose a cozy Italian restaurant, with strolling musicians.

When they arrived at Dominic's apartment, he prepared two brandies and instructed Regina to take her gift into the bedroom and model it for him. When Regina opened the box, a flush of heat rose upward from her chest to her face and her heart pounded fiercely. She realized, for the first time, what saying "yes" to spending the day and night with Dominic meant.

The only light came from the fireplace, in front of which a large white bear fur rug was placed. When Regina entered the room, she truly looked like a "Madonna" as the flicker from the fireplace cast a halo about her. She was the perfect little "virgin queen" in her new white lace negligee.

She came to him shyly. Dominic was very, very gentle as he laid her down on the rug. He took his time, admiring every little curve and dimple on her beautiful, young body. When he entered her, she cried out, lashing out at him with her fists.

"Oh, my baby, I am so sorry, I hurt you," Dominic withdrew immediately. "It's all right, my sweet Gina." He kissed each tear as he tenderly stroked her face. "We will go slow and take this nice and easy, Okay? You will get used to it, and then, you will enjoy it. You will see."

Dominic's soothing voice did not comfort the hysterical Regina, however.

Everything was so perfect. Oh, why did he have to ruin it? Is this what sex is like? Why did the girls at work tell me it was fun? Well, I don't like it at all. It was awful and it hurt! Regina cried to herself.

But because Dominic was such a good lover and taught her so much, that as time went by, Regina began to trust him and to enjoy their lovemaking.

Dominic was content. He had turned his little caterpillar into a magnificent butterfly. Dominic treated her like a queen. Never before did she feel herself so appropriately named. (Regina means "queen" in Italian.)

Dominic showered Regina with expensive perfume and

jewelry. For her nineteenth birthday, he bought her a twenty-carat emerald-cut blue topaz ring, her December birthstone. He took her shopping in the finest stores and Regina walked out with exquisite gowns and smart suits and dresses. When he saw Regina shivering in her lightweight spring coat in December, he replaced it with a full-length golden fur coat with a matching hat.

They made such a handsome couple as they paraded down the city streets. Regina in her fur coat and Dominic in his long black leather coat and leather fedora. When men turned to admire her, Regina squeezed Dominic's arm. Dominic smiled at his prize.

Regina was not accustomed to so many clothes. When Regina appeared in the same gown two nights in a row, Dominic teasingly chided her.

"Gina, you don't have to wear the same clothes you wore last night. You do have many more to choose from."

When Dominic leased a furnished apartment for Regina, he told her to quit her job so they could spend their days together. Their days were exciting, filled with surprises; ice skating in the Rockefeller Center, attending Radio City Music Hall to see "The Rockette's." He exposed her to museums, and all the cultural events. He was her mentor. He taught her about life. He was her life!

Regina felt like Cinderella. Each evening, at five' clock, she put her old clothes on and went home to her mother's. Each morning, she returned to her apartment and changed into her new clothes. Her mother never knew she didn't go to work. Soon her conscience tormented her lying to her mother. If her mother ever found out, it would kill her! She knew she could never tell her mother about Dominic—not after all this time—not after all she had done. When Dominic told her to spend the night, she lied to her mother again, telling her she was spending the night with Angela. Her Mother never suspected a thing.

They ate at the finest restaurants where Dominic had a

reserved table. Regina feasted on foods she'd never tasted before and sipped Cabernet Sauvignon for the first time. Regina waited for Dominic to start eating so she could see the proper utensil to use. When the fingerbowl arrived, she panicked. Was she supposed to drink it? She then relaxed when Dominic dipped his fingers in it.

Regina was content with her life and thought it would go on forever, so she wasn't prepared when Dominic told her he was moving out of New York City for business reasons. He would be leaving in a few weeks. How could he do this to her? He never discussed his business with Regina, and she knew not to ask.

Even though Dominic paid a year's lease on the apartment and sent Regina money, it did not ease the ache in Regina's heart. It felt so heavy, she thought it would break. Regina felt her whole world had fallen apart. She could not bear to live without Dominic.

Regina returned to work and resumed her life with her mother. She visited her apartment occasionally. It held so many memories for her. She walked around the rooms modeling her beautiful clothes. She admired herself in the mirror remembering the happier times she wore them. She then put her old clothes on, locked the door, and went back to her other life.

CHAPTER 16

Dominic didn't waste any time making new female friends. But after six months, he realized how much he missed Gina. He really was very fond of her, perhaps even loved her. He knew he broke her heart when he left her. He felt sorry for her, and out of this pity, sent for her.

Regina didn't hesitate for one moment. Her obsession for Dominic was too strong. Amazing how much she had changed— no longer that sweet little Catholic girl. She was now a woman. Dominic had made her into one. She was too ashamed to live with her mother any longer. There were just too many lies; too much guilt in hurting her.

She left her mother a brief note...that she was going away with someone she met. She didn't tell her mother she had known him for the past year and had lied to her all that time.

Regina moved into Dominic's ten-room, two-story home, complete with swimming pool, tennis courts, exercise room, Jacuzzi, sauna and live-in housekeepers. They lived a grandiose lifestyle, and this time Regina became part of Dominic's world and was introduced to all his friends and business associates. Regina entered this opulent life with abandon. As lady of the mansion, she was a charming hostess. Dominic presented her with charge accounts at all the chic boutiques and she had a limousine at her disposal. She should have been happy, and she would have been if not for Dominic's philandering. But she loved him and believed he loved her, in his own way, so she went along with it. It was very easy for her to do because she was so comfortable.

Then that day came, which changed everything. Dominic was going to San Lucci Island on business. He told her to stay in the house until his return. He didn't expect to be gone more than eight months and his Godfather and business partner, Salvatore, would bring her over when he came on business. Regina didn't want to complain to Dominic, but she was so lonely in the big house without him. She had no one to talk to. No one to share her feelings with.

Oh, how I miss Angela and wish she was here with me, Regina sighed.

With all the different events on San Lucci Island, the time passed quickly. There was the Art Festival in September; the canoe Boat Club Races from Meadowbrook to San Lucci in August; the Jazz Festival in October and the Christmas party for the Islanders in December.

But the biggest event of all was the day Dominic and Regina got married. The extensive guest list included all of Dominic's business and social associates from Meadowbrook and some of the fortunate Islanders.

Regina asked Angela to be her Maid-of-Honor. Salvatore would give Regina away, in place of her mother, who died shortly after Regina left. The official cause of death was listed as heart disease. But Regina knew deep down that she was the cause of her mother's death for literally breaking her heart. This would remain a wound in her heart for her the rest of her life.

Angela was ecstatic when she received Regina's letter. Of course, she would come. She was so glad to get out of her hellhole. Like Regina, Angela lost her father at a young age. Unlike Regina, however, she didn't have a mother a girl could be proud of. While Angela was growing up, her mother married and divorced four times, with a lot of boyfriends in-between.

One night, her mother and husband number four came home drunk. Angela was awakened, in the middle of the night, by a heavy weight on top of her. She stared up into her stepfather's face. It was brutal and it was quick, and she was only twelve years old!

The two were closer than sisters. Their complexion and features were so similar that they looked like they were related. They told everyone they were cousins, which made their bond even stronger. When times were hard at home for both, they clung to each other for moral support. They shared all their dreams and hopes. They both fantasized about a rich man coming along and taking them out of their drab existence. When this actually happened to Regina, Angela was thrilled for her and gladly covered for her, whenever she spent the night with Dominic.

The day Angela received Regina's letter, she quit her job at the beauty shop and left her mother a brief note.

"Just in case she 'happens' to miss me," she told herself, with a smirk. She knew no one would miss her and she wouldn't miss anything or anyone else either. She had been on her own ever since that ill-fated night when she was twelve and couldn't tell her mother. They didn't have a close relationship, and her mother would have even accused her of seducing her husband! That's why Regina was the only one she confided in. Angela was a survivor, and she became streetwise, unlike Regina. She was the one that always looked after Regina and was happy that she asked for her now. She could tell from her letter how much Regina missed and needed her.

CHAPTER 17

Dominic supported Regina's close relationship with Angela, even after he paid those huge phone bills. He understood loyalty among friends, and he encouraged this friendship. Johnnie was sent over to the mainland to escort her aboard the ferry for San Lucci.

Dominic and Regina were at the boat dock when the ferry pulled in. Angela was waving to them as the boat docked. Johnnie had his arm around her and was smiling broadly. Seeing them standing so close together and looking so cozy made Dominic smile.

"That hot Sicilian didn't waste any time," he murmured.

The ladies ran into each other's arms, kissing, hugging and laughing like two schoolgirls. When Dominic witnessed Gina's radiant face, he realized for the first time how lonely she must have been. He was glad to see his little Gina so happy.

Everyone in town was hoping for a wedding invitation. Some of the invited Islanders were Father Albert, who would be conducting the ceremony. Remo, "a customer" and sometime worker for Dominic. Reginald was coming as Remo's guest. Betsy, Maggie, and Roxanne, Charley's girlfriend. Aaron and his Swedish housekeeper, Ingrid. The Farnesi brothers and Paula. The musicians were Charley and Eddie. Special escorts of "Rent-a-Cop" were brought over from Meadowbrook to keep out any intruders.

The employees decorated the Pizza Palace where the reception would be held. Glass lanterns sat on the outside patio tables. Balloons and fresh flowers filled the room. A bride and groom centerpiece was placed on each table. The bridal table was set up for the bridal party. Baskets of carefully wrapped confetti sat nearby. Expensive champagne chilled in silver ice buckets. The "Closed for Private Party" sign hung in the window.

The limousines lined up in front of The Hotel Capri waiting for the wedding party to depart for the church. The out-of-town guests came out first. Then the groom with Guido, his best man. They drove off in the first limousine. Regina and Angela followed in the second one. They passed Heather's house on the way to St. Mary's. Heather watched from her window.

Wish it was my wedding day, she let out a forlorn sigh.

Regina was a beautiful bride in her beaded gown and long train. Her long dark brown lustrous hair framed around her exotic Italian features and complexion. Dominic requested the ceremony be short, and the priest accommodated him. Dominic was, after all, making a sizable contribution. After the ceremony, he slipped a fat envelope into Father Albert's hands.

I may use him someday, better break him in right away, Dominic told himself.

Islanders and tourists alike both stopped and watched with envy as the limousines passed through the town honking their horns on their way to the Pizza Palace.

Charley and Eddie were playing "The Anniversary Waltz" as the bridal party walked in. Dominic waltzed Regina over to the polished floor. After a few twirls around the dance floor, Dominic motioned for the guests to join them. Soon the dance floor was filled with couples. The food was brought out and Guido called for everyone's attention.

"A toast to the bride and groom."

They all raised their champagne glasses and toasted the

couple.

"**Buon Fortuna, Buon Fortuna.**" Salvatore wished the couple good luck.

After they ate, the dancing resumed. Mario and Louis danced the Italian dance, The Tarintella with Betsy and Maggie. Remo was talking, excitedly, to one of the guests, hitting on the unsuspecting newcomer. Reginald was standing near his "date." Aaron was telling everyone that Ingrid was just his "housekeeper," but he was keeping a close watch on her all the same.

After the wedding toast, Vincent left for the gym. Sammy made the rounds of the guests, targeting the ladies without escorts.

Paula wandered out onto the patio with her champagne. She was surprised to be invited but upon inquiring, discovered why. Dominic had sent an invitation to all the members of the Salmon Club.

Guido was so busy making sure everything went well, he never noticed her. He made sure the champagne kept flowing and the pizzas were hot. When the kitchen help informed him that they ran out of sausages for the pizzas, he called the emergency number for a delivery. Entering Dominic's office to make the call, he walked in on Johnnie and Angela on Dominic's eight-foot black buffalo sofa.

"What the hell? Johnnie, you crazy or somethin'? Dominic will kill you if you come all over his sofa!" Guido raised his foot to kick Johnnie's backside out the door—but Johnnie was too fast for him, and he missed.

"What the hell. Everyone wants to do it on this couch!" He yelled out after them.

Guido made sure the door was locked when he left. Johnnie and Angela had disappeared from sight, but he knew that Johnnie was scared he would tell Dominic and then Dominic would tell Salvatore. Guido, for his part, was glad he scared the shit out of him. He needed some fresh air. He poured some champagne and wandered out onto the patio. Lost in thought, he didn't notice Paula at the other end of the patio.

Guido Gambino had been with Dominic for the past twenty years and moved out here with him when he re-located. They had been through a lot together over the years. Guido lost his wife twenty-five years ago and never remarried. A meticulous man, like Dominic, Guido went first class wherever he went. A small man, only five-five, sensitive, even-tempered, slow to anger...the one who kept the hot-tempered Dominic calm. He knew him better than anyone and Dominic depended on him. That was, until Regina came along. Not that he wasn't happy Dominic married her. He was. After all, he was the one that always encouraged this union but now he couldn't help feeling alone.

All that anger directed at Johnnie wasn't really about that sofa! Nah, he was jealous. After all, he was already in his fifties, and he had no one. Dominic had Regina. Johnnie had Angela. Who did he have? He had dedicated his life to Dominic, was always there for him. It was Dominic this, and Dominic that. But what about him? What about his life? Why couldn't he have something for himself? Why couldn't someone belong to him?

Dio mio, fermata, fermata*, stop, stop, that's enough*, he scolded himself. Must be the wedding. Yeah, I'm acting like a whimpering schoolboy, feeling sorry for myself.

Guido took in a deep breath of fresh cold salt air, sipped his champagne and felt better. Then he saw her. He studied her for a while before approaching her.

"You enjoying yourself, Ms...?" He let the question dangle hoping she would say her name.

"Oh, yes, yes, thank you."

"Allow me to introduce myself. I am Guido Gambino," he waited for a reply. Nothing.

"And you are...?"

"Oh, excuse me. I am Paula, Paula Winchester."

"I know most of Dominic's friends," said Guido. "Perhaps

you are Gina's friend?"

"Neither. What I mean is, my husband and I belonged to The Salmon Club and Dominic sent me an invitation." She had difficulty composing herself, his presence unnerved her.

Sorry to hear her mention a husband, he decided to end it.

"Well, I hope you and your husband had a good time." As he turned to leave, she spoke.

"Oh, I don't have a husband...that is, not anymore."

Guido turned back and with a smile said.

"Well, I don't have a wife anymore, either." They both laughed to relieve their tension.

The ocean air was turning cool, and Paula said she would like to go back inside. On impulse, Guido asked her to join him in the office for a drink. It would be quieter, and they could talk and get to know each other. When Paula accepted his invitation, Guido grabbed a bottle of champagne and two glasses.

Guido led her to Dominic's eight-foot black buffalo leather sofa. They talked and they laughed. They finished the champagne and Guido brought in another bottle. Soon Paula's inhibitions opened up and she told Guido all about her past, about Neal and Cameron...details she never told anyone before.

Guido was thinking, *I will move slowly, now. This is a very classy lady. I like her already and I want her to like me. So, take it easy now, Guido, just talk for now. Someday, you will do something else on this sofa!* He looked at Paula, his dark eyes burning with desire.

CHAPTER 18

Regina threw her bridal bouquet and was glad Angela caught it. The couple postponed their honeymoon. They would take their honeymoon at a later date. They spent their wedding night in Dominic's penthouse at the hotel.

The private elevator to the penthouse was covered with plush red velvet brocade. The door opened to a large circular glass-dome room where the ceiling was one giant skylight. The penthouse was magnificently decorated with black and white leather furniture...a white bear fur rug laid in front of the marble fireplace. The sweet scent of dozens of roses filled the room. A basket of fruit, nuts, cheese and chilling champagne rested on the marble coffee table. Two brandy snifters with a bottle of brandy were placed on the marble end-table, for afterwards. The sounds of the bubbling jets of the Jacuzzi beckoned. A 12-foot circular bed sat in the center of the large bedroom. A black mink comforter covered the black, satin bed sheets.

They made marvelous love, under the twinkling stars, as the Universe looked down on them. They knew how to please each other, but this lovemaking was different tonight, at least it seemed so to Dominic. It was sweeter. He had never experienced this feeling after making love to Regina, before. These were all new, wonderful feelings. He felt good inside, whole... like he really belonged to someone. For the first time, he understood what it meant to be one.

Marrying Gina was a good decision, he told himself. He knew, in his heart, there would be no other women from now on. He later told Guido.

"**Perche andare fuori per hamburger quando io avere bistecca mio casta**." (Why go out for hamburger when I can have steak at home.)

The day after the wedding, Dominic went back to work, eager to complete the assignment Salvatore gave him; to recruit new help from the cruise ships. Salvatore was right, the locals were unreliable. He tried to give them a break, a chance to make some money, and what did Sylvia do? Repay him by stealing. "**Disgrazia**," he cursed her, under his breath, each time he remembered. She made him look bad in front of Salvatore, and there was nothing worse than a Sicilian losing face.

Salvatore and his "boys" stayed with Dominic for a couple of weeks after the wedding. Angela's room was adjoining theirs. Dominic was an excellent host, and they were all made comfortable. However, Salvatore eventually tired of the sleepy little island and decided to leave.

"Dom, thank you for your wonderful hospitality, but it is time for me to leave."

Dominic was sorry to see him go.

"My pleasure, Sal, anytime."

"By the way, Dom. The boys will be saying on here for a few days, if that's all right with you."

Dominic hesitated to answer him...he thought there was an ulterior motive here. Maybe Sal didn't trust him and wanted his boys to look over his shoulder to make sure he didn't blotch up again.... Because of the last incident.

"**Dom cos ha**?" (What is the matter?) Salvatore asked.

"Tu non speranza me," Dominic's head dropped, and his words were barely audible.

"Dom, what do you mean I don't trust you? You are my Godson. Me and your poppa were like this." He held up two fingers touching, indicating their closeness.

"Then why are you leaving the boys behind?"

"Is that what is bothering you?" Salvatore's face opened up into a big smile and he pinched Dominic's cheek.

"Johnnie had the hots for Angela and wants to hang around here, capise? Vinnie and Sammy can't leave without Johnnie. You know how it is with them. They're the 'Three Musketeers.'"

That settled it in Dominic's mind, and the men embraced and said their good-byes.

"**Arrivedenci, Sal**."

"**Arrivedenci, Dom, e stato un soggiorno molto piacevole**."

Salvatore thanked Dominic again for a very pleasant stay.

CHAPTER 19

Guido pursued Paula like a schoolboy's first love. The more he found out about her past, the more he loved her. Not because he felt sorry for what she had been through, no, it was much more than that. She was a loving, sensitive woman who still had so much to give.

Paula was not sorry for her past. In fact, she was grateful for it, because out of it came an understanding of her own character. She knew that she could handle anything now because out of her weakness came her strength. Strength she never knew she had. She now knew the meaning of real love...for the first time. Oh, she did love Neal but her relationship with him was like a father to a daughter, considering their age difference and her immaturity. With Cameron, it was a need for comfort during a lonely time. She was vulnerable when Cameron came along, and she had ended her long vigil for him.

Her relationship with Guido was different. She had weathered the storm; she had come out of it a more mature and stronger woman. She had survived. She was a survivor. This time, she had much more to offer a man. This time it would be an interdependent relationship. They would be equal. She was with Guido because she wanted to be, not because she had to, out of fear or loneliness. She wasn't financially well-off anymore, but she

89

had a little job and lived with her friend, Yvonne, so she was managing. No, she didn't need him for that. She didn't need any man, again.

Oh, I do deserve happiness again, she told herself. With this new confidence, Paula entered her third relationship. Paula approached this affair with abandonment, but not in the immature way she had with Cameron.

She never knew what was happening to her then. She had allowed herself to become a victim. This time, she was in control. This time she was the aggressor. She knew what she wanted, and she was going to get it! This new Paula was a strong, self-assured woman with great passion and determination. Her long years of pain and torment had finally come to an end. She was now a free woman!

Guido was enamored with Paula. He asked her:

"Where have you been hiding on this island that I never found you?"

He then kissed her, passionately.

...

Guido arrived in San Lucci two years before, the time Paula made her last trip to the ferry boat and the same night she met Keith Wilson, Cameron's son. After that night, Paula lived a quiet life, rarely going out. Until the wedding invitation came, she never knew Dominic or Guido. However, she heard of them, from the rumors circulating around town.

Paula underwent a metamorphosis over the next two weeks. The couples went everywhere together making quite an impression. They dined, drank, and danced the nights away spending their money freely throughout San Lucci. Large tables were set up to accommodate them, Dominic, Regina, Guido, Paula, Johnnie and Angela. Sammy with his date for the night and Vincent going solo.

Guido respected Paula. He was a passionate, sensitive man but he never tried anything with her. They cuddled together, kissed passionately, but then he would stop.

"No, I want this to be right. It will happen at the right time."

That was how he explained his hesitation away in the face of Paula's puzzled look. But she had been living a celibate life for too long and was now ready for more. Something ignited within her, something raw and elemental, a force that engulfed her body whenever she was with Guido.

...

The day was warm and sunny when the limousines lined up in front of The Hotel Capri, two of them decorated with white pom-poms. Paula emerged first in a long-sleeved champagne silk suit with matching stockings, shoes, and veiled hat. She was all aglow and looked ten years younger than her age.

Angela followed with a long bridal gown and train. The others filed in the remaining limousines for the downhill ride to St. Mary's by the Sea Catholic Church.

Heather watched as the wedding passed her window. She remembered Regina's wedding.

Two more brides, she thought and sadly closed her drapes. Heather had been keeping long hours at the store to avoid coming home to an empty, lonely house. Sometimes, she touched herself, then cried on her pillow.

Was this it? Was this the way I will live the rest of my life? she asked herself.

The whole wedding ritual of just one month ago was repeated with the reception at Dominic's Pizza Palace. The two bridal couples opened the dancing with "The Anniversary Waltz," played by Charley and Eddie. The guests were thrilled to be repeating such a festive occasion, so soon. The food and champagne flowed. The Farnesi brothers were dancing the Italian dance, The Tarintella with Betsy and Maggie. Aaron was still trying to convince someone that Ingrid was just his "housekeeper." Reginald was jealous because Remo was engaged in conversation with another male guest. Remo was just hitting the poor sucker for a loan. Roxanne was getting drunk.

Guido and Paula walked onto the patio with their champagne glasses and toasted each other. They watched the sun set over the water and the harbor lights come on. A full moon was making an appearance.

Ah, it was a beautiful night, and everything was perfect, thought Guido. He had been waiting a long time for just this moment.

"I love you, my precious wife." Guido leaned over and kissed Paula, tenderly.

"I love you, my tender, sweet husband." Paula pressed his fingers to her lips.

After all the toasts were made, Guido knew it was time. Paula watched as he whispered into Dominic's ear and saw Dominic's surprised look as he nodded his head and smiled agreeably.

With a big flourish of his hand, Dominic indicated his guests to follow him.

"Come on everyone, grab a bottle of champagne and follow me. We are taking this party to the hotel. Yes, that means you two."

He looked over at Johnnie and Angela.

"We will let you two have the penthouse for your wedding night, now, how is that?"

Dominic grinned from ear to ear as he thought about Guido's request.

...

Guido locked the front door after them, took Paula by the arm and led her into Dominic's office where he locked the door.

"Now, my darling, we will continue where we left off about a month ago right here on this sofa."

He came to her slowly, unbuttoning her jacket and unzipping her skirt. He watched as she stepped out of them and stood in front of him in her satin bra, high heels and stockings with the white satin lace garter belt. He buried his head in between her firm, rounded breasts as he unsnapped her bra. He took a deep, shuddering breath and exhaled it slowly as his palm traced the dark brown circle of her hardened nipples.

They undressed each other with care and tenderness. Guido lowered Paula down on the buffalo leather sofa.

Ah, my dreams are about to be fulfilled, Guido smiled, joyfully.

Paula's passion was urgent, powerful. An unbearable sexual intensity overwhelmed her. Lovemaking with Guido was different than with her other lovers. Neal was sweet and tender but lacked passion. Cameron was too rough. Guido had the right amount of passion with all the tenderness to go with it. Paula had finally found her perfect mate!

CHAPTER 20

The "Three Musketeers" three-day visit ended up being an indefinite stay and Salvatore no longer expected them to return to Meadowbrook, especially when Dominic told him he was taking his postponed honeymoon and he had invited the others to come along. He planned an extensive trip on The Regina, crossing the oceans and stopping off wherever they desired. Paula returned to a familiar lifestyle of luxury, one that had been taken from her a long time ago. Guido was worth more than Neal financially and showered his new bride with everything she wanted. In every port they visited, Paula joined Regina and Angela on shopping sprees.

They sailed to the French Riviera and docked at Monte Carlo. The ladies shopped in the classy St. Tropez boutiques and walked out with three sexy evening gowns which they wore to the casinos that evening. The next day, they modeled their expensive skimpy bikinis to the delight of their spouses.

From the French Riviera, they sailed to the Island of Crete where they sunbathed on the white beaches that covered Crete. Vincent visited the Greek Ruins and The Archaeological Museum. When he tried to share his experiences with Sammy, he was met with bored indifference.

Venice was everyone's favorite. Dominic hired a gondola that came with a picnic for the two-hour ride down the Grand

Canal. An impressive history was attached to the fifteen century palaces that bordered the Grand Canal. Dominic was especially interested in one constructed of marble slabs and intricate stonework. It looked vacant. When he asked the guide about it, he was told that The Palazzo was for sale but that it was bad luck. When Dominic asked him to explain, the guide waited until they were past The Palazzo before answering. When he did, he spoke in a low voice.

"It has been for sale for a long time...no one wants it...it is haunted!"

At this, the others turned their attention toward the guide.

"Horrible things have happened to all five owners. The first owner died in his sleep. It was strange because he was young, in good health. They never found anything wrong with him. The second was electrocuted in his bathtub. The third was stabbed to death in his study.... The fourth owner died of a drug overdose...they don't know if it was intentional. The fifth was found with the dagger still in him and the last owner fell out of the fifth-floor window to his death. Now this was really strange because he was the fifth owner and there were six floors and he fell out of the fifth!" From the excited animated look on the guide's face, they could tell that he enjoyed telling this story.

Everyone was dumbfounded when Dominic asked.

"How can I contact the broker handling this property?"

Dominic was indeed impressed with the story and perhaps because of it, decided he must have it. The asking price was $7.5 million. When Dominic offered $5 million, it was readily accepted.

It was a pleasantly leisure cruise. They played friendly board games, talked and dined. The couples pursued their own interests. Dominic and Regina spent many hours in their stateroom where Dominic felt at home on his familiar black buffalo leather sofa...a duplicate of the one in his office except this one was only six feet.

Johnnie's insatiable appetite for Angela kept them in their cabin for hours on end. Guido and Paula spent their moments alone, lounging in the deck chairs, holding hands and silently enjoying just being together. Sammy sat topside at his private table, playing solitaire while Vincent read in his cabin.

...

The "Three Musketeers," Johnnie, Sammy and Vincent grew up together in the Bronx. They attended grade and high school together and could easily be mistaken for brothers with their dark features and olive skin. But that's where the similarities ended.

They were a perfect balance, with their three distinct personalities. Johnnie was the designated leader, at least of Sammy. Vincent was the independent one. Johnnie had a large persona and was aggressive, ambitious, fearless, ruthless, impulsive and had a very hot temper. This would explain the deep scar on his right cheek, extending to just below his jaw line.

Sammy was the follower, leaving all decisions to Johnnie and Vincent. All Sammy thought about was sex!

"Sammy, you really should think more with your head," Vincent told him, pointing to Sammy's head..." instead of with your other head," with a grin, Vincent gestured toward Sammy's groin.

Vincent was the "thinker" of the pack. He was called "the college boy". He was the smart one of the three, the only one who attended college; even though it was a junior college. The other two were impressed with his articulate way of speaking and the way he had with words. Vincent could have been anything he wanted to be. He knew that someday he would leave this business but for now he was very comfortable with all the amenities this lifestyle provided.

...

The following days and nights were the happiest that Paula had ever known. Guido was a tender, considerate lover, not stopping until Paula was completely satisfied. He feasted himself from her banquet and tasted the nectar from her sweet being until tumultuous waves of joy overtook her. When they were both stated, they fell asleep in each other's arms. They awoke in the middle of the night and quietly made their way topside. The air was crisp, and the star-filled sky was aglow with a half-moon. Guido wrapped a cover around Paula. In the still night, they sipped their brandies and made plans for their future.

Guido told Paula about the beautiful house he was going to build for her on San Lucci Island. He planned on purchasing five acres of land on *High Mountain*, overlooking the harbor. He had a site in mind, and once they returned to San Lucci, he would begin fulfilling their plans.

...

The loud gunshot noise, signaling a catch, echoed throughout San Lucci Harbor as The Regina slowed down as it neared its mooring. The church bells chimed announcing the eleven o'clock Sunday Mass.

It had been a long fun-filled honeymoon, they all agreed. Dominic, however, was glad to be back. He had work to do and was eager to get started. He remembered the suggestion—no—it was really an order that Salvatore had given him. He would begin first thing in the morning.

Early the next morning, Dominic was at his office while everyone was still sleeping back at the hotel. He was planning his strategy on hiring the right kind of help to expand the territory to the neighboring islands.

The first thing Dominic did was buy The Lei from Russ located just across the plaza from his pizza palace. This way he could interview prospective employees, conveniently. Dominic believed in keeping this part of the business separate. It was a nice atmosphere for mixing business with pleasure. The Polynesian ambience was popular with the locals and the tourists-standing room only on weekends.

The Islanders were surprised when Dominic bought The Lei. They didn't know Russ was selling it. He wasn't, but Dominic had a nice long talk with him and made him an offer he couldn't refuse! He convinced Russ that with the money from the sale, all tax-free cash, he could meet up with his buddy, Jamaica Benny and retire. Russ broke out in a cold sweat when Dom mentioned Jamaica Benny. *Had he hit on Dominic too? Did he think he was in on that scheme?* Russ decided to sell and as soon as the deal closed, he was on the first ferry off the island.

By the time Russ reached Meadowbrook, he felt safer. In fact, the more relaxed he was, the more indignant he became. *What right did Dominic have running me out of town like that and why did I feel so intimidated? After all, I am not guilty of anything. I had nothing to do with Jamaica Benny's scheme. Why didn't anyone in San Lucci believe me? It isn't fair.* Thinking about this made Russ morose.

I know what's going on over there. I know all about Dominic and his "business". I'll show him. I'll show all of them for treating me this way! Russ had a plan.

CHAPTER 21

The Meadowbrook Police Station was buzzing. The narcotics team made a big bust and the department was crowded with police officers filling out their reports.

Annette Kelsey had worked in narcotics for three years.

"So, what have you got for me today, Captain?" Annette walked into Captain Bill Sheridan's office. Bill thumbed through his over-flowing "inbox" and pulled a report from the bottom of the pile.

"Here's a good one for you," the captain handed Annette the report and she walked out reading it. It took only a few seconds and she turned on her heels and marched right back into his office.

"What the heck is this?" Annette read the report out loud.

"Woman's body found dead in hills in remote area of San Lucci Island. Big conspiracy in town, no proper investigation, drug ring suspected, etc, etc." Annette was upset that the captain picked her to go to the island. Although she had never been to San Lucci, she heard a lot about it, all negative, and didn't have the slightest desire to go there.

"Now don't get too worked up, Annette. San Lucci Island is really a nice place. I can remember when Irene and I spent a lovely vacation there and—" Bill stopped when he saw Annette contorted her face in annoyance. He continued.

"Some nervous little guy walked in here stuttering about an important story he had for us—thought it might be of interest to the department."

"Well, it sure isn't of interest to me!" Annette pondered the assignment.

"And how come you gave it to me—from the bottom of the pile—no less?" She didn't wait for an answer. "No one else wanted to get stuck on no man's land, huh?"

"Now Annette, it's a good chance to get out of the city and breathe some of that healthy ocean air. Why, you can even take Kay with you. You two can make a nice vacation out of it."

And with that, Captain Sheridan went back to his paperwork.

Annette stood staring down at Bill with a frown on her face.

Hmm, I bet he wouldn't get away with this with any of the guys, she thought to herself as she stormed out of his office.

Annette was five-nine, attractive, in her late twenties with wiry red hair, hazel eyes and a svelte figure. She also had a temper to match her red hair. Annette thought about the captain's suggestion of taking Kay with her. She liked Kay but didn't think she had enough experience. She had only been in narcotics a year and all of it behind a desk. At least, Annette had field experience. Well, if she was going to get stuck on a little island, for who knew how long, she may as well have company. Annette really didn't expect Kay to be of much use.

Annette researched San Lucci and planned her strategy carefully. She decided that they would go to San Lucci on the cruise ship that made its port stop there every week. This way they would blend right in with the passengers as they walked into town and not stand out as newcomers. She booked two first class tickets on the cruise ship and a suite at the best hotel in San Lucci. She would go first class all the way—her way of sticking it up to the department—make them pick up the tab!

...

Annette and Kay watched out their cabin window as the island loomed up before them. They gathered their belongings, informed the captain they would not be returning to the ship that night and boarded the waiting shore boat with the rest of the passengers.

"So, this is San Lucci Island." Annette emphasized each word, sarcastically.

"Oh, it looks pretty nice to me, Net," Everything was always nice to the good-humored even-keeled Kay.

What a bore! thought Annette.

The women were the complete opposite of the other. Annette was self-disciplined, self-assured and conservative. Kay was Annette's age but seemed younger because of her gullible personality and shyness. With her buxom body on her five-foot two-inch frame, rosy cheeks, crystal blue eyes and short blonde hair, Kay resembled a cherub.

They walked to the hotel but even with just a weekender suitcase, the trek up the steep hill proved exhausting. When they reached the top, the reflective glare from the chalky white hotel blinded them.

After unpacking, they took a walking tour of the town. Annette's plan was to find someone who would love to tell her about the murder—in other words—the town gossiper. Being raised in a small town, herself, she knew every small town had one.

They meandered through the charming shops, then stopped for lunch. Normally, the diet conscious Annette would have passed up the pizza and beer but the aroma floating past them as they strolled by Dominic's Pizza Palace was just too overpowering to resist...and they went inside.

"Oh, this is so delicious," they both agreed. It was the best pizza they ever had. Annette, always watching her figure, refused to feel guilty. Kay, never considering her figure, ordered another slice.

After they paid their bill, Annette asked the waiter to recommend a nice dinner house that had entertainment.

"Oh, The Lei. It's right across the street. You can see it from here."

That night, the women dressed as voluptuously as possible, considering they each only brought one good dress with them. They wanted to attract attention and they did. Annette needed to find some friendly, talkative local to fill her in.

Charley and Eddie were just setting up when they walked in. Being a weeknight, it wasn't too crowded and they got seated immediately. Their table gave them a lovely view of the harbor and they settled back to enjoy themselves. The music floated throughout the restaurant and couples filled the dance floor.

After dinner, the women walked into the lounge and found a table just off the dance floor. They ordered two Mai Tais and listened to the music. It didn't take long for the drinks to catch up to them. They had had wine with their meals and now these cocktails. It made them giddy, and they looked at each other and laughed for no reason. The music drifted through the open windows into Dominic's Pizza Palace across the plaza.

"Oh, Johnnie, I wanna dance. Take me dancing, please," Angela rubbed her breasts seductively against Johnnie's arm. The sight of Angela's erect nipples protruding through her thin blouse aroused Johnnie.

"Yeah, yeah, you always wanna dance. I know what you really want. You just wanna feel my hard cock pressed up against your body. Yeah, I know that's what you want." They both laughed.

"Hey, Vin, Sam, you two wanna join us for a drink? Johnnie always included his comrades.

...

Sammy noticed them first as soon as they walked into The Lei.

"Mamma mia, che bello gamba."

Sammy nudged Vincent as he admired Annette's long legs as she crossed them under her short tight dress.

Johnnie and Angela got up to dance while Sammy tried to get up the nerve to talk to the women.

"Hey Vin, which one do you want, huh?"

Vincent took his time looking them over, then shook his head.

"Not my type, Sam."

"What's the matter with you? Don't you like women no more? Maybe you been on this island too long, huh?" Sammy never could understand him. Vincent would rather be in his room reading a good book right now, but he was congenial enough to accompany his friends.

Sammy took his time approaching the women and when he did, he invited them over to his table. The women studied them for a while. Kay decided they were cute and was happy to join them. Annette was not so sure. She reminded Kay that they were here on business, not pleasure.

"Well, I thought you wanted to get to know the locals. And the way they knew and spoke to everyone when they came in—oh yes, I noticed—seems to me they're as local as you're going to get." Annette was surprised Kay noticed them and yes, she was interested, especially in Vincent. Agreeing with Kay's rationale, Annette accompanied Kay to their table.

As the four sized each other up, Sammy decided Annette was definitively not his type.

She talks like Vincent, all those big fancy words. Now Kay seems just right, with her sweet smile and her plain talk, Sammy thought he was satisfied with his choice.

Vincent and Annette faced each other, engrossed in conversation while Sammy leaned in toward Kay. Someone ordered another round of drinks and they hardly noticed when Johnnie and Angela said goodnight.

At midnight, Charley and Eddie played "The Party's Over."

"It's been a lovely evening, and we thank you both. So nice meeting you," Annette extended her hand to Vincent. They declined the men's offer to accompany them to the shore boat. They didn't bother to tell them they were staying in San Lucci.

They decided against taking a cab and walked up the long, steep hill. They had more than enough to drink and needed fresh air. By the time they reached their room, they were pleasantly exhausted and welcomed the smell of freshly laundered sheets as they turned down their beds. They would have plenty of time to go over the night's events in the morning.

CHAPTER 22

They awoke early the next morning and went downstairs for the hotel's continental breakfast.

"Yes, we had a great time last night, but now we must get down to business," they both agreed.

Annette didn't have much to go on as Russ didn't supply them with many details nor names. He seemed to get a sinister satisfaction out of making law enforcement gather the information on their own.

Damn him, Annette swore under her breath. *He could have saved me a lot of trouble. Besides, who knew if his story was even true.*

Annette decided to stroll through the town alone and find the locals' gathering place. One new face asking questions would attract less attention than two. Kay was happy to have the day to herself and headed for the beach.

It didn't take Annette long to find the local hangout...the hotel desk clerk filled her in. When Annette walked into Al's Coffee House, all eyes turned towards her, bodies frozen in place as all action stopped. Annette stood motionless for several seconds and waited until the chatter resumed. Annette chose a vacant seat at the far end of the counter and ordered coffee. With her head in her coffee cup, she discreetly peered over her cup and surveyed her companions.

Not too promising. They seem too cautious of strangers, thought Annette. Several were preoccupied with their own thoughts and weren't interested in her. Then she noticed an animated talker who seemed friendly.

Reginald was talking about how Aaron had come home and found Ingrid in bed with another man.

"When they heard Aaron at the front door, her lover ran out the back door into the dark night. Aaron ran after him yelling obscenities. Ha, ha, I would have loved to have seen that! Aaron said that when he found out who it was, he will cut off his..." Reginald lowered his voice, cupped his hands and shyly continued, "...his you know what!" Reginald laughed.

Annette moved into the newly vacant seat next to Reginald. At first, he didn't notice her but when she ordered more coffee, he turned to her.

"Hi, my name is Reginald. Did you just get in?"

This will be easy, Annette thought as she introduced herself. When she ordered breakfast and asked if he would like to join her, he warmed up to her immediately. Reginald loved "freebies" and was happy to tell her everything she wanted to know about San Lucci.

Annette learned about Dominic Visconti's unscrupulous reputation—that he had a lot of money and controlled the town.

"He has his own entourage, you know his 'boys.'"

Reginald told her about the weddings and Dominic's acquisitions on the island. Restaurants, a hotel (of which he didn't bother to name) and other real estate.

"You know Dominic's Pizza Palace was rumored to be the front for his real operation," he leaned over and whispered in Annette's ear.

"You know, drugs. I just happen to know that a big shipment was about to be dropped here in San Lucci, any day now!" Reginald sat back, arms folded, with a smug look, so happy was he to be the possessor of so much information.

Annette asked him about Sylvia Lawson's death. Reginald's eyebrows shot up in surprise which made Annette's heart skip a beat. Too late—she realized her error!

"Now, how did you know about that if you just arrived? Who told you about her?"

Annette thought quickly and said that she was going through some old newspapers at the library and happened to come across the story.

"Oh, I see."

Reginald was relieved that he hadn't been superseded by another local. But in reality, there was no such story on Sylvia Lawson, just a three-line obituary. Anyway, why would a newcomer read the obituaries in a strange town? This all slipped past Reginald in his quest to enlighten Annette about his island.

By the time Annette returned to the hotel, she had a sickening headache from talking so long with Reginald. He would have talked forever if Annette hadn't decided she had enough information. When Reginald drifted away from Dominic and his affairs to meaningless small-talk, she brought the interview to a close.

It was three o'clock and Kay was still at the beach. Annette took two aspirins, laid down and dozed off. The sound of the door opening roused her quickly from her light sleep.

"Kay, is that you?" Annette glanced over at the clock. It was six o'clock.

"Yes, Net," Kay answered in an anguished voice.

"What's the matter, Kay? Oh, my goodness! You look like a lobster!"

Kay was beet red all over and was on the verge of tears as she gingerly lowered herself onto the bed.

"I fell asleep and when I woke up, I couldn't move," the tears ran down her red-hot cheeks.

Annette jumped up and grabbed her purse.

"I'll run down to the drugstore and get you some

108

calamine lotion. Now, you just stay put, I'll be right back."

Kay watched her, thinking.

She didn't need to tell me to stay put! She would have laughed if she wasn't in such pain.

Annette saw a deli next to the drugstore and picked up some food to go. They wouldn't be going out for dinner tonight. It was one long, hot, painful night for poor Kay and the next day she was quite content to close the drapes and spend the day alone in her dark hotel room.

...

Annette decided to check out the local library and see what had been written about the dead woman.

The three old librarians eyed Annette suspiciously since she wasn't a local. When she asked to review the old newspapers that dated around Sylvia's death, they looked at each other and then at her with squinted eyes.

Wow, these women are weird, Annette thought to herself.

As they brought her the newspapers, they wondered among themselves why she was so interested. When the news was outdated, it stayed old, and nobody cared. Besides, it was a bother to search those files in the back room.

"Sure hope she appreciates it!" they whispered to each other. The locals did not like having their routines disturbed...it made them uncomfortable.

The three pasty looking women were not your ordinary librarians. One had a consistent, hacking cough. She grabbed her walker each time she went into spasms for fear of falling from the intensity of her cough. Another was connected to an oxygen tank. The oldest, a lady in her eighties had Alzheimer's disease and was talking to herself.

I feel like I am in a sanitarium instead of a library, Annette thought.

Annette had to scan several newspapers before she found what she was looking for. She couldn't wait to get out of that small, stuffy library. She felt three pairs of eyes constantly watching her and she felt that she could practically slice their animosity with a knife.

The information wasn't much.

"Sylvia Lawson, 29, died June 16, 1963. Cause of death: Brain hemorrhage due to a fall. No known survivors. Funeral to be held at gravesite on June 18, 1963."

She thanked the women and left. She was glad to be out in the fresh air where she could breathe. Her next stop was the Sheriff's Office.

Sheriff Dawson was settling down at his desk with a cup of coffee when Annette walked in. She introduced herself as an old friend of Sylvia Lawson's. Just then, a loud crash was heard coming from the back room.

Ernest Frye dropped his coffee cup when he heard Sylvia's name mentioned. Annette looked up to see a handsome deputy with a frighten look on his face enter the room.

"I didn't know Sylvia had any friends," said Dan.

"Oh, yes, Sylvia and I were old friends, college friends. After college, we drifted apart and didn't see much of each other, just letters, phone calls, you know." She hoped this was enough to assuage Dan's questions, doubts.

"She's been dead three months now. What took you so long to find out about your old school friend's death?' Dan didn't buy her story. He wondered why she was so curious about Sylvia Lawson's death.

"Well, I've been out of town, out of the country, actually. You see, I'm a teacher and I was on a sabbatical doing research for my thesis. I'm going for my Masters and..."

"Okay, okay," Dan cut her off having heard enough of her rambling.

"So, get to the point, lady. What was it you want?"

"Well, I really would like to hear the details of how she died. She was so young."

"Yeah, well, young people die too, lady!"

Dan became increasingly annoyed with Annette but decided to appease her so he could get rid of her. He told Annette his theory—the one he told Ernest and everyone else in town, about Sylvia falling down the ravine and hitting her head on a rock which killed her, instantly. Dan had repeated that story so often that even he believed it.

Annette thanked him and walked out, stealing a backward glance at Ernest, who had stared nervously at Annette the entire time.

CHAPTER 23

The women spent another evening in their hotel room, dining on take-out food and watching re-runs on T.V. The following morning found Kay feeling better but looking more like a bronze Indian instead of a red lobster.

Annette grew weary of all the research and questioning she had been doing and suggested they take a holiday.

They booked the three-hour tour of the Interior and settled in their seats for the long ride ahead. Their bus driver introduced himself and began his spiel.

"Hi, my name was Bert, and I will be your tour guide for this trip," Bert had repeated his introduction so many times over the past eight years, he sounded like a wind-up toy.

The view was breathtaking as they climbed higher and higher. The women kept nudging each other excitedly as they each made a discovery. Their first stop was the heliport and hotel, Inn in the Sky. They lunched in the Inn's restaurant and shopped in the souvenir store. When they re-boarded the bus, Bert filled them in on the details of the recent accident that occurred at the heliport.

"It was a foggy morning, and the helicopter was just taking off for the Mainland when another helicopter was coming in. They collided—the blade of one of the helicopters sawed right through the other plane, decapitating a man sitting by the window. His head rolled right out of the plane and landed right there just a few feet from the restaurant." Bert pointed in the general direction of the tragic incident.

"Oh, ah, oh no." Anguished sounds were heard throughout the bus.

"Yes sir, there were bodies spread all over the place and lots of blood and body parts." The groans grew louder and Bert grinned.

The two women turned to each other; disgust written all over their faces. They got the distinct impression Bert just loved telling this gruesome story. They were only glad he had waited until after they had their lunch.

A rare glimpse of a soaring bald eagle perked everyone's spirits up.

"Okay, everyone. Start looking for the buffalo herd. See that one over there. Yeah, that one. It's about ready to give birth."

The women thought that was amazing, as the buffalo all looked alike, big and fat, but no one was challenging Bert. They stopped for refreshments and a horse show at the Chandler's Arabian Horse Ranch—at one time a horse breeding ranch—now a tourist attraction.

On their way back to town, they caught glimpses of deer and island fox.

When they arrived back at their hotel, they decided to sit out on the hotel's sun deck. They pushed the up button for the elevator and waited. Meanwhile, down in the lobby, Vincent and Sammy were just returning from a long day's fishing trip and were dirty and tired. They watched as the elevator went up to the sun deck.

From the sun deck, the women spotted Dominic's Pizza Palace, The Lei and even the little deli. They were looking forward to going out tonight as they hadn't been out since Tuesday, when they met those two guys.

"Oh, what were their names? I wonder if we will see them

tonight?" They asked each other.

Annette put on the new navy-blue lace dress she bought at Roxanne's boutique. It had long sleeves and a sweetheart neckline. Annette looked demure in it, with just the right amount of sauciness. The salesgirl was right. It was perfect with her coloring and set her raven red hair right off. Kay wore a simple dress that she had brought from home. It had a big circular skirt that camouflaged her figure.

When they arrived at The Lei, the place was packed. Being a Friday night, the place was filled with weekend tourists. All the tables were taken, except for a big booth in the rear with a reserved sign on it. The hostess took their names and told them it would be an hour's wait.

"However, there are two stools left at the bar and you can have your dinner there, if you don't want to wait."

They didn't want to wait and accepted the bar stools. At that moment, Vincent and Sammy walked in, past the hostess desk and bar and headed straight for Dominic's reserved table. Dominic always had his table set up for his party and guests from the Mainland.

The women enjoyed their delicious fresh salmon dinner, the best dinner they had in two days. They brought their wine with them to the lounge and that's when Sammy spotted them.

"Look, Vin. Those two broads are back," Sammy was excited to see Kay again. Vincent was also delighted to see Annette but hid his feelings.

They ordered a bottle of Cabernet Sauvignon and had it sent to the ladies.

"It's from Vincent and Sammy," the waitress answered their puzzled look as she pointed to the rear of the restaurant. Annette nervously fidgeted in her seat as the men approached their bar. *Well, at least I know their names again, thanks to the waitress,* she thought.

"How nice to see you again, Annette—Kay." Vincent

114

greeted them, warmly.

He remembered our names, how sweet, thought Annette.

"Thank you, and nice to see you also."

"So, when did you ladies get back into town?" asked Sammy.

"Oh, we never left. We've been here all week," Kay replied.

Sammy slapped his knee, in excitement.

"You're kidding! We thought you were going back to the cruise ship that night we met you," Sammy was so happy to see Kay again that he didn't give her a chance to explain.

"I can't believe you were here all week, and I didn't see you. How did you manage that? Where were you hiding? After all, this is a small town."

"Well, I went out on the beach and got a sunburn, so I spent the next few days in my hotel room."

Sammy then noticed the bathing suit strap tan marks that her dress couldn't hide.

"That's a very pretty dress, Annette," Vincent complimented her.

This time, Annette paid closer attention to Vincent. She observed him to be handsome in a reckless, devil-may-care way. He had an abundance of thick, wavy brown hair that tumbled across his forehead begging to be smoothed back by a female hand. He was very sexy, in a rugged sort of way. He was the perfect height, five-nine to her five-seven. Annette could tell because her two-inch heels brought her in line with his forehead. She always liked being even with a man! She was also impressed with his mind—an intelligent man could arouse Annette. He had interesting things to say about life and human nature and was especially fond of repeating famous quotes.

Such as, "If we could only be born with the age old wisdom of eighty, and then gradually age to the youthful age of eighteen," which he quoted from Emerson.

By the time their conversation got around to the study of astrology, Annette was enamored. Now she understood his strong, silent attitude, reminiscent of the Taurus sign. She knew they were solid, steady, practical and lacked superficiality. Yes, he was a perfect match for her Virgo sign. She had read that the bull was deep and sensuous, and she felt an involuntary jerk between her thighs. Annette felt the heat rising throughout her body and had a hard time concentrating on what Vincent was saying. As fascinated as she was by his profound perspectives, she couldn't stop looking at the cute little mole near his lip. Each time he spoke, it moved right along with him. This mole, coupled with his deep baritone voice, mesmerized Annette.

Vincent noticed her rapt attention and mistook it for deep interest in what he was saying.

Now, this lady is really smart, Vincent thought. *She's in touch with my intellectual side. I like her already!*

Sammy was in a euphoric state holding Kay close as they moved in rhythm to the slow music. But when Kay felt herself being poked by something hard in her lower abdomen area, she blushed and suggested they sit down.

Since it was Friday night, Charley and Eddie played until 1 A.M. and the couples stayed the entire evening.

"So, where are you ladies staying?" Sammy asked when it was time to leave.

The Hotel Capri, Annette answered.

Sammy and Vincent exchanged stunned looks, then laughed.

"What's so funny?" The women asked.

"Oh, it's nothing, really. It's just that we always laugh when tourists mention that hotel. You see, we're not used to hearing it called that...it's known among the locals as the Milk of Magnesia, because of its chalky white appearance."

They strolled up the hill, hand in hand. Sammy's mind raced ahead as he imagined sneaking into Kay's room late at night, just like Johnnie used to do with Angela, before they were married.

When they reached the top of the hill, Annette turned to bid them goodnight, but the men continued walking passed them through the lobby towards the elevator, nodding at the desk clerk in the process.

Annette stood with mouth gaping, dumbfounded as she watched them enter the elevator. She was infuriated and insulted as she clenched her fists and turned to Kay in an agitated whisper.

"Why do these creeps think they can get us in bed just because they bought us a bottle of wine? Who the hell do they think we are? Some little floozies? And they even acknowledged the desk clerk. Did you see that, Kay? The nerve! I wonder how many times this scene has been played out?"

Kay giggled, but tried to squelch it when Annette gave her an angry glance.

Vincent and Sammy were obviously enjoying the confusion they had caused while holding the elevator door open.

"You ladies going up? This elevator can't wait here forever, you know, and Sammy and I would like to get to our rooms!" Vincent delivered all this with a straight face looking directly at Annette.

"Come on Annette, it's okay. We're staying on the fourth floor." Vincent took Annette's hand and Kay followed.

The elevator stopped on the third floor, let the ladies out and abruptly closed the door after them. The women stared at each other, then burst out laughing, somewhat relieved with perhaps a tinge of regret that they weren't going to be taken advantage of, after all.

As soon as the elevator closed after them, Sammy paced back and forth like a caged animal.

"Gees, Vin, doesn't it make you crazy not getting them in the sack? I mean they're right below us, so close. Man, I don't know about you, but I've been going crazy on this damn island without a woman. I wake up every night with a hard-on! Every night, in the middle of the night, I hear those two next door, Johnnie and Angela going at it and her loud screaming."

Sammy was still talking as they stepped out of the elevator.

"Gee whiz, Vin, I can't get back to sleep until I jerk off, know what I mean?"

"Sammy, Sammy, I told you to take up reading. If you could get interested in a good book, you'd be amazed how it subdues the carnal desires." Vincent was aware his condescending manner drove Sammy nuts. Sammy shook his clinched fists at Vincent. He wanted to hit him so badly.

...

The sound of the phone ringing the next morning woke the women. Annette glanced at the clock. It was seven o'clock A.M.

Now who would be calling this early? Annette wondered.

"Hello."

"Oh, I'm terribly sorry, Annette. Did I wake you?" Vincent could tell from her voice that he had.

"Oh, no, no, I'm awake." Annette recognized his voice and immediately sat up in bed and stretched her face to widen her eyes.

"I just called to apologize for the way we led you ladies on, last night. We just couldn't resist having a bit of fun with you when we realized where you were staying." Silence.

"Hello, are you still there?"

"Yes, yes, I'm here." Annette was still trying to wake up.

"Well, I just wanted to invite you ladies to be our dinner guest tonight, say at eight o'clock at The Lei? Just to show there's no hard feelings."

Annette hesitated for a moment, then looked over at Kay

who was now sitting up straight and rubbing her eyes.

"That would be very nice. Thank you. We would love to have dinner with you."

Annette smiled as she hung up the phone.

"So, what was that all about, Net?"

"That, my partner, was a dinner date for tonight. Oh, dear, what will I wear? I already wore my only new dress I had last night. Now, why didn't I bring more dressy clothes?" Annette was all a-glow as she rambled on.

"I know. Let's go shopping again, back to that little shop where the salesgirl was so nice. Let's buy some really sexy dresses this time!"

CHAPTER 24

Since the shops weren't opened yet and the women were now wide awake, they decided to pass up the hotel's continental breakfast for a hardier meal.

There were two empty stools at the counter when they entered Al's Coffee House. When Ernest Frye looked up to see Annette sitting next to him, he spilled his coffee. That caught everyone's attention at the counter, especially Annette's.

"Well, hello. Remember me?" Annette asked, wondering why he was so nervous.

"Yes, yes, I...I do." Ernest stuttered.

"Is something wrong? Are you all right?"

Ernest broke out in a cold sweat.

"You don't know me, do you?" Ernest asked, timidly.

"Well, I did see you at the police station the other day. I'm sorry, I never did get your name."

"My name is Ernest Frye. I mean, before that day?"

"Well, no. Should I?"

Ernest took a deep breath before continuing. "I worked in the Meadowbrook Station before transferring here. I was assigned to the Juvenile Division and paid visits to the Narcotics Division to drop off the paperwork. You were in the office each time I came in. Guess you never noticed me."

Annette looked around anxiously to see if anyone was

eavesdropping.

"I was afraid this would happen. I knew if word ever got out about Sylvia Lawson and that we didn't do the proper investigation, someone would come over here to investigate. I tried to tell Dan, but he wouldn't listen," Ernest's hand shook as he took out his handkerchief and wiped the sweat from his brow.

Annette placed her hand over his. "Ernest, calm down. It's okay. I didn't come here to check up on you. I'm here on a special assignment and it had nothing to do with you, but you must not tell anyone who I am, understand?"

Ernest was so self-absorbed that he really wasn't listening to Annette, nor did he feel placated. "Look, I didn't approve of the way Dan handled the case. I tried to tell him we didn't do a proper investigation, but you can't tell him anything. I mean, you saw what he's like, didn't you?"

Ernest sounded like he needed more reassurance.

"Ernest, no one is holding you responsible for this and I can see that working with Dan must be difficult for you." Annette placed a comforting hand on his arm. "But you can be of real help to me, Ernest."

"I'll tell you anything you want to know," Ernest let out a sigh of relief. "This whole thing stinks. These people are ignorant, you know?"

Ernest finally found someone he could trust, someone to express his frustration to.

"I do understand. I've been here long enough to see how it is like here and what these people are like, and I do sympathize with what you have to endure. Okay, Ernest, what can you tell me?" Annette lowered her voice, and they became so engrossed in their conversation they didn't see Dan walk in.

"Ernest, we have a department to run so if you've finished up here, get your tail back so I can have my breakfast!" Dan sat down on the newly vacant seat next to him.

How uncouth, thought Annette. She paid for their coffee

and left, not staying for breakfast, after all.

"So, what were you two talking about, huh?"

"Nothing that concerns you, Dan." Ernest answered, scornfully. Talking to Annette gave him the courage to speak to Dan in that tone of voice. He paid his bill and smiling to himself, walked out briskly.

...

Heather was busy ticketing her merchandise when the bell over the door sounded. "Oh, hello." She recognized Annette. "I hope the blue dress was a hit."

"Oh, yes, it certainly was. Now, we need two more new dresses for our big date tonight."

They both tried on short, sexy, tight dresses. Kay admired herself in the dressing room mirror as she modeled a red, sequin, off the shoulder dress. It was a tight, close-to-the-body dress. Although this style didn't do anything flattering to Kay's Rubenesque figure, she knew it would meet with Sammy's approval.

"He told me he liked his women with meat on their bones!" she explained as she attempted to ward away Annette's critical stare.

Annette chose a classy, black knit, long-sleeved dress that hugged her trim body. It had a plunging neckline and a back of crisscross straps that were tied at the waistline. The women agreed it was beautiful from the front and back. Annette looked at the $150.00 price tag and gulped. "This is definitely the one," she said with her heart racing. "We'll have to list these receipts as working clothes when we send the bill to the captain." They laughed.

Heather sighed, with envy, as the happy women left with their purchases.

Saturday night was a big night at The Lei. There was a

123

two hour wait for those without reservations. When the women gave their names to the hostess, she smiled and led them to the big booth in the rear of the restaurant. They had to make their way past a long line of hungry couples waiting to be seated. Envious eyes followed them as they walked through the crowd.

"So, this is what it feels like to be treated like a VIP," Annette whispered to Kay. Annette felt very special this evening. As they approached the table, three other couples were with Vincent and Sammy. They had already met Johnnie and Angela.

"That's them...the dames we were telling you about," Sammy excitedly whispered to Dominic. Vincent, always the gentlemen, rose to greet them and introduced them to Guido, Paula, Dominic, and Regina.

Annette's heart skipped a beat when she heard him say Dominic's name.

So, this is the infamous Dominic Visconti that Reginald told me about she thought, and his entourage, his boys, and here she was in the center of all this notoriety. Annette looked at Vincent differently the rest of the evening. She sat back, surveying the group, thinking. *Boy, would they be surprised if they knew who I am and what I came here for*. She could hardly wait to make her weekly report to her captain.

They were a happy group that night as the food and wine flowed freely. When the women got up to go to the powder room, Sammy let out a long, low whistle. "Mamma mia, did you get a load of that Vin? Did you see the back of Annette's dress? She's not wearing a bra!"

"Calma, calma," Vincent told Sammy to calm down.

"**Su two asino**," Sammy told him to shove it—performing the Italian obscene expression of crossing one arm over the other, then making a fist and raising it.

"So, what do you think of those girls, huh, Vinnie?" Dominic turned to Vincent as he was the one who used his analytical head instead of his other one, unlike Sammy.

"They seem to be nice ladies, Dom."

"Maybe too nice, was that what you're telling me, Vinnie?"

"Time will tell, Dom."

Vincent didn't like where this conversation was heading. He liked Annette and didn't want her mixed up in Dominic's operation. Not that he thought she would—she's too decent to ever go for anything like this, thought Vincent.

"Give me time to get to know them and I will let you know. Okay, Dominic?"

Whenever Vincent refused to shorten Dominic's name, Dominic knew that meant fermata—stop! He was satisfied. He trusted Vincent to make good judgments about people. He would forget about business for tonight.

When they finished dinner, Dominic ordered several bottles of wine to be brought to his reserved table in the lounge. Charley and Eddie were playing his favorite tune, "Satin Doll."

"Look at Eddie play that guitar. Isn't he great?" Dominic put a twenty in the tip jar and whirled Regina on to the dance floor. The others joined in. As they danced the night away, they were unaware of the time until they heard "The Party's Over" being played. No one wanted the evening to end, so Dominic invited them back to his Pizza Palace.

They put coins in the old juke box and continued their dancing. As Annette surveyed the front, Vincent noticed her interest and offered her a tour of Dominic's office. Guido and Dominic overheard Annette's admiration of Dominic's eight-foot sofa. Guido grinned, thinking. Ah, ha, another one likes this sofa. He caught Dominic's eye and they both laughed remembering Guido's unique request on the night of his wedding.

The two couples wandered out onto the patio. The fog was just rolling in and the damp air sent chills through Annette, and she shivered. Vincent noticed and put his arm around her. She turned her face toward him, and he kissed her. A sweet, short, friendly kiss. Not so with Sammy and Kay who were at the other end of the patio with Sammy leaning against the wooden rail and Kay pressed up against him kissing passionately and making blissful sounds.

It was four in the morning when the couples left Dominic's and strolled leisurely up the hill. Sammy and Kay made periodic stops along the way to kiss and hug. By the time Vincent and Annette reached the top, they were shrouded by the fog.

They sat in the lobby and waited, all the while, reading each other's eyes. They wanted each other, it was obvious, but they were both afraid of losing control. Annette was aware of sending out mixed signals. She dressed in a sexy way, telling the world she was a passionate woman and would love to lose herself in the moment. Yet, Annette had a tough veneer and behaved in a way that discouraged any improprieties. Annette realized she had this complex personality. But underneath all that exterior was a passionate embryo just waiting to be born. Vincent felt the urgency of this yearning between them.

Sexual tension engulfed the couples as they entered the elevator. The women reluctantly got off on their floor. Even the elevator door seemed to hesitate in closing after them.

The ladies undressed speechlessly, almost as if they were afraid of breaking the invisible spell that surrounded them. In the middle of the night, Annette woke restless and wondered if Kay was asleep. She looked over to find her bed empty. Her robe and slippers were gone, and the door was unlocked.

"What the hell," Annette said out loud to the dark, empty room. "I don't believe this." Just then a soft knock at the door startled her. "Who is it?"

"It's Vincent, Annette. May I come in?"

Annette grabbed her old robe, thinking. *Darn, I wish I brought a sexy robe.* She opened the door and found Vincent standing there in his pajamas and robe.

"Hi, sorry to bother you, but can I borrow a cup of sugar?" They both laughed at the awkwardness of the moment.

When Annette didn't invite him in, he grinned and asked.

"May I come in, Annette? I feel silly standing out here like this," he said, sheepishly.

"Oh, of course, I'm sorry. I wasn't thinking. I didn't expect to see you here, like this." Annette was very uneasy about the situation.

As soon as he entered, she turned all the lights on, pulling her robe more securely around her in the process.

"I guess you know where Kay is," Vincent grinned, apologetically.

"Yes, and I am surprised. I never thought she would just go off like that in the middle of the night to a guy's room like a..." Annette stopped herself from calling Kay a "tramp". She was embarrassed. She hoped her jealousy didn't show. She didn't want to admit that Kay had the courage to go after what she wanted. She couldn't help but admire her for that.

"I am sorry, Annette, for coming here now, but I thought you wouldn't mind...that you would understand if I stayed here awhile to give them a chance to be alone."

They sat together on the sofa, without saying a word. The silence became so uncomfortable, they let out a small nervous laugh. They looked at each other sitting together on the sofa in night clothes and burst out laughing. The sound of their laughter tore through the silence of the room and relaxed them. Soon they were conversing and lost all track of time until they heard Kay at the door.

...

The next morning Kay woke up, smiling. "Good morning, Net. Isn't it a glorious day?" She stretched herself awake.

For heaven's sake, has she no shame? thought Annette, resentfully. *I'm the one who should be freer, more liberal.* Annette was surprised to discover Kay's free-spirited nature, when she seemed so shy. *Heck, you can never tell when it comes to people*.

After that night, Sammy and Kay behaved like lovebirds, not trying to hide their feelings for each other. Sammy was finally *calma*, as Vincent would say. Except for the strained sexual tension between Vincent and Annette, the couples enjoyed each other's company.

Even so, Annette told herself, she could not get involved with such an objectionable person. *I'm supposed to be putting him away not laying him!* she reminded herself. But she felt so vulnerable whenever she was near Vincent. Annette wasn't so sure now about making her weekly report to her boss. She was confused!

CHAPTER 25

Annette was from a family of police officers. She was the only daughter of Brendan Kelsey and the youngest of five children, the rest, all boys. Annette's mother died when she was just a baby, and her older brothers took turns diapering her and watching her grow into the lovely woman she had become. From an early age, Annette knew what she would be when she grew up.

When she was eighteen, after graduating from high school, she entered the Police Academy. She graduated with honors and became a Narcotics Agent. Since she was surrounded by men, both at home and on the job, she never felt she needed any one man in her life and besides, she never found that special man who could crack her defensive wall. She had great plans for her own life, and it didn't include a husband and children. Sure, she dated, but her relationships were short-lived. Whenever a beau showed too much interest, she ended it. Annette was tough, self-confident and self-assured. Her co-workers often accused her of obstinacy.

"That's it! I'm making that phone call!" she proclaimed loudly. Her self-appraisal reminded her of what a sensible woman she really was.

"This is Sergeant Annette Kelsey. Put me through to Captain Sheridan, please."

"Captain Sheridan, here."

"Bill, have I got a report for you!"

Annette filled him in on her meeting with Dominic, carefully filtering the circumstances of their meeting...she omitted mentioning Vincent. She told him about Reginald and the information he gave her—that Dominic's Pizza Palace was a front for his drug operation.

"Oh, one more thing. A big drop is supposed to be made, any day now. Yes, I got it from a reliable source, Deputy Ernest Frye. He worked at the Meadowbrook station before being stationed here. No, I didn't know him either, but he recognized me. Well, I'll keep you posted. Yeah, yeah, I know I'm doing a good job." Annette smiled as she hung up the phone. Bill rarely gave out compliments.

Annette felt a heaviness come over her. What had she done? She felt like a traitor. What was happening to her? Was it the island that made her want to loosen up? To free herself from her responsibilities and to live and love? That was exactly what she wanted to do...make love to Vincent. She could hardly believe she admitted this to herself. The thought increased her heart rate. Annette never thought she could hate her job, but she did hate this assignment, she hated being a spy! She wanted to abort the whole thing, get on the first ferry off the island, and never look back. She liked these people—even Dominic, and of course, his group. And she didn't want to hurt any of them, especially Vincent.

...

Heather was happy to see Annette back so soon. She had become her best customer, lately. Annette knew exactly what she wanted and went right to it.

Kay was coming out of the shower when Annette walked in with a box under her arm.

"What's that, Net? Not another new dress?"

130

"No, not this time," Annette answered and smiled secretly.

That night, after dinner, the couples retired to their respective rooms. Annette claimed she was tired and went right to bed. When she thought Kay was asleep, she quietly rose, put on her new purchase and admired herself in the mirror. Annette was amazed at how her thoughts, over the past week, had changed her looks. Before, she saw herself as rigid, controlling, even old. This woman staring back at her was sexy, charming, softer and younger looking.

"Oh darn!" Annette whispered, softly, at the reflection of her hair-a mass of kinks from the damp ocean air. She threw her uncompromising hair back indignantly. As she quietly let herself out of the room, Kay rolled over and smiled.

The soft knock on the door stirred Vincent easily, as he wasn't asleep.

"I'm sorry to bother you, but can I borrow a cup of sugar?"

Vincent knew it was just a matter of time before one of them would go to the other. He was happy Annette was the one to make the first move.

Vincent roused Sammy.

"Hey, what the hell is going on? I'm asleep, for Heaven's sake." Sammy sat up abruptly, rubbing his eyes. He dimly made out a beautiful figure, with ravishing red hair, wearing a black lace negligee. As he grabbed his robe and slippers, he thought. *Damn it, if that college boy isn't finally gonna get laid!* He threw out a "have fun" as he closed the door behind him.

As Sammy ran down the stairs, he thought. *Hey, this was just what Johnnie used to do, before he married Angela—and what I've always dreamed of doing.*

Kay was expecting the knock and with a mischievous smile, opened it to receive her caller.

...

As soon as the door closed, Vincent moved slowly toward Annette, removing his pajama top. His hard body delighted Annette. The first time she saw it was that day on the beach and she remembered thinking at the time. *What a shame to cover up such a smooth, hard, perfect physique.*

Vincent gently removed her negligee, picked her up in his strong arms and carried her over to his bed. Annette surrendered herself as they entered into a world of passion. Vincent was a smooth, romantic, experienced lover. He caressed every inch of her firm body, leaving Annette tingling with joy. He traced her breasts with his long fingers, smiling when her nipples hardened. He took one in his mouth and swirled his tongue slowly around it all the while kissing and sucking it. He repeated this pattern on the other nipple. His massaging fingers then made a more intimate search below until he felt her warm moistness.

Annette reached down and gasped when she found her hand holding a very well-endowed organ. She was no longer a complacent recipient. She had now become the aggressor as she lowered herself to meet this wonderfully, corpulent, elongated piece of flesh. She formed her moist lips in a wide circle to accommodate Vincent's large, luscious head and with the first taste, he shuddered and fell back in complete ecstasy. She found his juice warm and full and took it all in, not losing a drop. He brought her face down to his, cupped it with both his hands and gave her a long, passionate kiss and whispered something in her ear. Annette thought she heard "thank you." This touched her deeply.

They drifted off to sleep. Annette woke with the delicious sensation of Vincent's lips on her loins. He separated her legs gently and kissed her inner thighs. He moved slowly up her smooth flat stomach and then back again to her pubis. His long tongue moved masterfully around her red juicy lips until a combustion was imminent and Annette's whole body was thrown into a frenzy of convulsive jolts. As the throbbing ripples receded, she kissed him gratefully.

They fell asleep once more, holding each other. Hours later, they awoke refreshed and hungry. This time, Annette had the complete joy of experiencing Vincent's marvelous penis in her. She wrapped her long legs around him, tightly, urgently. He filled her up completely and Annette let out a piercing scream. Vincent silenced her with his kisses.

After Vincent dressed her, he poured two brandies.

"By the way, Annette, you look ravishing in that negligee."

...

The following days and nights were filled with joy. There was freedom in their lovemaking as the couples no longer hid their feelings for each other. Annette knew she was fooling herself to allow this to continue without any repercussions, but she was too involved to care. She didn't know how to unravel herself from this involvement with Vincent nor did she want to. Little did she know that soon she would be forced to make a decision.

The phone rang. She knew who it was and hesitated to answer until the fourth ring.

"Oh, Bill, how are you?" Annette sensed her boss's perturbation.

"How nice of you to remember me," Bill said facetiously. "Haven't heard from you in over a week now, however, I did receive your receipts from that boutique shop. All $500 worth! What the hell are you buying? And what do you think you two are doing out there—on a holiday?" Bill was now raising his voice.

133

"Now Bill, calm down. Kay and I needed some dressy clothes so we could go to The Lei. You know, the place I told you about. Dominic's place. Now, how can we attract the right people without the proper attire? Besides, whose idea was it we come here? And who was the one to say we could make a nice vacation out of it? Remember?" There was silence on the other end. *Good strategy. I now have him on the defense*, thought Annette. "Now, the reason I didn't call sooner was because, frankly, I had nothing new to report. These Islanders are very cautious about strangers and don't open up too easily, so I needed to take it nice and slow and get them to accept me. To trust me, you know." Another length of silence, then...

"Yeah, okay. So how is Kay doing? Put her on."

"Oh, Kay is in the shower. But she has been such a help. Glad you suggested I bring her."

As soon as Annette hung up the phone, she put on her bathing suit, grabbed her beach bag and ran out the door to catch up with the others at the beach.

CHAPTER 26

The couples were eating pizza and drinking beer in a booth near the back of Dominic's Pizza Palace when Dan Dawson walked in. He looked up when he heard loud laughter coming from the rear of the restaurant.

"Hi Dan, nice to see you. You haven't been here for some time," Dominic greeted Dan, with a smile.

"Yeah, well, we've been busy," Dan responded, without taking his eyes off Annette. "I see you've met Ms. Snoopy," Dan nodded toward Annette.

Dominic looked puzzled. "You mean Annette Kelsey?"

"Yeah, that's her all right."

"What did you call her, Dan?"

"Ms. Snoopy. She dropped in the department the other day asking a lot of questions about Sylvia Lawson."

Dominic stared intently at Dan not wanting to interrupt him. "Go on."

"And the other day," Dan continued, "I found her in a huddle with my Deputy, Ernest Frye. They were going on about something and you could sure as hell tell they wasn't talking about no weather!" Dan watched Dominic's face turn ashen as he turned his head to look at Annette.

As Dan got up to leave, Dominic snatched up his check. "This is on me, Dan." For the information you supplied, Dominic added to himself.

Dominic waited in his office, leaving the door ajar, so he could watch when the foursome got up to leave. It was midnight when they passed by his office. Dominic called out to Vincent.

"Vinnie, can I see you a minute?"

"I'll see you up at the hotel," Vincent kissed Annette on the cheek.

"Close the door, Vinnie," was the last thing Annette heard. All the way up the hill, she kept looking over her shoulder, hoping to see Vincent and becoming increasingly anxious when he didn't appear. *Why did Dominic call him in so late at night?* Annette asked herself. *They always discuss business during the day. Never at night and never this late.* It must have been important.

...

"What's the problem, Dom?" Vincent wondered why Dominic wanted to see him so late at night. Dominic had a concerned somber look on his face.

"Vinnie, something real bad is happening here," He poured them a scotch and soda. "Your girl has been snooping around, asking questions around town about Sylvia Lawson."

Vincent flinched. "You're not talking about Annette, are you?" Vincent knew that was a rhetorical question.

"Yeah, Vinnie. Your Annette Kelsey. I don't think she's just an innocent tourist. I know you two have been getting pretty

136

close lately and damn it, I wish this wasn't true, but I got it from reliable sources." He paused to study Vincent, whose head was bowed, the color drained from his face.

"You know what you have to do, Vinnie. Nothing comes between our business—no broad-no relative—nobody, caprice?" Dominic placed his hand on Vincent's shoulder.

"I know you to do the right thing, Vinnie."

Vincent walked outside and felt like a beaten man. He went straight to his room and laid on the bed. He stared wide-eyed at the ceiling and thought about what had transpired.

Annette lay wide awake staring at the ceiling and wondered why Vincent didn't come to her room to say goodnight. *That's not like him. Something must be wrong.* Butterflies of anxiety were fluttering in Annette's stomach.

Their plans for the following day were to rent two bicycles-built-for-two and cycle around the island, however when Sammy knocked on their door that morning, Vincent wasn't with him.

"He had some business to take care of for Dominic," he told them. "He told us to go ahead without him." Kay thought nothing of it, but Annette knew something was wrong and decided to spend the day alone.

She took a book up to the sundeck. She stared at the first page, thinking. It isn't like Vincent not to call me this morning about the change in plans. Her book slipped from her lap as she fell asleep. Hours later, a cold wind drifted in from the harbor awakening her and she woke up shivering. She glanced at her watch, 4 P.M. *Was it still on?* She wondered.

The evening plans were for dinner and dancing at The Lei, but when the men came to pick them up, Vincent said there was a change in plans. He had made reservations for them at Pelican's Beak. Everyone was happy, except Annette. She didn't like this change, one bit. She felt apprehensive being ten miles from town. Ordinarily, she wouldn't give it a second thought but tonight was different. Vincent was different, tonight.

Vincent was driving Dominic's big black Cadillac wild and furious on the long winding mountain road and too close to the edge of the cliffs.

He doesn't usually drive Dominic's car anywhere. It's mainly used for business. Annette's mind raced ahead competing with Vincent's erratic driving. The nervous passengers were glad when the thirty-minute ride was over, and they arrived at Pelican's Beak.

Vincent had reserved a window table overlooking the harbor below. At any other time, Annette would have been thrilled to be here—it was more sophisticated than The Lei—but not tonight. A heavy gloom hung over the couples. They ordered lobster tails and their favorite wine.

If only Vincent wasn't so melancholy and in such a pensive mood, Annette thought. She tried small talk, but Vincent looked right through her. Kay and Sammy noticed but rationalized it to each other. "Oh, they're just having a lover's quarrel, that's all."

Perhaps she should have confided in Kay—tell her what she suspected, but she felt so guilty for allowing herself to become so involved with Vincent. She was so ashamed she had let this assignment get out of hand. After all, she was supposed to be the responsible one here. She wasn't supposed to get involved. She was supposed to do her job and get out! Alas, she stayed too long, and she got caught!

Annette didn't know what Vincent was thinking or what Dominic said to him, but she knew she shouldn't be here now. She should have left yesterday after reporting to her captain. She should have packed her bag and left on the first ferry off the island that morning. She hadn't shared any of this with Kay. *Why scare her? Anyway, Kay never planned on making the department her career, she was just waiting for someone better to come along, and it looked like he did. Kay would probably resign when this mess was over with. Oh damn!*

All these anxious thoughts gave Annette a migraine. She excused herself and went to the ladies' room. When she saw an outside door, she decided that was what she needed, some fresh air. When she stepped outside, she discovered she was on the side of the restaurant, without the protection of a rail. She leaned over the mountain side, two-thousand feet above San Lucci, and shuddered. The pitch-dark night gave off an eerie silence.

Was this what it was like for Sylvia Lawson? Annette asked herself. Reginald had told her that an Indian, Pipe, while drunk told him about a dark night—a mountain—edge of a ravine—a rock—a fall. Just fragmented pieces. Annette's head was swimming, and she didn't realize how close to the cliff's edge she was. As she turned to go back inside, she twisted her ankle on a loose stone and lost her balance. Falling backwards, she felt hands pressing against her. Was she being pushed...or being pulled back to safety?

She fainted and when she came to, she was lying on the cold ground staring up into Vincent's face. "You almost fell, Annette. Good thing I came out looking for you."

As Vincent helped her up, Annette studied him, thinking. *He still cares for me, I know it!*

"Oh, Vincent, please talk to me. Tell me what you're thinking, please!" Annette pleaded with him.

Vincent looked at her and took a deep, sad sigh. "Why Annette? Why did you lie to me, lead me on? How long did you expect to get away with this deception? Don't you know how fast rumors travel here on San Lucci. Surely you knew it was only a matter of time before I would find out who you were, Sergeant Annette Kelsey," Annette blanched when he mentioned her name.

"And why would you book a room in Dominic's hotel, the very man you were investigating?"

Annette stammered as she tried to explain but Vincent put his hand up to stop her from interrupting. "And those phone calls between you and your boss. Tsk, tsk."

Vincent had spent the entire day investigating her and picked up the long-distance phone charges at the hotel. When he called the phone number listed, a male voice answered. "Meadowbrook Police Department, Narcotics Division, Sergeant Snyder speaking." Then he recalled the first night they met at The Lei. He assumed they were going to the boat dock since Annette never told him they were staying on the island. Then he remembered it was past midnight when they left, and the last ferry left the island at eleven. He never thought about it then. He was insulted that she led him on, especially when the hotel clerk told him they had checked in at noon on that day!

"You really fooled me, Annette. Coming to my room that night we made love for the first time. A real smart move. And all those nights afterwards were just part of the job, right?" Vincent's voice broke and his eyes became misty as he remembered their passionate times together.

"Oh, no, it wasn't like that, at all. I loved our times together; they were real, special," Annette felt the urgency to make Vincent believe her. She spoke rapidly for fear Vincent wouldn't let her finish. "I never planned to stay in San Lucci this long... I never planned to meet you. I didn't know Dominic owned The Hotel Capri. That night you invited us to dinner and Dominic Visconti was our host...I was shocked. I never knew you were associated with him. I never suspected you were one of his boys.

"By then, I had all the information I needed and was planning on leaving the next day, but I stayed, Vincent, because you asked me to. Remember?"

Annette paused anxiously to study Vincent's demeanor, hoping for some encouraging sign but he remained emotionless. "Oh, Vincent, I never intended to get so involved with you. It just happened and then I was so deeply in lo—" Annette caught herself, "...so entangled that I didn't know how to get out. Oh,

Vincent, so many times I started to pack my bags, get off the island, forget about this place, about you." Annette was on the verge of tears. *Oh, why doesn't he speak? Why doesn't he say something? Why must he look at me so coldly? Oh, please speak to me, Vincent*, Annette silently prayed.

"What are we going to do?" Annette finally asked aloud, in desperation.

Vincent looked at her, solemnly. "I don't know, Annette. I really don't know."

No one said a word on the long ride down the mountain. Sammy and Kay fell asleep in the back seat. By the time they reached the hotel, Annette knew what she would do.

CHAPTER 27

The next morning, Annette woke up early, packed her bags and woke Kay.

"What's going on, Net?" Kay asked, sleepily then sitting straight up in bed when she saw Annette's packed bags.

Annette explained everything to her. "So, that's why we must get out of here, now."

"But what will you tell Bill?"

"Oh, I'll think of something. That I never found any proof of anything illegal going on here...that...that guy that came into our station made it all up—that he wanted revenge. And... that he turned out to be the town's liar. That he made it all up for the attention and that I found nothing to suggest foul play...and oh, I'll convince him, somehow." Annette answered nervously, unsure of herself.

When she saw that Kay didn't make any attempt to get up, she instructed her firmly. "Kay, get up! You have to pack. We need to catch the first ferry out of here."

Kay looked at Annette, anxiously.

"Net, I'm not going back with you," she said in a quiet voice.

"What?" Annette stared at her in disbelief.

"I'm going to resign. I never really belonged in the department—you always knew that Net. I'm just not cut out for this. You're tough and I'm so weak."

"Ha," Annette gave out an exasperated laugh. She didn't feel so tough right now.

"So, what will you do here?"

"Sammy said I can get a job here, no problem. Dominic knows everyone. And then me and Sammy could be together for good."

"Well, looks like you had it all figured out," Annette's eyes widened as it dawned on her. "Oh, for heaven's sake, Kay. You told Sammy who we were and what we were here for, long ago, didn't you?" One look at Kay's tense, frightened face told Annette she was right. "So, all this time, Sammy knew about us?" Kay slowly nodded her head. "How could you, Kay? Didn't you realize the danger you put us in? What if he told Dominic?" Annette couldn't get over Kay's irresponsibility. That's what love does to someone, she thought.

"It wasn't like that, Net. It was okay because I knew Sammy would never tell on us. He is not like that. He loves me and I love him. He knew I wasn't happy with this assignment, and he made plans for me to get out of it and stay here with him."

That was that. Sammy and Kay walked Annette to the ferry where the ladies, tearfully, said their goodbyes. They had become close, these past three weeks, despite their differences.

...

"You know, Vinnie, we have to make a decision here, you understand?" Dominic looked intently at Vincent. Vincent nodded in agreement. Vincent hadn't slept in two nights and had dark circles under his eyes.

"Now, if this was another Sylvia Lawson, I would have no problem deciding the outcome, caprice?" Vincent nodded again; his face visibly fraught with despair. "You know, Vinnie, I really liked that girl—the other one, too. I know how much you care about each other. I even thought we would have another double

143

wedding—you and Annette and Sammy and Kay. Ah, there was nothing I wanted more. Stupido donna! (stupid woman)" Dominic couldn't restrain his infuriation with Annette and calmed himself by pouring two drinks. He took a sip before continuing.

"Now, I have given this a lot of thought. More than I would if it was anyone else but you," he slapped the side of Vincent's head, affectionately. "I don't like to see you like this. You love this girl." Vincent tried to contradict him by shaking his head.

"No, no, don't interrupt me and don't you deny it! Do you think I was born yesterday, eh? I watched you two. I see the love you have for each other. No, I have decided. You belong together. I have a soft heart for love, what can I say? So, this is what we do," Dominic paused, finished his drink then continued. "First, bring her here to me, then I will tell you my plan."

Vincent looked at him, sadly.

"What is the matter with you? I tell you to bring your love here and you sit there and look at me like a sad puppy."

Vincent stared out the window at the ferry boat. It was loading up with passengers.

"She's gone, Dom. Sam and Kay took her to the ferry this morning. Sammy told me just before I came here.

"So, go get her. Bring her back here. The boat is still at the dock, I can see it from here. Now, if they pull out before you get there, you make them bring the boat back. You tell them Dominic ordered it. They know you are one of my boys. They will do it for me—they will not refuse. Now, matersi in moto. Hurry up and get outta here!" For re-enforcement, Dom gave him a swift kick in the behind.

...

Annette stared out the window watching the boat slowly make its way past the dock as it backed up. She was so engrossed

144

in her morbid thoughts she didn't notice the boat come to a stop. Her eyes were filled with tears and the ache in her heart was so heavy she thought it would break. He sat down next to her. She stiffened when he took her hand. She stared down at the familiar smooth hand with the perfectly manicured nails and was in a daze as she perked up with recognition. He took her arm and she rose as if in a trance and without a word followed Vincent off the boat.

Dominic was glad to see her. "Annette, please be seated. Can I get you something to drink?"

Annette stared apprehensively at Dominic. *Why is he so cordial with me after all I've done and why am I here? What do they want from me? What's going to happen to me?* Annette began to tremble as the tears ran down her face.

"**Povero bambino**," Dominic saw how frightened she was. "Oh, you poor baby. Don't be scared. No one is going to hurt you, Annette. That is not why we brought you here. Besides, if we wanted to hurt you, it would have been done already. Vinnie had the opportunity at Pelican's Beak."

Annette looked up in alarm.

"Oh, yes, you wondered why he changed the evening plans the last minute, eh?" Dominic paused to give Annette time to digest all that had happened. "He wanted to scare you, to teach you a lesson, that's all. He knew you would probably leave the next day. He scared you out-of-town!" Dominic laughed hilariously. "Vinnie's idea, brilliant, no? Okay, now we get down to business. Now, I'll tell you what I want. This is how we clean up your little mess." He smiled and patted her face.

...

Annette charged into her hotel room and caught Kay and Sammy in bed.

"Net, what are you doing here?" Kay reached for her robe while Sammy retrieved his pants.

"You really ought to keep that door locked, Kay. Never know who'll barge in!" Annette was all smiles, in charge once again and feeling great. "Okay, you two, out! I have an important phone call to make," she had a twinkle in her eyes. Oh, she was enjoying this. After they left, Annette poured herself some wine, settled back in her chair and took a few sips. "Okay, this is it!" She reached for the phone.

...

"Okay, Vinnie, now we have just seven days to complete our business, so you better get started. I want everything wrapped up nice and clean, **caprice** (understand)?"

Vincent began immediately staying busy day and night, with no time to spend with Annette. But she understood. She knew they would have plenty of time together later. Vincent paid a visit to Christopher's Rent-A-Boat on the wharf and told Christopher what he needed.

"No problem, Vincent. Consider it done, a piece of cake." Christopher grinned from ear to ear. This was the best assignment they had ever given him. He rubbed his hands together gleefully as he made his plans.

...

On the seventh day, they were all in Dominic's pizza palace, waiting. It was 6 A.M. and the sun was just rising over the water. The orange-streaked sky indicating a glorious day. They were in good spirits as Regina and Dominic made breakfast for everyone. Someone remarked, "This feels like a wedding—just like old times." But no wedding was taking place today.

Dominic looked around his restaurant, nostalgically. "This place holds a lot of fond memories, right Gina?" Regina nodded and smiled at her husband.

Rapid, loud knocking at the front door froze the group.

"Who could that be? It's too soon." Guido hesitated in answering the door, but the caller's persistent knocking indicated he was not going to stop. Guido pushed the drape aside, slowly, then gave a reassuring nod to the others as he opened the door and let the caller in.

"**Grazie, grazie**." Father Albert thanked Guido as he pushed past him heading straight for Dominic. "**Mi scusi, Senor Dominic, mi dispiace**," He apologized profusely for barging in on him but it was of extreme importance. Father Albert's hands shook as he took out his handkerchief and wiped his sweaty forehead and palms. He explained his predicament to Dominic while clutching a small black traveling bag.

Just as the sun was coming up, Dominic steered The Regina out of the harbor heading towards Venice where a new generation was to be born.

CHAPTER 28

The church bells tolled twelve times. The cruise ship was in. Charley and Eddie were playing their theme song. Betsy and Maggie were fighting for center stage again. Roxanne was putting her sale signs up. Heather was ticketing her new merchandise. Clyde was selling his newspaper, "The Seaport Gazette." Bandana Luke just made his third trip of the day to Rocky Beach. The retirement club had just initiated a new member and they were on their way to being inebriated.

The gun went off near Angie's Fish Market announcing a catch. Bert was welcoming a group of Japanese tourists on his tour bus. The aroma of buffalo burgers from Rodran's Buffalo Restaurant drifted through the town.

Tommy, Gilbert, Reginald and Remo were drinking coffee and gossiping at the counter at Al's Coffee House. Dan was berating Ernest for forgetting his onions, again.

The tourists were crowding the little town frustrating the Islanders as they sat on their benches.

The Farnesi brothers were clipping away while Mario Farnesi serenaded the passing women.

Aaron was walking rapidly down the street with Ingrid taking short quick steps trying to keep up with him.

Homer was drunk and banging on his door pleading for

Hetty to let him in.

Henry, the dentist, was sitting up on his balcony *on High Mountain* playing his trumpet.

Tony had his Marine Hymn tape on full blast.

Bobby was putting fresh duct tape on his boat. Uhrick convinced a tourist there was a 36-mile bridge connecting the Mainland to San Lucci Island and that next time he should drive over.

Mike just sold another dingy.

The paramedics and fire engine sirens were sounding throughout the town, on their way to The Bluff's. All the phones on the wharf were in use. Harry sold more condoms to some eleven-year-olds.

San Lucci had resumed its rituals, and all was well on the little quiet island until they showed up!

...

They appeared out of nowhere—in four sheriff's patrol boats, five men to a boat. Pandemonium ensued as twenty men marched through the town with guns bulging under their uniforms. Islanders and tourists alike stopped to watch the men. The Islanders knew something was not right, but the tourists thought it was a show staged for their benefit and they were delighted. Appropriately enough, just at that moment, the sounds of Tony's tape could be heard playing "From the Halls of Montezuma to the Shores of Tripoli."

Sergeant Bill Sheridan and his agents headed straight for The Hotel Capri where Annette told him they would meet. However, it was not as Annette had described to him. Instead of chalky white—they found a green building called The Four-Leaf Clover.

"Can I help you, gents?" A tall burly man in dark coveralls greeted them at the door.

"Yeah, what place is this? It's supposed to be the Hotel Capri, the one you people call the Milk of Magnesia. Where the hell is it? And where are my agents, Annette and Kay?"

The angrier Bill got the louder he became until he was literally shouting at Shawn...a big mistake!

Shawn Brandigan threw out his massive chest, raised his six four frame and glared down at Bill. "This here is The Four-Leaf Clover Hotel. The color is green, and the Islanders call it, Limeade and I am Shawn Brandigan, the owner. No Annette or Kay here!" He underlined each of his words firmly and sharply and with that, turned on his heels and slammed the front door in Bill Sheridan's face.

They walked down the hill with Bill fuming and cussing all the way. "Where the hell are those two? What's going on here, anyway?"

Their second stop was Dominic's Pizza Palace. Bill opened the door to find commercial washers and dryers and a Chinese man behind the desk.

"What is this? This is supposed to be Dominic's Pizza Palace!

"This Chinese laundry—best on island. You want I clean shirt?" He grabbed Bill's shirt.

"Stop that!" Bill slapped his hand. "I don't want my shirt cleaned. I want to know where Dominic's Pizza Palace is!" Bill was frustrated as he stormed out of the laundry yelling at his agents—he was taking it out on them.

"Okay, there's just one more place to check. The Lei. The place they had to buy those expensive dresses for!" Bill bellowed.

They found two Chinese men painting the outside red and putting up a sign that read, The Red Dragon Restaurant.

"What the hell?" Bill scratched his head, befuddled. "Isn't this The Lei, a Polynesian restaurant?"

"No, no, this Chinese restaurant. No open yet. You come

back next week." They resumed their painting.

Bill stood there watching them, speechless. Then it hit him! "Why those little bitches! They set me up! There isn't going to be a drop today or any other day... they skipped out!" Bill raved and ranted as he pulled his hair yelling obscenities. "I'll kill them when I catch up to them!"

Just then, four loud explosions coming from the harbor stifled the enthusiasm of Bill's threat. They ran to the dock just in time to see their boats go up in flames.

On the wharf by Christopher's Rent-A-Boat, a figure watched from behind the rail. Christopher rubbed his hands together and grinned from ear to ear.

CHAPTER 29

Dominic was at his desk in his stateroom talking on the phone.

"Um hmm, no kidding, ha! ha!" He looked over at Vincent, including him in on his merry conversation. "Good job. Okay, so tomorrow, you get started and when everything is liquidated, wire the money to my Swiss account. You have that information. And thanks again, Bernie, you earned your commission."

Dominic grinned at Vincent then laughed jubilantly as he relayed the big bust on San Lucci that his real estate broker, Bernie Goldstein described to him. "Come on, Vinnie, let's go topside and join the others. It's time to celebrate." Dominic threw his arm around Vincent and with the other grabbed his box of Havana's.

Annette didn't need to ask about the outcome. One look on Vincent's pleased face said it all.

"You were wonderful, darling. It worked exactly as planned," Vincent kissed her warmly.

"Okay, everyone, listen up. I have two announcements. You've all known about the affection these bambinos have for each other." Dominic looked at everyone, relishing the thought in what he was about to say. "Yes, yes, you know who I mean, you two over there,'" he gestured to Annette and Vincent and Sammy and Kay. "Now it is with deep regret that I can't arrange this like before. You know limos, church, the pizza palace, but this will have to do. And, since we have our priest here..." Father Albert spilled his red wine down his white shirt when he heard his name.

"So, what do you say? Let's have a double wedding, right now, right here, eh?"

The two couples looked at each other and their eyes said a definite "yes."

"Wait, wait, everyone." Regina ran down to her stateroom and brought back a bag of rice. "It's bad luck having a wedding without rice," she explained, handing out handfuls among the couples.

"Okay, now the other announcement," Dominic took Regina's hand in his and looked into her eyes with much love. "Gina and I are going to have a baby!" "Oohs" and "aahs" sounded throughout the boat.

Dominic told Father Albert to begin the ceremony, "And don't you forget, keep it short!"

Father Albert reached in his little black bag and took out his Bible and his stole, which he kissed, before placing it around his neck. He was happy to comply with anything Dominic wanted. After all, he was very grateful to him for taking him on board at such short notice. It was crucial that he got off the island immediately when Aaron found out he was the man with Ingrid that night Aaron walked in on them.

"I now pronounce you husband and wife. You may kiss each other." The champagne bottles were opened amidst hugs, kisses and tears of joy.

Johnnie cornered Dominic and whispered in his ear. He had been waiting a long time for this, for just the right moment. Dominic appeared puzzled, then grinned as he nodded his head, "yes." Johnnie smiled, smugly at Guido and grabbed Angela's hand, a bottle of champagne and headed swiftly towards Dominic's stateroom.

Ah yes, of course, thought Guido. Johnnie never did

forgive me for barging in on him and Angela the night of Dominic's wedding and finding them making out on Dominic's black leather sofa. Well, I hope he's satisfied now and maybe bring an end to this obsession with that sofa! Unless the other two couples have a taste for leather. At this thought, Guido's eyebrows shot up, in amusement.

"So, you thought I was pazzo, crazy, when I bought that haunted place in Venice? Dominic asked them. Somehow, he knew that one day it would come in handy. Dominic was looking forward to this new life with Gina, the baby and all his amicos (friends). As they neared Venice, he called his broker to open up The Palazzo and hire the necessary servants for their arrival.

...

Back on San Lucci Island, per Dominic's instructions, Bernie Goldstein paid a handsome bonus to the Chan family and Shawn Brandigan for their part in the charade. Then he hired local painters and maintenance workers to reveal the booths and tables in the Pizza Palace. The Hotel Capri was restored. The Chinese lanterns and red paint were removed from The Lei and the Polynesian décor was returned. When all the buildings were back in their original state, Bernie put up "For Sale" signs. He would receive a huge commission from the sale...as the whole town had profited from Dominic's departure.

...

Though each member of Dominic's group knew they could all live happily in Dominic's comfortable twenty room Palazzo, two couples were making their own private plans.

Vincent had decided to make that change he always knew he one day would. Now that he had Annette in his life, he was ready to live a respectable life. He shared his dreams with her. He had always had a penchant for metaphysical studies and wanted to go to school in England and become a professor. Annette loved the idea of being a professor's wife living in England.

Guido and Paula were looking forward to their new life together, even though Paula was disappointed Guido couldn't build their dream home on San Lucci Island. She had had an ambivalent relationship with San Lucci over twenty years but now she was ready to end those chapters of her life. It really didn't matter where she lived as long as she was with Guido. She confessed to him that she always dreamed of living in a beautiful chalet, high in the Swiss mountains. Since the borders of Switzerland and Italy kissed, Guido was happy to fulfill Paula's dream as long as he remained close to Dominic.

She then told him that she wanted to write a book. She visualized spending her days sitting on her bedroom balcony, overlooking the lush green valley below, writing her novel, "My Life on San Lucci Island."

THE SEQUEL

CHAPTER 30

"Please Dominic, tell him he can't go!" Regina desperately pleaded with her husband. "I keep having the same dream that something terrible happened to our son and he doesn't come back to us." Regina's premonition would later prove correct.

"Gina, Gina, you worry too much. It will be all right, you will see. After all, he is 25 years old, for heaven's sake. No longer a baby. Now, what is this? You still trying to keep him tied to your apron strings, eh? He's a man, now. He's gotta leave sometime."

Still, Dominic had some doubts knowing how psychic Regina was. He learned to respect her predictions. However, this time, he would stand his ground. This was their only persistent argument. Dominic knew he would not be sleeping in his bed tonight. Regina would lock him out!

He fixed himself a brandy and settled down on his eight-foot black buffalo leather sofa. He shook his head, in exasperation, and talked out loud to the empty room.

"Darn! That woman drives me to drink with all her superstitious." He let out a long sigh and pondered. "How is it possible that Joey is now 25? Where did the time go?"

...

What a day it was when he first saw his Joey in the hospital nursery at The Holy Immaculate Catholic Hospital in Venice.

"I'm a father for the first time-a father-at my age! Can you beat that? And it's a boy, a boy, at that!" He announced to all the people while handing out cigars.

It was a very special, scared thing, when the first child was a boy in an Italian family. Dominic was looked upon with even more respect. Dominic surprised himself when he saw how fatherhood affected him. He lay awake at night, wide-eyed and ears cocked for Joey's cry. Gently waking Regina, they entered the nursery. The love on Dominic's face was so real, so beautiful as he watched Regina tenderly breastfeed Joey while rocking him in her arms. This bond with Joey was formed the day he brought him home from the hospital. He remembered what kind of day it was.

The skies had threatened to rain all day and by nightfall, it fulfilled its promise by letting out a roar that tore throughout The Palazzo. Dominic recalled how frightened Joey was and how he cried at the top of his lungs. But when Dominic spoke softly to him, he immediately quieted down. Dominic's eyes filled when he saw how safe, secure, and loved Joey felt just hearing his voice. *So, this is what it means to be a father,* he reflected. As the brandy slowly worked its way down his throat, his legs and arms straightened in complete surrender. Dominic reminisced back to that time almost 26 years ago prior to moving into The Palazzo.

...

Dominic Visconti was well respected in the small island of San Lucci. His Pizza Palace was a haven for the homeless as they always counted on a free meal from the benevolent owner. The local priest also benefitted from his generous donations at Sunday

Mass. His real estate enterprises: hotel and nightclub, The Lei, brought in tourists and employment to the Islanders. So, when he made a hasty retreat out of San Lucci Harbor one Sunday morning aboard his yacht, The Regina, the town was devastated.

The culprits responsible were two NARC agents, Annette Kelsey and Kay Riley, who were from the Meadowbrook Police Department on the Mainland sent to investigate the cover-up of a young woman's' body found in the hills of the island. Annette reported to her captain that Dominic was involved. She later regretted her decision to do so when she met Vincent, one of Dominic's boys, at The Lei, Dominic's nightclub, and became romantically involved with him. She pretended to go along with her captain's plan to embark on the island with his agents in a surprise raid.

When the captain and law enforcement arrived, nothing was found that was reported, while Annette and Kay were nowhere to be found.

...

The entrance to The Palazzo was through the front courtyard up six steps to the second level, which consisted of a formal dining room, a drawing room and a ballroom. The third level was Dominic's private library with a secret door leading up to his bedroom, and a billiard room. The first level was the kitchen and housekeepers' quarters. The rooms fronted the Grand Canal with balconies extending the length of the rooms. The Palazzo was considered conservative, with only 20 rooms, compared to the 40 rooms of the other Palazzos along the Grand Canal. However, The Palazzo was not lacking in gaiety and comfort.

As they entered through the ornate, engraved, solid mahogany front doors, Dominic's servants, Cosmo and Celeste greeted them.

"**Benyenuto tutti**, welcome Senor and Senora Vincent and Annette Candiotti; Senor and Senora Sammy and Kay Santori; Senor and Senora Johnnie and Angela Compto; Senor and Senora Guido and Paula Gambino." When they came to Father Albert, they eyed him, suspiciously.

The sounds of their footsteps echoed throughout the entryway as they made their way down the long richly inlaid multi-colored marble floor. A chandelier of Murano glass hung at the base of a marble staircase that was decorated with trompe-l'oeil frescos.

The nine bedrooms were on the fourth floor and the master suite on the fifth. The sixth floor was the seamstress's room. The couples took the elevator and within seconds ascended to the fourth floor. They decided earlier which rooms they would occupy after Dominic informed them that the original owner was very religious and assigned a saint's name to the bedrooms.

The saint's name on Johnnie and Angela's door was St. Jude, Patron of Hopeless Causes. Angela had been trying to conceive ever since her wedding night. Johnnie felt he was to blame and lamented to her.

"Jeez, Angie, what kind of a man am I that I can't get you pregnant?" Johnnie was embarrassed by Dominic's constant nagging.

"So, Johnnie, what's the matter with you, eh? What kind of an Italian stud are you? You were married before Vincent and Sammy and already their Italian bread is in the oven and rising!"

The couples were amazed at what they saw in The Palazzo. Velvet tapestries and frescoes hung everywhere. The ceiling murals were painted by the leading Venetian painters and were known for their luminous sensual quality that reflected the Venetians' enjoyment of life.

Since The Palazzo's construction was U-shaped, the bedrooms wound around the building and each bedroom window had a direct view into each of the other bedrooms and down into the front courtyard. Each of the rooms were extravagantly decorated with silk damask wall coverings and drapes. The settee in the adjoining sitting room was richly covered in thick plush brocade material of many striking colors. Next to the marble fireplace hung a gold braided cord to summon the servants.

The Palazzo was of renaissance architecture, its style was round, geometrically astute, symmetrical, domed and balanced. Although its architectural attire was quite regal, it managed to combine nobility with frivolity. No fastidious woman dare find fault with the bath/dressing room. In the middle of the room surrounded by urns and obelisks sat a huge roman tub, large enough to comfortably hold six people. The ceilings were rich plaster. A ten-foot circular marble vanity lined the fresco covered walls.

"So, that's why Dominic asked my size and my favorite color," Annette excitingly told Vincent after discovering a black negligee set hanging in the bathroom closet. That was just like the thoughtful Dominic to make a woman feel so special. It resembled the one Annette wore the night she and Vincent made love for the first time in his hotel room on San Lucci Island. Annette smiled when she recalled what Vincent said to her after they made love.

"You look ravishing in that negligee, Annette".

"Net, are we dressing up for dinner? I just can't decide what to wear," Kay shouted out of her bedroom window.

"By all means, Kay. Dress up! You know how Dominic insists on a well-dressed table and that includes his dinner companions." It amused Annette how dependent Kay still was on Annette's opinions. *She is still so unsure of herself*, Annette thought, shaking her head. Still, she was pleased with the close friendship with her that developed after Annette took that break from her former life and married Vincent.

Annette decided, well—Vincent did, to wear her long-sleeved black knit dress, with its plunging neckline and crisscross straps that went all the way down her back to her waistline. This was the same dress she wore the night Vincent invited her to dinner at The Lei, and the first time she had met Dominic. Vincent always loved that dress and beamed when he saw her in it.

"You know, Annette, you won't be able to wear that dress much longer". Vincent gently patted her stomach smiling proudly.

Annette was just two months along and not "showing" but that didn't stop Vincent from checking her stomach daily.

"I think you are beginning to show. Don't you think you and Kay should start shopping for maternity clothes?"

Annette had to stifle a chuckle before responding. "You know, Vincent, I believe you are right. We will go shopping first thing tomorrow".

CHAPTER 31

When the couples entered the marbled column alcove leading into the dining room, they gasped. A 20-foot walnut, rococo style table with matching high-back tapestry holstered chairs sat majestically in the center of the room flanked on both sides by two buffet tables the length of the main table. The floor to ceiling marble fireplace at the far end of the room greeted them with a crackling fire. The rare and valuable religious scenes painted by noted Venetian painters in the 15th century filled the walls. The high dome ceiling was covered in colored mosaics, depicting "The Last Supper".

The formal table setting was flanked by silver tiered candelabras placed strategically along the table. The silverware was of the finest silver. The china bore the signature of a local craftsman. The pattern, "The Venetian Rose', was of the high renaissance era, at that time. The centers of the china were embossed with 18K gold roses encased with wide bands of 18K gold trim. The white starched linen dinner napkins were respectfully embraced by 14K gold napkin rings. Heavy tooled crystal wine glasses, with gold band trim, completed the setting. It was a table setting fit for a king. It was quite befitting the proud, somewhat egotistical demeanor of its owner. Dominic was the quintessential renaissance man. Ironic, slightly disdainful, supremely confident of his own powers.

The couples found their name card and commenced with the seating.

"I make a very warm welcoming toast to my familia, my family," Dominic always referred to the couples as his family, even though none were related. They went back many years together and were like flesh and blood. He practically raised "The Three Musketeers" as they were fondly nicknamed by him and his Godfather, Salvatore. They were the sons Dominic never had. He was a widower for 20 years before marrying Regina. Guido was like a brother to him. They grew up together in Brooklyn, New York and went into business together and were inseparable. Guido was also a widower with no children. Dominic insisted they regard each other as cousins; brothers and sisters; aunts and uncles.

"It's a matter of respect," he said. Respect was indeed paramount in the Italian tradition and Dominic would make sure this tradition continued into the next generations.

After everyone's wine glass was filled, Dominic lifted his glass in a toast.

"This is truly a wonderful night for all of us. We are all here together and have much to be thankful for". He paused and with a wide grin, continued. "Yes, we must be thankful we all survived San Lucci Island". A loud burst of laughter filtered from the long table. "Now, before we eat, I would like our very own dear priest, Father Albert to give the blessing".

Father Albertelli, Albert for short, was no longer a Father, having been stripped of his priesthood and excommunicated from the Catholic Church. This occurred after he abandoned his parish, St. Mary's by the Sea Catholic Church on San Lucci Island, in the middle of the night, when Aaron caught him in bed with Ingrid, his Swedish housekeeper. He managed to escape through the backdoor just as Aaron walked in. He hid out until he found out Dominic was leaving the island. He made his way to Dominic's for help and Dominic took him aboard The Regina as they sailed off for Venice. He owed his life to Dominic.

"**Nome Padre Figlio Spirito Santo**." They made the sign of the cross. "**Dio Benedire questo mangiare and tutto a case di Dominic**". After blessing the food and everyone in Dominic's house, he again made the sign of the cross. "**Nome Padre Figlio Sirito Santo**".

"Now we eat!" Dominic motioned Celeste and Cosmo to start serving the eight-course dinner.

The first course was the antipasto tray, followed by the soup, salad and vegetable courses. The main course consisted of rack of lamb, served with twigs of rosemary. The customary fruit, cheeses and nuts were dessert.

With the buzz of delightful chatter, a close camaraderie was felt throughout the room.

Annette glanced over at Kay and shook her head in amusement. *Poor Kay, she never could make good choices when it came to clothes, especially now, in her condition*, she thought. Kay was wearing a red sequin, off the shoulder dress with short cap sleeves much too small for her now. This was the same dress she wore the night she met Sammy at The Lei on San Lucci Island. Sammy fondly looked at Kay and smiled in his approval. That dress made Sammy hot for her! Kay saw the lustful look on Sammy's face and her face turned as red as her dress.

Dominic scrutinized his family as his eyes made a sweeping glance around the dinner table. He was satisfied with what he saw. They had honored his dinner table by being properly attired.

Dominic called for their attention.

"I have to tell you ladies. You look radiant. You have such a beautiful glow on your faces," Dominic appreciated women, stemming from his own close relationship with his mother and he was not ashamed to profess it here.

"There is nothing in the entire world more beautiful than a woman bearing a child, eh? You all know that?" This was a

164

rhetorical question, and he didn't need anyone's confirmation, but he looked at each one of the men, anyway. They nodded in agreement. He continued.

"You ladies look like Madonna's, especially my little queen, my Gina." Dominic reached over and gave her a kiss on the cheek, while Angela, sitting next to her dropped her head, sadly. Regina reached under the table and squeezed her hand, in empathy.

"Oh dear, why must Dominic bring this up? Doesn't he realize how much this hurts Angela", Regina mentally anguished. She knew how proud Dominic was, but she was sad when her best friend suffered. Angela was the only one of the ladies, other than Paula, who couldn't get pregnant.

Johnnie, who was sitting next to Angela put his arm around her, meanwhile seeking his own solace in his wine glass.

"So, when are you and Annette leaving for England?" Sammy turned to Vincent who was seated next to him.

Dominic interceded before Vincent responded.

"What kind of question is that, huh, Sammy? They just got here, for Christ's sake! **Bosta**, enough. Leave him alone and manigare and beve la su vino, just eat and drink your wine, okay"?

Dominic was annoyed with Sammy. He loved having his family around and if he had his way, that's the way it would stay. He knew, however, that Vincent and Annette had made their plans long ago, to move to England. Vincent planned to finish college and become a professor at one of England's universities.

"After the baby is born", Vincent answered, "Dominic wants us to stay since our baby is due a few months after his and he wants all the babies to be baptized together at The Basilica San Marco. Dominic is going to be the Godfather to our baby. You knew that didn't you?"

Sammy's face dropped. "No-no, I didn't know that. He never mentioned that to either me or Kay." Sammy thought he and Kay would be the Godparents to Vincent's baby, since Vincent

165

and Annette were going to be Godparents to their baby. Once again, Sammy felt slighted. Dominic always consulted Vincent first, about everything, personal and business. Sammy and Johnnie knew Dominic respected Vincent because he was more educated than either of them. Sammy loved him like a brother, even though he was jealous of his close relationship with Dominic. His meditative complaining continued.

"So, what about you and Paula? When are you two moving to Switzerland?" He asked Guide. He couldn't resist the desire to have the couples move on. Maybe then he and Dominic can get closer, he reasoned. With most of the family gone, Dominic would have to pay more attention to him. Sammy was desperate for Dominic's approval.

Dominic overheard Sammy's question while listening to Annette thank him for the black negligee set.

What's the matter with him? Why does he continue to ask these questions? Why does he want my family to leave me? These thoughts raced through his mind as he became increasingly upset with Sammy.

"Oh, we're in no rush. We're staying for the baptism. We are going to baptize Dominic's son, you know?"

Oh, that did it. That was the last straw. Sammy thought "he" was going to baptize Dominic's son. Sammy fell silent for the rest of the dinner.

"What makes you think it will be a boy?" Kay chimed in.

"Of course, it will be a boy. Italians always have sons-at least for the first one. Don't you know that?" Dominic raised his already natural booming voice, emphatically.

Cosmo and Celeste prepared to clear the table. "**Sono fantastico banchetto**." Dominic complimented them on a fantastic dinner. He was fortunate in having found this couple. He told his Venice broker what he wanted. An older couple, with no children at home, as he wanted them to live in the Palazzo and to speak only Italian (that wasn't difficult) and to make themselves part of the family and not just their servants. They fit the bill. They felt very much at home with Dominic and regarded him like a son. Dominic, in turn, treated them as his parents.

Dominic loved the fact that his family's children would learn their heritage and language. It pleased him to keep his roots alive through the children. It was a good arrangement. The children would call Celeste and Cosmo Nonna (grandma) and Nonno (grandpa).

"La signori volere espresso qui liberia. La signora volera espresso qui salottin." Dominic instructed Cosmo to being the espresso into the library for the men and into the drawing room for the women.

As they left the dining room, Father Albert humbly bade them all goodnight.

"**Buona notte, tutti**," as he retreated to his quarters. He had great respect for Dominic and knew when to make himself scarce. He was careful not to impose. He found a very comfortable home here and wasn't doing anything to spoil it. He was, therefore, the quintessence of humbleness, which went well with his small, meek-looking frame.

"**Si according**," Dominic told them to make themselves comfortable by directing them to sit on his eight-foot black buffalo leather sofa, while he sat in a matching high-back side chair. He poured brandy for them and passed out his imported, expensive cigars. He noticed Johnnie in a brooding mood.

"So, what's the matter, Johnnie? You didn't say one word all through dinner. Maybe something was wrong with your dinner?" Dominic asked, with a laugh. He knew the dinner was not at fault, here.

Johnnie looked up at him with a cold stare. *Damn him! He can be so good, so generous, but sometimes he is an ass, with his big mouth.*

"So maybe I had nothing to say, okay?" The sharp tone of Johnnie's voice startled Dominic and his head snapped back in surprise. A few quiet seconds went by.

Dio mio. Oh, my God. Johnnie is mad at me for bringing up the babies. Me and my big mouth!

"Okay, Johnnie, okay. I understand. Sure, I understand."

Dominic delivered what appeared to be an apology, in a very soft tone. Guido stepped in to soothe the sting he knew Dominic was feeling by changing the subject. He was good at this. He had been Dominic's business partner, confidante, and good friend for over 40 years.

"So, what's the latest news from Bernie, Dom?" Guido was referring to Bernie Goldstein, Dominic's broker on San Lucci Island. Bernie divested all of Dominic's properties after he and the family left the Island. Dominic appreciated Bernie's smooth and lucrative transactions and being his generous self, gave him an extra bonus besides his already substantial commission.

Ah, just the mention of Bernie conjured up some very happy memories for Dominic. He let out a long sad sigh for the past that could no longer be. He remembered his dear **padrino** (Godfather), Salvatore Sangelli who raised him like a son, after his father died, and taught him everything about the business and later brought him into it. Salvatore was the one that sent him to San Lucci Island to start the new operation. When Salvatore passed away, he left Dominic his big estate. This estate, coupled with Dominic's own investments, made him a very, very wealthy man. He should have been happy, content in his retirement, but instead he was restless. Each day, little by little, he felt like he was dying, and he did not like this feeling at all. Ah, yes, how he missed those days. Bernie was his only link, his last connection to that life on San Lucci Island and he welcomed his call, at least once a month, to fill him in on all the gossip. True, it was meaningless talk, but what the hell, it was better than nothing and it brightened his day.

They sensed Dominic's thoughts by his solemn countenance and in the silence that followed, each man reminisced about his own private memories of life on San Lucci Island.

Guido was thankful that Dominic had business there or he would not have been there. Then, he would not have met Paula. It happened at Dominic's wedding. He stepped out onto the balcony of Dominic's Pizza Parlor and there she was. It was love at first sight for him. She looked so regal, so demure, aloof and pensive. Later when they sat in Dominic's office on his eight-foot black buffalo leather sofa, he knew he would one day make her his own.

Johnnie remembered the first time he set foot on San Lucci Island. He, Vincent and Sammy came with Salvatore on his yacht "**Buno Fortuna**" (good fortune). Salvatore had business to conduct with Dominic and invited them along. "The three Musketeers," as they were fondly called by Salvatore. They were "his boys" until they decided to stay on the Island, and they became Dominic's "boys."

Johnnie was sent to pick up Angela, Regina's best friend from the Mainland and accompany her to San Lucci. Angela was to be Regina's maid-of honor and Johnnie a groomsman. They hit if off right from the start and felt very comfortable with each other by the time their ferry docked on San Lucci Island.

Vincent and Sammy met Annette and Kay while dining at The Lei, a Polynesian night club Dominic owned. Later, they discovered the women staying at their hotel, The Hotel Capri, another of Dominic's acquisitions. It was because of these two women that the family had to make a hasty retreat off the island.

Annette and Kay were NARC agents stationed at the Meadowbrook Police Station on the Mainland. Their assignment was to uncover the murder of a young woman found in the hills of the Island. When they discovered Dominic's involvement, they reported this to their captain. Shortly after, they entered into a romantic relationship with the two men. When the women's covers were exposed, they decided to join Dominic and his "boys" and fake a drug drop which they passed on to their captain.

Captain Sheridan arrived with his team in five boats only to discover San Lucci Island not as Annette described and both agents gone.

"You're gonna get a real kick out of this," Dominic's hardy laugh brought them all back. You remember Ingrid, the Swedish housekeeper that worked for Aaron?" Dominic waited for a sign of recollection from them, but they screwed up their faces in a perplexed frown. Dominic sighed, exasperatedly.

"Oh, for God's sake, you know the pretty young girl Father Albert had a passione **amori** a love affair with ..." Recognition set in.

"Oh, yeah, sure, sure, I remember now."

"Yeah, I remember too."

"Okay, well, Aaron kicked her out after he found out she was pregnant with Father Albert's baby and since she had nowhere to go, she left the island."

"Ha! HA! Ha!" They commenced laughing remembering hearing how Aaron chased Father Albert half-naked down the dark street. That was all the town talked about for days. It was only much later that Aaron found out who the seducer was.

"So, what?" Johnnie sarcastically chimed in. "And what makes you think it was his baby, anyway. Knowing that island like I do, it could have been anybody's. We all know the way of life on San Lucci. Everybody screwing everybody else's wife or girlfriend." Johnnie couldn't care less whose baby it was, in fact he wasn't even interested in the latest gossip. He just couldn't resist injecting animosity into whatever Dominic said.

Dominic was determined not to react to his foul outburst. He would not encourage his antagonist behavior. Hmm, he thinks I'm gonna get angry. Well, he is wrong. I won't give him the satisfaction, Dominic mentally told himself. The usually hot-tempered Dominic surprised everyone, including himself, when he didn't react to Johnnie's remarks. It was times like this, which wasn't often, that he felt good with himself for staying cool and in control. The approving look on Guido's face confirmed this.

"Bernie told me that Ingrid returned to San Lucci after she found out Aaron had passed away." Dominic continued with his news as if Johnnie had not spoken.

"And guess whose housekeeper she is now?" Dominic sat back in his chair with a big grin on his face, taking his time relishing the moment, before continuing.

"She is now the new housekeeper of the NEW PRIEST." He raised his voice in emphasis.

The barrage of laughter unleashed from the men carried directly beneath them into the drawing room, below. Despite the well-insulated rooms and floors, the muffled chuckles did not go unnoticed by the women.

"Well, it seems the men are really enjoying themselves up there. Dominic is probably telling them another one of his dirty Italian stories," Regina remarked as their heads turned upward toward the ceiling.

"Or just maybe Dominic is telling them about a secret love affair of his. Hmm, what do you think, Regina?" Angela teasingly said as the women laughed.

"Oh, Angela, don't be silly. My Dominic would never cheat on me. Why, he loves and respects me too much," Regina was adamant about this.

"How can you be so sure, Regina?" Angela pressed her. "I mean, how do you know if Dominic ever cheated on you or not, since you've been married. After all, you know how much he loves his women and had many of them, at the same time he was involved with you. Don't you remember, Regina? You used to write and complain to me about his womanizing?"

"Yes, yes, that's true. But that was before we were married, and I understood because he is Italian and full of passion. Dominic makes love to the whole world!"

"So, you're telling us, he has never made love to another

171

woman since you have been married?"

"Yes, I can swear to it …however," Regina hesitated. "Well, he may have made love with his eyes, and his mouth. Do you remember that maid…her name was Francesca, at our hotel— The Hotel Capri?" They nodded yes. "Well, I did catch him kiss her hard on the lips, but just once. Yes, I guess you could say he has made love with his mouth but never, no, never, with his privates." Regina raised her voice, defiantly. "I can tell you all this right now. THE PRIVATE NEVER LEFT THE BARRACKS!"

The women laughed so hard; tears rolled down their cheeks. When the laughter subsided, Annette brought their attention back to their previous conversation.

"Okay, ladies, so it is agreed. We will all go shopping tomorrow."

"Please excuse me if I don't join you, but I really would like to get some writing done. I have been putting it off long enough." Paula decided to leave the shopping to the younger women as they would be shopping for their maternity clothes.

"Oh, that's right, Paula. You always did have a desire to write that book." Annette remembered Paula confiding in her while aboard The Regina. Paula shared her past life with her, the life she lived on San Lucci Island prior to meeting Guido.

"I thought you envisioned yourself sitting on your balcony in your Swiss chalet home in Switzerland to write it, Paula." Regina smiled, remembering Paul telling her of this dream of hers.

That's all Paula thought it would be, just a dream. It was only after she learned they could not stay on San Lucci Island, did she dare to share this dream with her husband.

Guido was sorry they had to leave the Island as he wanted to surprise her. He planned to build a large estate on *High Mountain* with its endless vista of the ocean as a wedding gift for Paula. He purchased 15 acres and had the plans drawn up. The builders were to commence as soon as they returned from their honeymoon. Then everything came to a halt when Dominic closed his businesses and they all sailed on The Regina to Venice.

Paula told Guido that if they could not live in San Lucci, she wanted to live in Switzerland. Realizing that the borders of Italy and Switzerland kissed, he gladly gave his consent. It was imperative to him, as well as to Dominic, that the families remain in close proximity.

"Guido promised me we would leave for Switzerland after your baby is born, Regina. But I'm so eager to begin my book, I have decided to start now."

"Oh, ladies, not to change the subject but since our plans are now settled, I will." Annette couldn't wait to discuss Dominic's gift to her.

"So, my negligee set is black. What color is yours, Kay?"

Kay grinned, sheepishly. "Oh, mine is red."

"And how about yours, Regina?"

"Oh, mine is white," Regina answered, with a blush remembering the very first time she put on a white negligee set.

It was her 19th birthday and Dominic showered her with gifts.

This one is a very special gift and this one you wait until tonight to open." Dominic told her.

Regina will never forget that night, that night she became a woman. Dominic was her first and would remain her only lover.

Having her for the first time was a very special, sacred moment for Dominic, even though he chose not to marry her first. She would always remain his very own virgin. From then on, every birthday and every Christmas, he presented her with a white lacy chiffon negligee set. Even now, four months pregnant, he only saw that sweet young 19-year-old virgin.

"Naturally, it would be white, what else?" Angela smiled when she recalled Regina telling her about that night and crying on her shoulder. Regina shared everything with Angela, especially this momentous occasion. They promised each other that

173

whoever lost their virginity first, they would tell the other. Angela was the first one to tell. She lost her virginity at the very young age of 12, under very different circumstances. Angela could empathize with Regina. She understood the sadness and emptiness that Regina felt after losing her innocence, the funny feeling she had when she looked into the mirror. She knew that these feelings would pass for Regina, as they eventually did for her.

Even now, looking back, Regina wondered why she didn't refuse Dominic. She could have, as she knew he would never force her. He was always so gentle with her. She remembered feeling so guilty after that night and that nothing could ever be the same between them again. What would her mother say if she knew? She was brought up in a very strict Catholic home. She was a very good Catholic girl, never missing Mass on Sundays, and weekly confessions. She attended weekly novenas with her mother. There was never a moment when she thought she would not remain a virgin until she married, in the church. So how could she have let this happen? How could she forget all this upbringing, in just one moment of passion? She knew her mother would die if she found out. Her mother passed away before Regina married Dominic. She felt she was the cause of her mother's death, and this would remain a heartache for her the rest of her life.

CHAPTER 32

The next day, everyone was up bright and early and eager to start their day. The four women were going shopping for their maternity clothes. However, at the last minute, Angela decided not to go. It would be too painful for her.

"Oh, Angela, you simply must come. How can I shop without you? How will I know if I made the right selection?" Regina insisted.

Celeste had the buffet tables lined with food by the time they entered the dining room. It was a hardy repast. Eggs, waffles, all kinds of meats and potatoes and a large variety of fruits, cheeses and sweet breads filled the tables.

Happy light-hearted conversation filled the room. The women were all excited about their "no limit" shopping spree from their generous husbands. They were fortunate to be so loved and so well taken care of.

After Sammy's parting reminder to Kay, "Now, remember Kay, buy a lot of nice outfits and be sure to buy something red," they were on their way.

Once they stepped outside, they immediately pinched their noses, an automatic response to the stench from the Grand Canal. The overhead clouds predicted another hot, humid summer morning and the pollution in the air hung heavily over the city. The oppressive weather was not felt inside the walls of

The Palazzo. This was accomplished by the windows always being kept shut, except when the women forced them open, much to Dominic's dismay. He had installed a highly sophisticated air conditioning system which operated only when the windows were tightly closed. The system was designed to allow the occupants of each room complete autonomy in controlling its temperature.

The Palazzo sat right on the Grand Canal and Dominic's Captains' gig was docked a few yards from the front of The Palazzo, along with all the gondolas lined up, for hire. His yacht, The Regina, was anchored in the outer harbor. The family still took some local excursions now and then, but not like the past when Dominic took the entire family with him on his honeymoon. They had sailed across the ocean stopping off at various ports so the women could shop. Yes, the family's lifestyle had changed drastically since those days. Now that all the babies were due, Dominic settled down and enjoyed his family living at The Palazzo. It was a good life, at that. They spent the long winter evenings in the billiard game room playing their favorite card games. Vincent tried to teach them how to play chess, but they weren't interested.

"So, what's so exciting about moving a bunch of pieces on a board one by one, anyway?" Sammy wasn't going to admit that chess took too much thinking for him.

...

Their gondola wound around the serpentine canal, past the numerous churches, shops and outdoor cafes. They disembarked at the Piazza San Marco.

"Oh, let's go in this shop. I have always wanted to go inside."

They turned to see where Regina was pointing to.

"But why, Regina? This is not a maternity shop. Why do you want to go in here?"

Regina knew just what she wanted and was delighted when she found it.

"Oh, look, Angela. We found them. We have been looking all over for these, haven't we, Angela? They are perfect!" Regina held up the most exquisite Point de Venise handmade lace kerchiefs they had ever seen, Regina chose a white one and Angela, a deep rose color one. They would wear these to church to their weekly novenas to the Mother of Perpetual Help.

Regina discovered the small parish of St. Josefina while out shopping one day. She was attracted to the plain, unpretentious church for two reasons. First, Josefina was her mother's name, and it was also the name of the church where she had her first communion at the age of seven in New York City. If her ancestors were with her now, they would tell her that this was a sign, a reason she found this church. They never believed things just happened by chance, no, they did not believe this. They believed that everything happened for a reason and that this was a divine intervention. They would have told her this meant her mother was with her. Regina wasn't so sure she liked the idea. Was this good or bad? Did this mean her mother was still angry with her? Or did it mean that she forgave her for all the hurt she caused her? Yes, she decided she would accept this latter theory. Perhaps this was a good sign after all, she concluded. Maybe this meant her mother would pray that her fervent prayer would be answered. Had Regina known that her prayer would be answered, but at a very high cost, she would have accepted the former theory.

From the first moment Regina stepped inside the church, she fell in love with its humble décor. There were no marble columns, bronze statues, mosaics or frescoes. Only wooden angels and plain ordinary cherubs surrounded the otherwise unadorned, unornamented wooden altar.

The women continued along the Grand Canal passing cafes and expensive boutiques and dozens of churches, with their shiny golden mosaics, including St. Theodore, the first patron saint of the city proudly wielding his shield and spear.

The chimes from the 323-foot bell tower at the Basilica of San Marco chimed 12 times. It was noon. They had been shopping for three hours and were so thrilled with their selections, they forgot about eating. Now the chimes reminded them they were hungry.

"How can we be hungry after the huge breakfast we had?" they wondered.

"My, shopping sure makes me ravenous!" Kay's appetite was as voracious as ever and she ordered a full meal including dessert. She knew her doctor would scold her at her next appointment, but she didn't care.

The women had lunch at one of the outdoor cafes, along the Grand Canal, located in the piazza, surrounded by shops selling expensive designer clothes.

"My goodness, it's so hot!" Regina took out one of her purchases. A handmade white cotton lace trim fan. The muggy air made the women quite uncomfortable despite their crisp, sleeveless cotton dresses. The overhead clouds began to reveal the scorching sun.

"When the sun smiles, Venice becomes one of the most beguiling spots," Annette smiled, smugly, at her outburst of eloquence. She didn't recall where she read this quote but was happy, she remembered it now. *Hmm, Vincent's intellectual side is rubbing off on me*, she mused to herself. Annette discovered this about Vincent the first night they met. He was fond of sharing quotations with her. *I must remember to tell him this. He will be impressed*, Annette made herself a mental note.

The Piazza San Marco was home for the many pigeons that huddled under the damp wings of a marble angel who seemed to be weeping. The women choose a beautiful setting for their lunch. Surrounding them, everywhere they looked, history stared back at them. The Basilica di Marco with its four famous gilded horses above the main door seemed to be riding towards them.

After lunch, the women walked along the labyrinth of canal laces, past the three well-known bridges of Venice. The Salkzi, The Rialto, and The Academia. They stopped at The Rialto Market and spotted Celeste buying fresh produce and fish for their dinner that evening.

"Oh, let's have some gelato," Kay didn't wait for the others as she purchased her cone. They all enjoyed the cool, smooth taste of the Italian fruit ice cream, as it slid easily down their parched throats.

They were exhausted with all their shopping and were ready to go home. A **vaporetto**, water bus, slowed down as they waited by the canal, but they didn't get on. The vaporetto was the cheaper public transportation the working class used. When a traghetto, ferry gondola, appeared they got on. This was the expensive, private mode of transportation.

The chimes from St. Mark's bell tower struck 4:00 P.M. as they stepped inside the gondola. The searing sun beating down on them from the open exposure encouraged Regina to take out another of her purchases, a handmade white lace trim parasol that matched her fan.

Regina was pleased with herself. She made good purchases. Just before boarding the gondola, she bought a dozen red roses, her favorite flower. *These roses will dress up my boudoir tonight and their sweet smell will really please Dominic*, she smiled as she imagined Dominic's reaction. Regina knew that this little touch of femininity would affect Dominic's feminine side and arouse his emotional sensitivity.

"Oh, Angela, I just love my purchases. Thank you for coming with me and helping me decide. Did you have fun? Oh, I do hope so." Regina was so sensitive to Angela's feelings.

"Yes, yes, Regina, it was just great. Thanks again for my lovely veil. I will cherish it always."

Angela made an effort to sound happy for Regina's sake, but she really wasn't. Her heart was so heavy. She was coming home with nothing to show Johnnie. She knew the women would be giving a fashion show for their men, after dinner, and then make love. That was another problem poor Angela had to face with her husband. Johnnie was not the same hot Johnnie she knew on San Lucci Island. She remembered how he couldn't keep his hands off of her, even reaching under the table at Dominic's Pizza Palace to stroke her thighs. Dominic teased him.

"Johnnie, you know what? You gotta problem. Yeah, and you wanna know what that is?" Dominic doesn't wait for an answer. "You gotta long hands, that's what!" Dominic added with a grin. A big burst of laughter is heard from the others.

Angela loved all the instances their bodies rubbed against each other on the dance floor, at Dominic's nightclub, The Lei. Not a day went by when they didn't make love. Now, they hardly made love anymore. Oh, how she missed those times. Even so, she knew that Johnnie still loved her. She understood that Johnnie was tense and pressured to perform to make her pregnant. So, she decided to see a doctor and find out what was wrong. She didn't think anything was wrong with her, still if she went first and nothing was wrong, then maybe Johnnie would agree to go. So far, he wouldn't hear any of it. Every time she brought it up, he got angry and stormed out of their bedroom. The truth was that Johnnie was afraid to hear what he felt in his heart—that he was sterile.

"Oh, I can't wait for tonight to model these clothes for Sammy. I hope he likes them. What do you think, Net?"

"Yes, Kay, I'm sure he will. Why shouldn't he? You bought everything you saw, in red!"

They burst out laughing remembering the look on the saleslady's face when she saw Kay try on only red fashions. The bright red color only accentuated Kay's pregnant figure. She resembled a little short cherub with her butterball figure and round rosy cheeks.

"Perhaps Madame would rather try on a more subdued color?" The saleslady tentatively asked her in her heavy Italian accent.

The women rapidly disembarked the traghetto and hugging their precious treasures went straight to their rooms. They had just enough time to bathe and get some rest before dinner. Dinner at The Palazzo was served promptly at 8:00 P.M. and lasted exactly two hours. No one dared be late.

...

Vincent entered the courtyard to find Paula hunched over a pad in deep concentration.

"Hello, Paula. I didn't expect to find you here. I thought you were out shopping with the women. I hope you don't mind if I join you. I see you're writing. Please don't let me stop you. I was planning on catching up on some reading I've been meaning to do. You know it's not too easy to get off by yourself when you're in Dominic's Palazzo," Vincent smiled at her with an expected understanding.

"Oh, yes, I do know what you mean, Vincent. Dominic can be demanding, always expecting us to provide social intercourse with him."

Paula was also surprised when Vincent walked into the courtyard. She thought he was going with the men to see about a business investment Johnnie and Sammy were thinking of entering. Dominic was the backer and he wanted Vincent's input. He always trusted his business sense. But Vincent was no longer interested in the family business interests. He separated from them when he married Annette. This was a promise he made to himself a long time ago. "When I meet the right woman, Dominic, I'm out."

"There's something I need you to pick up for me, if you

don't mind, Dominic."

Upon hearing what Vincent wanted, his face lit up and broke out in a wide grin. *Ah, Vinnie thinks like me*, he chuckled to himself.

This new business of Dominic's was not like his other businesses that brought him to San Lucci Island. This business was strictly legitimate. It was a small privately owned bank that ran into trouble, bad management. They were open to all offers. Dominic got it for a steal, so, what did he care if he knew nothing about the business. It was for Johnnie and Sammy, and they convinced him they could make a profit. They were living comfortably off Dominic's money all this time, but they were restless. They needed something for themselves. *Besides, maybe now, Dominic will have more respect for me when he sees I can be smart in business like Vincent*, Sammy thought.

Vincent seated himself across from Paula on one of the several wrought iron benches. He took a moment to survey his environment. The courtyard, with its solid concrete foundation, was plainly designed with the simplest maintenance in mind. The sole adornments were two bronze statues of St. Theodore, patron saint of Venice and St. Jude, patron saint of hopeless cases with hands outstretched in an animated pose as if in conversation with the angel waterfall that rested in the center. There were no flowers, no plants, except for a 45-foot bay tree at the rear of the courtyard. With so few distractions, it was an idyllic setting for reading and contemplation.

Perhaps this was what the original owner had in mind, Vincent thought. He was pleased with his surroundings. It was quite suited to his frame of mind at the moment and with a nod of approval, he opened his book.

...

A strong gust of wind carried some bay leaves across the

courtyard and landed against Paula's feet with such force, it awakened her. She was startled to discover she had dozed off. *Hmm, must have been the quietness and the hypnotic sound of the waterfall,* she reasoned. She glanced down at her pen still poised against her pad and showed very little progress.

"Well, it's a start," she murmured. She looked over at Vincent who had succumbed to the stillness, also, and was fast asleep.

CHAPTER 33

The ladies were eager for dinner to be over with. They had plans for their men this evening and grew tired of all the small talk.

"So, who do you think invented the fork, eh?" Dominic asked smugly, assured none of them knew the answer, when no one responded, he asked again.

"Well, anyone? Speak up. No one knows?" Dominic paused, turning his attention towards Vincent.

"Vinnie, you are a college boy, surely you know the answer?"

Vincent shook his head, confessing he didn't. He didn't add that it was trivial information, then,

"Okay, okay, I tell you. THE ITALIANS." Dominic rubbed his hands together, gleefully, while waiting for a response. When none was forthcoming, he continued.

"Now, you listen to this." Dominic leaned into the group as if to keep it confidential.

"The FRENCH adopted it!"

Dominic roared, with laughter, enjoying the moment.

"So, now who are the superior people, eh?"

The men followed their after-dinner ritual by retiring to Dominic's library with their espresso and brandy, while the women adjoined to their rooms on the fourth floor. Regina's room occupied the entire fifth floor. The master suite was just as richly decorated as were all the other bedrooms, except on a more grandiose scale. The middle of the room was taken up by a king size canopy bed. The bed covers were made in white satin with lace trim. The Palazzo came completely furnished even down to the linens.

Marble column alcoves separated the sleeping, sitting and bath areas. The bathroom had marble basins and an ostentatiously silver bathtub sat majestically in the center of the marble setting. Bottles of aromatic essence oils, lavender, orange blossom, rosewater and sandalwood surrounded the tub and added a dignity to the bath. Regina chose rosewater for her aphrodisiac bath this evening to complement the strong aroma of roses in the bedroom. Her body went limp as the warm sweet-smelling water encompassed her. She felt herself sinking further down into the relaxing water and dozed off.

The chimes of the grandfather clock in her bedroom woke her. It was 10 P.M. She dried herself off and lavishly splashed herself with Chanel #5, Dominic's favorite perfume and now hers. This perfume was the first gift Dominic gave Regina when he met her and ever since, Dominic made sure she never ran out of it. She put on the white lingerie set Dominic bought her and settled down in the chair by the fireplace.

The warm secure feeling of a blanket being placed gently around her woke her up. She looked up into Dominic's smiling face.

"Gina, mia bella bambino. My beautiful baby. You fell asleep and you feel like ice. Why didn't you light a fire, eh? Ah, mia prezioso bambino. My precious baby always waits for me to do these things. Tsk, tsk, what will you ever do without me, eh?"

Dominic didn't expect Regina to light the fire. He always took care of these things. He enjoyed Regina's dependence on him, and he enjoyed babying her. After Dominic was satisfied the fire was off to a good start, he pulled the gold braided cord to signal the kitchen. It was midnight. Celeste and Cosmo were having their nightcap when the bell sounded. They knew, without looking up, which room it was at this time of night. They looked at each other and laughed, knowingly.

"Questa sera, il padrone fare l'amore con signora." Cosmo didn't need to ask Dominic what he wanted. He knew his habits. Dominic was the only one to ring up so late on the nights he made love to Regina. Cosmo went into the wine cellar and brought up a bottle of Christian Brothers brandy and placed it, along with two snifters, on the dumbwaiter.

Dominic made himself comfortable on the settee. He sat back, with eager anticipation as Regina enthusiastically modeled her new outfits. Dominic was amused at how thrilled Regina still was about her life with him and all the comforts she enjoyed. She appreciated everything he did for her.

When Regina saw Dominic's protruding member just straining to be released from his tight pants, she dropped down on her knees to acknowledge its call. As he unzipped his pants, her long, dark brown wavy hair fell over her face, covering it. Dominic reached over and brushed her hair away from her face to reveal a pair of large, dark brown eyes looking lovingly up at him. He cupped her face in his hands.

"Mia moglie tu na mio uno po' bambino. My wife, you are like my little baby!"

Dominic made a move to get up to go into the bathroom when Regina pushed him back down.

"No, no, don't get up, Dominic. I want to love you, right now, like this," she put her hand into his pants and cupped his testicles.

"But my darling, I want to prepare myself for you." Dominic was a fastidious man and would never make love to Regina without first freshening up.

"No, Dominic. Not this time. I want to love you now, just like this. I want to taste you, the real you, and not that clean smelling soap. This will only make me more aroused and desire you more. I have to confess. I wanted to do this for a long time, but you always wash up before I have the chance."

Dominic was enamored with this new Regina. True, she never refused him and always enjoyed it, but she never took the initiative. Regina's aggressiveness excited Dominic all the more and when Regina opened her mouth wide to accommodate Dominic's rigid, enormous penis, he fell back on the settee in complete surrender.

This time, Dominic tasted sweet and moist and hot on her lips. The more she sucked him, the more his penis seemed to swell and because of its length and fullness tended to bend a little to the side. It seemed to be thanking Regina for freeing it from its confinement. The natural smell and taste of Dominic's penis aroused her. This evening his penis reminded her of the only other time she tasted Dominic *ah natural*.

Dominic had set up business on San Lucci Island when his Godfather, Salvatore Sangelli paid him a visit. He brought Regina and his "boys' Vincent, Sammy and Johnnie with him.

She took him in the mouth right in Dominic's Pizza Parlor on his eight-foot black buffalo leather sofa. Regina felt guilty afterwards because they weren't married. But she had to admit, it was more fun then. Maybe because it was sinful, wrong. Regina was experiencing those very same feelings tonight and it excited her!

Dominic couldn't hold it in any longer. When he saw how excited Regina was becoming, he let out an outburst of joy and his warm juice spilled all over.

"**Io mio, Gina, sona fantastico**." While kissing the semen from her face, Dominic told her how fantastic she was.

When Dominic entered the room earlier, it was dark. The only light that shone through was from the lights in the courtyard. Now, he put on a night light. Regina tried to stop him.

"Please Dominic, no light. You know I don't like the light

on when we make love," Regina felt ashamed of her swelling stomach and since becoming pregnant, insisted they make love in the dark.

"No, Gina. Not this time. I want to see you and my **bambino** growing inside of you. Don't you know, my darling, I think you are even more beautiful now than the day I married you."

Dominic went over to the dumbwaiter and removed the brandy. He placed it on the marble table and poured two glasses. "I toast my beautiful wife and our precious son." Dominic patted Regina's stomach, tenderly. They sipped their brandy slowly while holding each other close and staring into the fire. There was no rush. They would make love again. Years ago, when Dominic was younger, he could make love three, four times a night. Now, he needed to take a little break, take his time between their love sessions. That was all right with Regina. She knew that Dominic would thoroughly satisfy her before the night was through.

They finished their brandy. Dominic took Regina's glass and placed it on the table, then took her hand and led her to their bed. He turned down the cool white cotton damask sheets.

"Okay, my sweet Gina. Now, I satisfy you."

Dominic knew how to please his wife. He knew she enjoyed all the many ways they made love, but he also knew the way she enjoyed it the most. It wasn't always like this. He remembered the first time he made love to her.

She was only 19, a virgin and innocent. Perhaps he shouldn't have taken advantage of her, but he couldn't help himself. He fell in love with her the moment he laid eyes on her as she worked behind the toy counter at Lee's Department store in Brooklyn, New York. Even now, after all these years, Dominic blushed, in shame, when he recalled the evening he forced himself on her.

Before Regina cried out, he knew his corpulent penis would never penetrate Regina's small tight vagina, without hurting her. When Regina cried out, he immediately withdrew. Dominic was neither callous nor selfish. He would go slow, and each time go in further, inch by inch, until one day, he would "break through."

Dominic still teased Regina about that night, how loud she screamed and how ferocious she was clawing him like a wild tiger.

"Look, Gina. I still have the scars from that night," they both laughed.

Regina laid back on the cool, clean smelling sheets, in happy anticipation as Dominic settled down alongside her. He began kissing first one ear, then the other. He kissed each dimple on her cheeks, before moving down her neck leaving a pathway of feather-like kisses. He took each swelling nipple and rolled it masterfully with his tongue.

Ah, Gina's breasts have gotten larger since she became pregnant, Dominic mentally noticed. He loved this positive change and hoped it would remain. His lips came to rest on her swollen stomach. He was careful not to rest his head on it but slowly and tenderly licked and kissed every inch of it. When he felt Regina's hand pushing his head impatiently down, he knew she was hot and ready. He saw that Regina's vagina had changed in color and texture. It was engorged with blood and now a deep red. All these changes excited Dominic as his tongue eagerly found her enlarged clitoris. It didn't take long before she felt the combustion building. It started as soon as Dominic's lips brushed by her clitoris while searching for it. The involuntary jerks were so strong, coming one right after the other, that Regina thought she would bounce off the bed. She always enjoyed good climaxes this way, but this time it was exceptional. She noticed that ever since she became pregnant, she enjoyed sex more and wanted it more often. This was very pleasing to Dominic when he saw this change in her and gladly accommodated her, all the time.

Dominic poured two more glasses for them. "We now

drink to our finale, no?" Dominic smiled as he handed Regina her glass. He was happy he made her enjoy it so much. This aroused him and he quickly emptied his glass. He positioned both their bodies sideways. He was very careful not to put his whole weight on Regina. Dominic moved slowly and rhythmically, in and out. He was thrilled when he heard Regina moan in joy. As if on its own velocity, his penis took off, frantically, faster and faster while Regina's screams became louder and louder.

"Oh, Dominic, Dominic, I came; I came again", Regina cried out in joy.

"Oh, my sweet Gina. I am so happy, so happy. I know this is the first time we have come together like this. **Mama mia**! This pregnancy is the best thing that even happened to us," he held Regina close and kissed her happy tears as they drifted off to sleep.

...

"So, what do you think? This is the last one. Did I do justice to your money?" Annette asked Vincent as she twirled around the room in her black sleeve-less A-line chiffon dress.

"Very nice, Annette. Yes, I am pleased. You are a smart shopper and have impeccable tastes. Now, why don't you put your black negligee set on?"

Annette glanced over at the marble table in front of the fireplace, where Vincent was sitting. She smiled when she saw the bottle of brandy and two glasses.

This is just like my romantic Vincent to want to duplicate the first night we made love, Annette thought back on that night.

Annette and Kay arrived on San Lucci Island as undercover narcotic agents to investigate a murder. They stayed at the Hotel Capri, Dominic's hotel, nicknamed Milk of Magnesia by the Islanders, because of its white chalky appearance. The women

190

were on the third floor and Vincent and Sammy on the fourth. One night, Annette paid Vincent a late-night call. When he opened the door, he saw a very gorgeous redhead standing in the doorway with the hall light streaming through her transparent black lace chiffon negligee set, revealing the curvaceous outline of her body.

After their lovemaking, they had their brandy and Vincent said to her,

"You look ravishing in that black negligee set, Annette."

Annette walked back through the marble alcove to the bath/dressing area. The room was now dim—the only light coming from the fireplace. Vincent motioned to Annette to come to him. She noticed a big white bear rug in front of the fireplace, which wasn't there earlier. This was the request Vincent made to Dominic that day. *It is so typical of Vincent to supply all the romantic touches to make our evening so special*, Annette smiled, thoughtfully.

Vincent placed Annette gently down on the rug as if he was handling a very rare, valuable gem. He savored the moment by studying her transparent form through her black negligee set. His eyes rested on her erect nipples which seemed to beckon him. His eyes moved down her body to her thighs. Her red curly public hair winked a welcome to him.

Vincent was very methodical in his lovemaking. He caressed and kissed Annette thoroughly before entering her. His endurance was phenomenal as he moved in and out, alternately between hard, fast thrusts and slow ones to give Annette ample time to climax. Annette's body became rigid, and her back arched upwards. Their mutual build-up and ultimate combustion were inevitable.

"Oh, yes, yes, yes, more, more, more, Vincent. Oh, oh, oh!"

They came down very, very slowly. Vincent moved gently off her; all the time cognizant of not putting too much weight on

191

her stomach. He kissed her tenderly.

"That, my darling was sublime. And, by the way, you look ravishing in that black negligee set."

Annette smiled, dreamily, and as she drifted off to sleep, she whispered to him, "I just knew you would say that Vincent."

...

A completely different lovemaking scene was going on just next door. Kay finished modeling her last outfit for Sammy.

"So, you like?" Sammy's smiling eyes told Kay what she wanted to hear.

"Yeah, that's great, Kay. Now, go put on your red negligee set for me."

"Oh, no you don't. I know you. You must promise me that you won't get too hot, too fast. Okay, Sammy?" Kay cautioned him as she left the room.

Kay considered it a compliment that Sammy was always so hot for her, but she wished they had more foreplay, like Annette and Regina. Not that the women ever discussed their intimate details. They had too much respect for their marriage to reveal what when on with their husbands behind closed doors. They did mention, however, how romantic their men were and how they prepared the "setting" for their lovemaking.

Kay could imagine this and was envious. Sammy never did anything like that. He was so hot for her all the time that he left out the foreplay, didn't think it was necessary. This wasn't anything new. Sammy had not changed since she met him. It was the same Sammy that made love to her on San Lucci Island. At the time, she was flattered that he found her so desirable. As time went on, she was not pleased. She was beginning to think that maybe it had something to do with Sammy's favorite color—red. *Perhaps it reminds him of a bull, ready to charge!* she contemplated.

Oh, my goodness. Is it my fault? Did I start it when I wore a red dress the first night I met Sammy? She remembered how fast Sammy came on to her and ever since, insisted she wear that dress!

That's it! I feel like a whore and that's exactly the way he treats me in bed with his quickies! Well, that's it! No more red outfits from now on. From now on, I'm changing my wardrobe color, Kay firmly decided.

Kay's resolution was confirmed when Sammy immediately ejaculated before even entering her. Kay pushed him off, in disgust.

"Gee, whiz, Sammy. Couldn't you have at least entered the portals all the way?"

Sammy's face turned his favorite color, in embarrassment.

"Gosh, I'm sorry, sweetheart, but you know how hot you get me in that red negligee. Just give me a minute and you know I'll be ready again."

Sammy kissed her and drifted off to sleep.

CHAPTER 34

Now that the women were all expecting, pressure was put upon Johnny and Angela to become pregnant. Finally, Angela agreed to see the doctor, but weeks went by and still no appointment was made. She did, however, do a lot of praying. She and Regina religiously attended Tuesday night novenas to the Mother of Perpetual Help. As they knelt side by side in the wooden pews at St. Josefina's Catholic Church immersed in their silent fervent prayers, Regina peered over at Angela and saw the tears running down her cheeks. This made Regina intensify her own special prayer. When they were not in church. Angela spent her days sitting in the courtyard in front of the statue of St. Jude, Patron Saint of Hopeless Causes.

Regina was now quite big and complained of swollen feet and backaches. Every afternoon, Dominic gave her a complete massage, lubricating her body with Jasmine oil. Regina watched this semi-balding 60-year-old man tenderly massage her feet and kiss her toes and was deeply touched.

One day as they were spending a quiet, restful afternoon in their room for Regina's customary massage, Regina glanced out the window and saw Angela sitting in the courtyard.

"Oh, look, Dominic. Angela is sitting down there again. She is always there. Oh, I do wish there was something we could do for her!"

"My dear sweet Gina. What can I do? You know I try to do what I can for the two of them. I already put Johnnie in the banking business. What does he know about banking? Nothing! So, maybe I take a loss. So what? I don't care about the money. If it makes him happy, that's all that matters. So, what more can I do, eh?"

Regina was due to give birth any day now, when Angela asked her to accompany her to the doctor. Regina was ecstatic that Angela finally decided to go. Angela did not want the others to know, especially Johnnie. They arranged the appointment at the same time Regina was scheduled for her monthly appointment, in this way; it appeared as if Angela was accompanying her. When Angela walked out of the doctor's office, she was pale and visibly shaken. Regina was concerned.

"Angela, what's wrong? What did Dr, Rosetti sat?"

Angela tried to speak but broke down in heart-retching tears. Regina put her arms around her to console her. Angela attempted to speak through her tears.

"Oh—Regina—Regina—it's me! It—it was never Johnnie. It was me all along. Oh—it's all my fault. Oh, Regina, what can I tell Johnnie? How can I tell him? How will he react?" Angela was grief-stricken.

"Angela, please calm down. It's going to be all right. Just tell me what happened. Tell me what Dr. Rosetti said to you."

"You don't understand. I am ruined, Regina, ruined I can't tell Johnnie, no, not ever. It will kill him. All this time, he thought it was his fault. Oh, Regina, he won't want me anymore if he finds out. Oh, dear, what shall I do?" Angela's hysteria frightened Regina.

"Angela, please stop this right now! You are scaring me. You must tell me what's wrong, please, Angela!"

Angela stared at Regina for a moment, then took a deep breath and let it out slowly as she wiped the tears from her eyes. Her words came out haltingly, with a great deal of effort.

"Oh, Regina—do you remember that time when I was 12 years old—and—and—what my stepfather did to me?'

Regina nodded as the tears welled up in her eyes remembering that traumatic time in their lives that neither of them would ever forget. Buried all these years, it now surfaced to haunt them.

...

Regina thought back to that time. Three days had gone by without a word from Angela. Regina grew alarmed when her phone calls went unanswered and when she went to her home, no one answered the bell. This was very unusual as they saw each other every day. Regina knew something was terribly wrong. Finally, her mother answered the door.

"She's in her bedroom," her mother told her, indifferently.

Regina found Angela in bed, in a fetus position with the covers wrapped tightly around her shaking body. Her face was flushed, and she was running a fever.

"I'm all right. I just have the flu and I am also late for my period, that's all," in answer to Regina's concerned look. She later confessed to her. It was about 2 A.M. and her mother and stepfather returned from a party, drunk. Angela was awakened in the night by a feeling of suffocation. A confining, heavy feeling. She opened her eyes to see her stepfather on top of her breathing heavily and reeking of alcohol. She tried to fight him off, but he hauled off and hit her. Just before passing out, she felt a searing burning pain as he forced himself inside her. It was quick and brutal.

...

"Regina, do you remember the time you found me in

bed, and I was so sick?" Angela waited for Regina's nod of acknowledgement.

"Well, Dr. Rosetti asked me if I ever experienced those very same symptoms. When I said yes, he asked me when. I told him everything. Then, he just stared at me for what seemed like a very long time with a sad expression in his eyes and then he told me."

Angela paused, groping for the words. "Regina, that night that I was raped—I—I—contracted gonorrhea and—and—now—I am sterile." Angela tearfully put her head in her hands. "And—and that's why I stopped having my periods.

Angela reached out and grasped Regina's hand. "Dr. Rosetti said if I had gone to the doctor right away, he probably could have cured me, but I never went and now it's too late."

That night at dinner, Angela was absent.

"Angela's not feeling well, and she is resting in her room," Regina answered their inquiries.

"I am sorry Angela is ill. So, how is my little Gina feeling? What did Dr. Rosetti say? Everything is all right with you and our son, no?" Dominic placed his hand on her stomach waiting for reassurance.

"Yes, yes, Dominic, everything is just fine with us."

Dominic did not believe her. He saw she was distracted and had a sad, painful look on her face.

"Please excuse me. I really must check up on Angela."

"Oh, sure, sure, you go see how she is." 'Of course, that's why she is so sad. My god! Those two are so close.' Dominic was relieved that's all it was.

"Angela, it's me. Are you all right?" She waited for no answer. "Angela, please open the door." Still, no response. Regina knocked softly at first. When no answer was forthcoming, she knocked harder, rapidly.

"Angela, please let me in." She waited, "Angela, open this door, this instance!" Regina was now shouting as she frantically

197

banged on the door.

Dominic quickly silenced the din of conversation with his outstretched hand when Regina rushed into the room, flushed and out of breath.

"Dominic, Johnnie, come quickly. Angela doesn't answer the door and it's locked, and something is wrong!"

"Gina, Gina, calma, calma. Calm down. What are you getting so upset about? You said she didn't feel well so she probably is asleep. Don't you know it is not good for you to get so upset? Not good for the baby, eh?" Dominic gently scolded her.

"Oh, no. You don't understand. She was really depressed all day and I thought if I give her a few sleeping pills, she would get a good nights' sleep, you know?"

"Yes, okay. But I don't understand why you are so worried when two pills are nothing." Johnnie couldn't understand her concern.

"But that's just it. She took more than that. My bottle was full when I gave her those two pills and when she didn't answer the door, I had a funny feeling, so I went to my room to check the bottle and it was empty! She emptied the entire bottle, Johnnie. She must have gone in my room when we were having dinner."

"But why, Regina? Why would she do such a thing like that? This doesn't make any sense." Johnnie didn't wait for an answer as he rushed up the stairs two at a time.

Meanwhile, Dominic picked up the extra key from the keyboard in the kitchen.

"**Celeste, portare una grand pignatta di forte caffe tu Signora Angelina's stanza**," Dominic instructed Celeste to bring a pot of very strong, black coffee up to Angela's room.

Johnnie pounded on the door. "Ange, open the door! You hear me, Ange? I don't know what's going on with you but it's okay, whatever it is. Please open this door now, Ange." Johnnie's loud voice competed with the loud banging on the door.

"Johnnie, she can't hear you, she's probably knocked out.

Here let me open it." When Dominic opened the door, they all rushed in.

Angela was lying on top of the bed, fully clothed. In her hand, she clutched a rose-colored lace head veil. She looked so peaceful. No one, except Regina, could have suspected what she had just been through, hours earlier.

"Ange, Ange, please wake up." Johnnie dropped to his knees and held her close to his body, rocking her and kissing her. He turned to Regina, in desperation, his eyes red.

"I just don't understand all this, Regina. Why? Why would she do such a thing? She is so religious, such a devout Catholic. You both go to church daily and you make those weekly novenas. You were with her today, all day. What happened today?" Johnnie looked, helplessly, at Regina, and waited for some answers.

"Go, go with Regina. She will tell you everything," Dominic suspected what this was about. He knew that Angela confided in Dr. Rosetti earlier that day about her problem because Regina told him. He remembered what Regina told him a long time ago about her being raped.

"Let's go sit in the courtyard, Johnnie."

Regina took Johnnie's arm and directed him to the most fitting place of all, the bench in front of the statute of St. Jude. Regina did not spare any details but paused, long enough to give Johnnie time to digest it and to study his demeanor.

Johnnie's body remained rigid, and his hands opened and closed as he clenched them tighter and tighter until all the knuckles turned white. His lips were tightly closed, and the colors of his face ranged from pale white to red as he became increasingly livid, with rage.

When Regina finished speaking, they remained quiet and motionless for a long time. When Johnnie finally spoke, his voice was low, then grew louder as his excitement and anger mounted.

"If that bastard was here right now, I would kill him. No, no, I wouldn't kill him right away. Oh, no, he wouldn't get off that easily. No, first I would cut off his balls and cock and shove them down his throat until he choked on his own dick, on his own lust!"

Johnnie hit the bench with his fist so forcefully to emphasize his point, he broke the skin of his hand. In his rage, Johnnie forgot himself using such foul language in front of Regina. The men had too much respect for their women. Regina understood, she knew Johnnie had a quick temper. She was not surprised by his outburst.

"She's resting now, Johnnie. Angela is going to be all right. Nothing to worry about." Dominic reassured him when they entered the room. He squeezed his shoulder.

"Okay, we go now. We leave you alone with your wife." Dominic quietly closed the door after them.

Johnnie stared down at Angela with compassion. She looked so pale and fragile.

"My poor baby. You have endured so much and all this time, I never knew." Johnnie spoke softly. He dropped down on his knees, hung his head and cried. Upon hearing the soft whisper of his voice, Angela opened her eyes to see Johnnie resting his head on her lap. She lifted her hand and weakly stroked his head. Johnnie grasped her hands tightly and brought them up to his lips, covering them with his tears and his kisses.

"Oh, Johnnie, I am so very sorry." Her words were so soft and weak, almost inaudible. Johnnie quickly put his hand over her mouth to silence her.

"No, don't you ever say that or think that again, Ange. I'm the one that is sorry for the way I treated you these past months. Hardly touching you or making love to you. I'm so ashamed of myself. I've been such a selfish bastard. Please forgive me."

Angela then noticed the red fresh blood on Johnnie's right hand. She didn't need to ask what happened. She knew Regina told him everything. Realizing Johnnie's hot Italian temper, she was not surprised that he expressed his anger by striking out.

She brought his hand up to her lips and kissed each knuckle, tenderly.

CHAPTER 35

The day dawned with the sun shining brightly. It was spring, a perfect day, warm but not stuffy. The family couldn't have picked a better day for the babies' baptism.

They walked up the white marble steps leading to the ostentatious entryway of St. Mark's Basilica. They pushed open the cylinder-shaped wood lattice 10-foot doors and made their way down the 100-foot mosaic tile aisle. The sound of the women's heels echoed throughout the empty church. The sun streaming in through the stain glass windows laid a rainbow path of reds, blues and greens at their feet. The glowing gold of the mosaics which formed the religious scenes that completely covered the ultra-high-domed ceilings looked down on them as they approached the altar. The church was adorned in magnificent splendor. The statue of St. Michael, along with the other statues, flanked both sides of the altar.

Monsignor Mazzarino stood waiting at the head of the elaborate gold byzantine altar. The large marble baptism font was filled with holy water. The Godparents disrobed their godchild for preparation for the babies' immersion into the water. Angela helped Paula take off Joey's gown, as Johnnie squeezed her hand, supportively.

Oh, God, please answer my prayer, for Angela's sake, Regina mentally prayed as she watched Angela turn away in an attempt to wipe a tear from her eyes.

They were grateful Celeste had made their job easier by sewing on just one big blue ribbon, tied around the neck, in place of small buttons. Regina instructed Celeste to make the babies baptism gowns, with matching bonnets. That was no problem for Celeste. She was an excellent seamstress, having made baptism gowns for all seven of her children. The babies' gowns were made of the finest imported white Irish linen cloth, trimmed in lace, with blue ribbon piping threaded throughout the lace trim, all the way to the neck, where it was tied in a big bow.

"**Accipe signum crucis tam in fron te, quam in corde, sume fidem caelestium praceptorum: et talis esto moribus, ut templum Dei iam esse posssis**."

Monsignor's melodious, high voice sounded as if he was singing Latin words, instead of speaking them. He now translated, meanwhile instructing the Godparents, Guido and Paula, to place their godchild in the water.

"Receive the mark of the cross on your forehead and within your heart. Embrace the faith with its diving teachings. So live that you will indeed be a temple of God. We beg you, Lord God, graciously hear our prayers. Guard your chosen one, JOSEPH DOMINIC VISCONTI, with the never-failing power of the cross of Christ, with which he has been marked."

Dominic nudged Regina, proudly, as he watched Joey being lowered into the water. He was mentally telling her. *Look, Gina. What did I tell you? Not a peep out of him. He is so calm. This is how a man like Joey takes to the water. I betcha the other babies' howl.*

After Joey was dried off and dressed, the Monsignor continued with the next baby.

"**Oremus. Preces nostras, quaesumus, Domine, clementer exandi: et hunc electum tuum MATTHEW VINCENT CANDIOTTI cricos dominicae impressione signatum**."

As soon as Matthew's Godparents, Dominic and Regina, lowered him into the water, Matthew let out a shrilling howl that echoed throughout the empty church. Dominic looked up at Regina and smiled, smugly, as if to say. *Ha! What did I tell you?* The fact that Joey was six weeks older than his cousins was not considered by the proud father.

FRANCES SAMMY SANTORI was the last baby to be baptized. His Godparents, Vincent and Annette, prepared him for his dunking. Sure enough, Frankie's shrilling howl filled the church. Dominic's smile broadened. The last ritual of the Baptism rite was the receiving of the salt.

"**Accipe sal dapientiae: propitiatio sit tibi in vitam aeternam. Amen**."

"Receive the salt, which is a symbol of wisdom. May it bring God's favor for life everlasting. Amen."

"**Pax tecum**. Peace be with you." "Et cum spiritu tuo."

"And with your spirit."

The babies enjoyed their salt as they smacked their lips in unison, ending the baptism ritual.

Monsignor Mazzarino was invited back to The Palazzo for the celebration feast Celeste and Cosmo prepared.

The women carried their sleeping babies to the nursery, next to Regina's room.

Regina and Celeste decorated the nursery months before the babies' arrival. However, they were not prepared for the surprise Dominic planned for them. They were greeted with dozens of colorful helium-filled balloons which covered the ceiling. Also, a dozen red roses were tied with a big blue bow to their babies' crib, with a card, congratulating the mothers. The nursery was furnished with all the essentials. The three babies were laid down in their own satin-lined bassinets with their names embroidered on the outside. The three wooden cribs were lined up nearby, waiting for their eventual use. There were three of everything; bassinets, dressing tables, highchairs, and prams.

Stuffed animals, musical carousals, trains, hobby horses, toy cars and trucks filled the rest of the nursery. These were very lucky babies and would certainly be spoiled growing up.

It was a very happy festive celebration, and the Monsignor was happy to be invited.

It was the first time he set foot in The Palazzo but had heard many fine things about it and Dominic's hospitality from the pastor at St. Josefina's parish. The Monsignor would never admit it, but he was envious of Father Tosca. After all, he was the Monsignor of the most respected church in all of Venice, whereas Father Tosca was just a humble priest from a poor parish. It seemed even the church was not immune to the sins of pride and jealousy among its clergymen! Before entering the dining room, the Monsignor asked if he could wash up.

"**Cosmo, mostra Monsignor Mazzarion il bagno.**" Dominic instructed Cosmo to show the Monsignor the bathroom.

Everyone was seated in the dining room when the Monsignor entered. When he heard Dominic conversing with Father Albert in his own native tongue, he felt comfortable enough to join in, after politely excusing himself, for interrupting.

"**Perdoni l interruzinone. Dominic dire mi conoscere San Lucci island**."

Father Albert had been deeply engrossed in conversation with Dominic when the Monsignor interrupted them. He was startled to see him. He gave Dominic an accusing look.

So, Dominic told the Monsignor that he met me on San Lucci Island. Hmm, I wonder what else he told him about me. He was upset Dominic didn't tell him he invited the Monsignor. He continued staring at the Monsignor, without speaking, while his already pallid looking complexion, from being indoors all the time, turned to ashen. He didn't need to worry. Dominic never told him he was once a priest and never addressed him as "father" in his presence. He only told the Monsignor that he had a house guest, staying at The Palazzo, whom he met on San Lucci Island.

But instead of answering the Monsignor, Father Albert excused himself and quickly left the room.

"**Scusa io aver bisogno partire adesso**."

The Monsignor looked bewildered as Father Albert made his hasty retreat. He turned to Dominic and with the surprised Italian expression of lifting his shoulders and placing his fingers together, he shook his whole hand in complete confusion and asked Dominic what just happened.

"**Cosa succede**?"

Dominic passed off the Monsignor's question by widely circling the air with his hand in the vicinity of his head.

"**Pazzo a temp**." Dominic told him Father Albert was a little crazy, at times. Dominic knew that Father Albert was uncomfortable around outsiders. Ever since he moved into The Palazzo, he became a recluse. Each night, he left the table immediately after dinner and went to his room. He never appeared in the dining room, if he knew Dominic had dinner guests.

"**Cosmo, portare bottiglia di vino molto vecchio**."

Dominic instructed Cosmo to bring him a bottle of very old wine, as he emptied the last of the wine into the Monsignor's glass.

"**Molto grazia**." The Monsignor had completely forgotten all about Father Albert, as he thanked Dominic for his hospitality.

Dominic had one ear bent to the Monsignor and the other to the whispers and laughter coming from Vincent and Annette.

"Did you see what I just saw?" Vincent whispered to Annette. They observed Johnnie lean forward with his body and reach under the table. Angela immediately jerked back, and her startled look and blushing smile confirmed Vincent's suspicions.

"Well, what do you know? Would you just look at those two? What a wonderful change. I am so happy they have rekindled their love for each other, Vincent. Ever since that time when

Angela …" Annette let her sentence drop. She didn't want to bring up that upsetting incident.

"You know, this reminds me of what I have always believed, Annette. Vincent paused to make sure he had her attention.

"Emerson once said, 'Every adversary contains,'" Annette heard this quote so many times from Vincent, she was able to finish it with him, "within it, the seed of an equivalent or greater benefit."

Dominic's attention wandered from his conversation with the Monsignor when he witnessed what Vincent and Annette were looking at.

Well, I'll be damn! That hot Sicilian is touching Angela under the table, just like he did at my pizza parlor on San Lucci Island.

"Bravo!" Dominic let out such a booming laugh, everyone turned to look at him.

Ah, this is good. Dominic enjoys my company. I made him laugh. Maybe, afterwards, I can talk to him about the Bishop's Fund. The Monsignor was convinced that "he" was the cause of Dominic's outburst.

A quiet soberness filled The Palazzo when the couples made their departure. Vincent, Annette and little Matthew left for England. Guido and Paula for Switzerland. Dominic was sorry to see them go and he made them promise they would stay in touch by frequent phone calls, letters and visits, as often as possible. Still, he would have been happier if he could have kept them all under his roof. He was thankful that the babies, Joey and Frankie's voices now echoed thoughout the empty Palazzo.

Regina and Kay were in the nursery getting the babies ready for their daily outing when Joey let out a big cry just as Dominic walked in.

"What is it, Joey? Why do you make so much noise, eh? Look, Gina, how he grabs on to my finger so tightly as if he wants to tell me something. What is it, Joey? What do you want to say to me, eh? Oh, I know. You want to go for a walk? Is that it? Gina, look how he stares right at me with those big brown eyes and long eyelashes. He has your eyes, Gina, you know? Ah, he knows his daddy. Don't you, my beautiful **bambino**."

Dominic was filled with pride as he pushed the baby carriage with Regina walking by his side. He greeted passersby with a jaunty tip of his hat, encouraging them to stop and admire Joey, and when they did, he beamed. He dominated the conversation in the discussion of bringing up children while Regina and Kay looked on, amused.

"Really, Dominic. Are you sure you need me to accompany you on our walks with Joey?" Regina teased him.

Their lifestyle had now changed. Dominic seldom went anyway, without Joey. He did not like leaving him, even though he was in the best of hands. However, he promised Regina that when the opera season arrived, in the fall, he would take her to see her favorite opera, Madame Butterfly.

The time arrived and they were attending the first opera of the season. Dominic was happy that Regina developed a taste for opera. When he met her, she knew nothing about them but eagerly absorbed all that Dominic taught her. Now, she could discuss all the operas with Dominic.

As soon as Dominic opened the door, the crisp sting of the cold autumn night air smacked against his face. His first thought was of Joey.

"Celeste, fare sicuro voi mettere un coperta su Joey. Suo molto freddo questa sera."

Dominic gave last minute instructions to Celeste to put an extra blanket over Joey.

As soon as the curtain went up, Regina reached into her beaded evening bag for her white lace handkerchief. She knew she would need it. It never failed, but no matter how many times Regina saw this opera, it always moved her to tears. She realized the reason it was her favorite opera was because it reminded her so much of Paula's life. Before Paul married Guido, she was in love with another man. One day, he left her but promised to return. Just like Madame Butterfly, Paula waited and waited, and the years went by. Her lover never returned.

...

Dominic found Regina sitting in the drawing room, warming herself by the fire and chuckling over the letter in her hand.

"Well, what does Annette have to say?" Dominic asked, wondering what Regina found so amusing.

"Oh, Annette was relating a conversation they were having at the dinner table one evening. Do you remember when we visited them last year and you mentioned how formal, even stuffy their mealtimes were?"

"Yeah, yeah, I remember. Too dull for me. I thought it was boring, to tell you the truth. There wasn't enough laughter. Everyone was too serious. Whatever happened to that funny Italian I once knew. The one who liked to tell jokes at the dinner table and make me laugh, eh? Maybe living in England turned Vincent into a proper 'Englishman.' Oh, **mamma mia**."

"Well then, you must remember Annette telling us that Vincent was determined to provide an intellectual environment for Matthew, and he wanted only stimulating, informative conversations at the dinner table?" Regina waited for an acknowledgment before continuing. When Dominic nodded in agreement, she continued.

"Well, the other evening while they were dining, Vincent told Annette that by exposing Matthew at such a young age to their adult conversations, he would become more comfortable when he grew up to partake in social intercourse with anyone." Regina paused, unable to contain her laughter.

"Okay, listen to this, because it is so funny. Matthew,

209

innocently, turned to his father and asked, 'Daddy, does this mean that when I grow up, I can make a baby anytime with anyone?'"

"What? Oh, no! Now, where did he get that from?" Dominic laughed so hard, he choked on his words.

"It seems that his friend from school told him that his father taught him about the birds and bees and that intercourse meant that daddies and mommies made babies together."

"What kind of parent teaches their child of six years old about sex? Jeez, what's wrong with those Englishmen? They can't wait for their kids to grow up before learning this stuff? Ah, but this is funny, no? Ha! Ha! Oh, I wish I could have been there to see the look on Vinnie's face." Dominic wiped the tears running down his cheek.

"So, what else does Annette say? Are they coming for Christmas?" Dominic asked, still laughing and visualizing the shocked look on Vincent's face.

"Oh, yes, Dominic. They will be here for the holidays. They are looking forward to it."

"Good, good. **Finalmente**! Finally, it's about time. Vinnie already missed five holidays with us. Guido and Paula will also be here. Ah, this will be a good Christmas. My whole family will all be together, once again."

The week before Christmas was spent decorating The Palazzo. The lights were up and the 20-foot Christmas tree was placed in the center of the high-domed ballroom with the presents for the adults under the tree. The children's toys would be placed there after they went to bed.

"Oh, Dominic, this time tomorrow they will all be here. I'm so excited! I can hardly wait! Do you realize we haven't celebrated the holidays together since the boys were born? All those short visits over the years just weren't enough. Now they will all be with us for two whole weeks, into the new Year!"

"Yes, I will be very happy to see Vinnie, again. I am so proud of that boy. He did what he said he would do. Go back to college and now he is finished. Maybe now, he will have some time for his 'family,' eh?"

Vincent did realize his long-ago dream. When he and Annette left The Palazzo, after Matthew's baptism, they moved to England and settled in the town of Cambridgeshire. Vincent was especially attracted to this country because of its people, which prided themselves on their independence and non-conformity. In fact, the important ingredient in the charm of the area was the opportunity to be solitary. Vincent applied and was accepted at Cambridge University and was proud to be part of its prestigious academic reputation. Chaucer, Milton and Darwin were all Cambridge graduates.

The Candiotti family lived a simple life. No servants, even though they could well afford them. Vincent had amassed a small fortune throughout the years working for Dominic and coupled with his own private investments, they lived quite comfortably. Annette preferred running the household, herself. She had thought of resuming her former career in law enforcement but for now, she was content taking care of her "men."

When Matthew turned five, he was enrolled in a private Catholic school for boys and immediately showed signs of taking after his father's quest for knowledge with his never-ending questions about life.

Vincent and Annette were looking forward to their trip to Venice. This would be their first trip back in over five years. Annette was especially eager to see Kay again.

"I wonder how much Kay's life has changed. I do hope it has been for the better, for her sake." Annette was referring to that time when Kay made that decision, when she was pregnant, never to wear red again. Annette wondered if a little change like that would make a difference in Kay's relationship with Sammy.

"Well, I certainly hope so too, Annette. But I know Sammy!" Vincent thought back to the time they spent on San Lucci Island when they first met Annette and Kay. Sammy's thoughts were always on sex, and he chided him about this.

"Sammy, you don't want to be so uncouth and scare Kay off, now, do you? She is a classy lady, so treat her, accordingly."

"Yes, it will be nice seeing everyone again, especially the little boys. I imagine they are quite big, by now. You must be looking forward to seeing Joey and Frankie again, right Matthew?"

Matthew hesitated before answering his father. His cousin, Frankie was okay, but he didn't care much for Joey. He found him to be a bully and a liar. He remembered how Joey got into mischief and then put the blame on him and Frankie.

"Yes—yes, I guess so, Father."

Vincent and Annette exchanged puzzled looks.

"What's this, Matthew? You certainly don't sound very enthused. What is the matter, son?" He pondered his son's less than happy response. Vincent knew his son well enough to know that something was bothering him. Perhaps it was the distinct differences in lifestyles. It was true; life at The Palazzo was a lot more hectic than in his household. His son was more reserved than his cousins. Dining at Dominic's table was a boisterous affair with all the passion, intensity, emotional characteristics that depicted the Italian culture. Small talk abounded with much excitement made over the littlest, insignificant tidbit. Whereas at Vincent's dinner table, the atmosphere was one of calmest and stimulating, informative, intellectual conversations. At Dominic's table, the children laughed and talked freely among themselves but were not allowed to join in the adult's conversation. Vincent encouraged Matthew's input and in fact, as Matthew grew older, was expected to learn something new each day and bring that information to the dinner table for discussion. At a very young age, Matthew had the benefit of his father's well-rounded knowledge of life. Matthew was a vessel, eager to absorb all that his mentor imparted to him. His father was fond of quoting from the bible and shared these quotes with Matthew.

"A shrewd man conceals his knowledge but the hearts of

212

fools gush forth folly." "The wiseman is cautious and shuns evil; the fool is reckless and sure of himself." "A wise son loves correction, but the senseless one heeds no rebuke." "He who loves correction loves knowledge, but he who hates reproof is stupid."

CHAPTER 36

"**Guiseppe, non tocco. Mandar via**." Celeste slapped Joey's hand while scolding him for touching the food she was preparing. She chased Joey around the large wooden kitchen table waving a big wooden spoon, ordering him out of her kitchen.

Joseph Dominic Visconti was a real handful for Celeste. This was the third wooden spoon she used on little Joey's behind, and it already had a big spilt in it. Dominic spoiled Joey from the moment he was born. However, Celeste would not put up with his bad behavior and never hesitated to give him a beating whenever he deserved it. Dominic never interfered with Celeste's disciplinary methods. He made it clear from the beginning that Celeste was family and would be treated as such. Joey thought of Celeste as his grandmother and from the moment he learned to speak, he respectfully called her nana, in Italian, for Grandmother. He was very fond of her and wanted her to put him to bed each night instead of his mother.

"I want my nana, Mommy. My nana reads me bedtime stories in Italian and you don't know how to read Italian."

It was true. Regina did not read or write Italian, nor speak it as well as Joey. By the time Joey was six years old; he could read, write and speak Italian better than his parents.

"**Guiseppe, tu parlare Italiano molto migliore di**
214

padre." Dominic was indeed proud of his son when he admitted to him that he spoke the language better than him. This was exactly as Dominic planned when he hired Celeste and Cosmo. Joey's and Frankie's first words were in Italian.

Joey spent a lot of time playing in the kitchen. He liked watching Celeste cook and pestered her until she fed him.

"**Nana, sono affamato**. I'm hungry, **nana**." The family was arriving the next day, Christmas Eve Day, and she was busy preparing all of Joey's favorite foods. On this day, Joey was literally underfoot.

"**Guiseppe, attento. Tu passo addosso mio piede**." Celeste scolded Joey for stepping on her feet. She later told Dominic.

"**Quando loro pccola, loro passo addosso suo piede; quando loro evilupparsi, loro passo addosso suo cuore**." "When they are little, they step on your feet; when they grow up, they step on your heart."

CHAPTER 37

"**Come stanno, Senor and Senora Candiotti**." Cosmo greeted Vincent and Annette when they arrived at The Palazzo. Then his attention turned toward Matthew.

"**Che bel bambino. Suo figilio il grande**." Cosmo complimented Vincent on having such a handsome boy and how big he got.

Matthew looked up at the tall, lanky manservant and wondered what he said about him. He knew he was talking about him but didn't understand Italian. While Dominic made sure Joey and Frankie learned their native language, Vincent made it a point to speak proper English, the "King's English," in his home. Since Annette was not Italian and only understood what Vincent taught her, Matthew had no opportunity to pick up the language. His cousins knew this and liked to make sport of him every chance they got. They did this by laughing and talking about him, In Italian, in front of him. That was another reason he wasn't too happy being at The Palazzo. He never shared his anxiety with his parents.

Vincent knew they were late when he heard voices and laughter coming from the dining room. When they entered the room, the family was seated for lunch.

"Vinnie, Vinnie, **finalmente**. Finally, you are here. I was beginning to wonder what happened to you." Dominic jumped up from the far end of the long table to greet them. He threw his arms around them and kissed them.

"Ah, Annette, still as pretty as ever. And, oh, who is this big boy? No, it can't be! Why, this must be Matteo, my little godchild."

Matthew tugged at Dominic's arm. "No, Uncle Dominic, I'm not Matteo. I'm Matthew. My name is Matthew," he repeated, emphatically.

Dominic looked down at his godson, amused.

"Oh, **mi bambino**. Ha! Ha! What's the matter with you, Vinnie. Couldn't you at least teach him how to say his name, in Italian?"

"It's okay, Matthew. Uncle Dominic was using the Italian name for Matthew." Vincent tried to soften Matthew's discomfort while his cousins laughed.

"Matteo, err-Matthew, you have grown so big since the last time I saw you. Why, you were only this high." Dominic indicated with his hand. "You look just like your father with your features and large Roman nose. Yes, yes, you look very Italian." Dominic was pleased with his assessment of his Godson as he continued to study him.

"Look, look, Regina. He even has Vincent's mole. I never noticed that before, but he's got a mole on right side of his lip, just like Vincent's." Dominic pinched Matthew's right cheek to demonstrate the mole moving upward, in compliance.

"Yes, but he does have Annette's thick curly red hair. Actually, I think he looks like an Italian-Irishman, which is exactly what he is!" Regina wagged her finger at Dominic, in annoyance, for his Italian narcissism. Annette looked on, amused.

Dominic dismissed Regina's correction by pulling Matthew toward him in a big bear hug.

"Matthew, give your uncle a big kiss, eh!"

Matthew looked uncomfortable as Dominic smothered him with his big frame.

"We're sorry we're late but our connected train out of Victoria Station arrived late." Vincent knew that Dominic did not like anyone late at his dining room table.

"It's okay, Vinnie, you are here. That is the main thing. **Sedere, sedere**. Sit, sit. **Mangiare, mangiare**. Eat, eat."

It had been a while since they had all been together so there was much catching up to do.

"Kay, you look great. Why, you look like you lost weight."

Kay had lost a little weight, however the dress she was wearing, a classic form fitting black dress, made her appear even slimmer.

Annette and Kay embraced warmly. Annette noticed that not only did Kay's figure change, but her attitude as well. She seemed aloof with Sammy and not so talkative. She wasn't gushing all over him, ready to do his bidding.

'Why, I do believe she is playing hard to get. Good girl! It's about time.' Annette mentally cheered her on. He noticed that Sammy had changed as well. He was now more attentive to Kay. She overheard Sammy ask Kay if there was anything she needed.

"Paula, congratulations on your book being a best seller. I always knew it was a winner. I understand you are now writing a sequel to it. That's great!"

Everyone was talking over each other and getting louder as they competed to be heard. The close camaraderie they shared together, over the past 25 years, was now evident. Dominic ceased talking, sat back and took a moment to enjoy all the commotion as he took a sweeping look around the table. He mentally pondered his family.

Ah, this is real nice. Everyone together, talking, laughing. **La dolce vita***! The good life!*

"Guido, you're putting on a little weight." Vincent patted Guido's expanding girth.

"Yeah, well, what are you gonna do, when you come to The Palazzo. You know how Dominic gets offended if you don't eat."

"So, how do you like living in Switzerland, Paula?"

"Oh, Annette, I just love it. It is everything I dreamed it would be. The mountain air is so clean, crisp and cool. And the countryside is so green and beautiful. I have such a beautiful view of the whole valley from my deck.

"Hey now, I thought you said San Lucci Island was the most beautiful place in the world. That's what you told me when I met you." Guido teased her. He knew it was never her decision to leave the island. Paula would have been content to have spent the rest of her life there. Her first husband, Neal, was buried there and she never thought she would leave him. After Guido and Paula married, Guido purchased a mountain view lot and made plans to build a home for her. All plans stopped when they left the island. That was when Paula confessed to him that she always dreamed of living in Switzerland even before she married Neal.

Well, at least they had the good sense to pick southern Switzerland for their home," Dominic told Regina. He was happy their home was located in the Italian speaking Ticino region and not far from Venice.

"So, when are you gonna come and see our new home, huh, Dom?" Guido asked, accusingly, with an unmistakable hurt in his voice. "After all, we've been there over one year, now."

"Guido, Guido. Non convenire arrabbiato con mi. Please don't be angry with me. You know how it is with us. Joey catches cold so easily when he goes into a new area. You remember, Vinnie, the time we visited you for my godson's birthday. Joey was just a little baby, and you remember how sick he got, eh?" Dominic looked to Vincent for confirmation. When none was forthcoming, he admonished him.

"Yeah, I had to come all the way over there in that cold damp England weather because you, Vinnie, never came to see me, all that time, not even once!" Dominic was becoming increasingly upset and his face turned crimson.

Vincent looked at Dominic and shook his head. Dominic knew very well why he never visited. He was busy attending the University. Dominic wanted to argue, but Vincent wasn't going to be a party to his silly pettiness.

Guido backed Vincent up by answering for him.

"Yeah, yeah, always some excuse. You wanna know what the trouble with you is, Dom, huh?" Guido doesn't wait for an answer.

"The trouble with you is, your baby Joey. Yeah, that's right. Ask anyone here, they will tell you." No one at the table was brave enough to confirm this. Guido was the only one that could talk to Dominic this way.

"And another thing. You wanna knew what else I think, Dom? I think another reason is because you are too lazy to leave The Palazzo. You wanna everyone to come to you."

"Okay, okay, Guido, what can I say? Ha! Ha! You know me better than anyone. We've been together a long time. Yeah, yeah, what you say is true," he had to agree with Guido.

"Well, now that Joey is getting older, I insist that you let my godson come and visit us." Paula turned to Joey who was sitting next to her and not paying any attention. He was more interested in drinking Paula's glass of wine, just as fast as Cosmo refilled it.

"You will really enjoy Switzerland, Joey. You know they have some of the oldest and largest castles in the world. And there is so much to do. We will go out on Lake Maggiore. Now, what is it you like to do, Joey? Sail, swim, water-ski?" She didn't wait for an answer. "Well, it doesn't matter. We will just do it all. We'll have such fun!" Paula became so excited in anticipation of Joey's visit, she never noticed how often Cosmo filled her glass.

"It's really good seeing you again, Vinnie. I really mean that. I missed you." Sammy's sincere smile and words were warmly received by Vincent. He remembered how they parted. Sammy had a chip on his shoulder. Vincent knew Sammy was jealous of his close relationship with Dominic and how he always turned to Vincent for advice. That had changed now. Ever since he and Johnnie went into the banking business and took it out of the red and made a profit, Dominic developed a respect for him and was now asking Sammy for advice.

"You're looking very well, Angela. Your cheeks have such a nice color to them. It looks like you've been out in the sun."

Annette chose her words prudently. She was careful not to bring up the past as Regina told her she still had depression bouts and was under a doctor's care.

"Oh, yes, thank you Annette. I have been getting some sun." The truth being that Angela sat in the courtyard every day at 12 P.M., in front of the statue of St. Jude and remained there until Johnnie came for her. Their relationship had improved. Johnnie was more considerate of his wife's poor emotional health. He could not, however, dissuade her from continuing to pray for a miracle.

"Who said the doctors are always right, huh, Regina? Who?"

"But, Angela. It's been so long."

"Well, I don't care how long it takes. With God, all things are possible. Why, didn't he say: 'whatsoever you pray for believing, you will receive' and what about this one. 'It will be done unto you, as you believe.' So, what do you say to that, huh?"

"Frankie, stop that now! How many times must I tell you not to do that?" Kay slapped her son's hand when she caught him reaching for her glass of wine. Frankie was copying his cousin, Joey. He wasn't as shrewd as Joey and got caught.

"It's okay, Kay. A little vino is good for him. I mean look at me. I was raised on wine, and I didn't turn out so bad, now did I?" Sammy smiled and gave Kay a loving hug.

Dominic was displeased seeing Kay slap her son's hand. *Ah, these non-Italian women don't understand our ways. It is*

221

good the children get used to drinking at home. This way there's no sneaking around afterwards. That's why the Italians don't have a drinking problem like the other cultures. Dominic mentally chastised Kay.

Frankie trembled when he saw his uncle look at him, then relaxed when Dominic winked at him as if to say, *It's okay, Frankie, I'm on your side.*

Dominic studied him as if seeing him for the first time. **Dio mio**, *my God, what a strange looking boy this is. He has his mothers' big blue eyes and his father's dark hair. So, what is he? He doesn't look Italian, and he doesn't look Irish. He's like Matteo, an Italian Irishman! Mamma mia! Why can't they look 'all Italian' like my Joey?*

Joey was a carbon copy of Dominic, in every way. From his dark brown hair to his thick bushy brown eyebrows and deep dimples and his large Roman nose. He did have his mother's big brown eyes. Joey would later display another characteristic of Dominic's, his explosive hot Italian temper.

Celeste and Cosmo kept busy throughout Christmas Eve Day serving up the foods that were traditionally eaten on this day. The main entrée included all kinds of fish, especially calamari "squid." There were bowls of nuts and trays of Italian anise and biscotti cookies.

"I toast all my familia. **Buno Natale, Buno Natale**." Dominic wished them a Merry Christmas and they clinked their glasses together, in response.

"Okay, now keep your glasses up. Cosmo, piu vino. More wine. Now everybody has had their glass filled? Good. Now, I make an announcement. I just found out that our Vinnie here is going to be il professore, Vincenso and teach at where you gonna teach, Vinnie?"

"Dominic, please. It's not official yet. I'm being considered for a professorship and if it happens, it will be at St. John's College at Cambridge University."

"What do you mean if it happens. Of course, it will happen and then maybe you have some time to come and visit me, no?"

As everyone downed their wine, Dominic cautioned them.

"Okay, now, don't you get too drunk. We will save that for later. After we all go to midnight Mass."

"Vincent, does he mean everybody? Even the children? Surely Dominic wouldn't expect the children to stay up so late," Annette whispered to Vincent.

"Sweetheart, you don't understand our tradition. Yes, all the children will go to midnight mass. That's the way it has always been. It is one of the most honored and respected Holy days in our religion. Don't worry, Matthew will probably love the change in his routine." Vincent patted her hand, reassuringly.

When Joey saw his father drain his glass of wine and pat his lips with his napkin and throw it down, he knew in another five minutes, his father would announce to Cosmo to bring the espresso into the library. Joey knew his father's habits well, by now. He immediately kicked Frankie who was sitting next to him to get up. He motioned Matthew to follow them.

"May I please be excused, Father?" Matthew obediently asked. Vincent nodded his head, in consent.

Dominic, embarrassed, called Joey and Frankie back to the table.

"Boys, what's the matter with you, huh? You forgot to ask to be excused. Where are your manners, eh?"

"**Cosa succede**, pappa? What's going on here, pappa? You know Frankie and I leave the table when we're through."

Before Dominic had a chance to respond, a young voice was heard speaking softly.

"He who loves correction loves knowledge; but he who hates reproof is stupid."

All movement ceased. No one spoke. All eyes turned

223

toward the little boy with the mole on the right side of his lips.

Matthew squirmed in his chair when he saw all eyes on him and looked up at his father.

"I—I—am sorry, Father. It just came out. I wasn't thinking about it, it just came out." Matthew's face turned a crimson red as the color rose upward covering his face.

Vincent looked down at his son, who by now appeared much smaller than his frame, as he slumped further down in his seat. Vincent patted his head, gently.

"Bravo, bravo, Matteo." His uncle broke the silence that filled the room.

"Now, Joey, why can't you speak like your cousin, eh? Vinnie, you have a very smart boy there."

As soon as the boys were out of the room, Joey hauled off and smacked Matthew hard across the face.

"You smart ass, showing me up in front of my father and everyone. I'll get you for that. Yeah, you just wait and see!"

Matthew rubbed his face as it began to redden and swell. He quietly turned, not saying a word, and walked up the stairs towards his room.

"Yeah, that's right. Go ahead. Run away you little ninny." Joey yelled after him.

They watched Matthew disappear down the hall. Joey turned to Frankie.

"Okay, now. This is the plan, Frankie. I'm going into the library and hide in the dumbwaiter for my father and my uncles to come in and have their espresso.

"Now, you be my look-out. If anything changes, you come tell me and I will tell you everything they say, okay?"

Joey loved listening to all the "man talk" about their past life on San Lucci Island which his father never failed to bring up. He liked watching his father light up his Havana cigar as he positioned himself, regally, in his high-back black buffalo leather desk chair behind his large walnut desk. It looked all so grown-up.

He made a vow to Frankie.

"Frankie, when I grow up I'll have my very own pizza parlor, just like my pappa. You just wait and see."

"And me too. Me too, Joey. I want to go with you. Take me, Joey, please."

Joey enjoyed seeing his cousin plead. A long cold silence followed as he stared at Frankie which caused him to start pleading again, exactly what Joey wanted.

"Please, Joey. I can be a big help to you. You'll see. It will be just like Uncle Guido and your pappa when they were together over there. We could be like that, Joey, right?"

Joey looked at Frankie, disdainfully, and with a condescending air broke the silence.

"Hmm, yeah. Yeah, maybe, that would be a good idea. Only you have to promise to do everything I say, because I will be the boss, capisce? Understand?"

"Yeah, sure, Joey, I understand. But, Joey, I was wondering. Why do you always get to go in the dumbwaiter? Why can't I ever get a chance?"

"Because I'm older than you, dummy, that's why."

"But, Joey, you're only two months older than me," Frankie countered.

"So, I'm still older!" And with that, Joey went into the library. He wouldn't be able to do this much longer, as he was getting too big to fit in the dumbwaiter. It was already a tight squeeze but if he rolled himself up in a real tight ball, he could still make it work. He's done this many times in the past, only this time would be different. Joey hadn't figured out a change of plans commencing right now in the dining room.

"We still have two hours before Mass, so before we go into the library, how about we go into the game room for a little card playing, eh? Maybe some poker? You ladies can join us, if you like, how's that?" Dominic was proud of himself for his generous invitation to the ladies. It was the custom to engage in men talk after dinner, but tonight, he was happy to include the women.

"No, no, you go ahead, Dominic. We women have a lot to catch up on." Regina kissed him tenderly.

Joey began to feel cramped and sleepy after all the wine he sipped. He wondered what was taking his father so long to appear.He nodded off. The sounds of loud voices and laughter woke Joey. He squinted his eyes through a small crack in the door of the dumbwaiter. He saw his father go over to the gold braided cord and pull it. A few seconds later, Joey felt a jerk as the dumbwaiter moved slowly down to the kitchen and abruptly came to a stop.

When Celeste opened the door and saw Joey, they both let out a startling scream!

"**Mi uccisione tuo!**" Celeste yelled at the top of her lungs at Joey that she was going to kill him, as she reached in the drawer for a wooden spoon.

Joey scrambled out of the dumbwaiter and ran as fast as he could with Celeste screaming after him. Joey didn't waste any time attacking Frankie who was still standing in the hall where Joey left him.

"**Studpido. Perche non dire mi padre andata stanze da caccia?**" Joey smacked him hard across the head several times, while reprimanding him for not telling him his father and uncles went into the game room. Joey was already showing signs of inheriting his father's habit of resorting to his native tongue whenever he became incensed.

CHAPTER 38

The week passed very rapidly but pleasantly for the women. They enjoyed shopping for their evening gowns, with matching gloves, for the New Years Eve gala, Dominic and Regina were hosting. It was to be a small, but very formal celebration. The guest list consisted of close church friends of Regina's and, of course, Monsignor Mazzarino and Father Tosca.

The grand ballroom provided the perfect background for the women's elaborate gowns. From its ceiling with trompe l' oeil frescos to its gilded chandeliers, it was indeed a room of baroque splendor. The ballroom ceiling was decorated with dozens of colorful helium-filled evenings and Regina proved to be the quintessence of courtesy, as she mingled among the guests making sure everyone had everything they needed. Even the children were allowed to participate and stay up past midnight to ring in the New Year. Celeste prepared the dining room table for their midnight supper and Dominic hired a three-piece band for the evening.

"Oh, if only Charley and Eddie were here now to play for us, eh, Guido?" Dominic was referring to the two musicians he hired to play at his Polynesian nightclub-the Lei-on San Lucci Island.

"Vienequi, Guiseppe. Come here, Joey. I show you how to dance." Dominic placed Joey's feet on top of his shoes and whirled him around the ballroom to the squeals of delight emulating out of Joey's mouth.

"Me next, Uncle Dominic. "Oh, please, me next," Frankie excitedly ran up to them when the music stopped.

"No, Frankie. I want to dance with my pappa, again. Go dance with your own father," Joey pushed Frankie away.

"Joey, what's the matter with you? Was that nice the way you treat your cousin? You shouldn't be so selfish." His father's scolding went unnoticed with him. He didn't care. He wanted his father all to himself. He was about to give Frankie another shove when he caught his father's eye. He was staring sternly down at Joey, and he knew what that look meant. A reminder that his father would not hesitate to punish him if he needed it. His father would have to be extremely angry at him to administer a beating. He will never forget the last time he received one.

...

He was five years old and he and Frankie were returning home from St. Joaquin's, a private Catholic School for boys, when Cosmo opened the door to have Frankie run past him, bawling. His mother was in the drawing room with Regina when she heard her sons' cries.

"Frankie, what's wrong? Did you get hurt at school?" Kay looked him over, anxiously, while Frankie tried to speak through his gasping sobs.

"Frankie, what is this? Why are you so upset?" Dominic came out of the library when he heard the commotion.

"It was—it—was," Frankie could only point his finger at Joey. Everyone looked at Joey who guiltily stared down at his feet.

"Okay, I wanna know everything. Speak up, Frankie. Tell me what happened at school today." Dominic came down the stairs and stood next to his son. Joey kept his downcast eyes riveted on his shoes aware of his father's hostile presence.

"Uncle Dominic, some kids were laughing and teasing me and—and—Joey was laughing with them and—then—and—then—he told them …" Frankie's trembling voice broke.

"And what, Frankie. Go on. What did Joey tell them?" Dominic lifted Joey's chin and fastened ominous eyes on him.

"What did Joey tell them, Frankie?" Dominic repeated the question, holding Joey's chin facing him. Joey's face turned pale, and his chin trembled.

"He—he—he told them," Frankie's face turned red.

"He told them that I—I—still—wet—the bed."

Kay's soft soothing words of consolations were barely audible over the din of Frankie's loud wails. No one noticed when Dominic took Joey by the hand and quietly led him away. Joey knew this was a very serious moment when they walked up the stairs and into his father's library.

Joey looked very small sitting in his father's high-back black buffalo leather side chair, across from his father. His father took his time, lighting his cigar, and pouring himself a glass of brandy.

Joey squirmed in his chair as he wondered if this was part of his punishment, to make him wait, when he was anxious for this to be over with.

"Guiseppe, do you know the meaning of familia, family?" Dominic didn't wait for an answer.

"Guiseppe, familia is a very special thing in our culture." Dominic got up from his chair, pulled up his pants, and walked around the desk, bringing his fist down hard on it. Joey's whole body jumped to attention.

"Nothing, and nobody comes between the family." Dominic raised his voice and pounded the desk again, for emphasis.

"If anyone does anything or says anything bad to a member of the family, well, this must never, ever be tolerated. And, you must never, ever go against your cousin, again. **Capise**?

Do you understand? You must stand up and fight, if necessary, to protect our honor, and you never, never, under any circumstances, tell anyone about our private business. Things that only the family knows. **Capise**, Guiseppe? You understand, Joey?"

Dominic looked down, coldly at his son, as Joey's eyes filled with tears and his lips trembled as he tried to speak.

"Y—y—yes, pappa."

"Okay, then, Joey. Take down your pants." Dominic took off his belt as Joey assumed the position. It tore Dominic's heart to inflict punishment on his son. He only resorted to such extremes when Joey committed a very serious offense. Only one other time was this the case, when Joey yelled out an obscenity to Frankie, in Italian, while at the dining room table. The fact that the Monsignor was present made his punishment imperative.

Joey's shrilling screams of pain were heard throughout the Palazzo. Kay looked in the direction of the library, then at Regina, horrified.

"My goodness, Regina, what is Dominic doing to Joey?"

"Oh, just giving him a very well deserved spanking, that's all." Regina patted Kay's hand, reassuringly.

"But it sounds like a big beating. Is that necessary? I mean, kids will be kids. I'm sure Joey didn't mean anything. It really wasn't that serious. Don't you think that Dominic overreacted?"

"No, no, Kay, not at all. You don't understand our ways. It really is serious. It is a big thing for us. This is the way we were brought up. First, it's the wooden spoon for 'venial sins,' then the belt for 'mortal sins,'" Regina used the church for her metaphors.

...

"Okay, Frankie. You can dance with my pappa, now." Joey walked away, resignedly.

At the stroke of midnight, they walked out on the balcony

to watch the fireworks being displayed over the Grand Canal. They added their own noise, with their noisemakers and the children joined in with the beating of pots and pans.

"**Buon anno, Buon Anno**." Shouts of Happy New Year resounded from all The Palazzos along the Grand Canal. As Regina said goodnight to her guests, the library door opened, and Dominic exited with the Monsignor and Father Tosca.

"**Arrivederci, e stato per me un vero piacere. Grazie tante, Signor Dominic**."

The Monsignor and the Father smiled broadly, as they thanked Dominic for a delightful evening.

Regina overheard them and wondered. Hmm, I'm sure they are thanking him for more than just the evening. I wonder just how much Dominic donated to their "fund" this time.

Dominic was known throughout Venice for his benevolent nature. He was a charitable man and took care of people. All they had to do was ask. And ask they did! Regina was happy he was so good-hearted, especially when it came to her own parish, St. Josefina, but sometimes felt the people took advantage of his generosity. He was the same with the people on San Lucci Island. Regina admonished him.

"Dominic, you must not be taken up by every sad story you hear. You are too good, too soft."

"Ah, my Gina. What else should I do with all my money, eh? My family has everything they need, so why can't I spread a little joy around, eh? After all, I have been so blessed. Look, I have you. So, now it is my turn to give back, no?" Dominic cupped her face in his hands and kissed her tenderly.

CHAPTER 39

The winter passed into spring, then summer, then fall and soon it was winter, once again. One year had passed since the entire family were together. Vincent was the only one who was always absent. This bothered Dominic so much that when he asked Regina what she wanted for her upcoming birthday, she replied without hesitation.

"I want to go to England to visit Annette." Dominic was delighted.

"Yes, that is a good idea and now that Joey is getting older and he will be on his winter break, I believe it can be arranged. Yes, I think we can go."

"No, Dominic. That's not what I want. I want just the two of us to go, like a second honeymoon. Well, come to think about it, we never had a proper first honeymoon, alone. Do you remember, Dominic?"

Of course, he remembered. How could he forget? What a wedding it was and what a honeymoon! They were married on San Lucci Island and postponed their honeymoon because Salvatore requested Dominic to take care of some business first. When Guido, Paula and Johnnie and Angela had a double wedding, it was the perfect time for everyone to take a honeymoon. Ah, those were the days, Dominic let out a long, sad sign. How he missed that time in his life.

"Dominic, Dominic. I have been talking to you and you haven't heard a word I said. You were miles away. Now, just where were you, Dominic?"

"Gina, I heard everything you said. You don't want to take Joey, okay, fine, I understand. We will leave him at home. Just you and me. Sure, why not? It will be like a 'first' honeymoon. Good, it is settled. I will make all the arrangements tomorrow and you can go shopping."

"Dominic, wait. There is something else," Regina hesitated. She didn't know how to bring it up.

"So, what is it, Gina. Anything for my baby. Go ahead and ask." Dominic pulled her toward him and sat her on his lap.

"Dominic, sweetheart," Regina stalled as she fondled his cheeks and placed a finger in his dimple.

"Dominic, I have always had this desire—this dream—but I never told you because—" Dominic motioned her to continue with a wave of his hand.

"Well, I'm asking now because this is the perfect time. I mean now that we live here in Venice, it is most convenient." Regina paused again.

"Gina, Gina, why do you take so long to tell me what you want? Have I ever refused you anything?"

Regina shook her head no.

"No, that's right, so what is it that you have a hard time asking me, eh?"

"Dominic, well, I wondered if instead of flying to England, or taking The Regina, that we take the train." She watched the color drain from his face. "Oh, not just any train," Regina spoke rapidly when she saw Dominic's countenance change from blissful contentment to extreme anguish.

"Dominic," she continued. "I want to go on the 'Orient Express.'" There it was out, she said it!

Dominic looked at her with dejected sorrowful eyes and when he finally spoke, his voice broke.

233

"Oh, Gina, Gina, of all the things to ask me. Oh, my baby, why that? You know how I feel about trains. You know. How can you ask me this? Why do you make me refuse you this one thing you ask me, why? Ask me anything, anything, and I never say no, but this. Oh, Gina, Gina." Dominic shook his head sadly and wrung his hands. He hated refusing her but what could he do?

"Dominic, oh, my darling, I am so sorry. I love you, so. I didn't mean to make you sad but Dominic, it was such a long time ago."

Dominic was a young boy, growing up in New York when the subway accident occurred, and when his nightmares began, he poured his heart out to Regina. Two trains traveling on the same track, coming from opposite directions, collided. They were seated in the first train car, which sustained all the damage. The severe impact ejected Dominic out of his mother's arms, hurled him in the air and he landed at the far end of the car. That's what saved his life. The seat where they were seating was completely demolished and his mother was crushed under it.

"Dominic, please say that you will, at least, think about it. You said I could have anything. Well, this is what I want."

In the days that followed, neither of them brought it up again. Regina knew Dominic was thinking about it and would tell her when he was ready. She felt so awful, so guilty putting him through this. However, she believed she wasn't being selfish. She believed she was helping him by forcing him to face his fears. She also believed that once he made the train trip, and nothing happened—which she believed nothing would happen—he would be relieved and then his nightmare would end. She was satisfied with her rationale, still, she brushed away her tears when she thought of how small her big, powerful, sensitive husband was made to feel by her request.

With the exception of Guido, Regina understood her husband more than the others. Having lost his mother at a young age, Joey's age, left Dominic insecure. This was why he had to have his family around him, always. Regina knew the family didn't understand his neediness, his possessiveness of having them around. No one, but herself and Guido, knew of his tragedy. Dominic, with all his openness, could be a very private man. This was one of the times when the pain was too great to share with the others.

...

Dominic stood on the balcony, off his library, watching the ominous clouds announcing the late October thunderstorm. Moments later, large drops of rain fell into the Grand Canal making ripples of waves, causing the row of gondolas to sway together, in unison.

Dominic turned when he heard a knock on the door. Guido opened the door and walked in.

"Guido, I have a little problem, here. Well, I believe it is a BIG problem for me. I need your advice." Dominic closed the French glass doors and sat down in his leather side chair, across from Guido.

"Sure, Dominic. What is it?" Guido was surprised. It had been a long time since Dominic asked him for anything, especially advice. Not since they were doing business on San Lucci Island. He was happy Dominic needed him again.

"Well, you know, I don't know what advice you can give me. I mean, I know I have to make the decision myself. Who else, right? I guess I just need to talk—because this thing—this request of Gina's' really troubles me."

After Dominic finished telling Guido of Regina's birthday request, he felt better, relieved. It was still early afternoon, but he poured them a glass of brandy, anyway.

"Dominic, you're right. What can I tell you? You know, maybe Gina's right. It's been a long time. Maybe it's time you face your pain, you know. Maybe then you can get rid of those nightmares you tell me about. Know what I mean, Dom?"

Guido thought back to that time in Dominic's life. It was very hard for him. He was so close, so devoted to his mother. He never knew his father. His father died when he was born. He was the only child and she spoiled him. So much so that the kids at school called him a "mamma's baby." That's why Guido understood why Dominic spoiled Joey so much. Dominic was 7, the same age Joey was now, when he lost his mother.

Guido and Dominic grew up together in Brooklyn, New York. They were so close, like brothers. After Dominic's mother died, Guido's mother took him in, mothering him and treating him like her son.

"Yeah, I know what you say is true. It's just so hard, Guido, you know? I feel like a little boy, right now. I'm too scared to get on that train and ashamed of myself, at the same time. But I want to please Regina. It breaks my heart to refuse her."

That night, after Joey was asleep, Dominic quietly entered his bedroom and took a seat next to him, watching him sleep. Joey looked like a little angel lying there with his long, dark eyelashes and his chestnut brown hair. His tight curly hair resembled springs, framing his rosy-colored round cheeks.

"Oh, my little Guiseppe, my little bambino. I was your age when your grandmother died. What if something bad happens to your parents and you lose both of us, and you—not even eight years old. Oh, mi povero bambino. Oh, my poor baby." Dominic whispered to his son, as he brushed a curl from his eye.

Two weeks went by and Dominic still not one word from him. Regina was concerned, because if they didn't leave soon, they wouldn't make it back for Christmas and she knew Dominic wouldn't dream of spending Christmas without Joey.

The family were seated for dinner when Dominic made his announcement.

"I just want all of you to know that this time next week, you will be dining here without me," Dominic hesitated, looked around the room and his smiling eyes came to rest on Regina.

Regina stared back at him, expressionless.

Can it be? Does this mean what I think it does? Regina's could feel her heart pounding in her chest.

Dominic continued. "On December 10, Regina's birthday. We will be dining on 'The Orient Express.'" Dominic raised his voice, for emphasis, in naming the train.

As everyone voiced their surprised happiness for them, Regina dropped down on her knees, at Dominic's side, took his hands and brought them up to her lips and kissed them, slowly, lovely, and passionately as the happy tears fell down her face. Dominic had just given her his deepest love by putting aside his own fears. No man could love a woman more.

Regina had only two days to shop and pack. She invited Kay and Angela to accompany her. She selected very special clothes as this was not your ordinary train trip. Oh no, this was a very special train. During the days, casual, but smart, was the expected attire. The evenings were very elegant and formal. Gentlemen wore tuxedos and the ladies wore long gowns. In fact, it was virtually impossible to ever overdress on The Orient Express.

Regina knew exactly what to shop for. She had been dreaming of this trip for ever so long and had colored picture brochures of The Orient Express all over her bathroom wall. Being cognizant of the era of the train's birth, Regina picked out a small black veiled hat and a black, heavily pearl-beaded evening gown, reminiscent of the 20's. She purchased a mink stole for the chilly evenings. The brochures went on to say that it was not necessary to dress up, it was, however, proper decorum to do so. It would certainly be considered bad etiquette not to. The Orient Express deserved to be honored and to act otherwise was a total breach of respect.

CHAPTER 40

The Orient Express offered two routes, between Venice-Paris-London, and Venice-Frankfurt-Dusseldorf. When Regina told Dominic of her request, he thought she just wanted to visit Annette. Now, he realized it was all about the train trip.

Well, if Regina wants this train trip so bad, I will make sure she has "all" of it. Dominic booked them on both routes. They would take the Venice-Frankfurt-Dusseldorf route first, then the London route, and at the end of their destination, stop off at Vincent's.

"**Buon viaggio. Buon viaggio. Buno divertimento**." The family accompanied them to the railway station, wishing them a good trip and a good time.

"**Soggiorno calma**. Stay calm Dominic, Stay calm." Guido, sensing Dominic's uneasiness, embraced him, forcefully.

"**Guido, lo sono lieto quel tu soggiorno a Palazzo con guiesppe**." Dominic told Guido how happy he was that he and Paula were remaining at The Palazzo while they were away, to look after Joey. This gave him a sense of security, and he even managed to laugh when a thought occurred to him.

"You know, Guido. I was just thinking. You know how you have been after me to visit you and see your beautiful home? Well, here I am finally stepping out of The Palazzo and will be passing through Switzerland, near your home, and you are not

238

there!"

They both enjoyed a good hearty laugh. This was good. It relieved the tension for both of them. Guido was feeling Dominic's anxiety, also. Whatever Dominic felt, he felt. That's the way it was with them since childhood.

"Good morning, Mr. and Mrs. Visconti. Welcome aboard The Orient Express." They were respectfully greeted, by name, by the steward.

As Regina stepped on the metal foot plate, she immediately realized she was about to enter another era. The thought made her heart skip a beat. She could hardly believe she was, at this instance, living her dream.

"My name is Enrico, and I am your cabin steward. You must call on me, at any time, for all of your needs."

Regina was mesmerized as she looked around her cabin. She gasped, in fascination, at all she saw. From the brass window lever to the original upholstered seats to the embroidered drapes to all the intricate parquetry, it was so difficult to take it all it.

They waved goodbye to the family as the train smoothly made its way out of the Santa Lucia Railroad Station. Dominic took out his hander kerchief and wiped away the beads of nervous perspiration now forming on his forehead. Regina reached over and took his hand. It was cold and clammy.

"**Dominic, mi amare tuo**." Regina squeezed his hand and told him she loved him.

Dominic sat tensely, with eyes half closed, trying to relax, while sneaking fleeting glances at the passing scenery of Verona, past old courtyard walls, cracked and vine covered.

When they entered the dining car, Regina was once more enthralled with her surroundings from the fastidious restoration of the 1920's and 1930's period in the beauty of the wood, drapery and glass to her cosmopolitan companions.

The Orient Express was indeed a luxury hotel on wheels and enjoyed a reputation for playing host to a prestigious list of very wealthy clientele, from princes and film stars to countesses and even spies! Their travel companions on this day were an Italian Nobleman, an actor, honeymooners and an elderly couple celebrating their 50th wedding anniversary. Everyone was united in the romance of the train.

By the time they sat down to dinner, the train had started its ascent up the snow-capped mountains of Switzerland. The exquisite food and stunning alpine scenery competed for their attention.

The food was superb from the lamb fillet, roasted with savory rosemary, Regina's choice, to Dominic's succulent beef tournedos complemented by a delicious claret sauce, all immaculately served with some aplomb by Italian waiters.

A cognac, after dinner, brought a beautifully soul-satisfying day to a finale, while consenting to being seduced by the strains of "After the Loving, I'm still in Love with You," coming from the baby grand.

As the day wore on, and with each mile of track, Dominic became calmer. The train moved along the tracks so gently, so smoothly, that by the time they had finished their cognac, Dominic was relaxed and feeling romantic.

When they returned to their cabin, they found it magically transformed by Enrico, to a cozy bedroom with heavy crisp cotton damask sheets, turned invitingly down. They were pleasantly exhausted and despite their best intentions to make love, fell victim to being swayed to sleep by the age-old rhythm of wheel on rail.

The next morning, Enrico's discreet knock announced the arrival of their continental breakfast. They enjoyed their coffee and croissants while watching the spectacular Rhine Valley drift effortlessly by as it made its way to Dusseldorf. The scenery was stunning as they passed landscapes of rugged peaks, forested slopes, sparkling lakes, turreted castles, ornate cathedrals and imposing landmarks. With every winding turn, a new breathtaking site captured their attention.

Their journey was rapidly coming to an end. Soon they would be in Paris. They spent the remainder of their days in stimulating conversation with their fellow travelers.

On Regina's birthday, Dominic visited the exclusive onboard boutique. He purchased a toy replica train of The Orient Express for his Joey and a very special birthday gift for his Gina, earlier that day, Dominic instructed Enrico to prepare their cabin for Regina's birthday. Enrico was given "carte blanche" to purchase whatever he needed, informing him of Regina's likes.

When they returned to their cabin that evening, Dominic felt a resistance in opening the door. Against the door, throughout the small cabin, were dozens of stuffed animals of all kinds and sizes. Balloons and party decorations covered the walls.

"Oh, my God! Dominic. What did you do? Oh, my, all this for me? And you remembered how much I love stuffed animals, but so many!" Regina picked up the large lion and hugged it in her bosom.

Sitting on their night table in the ice bucket was a bottle of champagne and two glasses chilling in it.

"Oh, Dominic, I can't tell you—I can't express how happy you have made me on this birthday. This is a very special birthday, Dominic. First, this train trip and now all these gifts. It is the best birthday ever. I mean that with all my heart and I will always remember it until the day I die." Regina's tears of joy streamed down her face as she buried her long silver-white hair on Dominic's lap.

"My **bellismo**, Regina. My beautiful one. My little queen. I love you so much."

While the lights of Paris gleaned through their cabin window, they made long, tender, passionate love.

"Oh, Dominic, that was wonderful." Regina cuddled contently in Dominic's arms, completely satiated.

"You know, Dominic. I must tell you something. This

lovemaking tonight was very different than usual. I mean, it "felt" different. Oh, I don't know how to explain it. I mean, tonight, well, tonight, it seemed very special. Almost sacred."

Dominic adjusted his arm around Regina and held her close.

"Well, sure, Regina, of course it was different. First of all, it is your birthday and secondly, here I am on a train—something I swore I would never do! So, of course, it is different and special."

"Yes, yes, I know all that—but it's more than that. I feel like 'something' very wonderful happened here, tonight."

"Okay, Regina, okay. Something wonderful happened here, tonight," Dominic knew not to argue with Regina over these "feelings", these "premonitions", of hers. Besides, most of the time she was right. Like the time she told him her mother would never see her get married. They learned, later, that her mother passed away on that very same day Regina told him that. Regina's premonition, this evening, would prove her right, once again.

"Happy birthday, **mi bambino**, Gina." Dominic kissed her warmly and presented her with her gift.

"Oh, sweetheart, another present? You have given me so much already. Oh, what is it?"

Dominic was amused at her childlike exuberance as she carefully opened the beautifully wrapped gift, so she could save the paper.

What a good woman this is. Never in all the years, with all the money, is she spoiled, never once. Dominic smiled at her.

Regina took her time opening her gift, relishing the moment. She behaved as if it was the first gift she ever received from Dominic. She knew it would be a very special gift, because of his fine tastes. When she opened the blue velvet jewelry box, she was not disappointed. The gleaming gold from the 14kt thick-link charm bracelet caused her to blink her eyes. Each one of the gold charms was an exact replica of the cars on The Orient Express. All were hand-crafted of exquisite workmanship. The fine-tooled doors opened to reveal the inside of each car. It was a work of art done with extreme care and precision and wonderment at the craft of placing a miniature washbasin in the cabin of its car to the miniature baby grand piano placed in the bar lounge car. It was one of a kind, only to be found on The Orient express on-board boutique.

"Oh, Dominic, I love it. I love it. It's so beautiful. I can't wait to show Angela. Thank you, thank you, Dominic. Here, put it on me. Now, I shall never, never take it off."

They drifted off to sleep, surrounded by all the stuffed animals. They arrived in Boulogne, in the morning, where they took a short sea-cat cruise across the channel and then boarded the gleaming umber and cream Pullman carriage that brought them into London's Victoria Station.

CHAPTER 41

The train slowly pulled into Victoria Station, as if sensing its occupants' reluctance to end a nostalgic, unforgettable adventure, back in time.

Dominic hesitated before disembarking, as he threw a backward glance at the train. Although he never voiced his sentiments to Regina, it showed in his supremely calm, contented countenance what he was feeling. He thanked Regina, in his heart, for putting a closure to his nightmares and for giving him an unforgettable memory of this train trip that would remain with him for the rest of his life.

"**Venzenco, Venzenco**. Oh, it's so good to see you again," Dominic pulled Vincent towards him roughly, kissing him on both cheeks.

It was a two-hour drive to Cambridge, but it went by rather quickly as Dominic monopolized the conversation relating to Vincent and Annette all about the Orient Express, making sure not to leave anything out, and before they knew it, they arrived in Cambridge.

Although having more than 101,000 inhabitants, Cambridge was an extremely compact place and distinguished itself by having the best array in English architecture of all its neighboring towns. Besides its noted fame of being an historic University town, it was also an agricultural market town, at heart.

It reminded Regina of Venice and the Rialto Produce Market, and she immediately warmed to it. Dominic confessed to Regina later that he found it too confining, as it was on the whole a quiet, secluded place.

Vincent gave them a tour of the Cambridge University, as well as St. John's College, where he was teaching.

After five days visiting, Dominic had enough. He told Regina they had to go back to The Palazzo. Regina didn't protest even though she would have loved to stay longer. She was more than satisfied with all that Dominic had given her. She knew how much he missed Joey. She missed him also, but not like Dominic. Regina never would admit this to anyone but her first and last love would always remain with her husband. Not even her son could take first place in her heart.

Angela was happy to have Regina home and they disappeared into Regina's bedroom for the rest of the day. Regina talked nonstop about her adventure on The Orient Express. She showed her all the mementos she bought at the on-board boutique and the lovely birthday gift from Dominic. She then gave Angela her gift. A beautiful gold locket with the inscription on the back, "To my dearest friend, Angela. Love, Regina." Angela put Regina's picture in it, alongside her own.

...

Regina was home a couple of weeks when she woke up one morning feeling violently ill. She dismissed it as stomach flu. However, Dominic insisted she see Dr. Rosetti.

"It's nothing, Dominic, really. I know what it is. I just have the flu. I just need lots of rest and time to get over it. That's all."

But Dominic had his way and the next day, Angela accompanied Regina to Dr. Rosetti's office.

Dr. Rosetti did not agree with Regina's diagnosis and

Angela wasn't sure what to make of Regina's behavior when she exited his office. She tried to read her face. *Were those retching sobs of joy or anguish coming out of Regina*, she wondered.

"Regina, what's wrong? What did Dr. Rosetti say? Are you all right?" Angela was so scared; she would die if anything was wrong with Regina.

"Oh, my dearest Angela. No, no, there's nothing wrong. On the contrary, everything is right. Oh, Angela, everything is so right!"

Regina wrapped her arms tightly around Angela and hugged her so fiercely, Angela let out a yell of discomfort.

"Oh Angela. It finally happened! My prayers—all my novenas to our Mother of Perpetual Help have been answered. She answered them for me—for you—for us!"

Regina paused, just brief enough to take in a deep breath before continuing. "Angela, I'm going to have a baby!"

Angela stared at Regina, dumb founded while thoughts whizzed through her head. *I thought she was through-past the age. She always complained of hot flashes–never went anywhere without her fan–how can this be? —how can she be pregnant?*

"I know, I know, what you are thinking. You can't believe it, either. You think I'm too old, don't you? Can't you see, Angela, nothing is impossible if you have faith, if you never give up believing. This is what you always tell me."

Just then, a "**Satori**," (an instant awakening, as they say in India), swept over Regina and she shook Angela, never having let her go through out this time.

"Oh, my God, Angela. I know when it happened. I know the exact moment I conceived!" Regina's face brightened, with added excitement, as she hugged her face with her hands. "It happened on The Orient Express. It happened as we were approaching France, in fact, I can remember seeing the lights from the Paris skyline shining into our cabin window. And—and..." Regina groped for words as she recalled that evening and everything they did and said. "It was my birthday and—and—oh, Angela, do you realize that? It happened on my birthday! You see what a sign the Mother of Perpetual Help sent me, you see? And—and—there's something else." Regina paused to catch her breath. "After we made love, I told Dominic that I felt something very special just happened. Well, he pooh-poohed it—you know how Dominic reacts whenever I tell him about my premonitions. Well, now, what's he going to say, huh? Oh, Angela, I can hardly wait to see the look on his face when I tell him!"

"Wa—wa—what—are you saying to me, Gina?" They were in their bedroom when Regina told Dominic the news. Dominic's loud, shocked voice could be heard echoing down the hallway to the fourth-floor bedrooms. He then grew silent, and stared at Regina, with his mouth opened, in disbelief. *Is she playing a joke on me?* he wondered. No, he could tell she was serious. His face lit up and a bemused smile creased his face.

"Oh, Gina. **Mia moglie**, my wife. You make me look like a sex machine; you know that? I mean, at my age. Now, what will people say, eh?" Dominic was proud that people would look upon this balding 68-year-old man, with renewed respect—that he still had it in him to produce fruit. Yes, Gina made him look good among his family. Wagging his finger sternly at Regina, he cautioned her.

"No more trains for you, my little darling. After all these years—no **bambinos**, no babies, and we take just one train trip—just one—and—Dio Mio—My God, it happened!"

It was true. They tried to have more children. Regina was a devout Catholic and never consented to any form of birth control—and yet, it never happened—and now in her mid-40's, she is having her miracle baby.

"Dominic, there's something you need to know. This baby I have been praying for all these years—well—it was not just for me—for us. I prayed to have a baby for my dear friend, Angela. This baby is for her, Dominic. This is my special gift to her. She will be the Godmother. I wanted this baby so Angela can think of it as her very own-and she must be made to feel like it is hers, in every way. Understand, Dominic?"

Regina was shaking, with emotion, convincing Dominic it must be this way. This was the commitment she made to the Virgin. She vowed that if the Virgin blessed her with a baby, she would give it to Angela in every way possible. This friendship she had for Angela was a promise spoken from the heart.

"Gina, Gina, **calma, calma**. Please calm down. You are shaking so much. Sure, I understand. It is as it should be. This does not surprise me, at all. What, you didn't think I knew this special friendship you have for each other. I have watched this grow deeper over the years. Yes, it will be Angela's baby, also. *My God, this woman loves so deeply, so passionately. No one could love a friend more.* Dominic admired Regina's loyalty to her friend.

Constance Angela Regina Visconti was baptized at St. Mark's Basilica by Monsignor Mazzarino with Angela and Johnnie as the Godparents.

Constance grew up surrounded by a great deal of motherly love and soon noticed her Godmother showering her with so much love and attention, she thought of her as a "second mother". This made her feel very special, boasting that she had "two" mothers while her friends only had one.

Angela loved taking charge of Constance, which Regina encouraged from the moment they brought her home from the hospital. She stood, in the background, watching Angela tend to her baby. The arrangement worked out very well for all of them and a sense of peace and contentment filled the Palazzo. Regina knew Angela was going to be all right the day Angela failed to make her appearance in the courtyard and all the following days thereafter.

CHAPTER 42

"Dominic, I think this would be the perfect time for my godchild to come to Switzerland with us."

Paula pestered Dominic again as she had been doing for years. Since Guido and Paula were at the Palazzo for Constance's baptism and Joey had one month left before returning to school, it seemed the right time. Dominic had to admit Joey had been getting to be a nuisance around the Palazzo ever since his sister was born. He created more trouble and problems as more and more attention was showered on his baby sister, by the women.

"Yes, I think you are right. This would be a good time for Joey to leave. Guiseppe e conveniente geloso con suo sorella. Dominic admitted to them that Joey was becoming jealous of his sister.

Joey was excited about going off to Switzerland. It was the first time he would travel without his parents. At eight and a half years old, this made him feel very big, and manly.

Frankie pressed his face against his bedroom window, tears marring his view, as he sadly waved goodbye to Joey. He would miss his cousin. They grew very close over the years growing up together in the same household. They were a miniature Dominic and Guido. Joey was the "boss" and Frankie, his shadow, following him everywhere and obeying every order Joey gave him. Joey really loved Frankie, no matter how many times he slapped him on the head and called him stupid. They developed a tight bond which would served them well in enduring the many trials they would be facing together in the years to come.

The bus took five hours to reach Ascona. Guido and Paula preferred traveling by train, but Joey wouldn't hear of it.

"No, no, I don't want to go by train. I won't—I won't."

"But why, Joey? It is such a long tiring trip by bus, and the train is so comfortable, and you will still enjoy the beautiful countryside."

Paula could not understand why Joey was so adamant about this. However, Guido understood.

"It's okay, Joey. I understand. But you don't have to worry. Nothing is going to happen with the train." Guido tried to reassure Joey to no avail. He realized why he didn't want to go on the train. *Hmm, he must have heard his father talk about that time he was in that train accident that killed his mother, and Joey's grandmother. Hmm, I wonder how he heard this. We never spoke of this in front of him, only while in the library. This is very strange.*

They arrived in Ascona at nightfall. The heavy aroma from the flowers that bloomed all year around in this subtropical vegetation permeated the air as they traveled up the long winding road leading to their magnificent chalet high in the mountains. They eventually came upon a large two-story chalet with full length balconies on both floors opening up to an expansive breathtaking view of Lake Maggiore and the town. This was Paula's dream home. Early each morning, before the sun came up, Paula stepped out onto her balcony to breathe in the fresh clean mountain air, welcoming in the new day. Guido brought up a tray with a pot of coffee and rolls, kissed her and left. Paula took out her tablet and pencil and began writing. This was Paula's daily routine and Guido respected it. Now that Joey was here, she altered her routine.

Ascona was once a tiny fishing port, a poplar place for painters, writers and celebrities. It was known for its active cultural life and Paula made sure Joey was exposed to all of it. They went to museums, galleries and lectures. They journeyed to the capital city of the Ticino area, Bellinzona, where they visited the oldest and the largest of the castles, "The Castello Grande."

One of the major attractions of Ascona was the New Orleans Jazz Festival, when the picturesque squares and alleys of the region took on a particularly lively and colorful atmosphere.

The time sped by quickly as they kept Joey entertained. They went horseback riding, swimming, windsurfing, water-skiing and sailing on their boat. They visited Locarno and shopped at the fine department stores. Joey bought a gift for Frankie. The clerks were impressed with Joey's command of the Italian language and the waitresses at the hotel restaurants thought him charming and were amused when he flirted with them.

"Joey, stop that! For heaven sakes! What is the meaning of this, at your age?" Paula was horrified when Joey leaned over and made a motion of pinching the waitress's behind, as she passed by.

"Can you believe this, Guido? Have you ever seen such a young child behave in such a way? Why, he acts like he is 19 instead of 9. How did he get so precocious at such an early age?" Guido laughed heartily. Just like his father, the womanizer, he mentally noted.

Joey had had enough, he was homesick. He missed his parents and Frankie. He had fun being away from home, but now he wanted to go home and share his experiences with Frankie.

Frankie was very happy to have him back and the two ran off to Joey's room to hear all about his vacation. Of course, Joey exaggerated everything. When Joey told Frankie about all the girls flirting with him, his mouth flew open, and his eyes widened in awe at his flamboyant cousin. Frankie was deeply impressed with his cousin's self-assured manner. He wished he was more like him instead of being so shy and lacking in self-confidence. He looked to Joey for his identity. In this respect, he was a lot like his mother, in her younger days, when Kay looked up to Annette as her idol.

CHAPTER 43

Joey hesitated before knocking. The sound of his father's favorite opera could be heard through the heavy, mahogany library doors. When he was sure he no longer heard it, he knocked quietly, timidly. This approach was highly unusual for the self-assured, cocky Joey, who, in the past, announced himself loudly and forcefully. However, tonight was to be a different kind of visit with his father.

"Avanti, entril," his father's loud, strong voice invited him to enter.

Joey nervously made his way to the side chair across from his father. He squirmed and adjusted himself trying to get comfortable. There was nothing wrong with the high-back chair. It was Joey who was uneasy. *Why was it*, Joey wondered to himself, *that in any other room in the Palazzo, I am fine and can speak right out to my father, without hesitation? What is it about this library that makes me feel like a small scared little boy within its portals? Ah, can it be my memories of those times I was punished in this room? Yes, that must be it.* Still, even now, at 25 years old and no longer that little boy that used to curl up in the dumbwaiter and eavesdrop on his father and uncles, he felt intimidated in this room. There was something about this room that made his father appear massive and formidable. He looked around to study the culprit. It was a warm room with its richly ornate mahogany wall panels. The bold plaques, along the bookcase wall, depicted the famous Roman scenes of Venice. Tintoretto's "Paradise," the largest picture ever painted in oils by this artist, hung on the wall over Dominic's desk. Two 18th century celestial and terrestrial globes were stationed alongside the desk. What Joey didn't see, nor did he know, was that behind the center panel in the bookcase was a secret doorway which led to his parents' bedroom closet. Dominic and Regina made sure their mischievous little boy never found out. This was Dominic's favorite way of slipping into his library late at night, when he couldn't sleep. He played his beloved music and fell asleep on his black buffalo leather eight-foot sofa. In making her morning rounds, Celeste found him, still asleep.

"Ah, Joey, listen. Isn't this beautiful? Did you ever hear anything more beautiful?" The sounds of music filled the room. It gives me such shivers each time I hear it. I don't know why. I can't explain it. But it fills me up and makes me feel so good inside!" The strains of Dominic's favorite classical piece, the "Bacarolle" by Jacques Offenbach filled the library and engulfed them. His father sat back in his chair with his eyes closed, a blissful smile on his face.

Joey tapped his foot, impatiently, and hoped this would be the last time he would play this music as he was anxious to talk to his father. He knew, however, that when his father was in this state of ecstasy, he sat for hours playing it over and over and did not want to be disturbed. The music ended and Dominic was temporarily satisfied.

"Okay, Joey. So, you want to talk to me? You know, Joey, I am glad you came to see me. Because I needed to talk to you, too. Your mother—well, she's been nagging me to talk to you. You know what she wants me to talk to you about, eh?"

Joey nodded his head. Yes, he knew. Lately, he and his mother had been at odds ever since he told her he wanted to go to San Lucci Island and open up a pizza parlor. This was his dream ever since he was a young boy, listening to the adventurous stories his father told him about the Island. He had to go and experience this for himself. Joey looked up to his father, he was his idol. He wanted to be just like him, respected, and the leader of his family. He wanted his own family, and he would start with his cousin, Frankie, a willing participant. Frankie stood in awe of Joey's magnetic personality. Joey was a great talker and a manipulator. He could get anything he wanted out of people, except when it came to his father. Joey had a charisma that people responded to, especially the women. He was also an astute business negotiator and since joining his uncle's banking business, while in college, the bank profited substantially through his shrewd business dealings.

"Yeah, Pop. I know. But what I don't understand is why Mom is so against me going to the Island. What's wrong with San Lucci Island, anyway? You were there and you had a good business and a good life. Well, didn't you?"

Dominic took a deep breath and studied this caricature of himself. Joey was looking more and more like him, every day. He had his dark brown hair, his deep dimples and his Roman nose. Unfortunately, he also inherited his hot Sicilian temper, along with his love of the ladies. These two traits worried his parents, especially his mother. As long as he was living at the Palazzo, she could protect him. He would be safe. But once he stepped on San Lucci Island—well, who knew what would happen to him. Dominic hid the fact that he was pleased and proud that his son took after him. He couldn't let Regina know that even these negative traits Joey inherited—even these made him proud. Should he tell his son that these traits were lethal on San Lucci Island? It was true the Islanders were tolerant of newcomers if they brought money to their Island, but they could also be very clique-ish and unless you fit in, they could make your life hell. Fortunately for Dominic, he knew how to endear them to him. He always had an open pocketbook for anyone that needed a handout. He knew it would be different with Joey. He saw how he operated in his banking business. He was a cold, hard businessman. He wouldn't be so free and easy with his money. On the other hand, perhaps it was about time he learned how to get along with other people, outside the family. Dominic knew it was a matter of time before Joey left as he saw how bored and restless he was becoming, and he knew he needed to spread his wings.

"Okay, Joey, so if you go, what is it you want to do there? How would you make your living?" Almost before Dominic asked him, he realized it was a rhetorical question. Even since Joey was a small boy, he told his father that one day he would move to San Lucci Island and open a pizza parlor and be a big "King" on the Island, just like him.

"Okay, so I'll make a phone call and then when we get everything settled, we will deal with your mother, okay?"

Dominic poured them a glass of brandy as if to cement his decision. Then he picked up the phone.

"Bernie, yeah, this is Dominic. How are you? Um-hum, yeah, I know it's been a while. But, you know, I gotta give you a chance to gather up some more juicy gossip for me, right? Ha, ha!"

Bernie Goldstein was Dominic's real estate broker on San Lucci Island. When Dominic left the island, Bernie liquidated all of his properties. Since then, he remained in close contact with Bernie. They talked on the phone at least once a month and Bernie filled him in on all the latest news. It was Dominic's way of staying connected with the Island.

"Bernie, I need a favor. I need you to find me a pizza parlor. What, oh, no, not for me, I wish, no, it is for my son, Joey. A real nice one, with an ocean view. You know, similar to the one I had, and—" Dominic was interrupted by Joey waving his hand trying to get his attention "What is it? No, Bernie, I'm not talking to you. Just a minute, Bernie, can you hold on a second?" Dominic put his hand over the phone.

"Pop, I don't want just any pizza parlor. I want yours, the one you had. It's got to be that one, pop."

Dominic studied his son and recognized the fire of determination in his eyes. The same fire he had once when he was young, while under his Godfather's guidance. He knew that look and respected it.

"Okay, okay, let me see what I can do." Dominic turned back to Bernie.

"Ah—listen, Bernie. I wanna buy back my old Pizza Palace." There was a pause.

"Yeah, yeah, that one. The one I had 25 years ago." He listened, patiently, while Bernie explained it wasn't possible because it wasn't for sale. He knew the owners and they had many offers in the past but refused to sell. Couldn't he find him another property?

Dominic looked at his son. In the silence that followed, he knew Joey would not settle for any other pizza parlor.

"No, Bernie, it's gotta be that one. You just make them an offer they can't refuse, okay? You tell them it's for the son of Dominic Visconti."

With that completed, Dominic relaxed and enjoyed the rest of the conversation with Bernie. He chuckled frequently.

"No, no kidding really? Well, now isn't that something? You see, even the bells have respect for the Visconti name. Ha, ha!"

Dominic smiled and shook his head, in amused disbelief, as he hung up the phone.

In answer to Joey's puzzled look, he explained.

"Bernie told me something very interesting, very unusual. You know, if your mother heard what I am about to tell you, she would say it had a special meaning. Well, Bernie told me that the bell tower chimes that sat high on the hill overlooking the ocean went out about 25 years ago, on the exact same day, the family sailed out of the San Lucci Island Harbor. And they remained silent ever since, as they couldn't find a clock man to fix it as it is a very old bell, and no one knew how to fix it. They needed to find the original craftsman who made the bell, but no one knew where to look. He left the island some 30 years ago right after making the clock. The person in charge of locating him traveled all over the world to locations where he thought he would be but to no avail. When he finally found him, the man was now 90 years old, and living in—guess where? You will never believe this."

Joey shrugged his shoulders.

"In Switzerland! In the same town your uncle and aunt live! And—what is even more funny is that now that another Visconti—you—returns to San Lucci Island, the bell chimes are working once again! Now, isn't that something? Ha, ha." Dominic wiped the tears from his eyes.

"You see, my Joey, even the bells honor the Visconti family, eh?"

CHAPTER 44

It was settled. Joey and Frankie were to leave for San Lucci Island in one month.

That's how long it would take Bernie to transfer ownership of the Pizza Palace to Dominic. The owners didn't want to sell but when they found out who made the offer, they changed their minds. They remembered when Dominic lived on the Island, 25 years ago, and were aware of his unsavory reputation for getting what he wanted no matter what it took. They heard stories of "bad things" happening when he didn't get his way. They recalled how Dominic acquired The Lei, the Polynesian restaurant that wasn't for sale. Shortly after, the owner Russ abruptly left the Island. Then there was the story about the murdered girl found in the hills above San Lucci Island. Rumors circulated that it wasn't an accident and that Dominic had something to do with it. No, they weren't taking any chances of "natural disasters" happening to them! When Dominic made them a very generous offer, they decided it was time to retire.

Frankie was elated to be going with Joey. He had been working alongside his father, uncle and cousin, Joey in the banking business for the past five years. He was eager to leave all this behind and start a whole new life with Joey. The men made their plans for their new life while they waited for Bernie to complete the arrangements.

It was decided that Joey would take the yacht, The Regina. He hired a ship's crew to accompany them. They were to remain with Joey for as long as he needed them. Dominic hadn't made use of The Regina for many years and decided it was time it went out to sea. Besides, he could appreciate the importance it was for Joey to duplicate everything "exactly" as it was 25 years ago when The Regina was anchored in the San Lucci Harbor.

Regina had finally succumbed. What else could she do? Dominic always had the last word, after all, he was the "boss" in the family.

Constance was devastated. The day before Joey was to leave, she locked herself in her room and cried her eyes out. Joey went to console her.

"It's okay, Sis. Listen, when you graduate from high school, next year, you can come and stay with me. You can take some time off before leaving for college, okay, Connie?"

Constance was a very lovely, sensitive young lady, an almost exact replica of her mother with her long, dark, silky, wavy hair and her big brown eyes and long thick eyelashes. However, that's where the resemblance ended. Her mother developed late at the age of 19, when she met Dominic, she was practically flat-chested with very slender hips. Constance, on the other hand, was fully developed at the age of 13. Her well-rounded breasts and her curvy hips were not missed by the young men in her little town. She was naïve and wondered about the turned heads and whistles she received each time she stepped outside the Palazzo.

Now that Joey was leaving, Constance needed her father. Dominic loved his daughter but was not aware of her feelings. He left that to the women. It seemed to Constance that the more she needed him, the more he seemed to absent himself from her life. These days, he was consumed with concern over Joey leaving. He never realized how hurt Constance was by his lack of attention towards her. It was obvious to Constance and to the rest of the family, that Joey was the apple of his eye. Despite this, she wasn't jealous of Joey. Instead, she felt sorry for him, the way he was babied and dominated by their father. She knew this only made him more determined to become his own man. She knew he had to prove to himself and his father he could be a success on his own.

Joey was the one Constance turned to more and more over the years for male advice. Joey became "her father." Since Joey was 9 years older, it was easy for her to accept his fatherly advice. Joey, in turn, adored his baby sister and always watched over her. He was the one to give his consent on her dating at the age of 14. They were afternoon dates and always chaperoned by her godmother, Angela. Nevertheless, Joey scrutinized all the suitors that came to the Palazzo. He warned the young men to treat his sister with respect, or they would answer to him. He scared most of them away, by his interrogation, before they even left the Palazzo. He was strict with Constance, just like a father would be. There would be no evening dates until she was much older.

Kay also relented in letting Frankie leave. Sammy never had a problem with this. He thought it would be the best thing for his son. In talking to Dominic about his leaving, he expressed his feelings.

"You know, Dom. I am glad he is leaving with Joey. I think this is the best thing for him.

Being on his own, maybe it will make him a man. You know, Dom. I never told anyone this, but I have always been disappointed in my Frankie. I know—I know—that sounds bad, but, you know, I kinda wish he took after me more—you know what I mean? The way Joey takes after you. I mean, Frankie is so shy, so withdrawn, nothing like me. Well, I guess he takes after his mother. Maybe, it's Kay's fault the way she raised him. The way she babied him and over-protected him. Yeah, no wonder he acts like a 'mamma's baby.'"

Dominic nodded, in agreement. He knew exactly what

Sammy was talking about. He too, thought the same thing about Frankie watching him grow up, alongside Joey. What a contrast! He certainly didn't take after his father, at all. Why, he didn't even look like Sammy. Dominic wanted to tell Sammy. "Eh, what do you expect when your Frankie is a mezzo, mezzo a half and half. Half Irish and half Italian." But he didn't want to make Sammy feel worst.

He remembered Sammy back in the old days on San Lucci Island. He was so impulsive, very talkative and always had his mind on sex. A real true hot-blooded Sicilian. Frankie, on the other hand, never seemed to look at women or care about them. He knew his Joey was sowing his oaks at an early age by dating a different woman every night. Frankie never dated. He was content to hang around Joey, waiting to do his bidding.

Yeah, Dominic agreed, Sammy was right. Frankie didn't have any pallones, (balls) like his Joey. Yeah, maybe this is just what he needs. Maybe when he gets away from home and his mother, he might become a man.

...

It was a beautiful, warm sunny spring Sunday morning when The Regina pulled into San Lucci Island Harbor. They were greeted by the dual sounds of the church bells ringing for the 12 P.M. Mass at St. Mary's of the Sea Catholic Church and the bell from the Angie's Fish Market announcing the start of the fishing derby. The gun sounds were heard coming from the green pier. This was the custom whenever a fisherman brought in his catch.

Joey couldn't have picked a more spectacular time to make his arrival on the Island.

In fact, if they weren't expected, the 250-foot grandiose size of The Regina would have been enough to capture the Islanders' attention as it smoothly made its way into its berth. As it turned out, everyone was expecting them. It didn't take long for the news to spread as soon as the Islanders found out who the new owner of the pizza palace was. They were well acquainted with the Visconti name and the old timers passed on his reputation to their children and to their children's children. The pier was crowded with the curious Islanders as they shoved each other to get a closer look at the two young men. Joey stood proudly on the deck of The Regina surveying "his Island." The sea gulls flew overhead and then straight for the pizza parlor, landing on the roof top as if to acknowledge its new owner. The cruise ships were docked out of the harbor and the shore boats brought the tourists to and from as the mouthwatering aromas from Rodran's Buffalo Restaurant welcomed them to the Island. The merchants were marking up their "sale prices" in anticipation of a lucrative day. Activity abounded everywhere.

CHAPTER 45

Joey took a long, slow drag on his expensive Havana cigar and smile contently as he stared out the window at The Regina resting in the harbor. He leaned back in his high-back buffalo leather desk chair and surveyed his office.

It was just as his father described it. A richly decorated office paneled in dark mahogany. It remained exactly the same after all these years, except for leather furniture. The leather on the arms were now cracked and the inside batting shone through. However, the strong smell of the leather was still quite potent, and Joey took a deep breath, luxuriating in it. This, too, Joey inherited from his father—this fascination—this sensual appetite for leather!

His pulse quickened as he eyed the infamous eight-foot black leather sofa. He remembered his father's voice in the library. He became aroused recalling his father and uncle talk about all the "good times" they had on that sofa. He remembered, at the time, blushing when he realized his father was talking about his mother, before they were married. It was the day that Dominic's Godfather, Salvatore Sangelli sailed into San Lucci Harbor on his 300-foot yacht "**Buno Fortuna**" (good fortune). Accompanying him was Johnnie, Sammy, and his mother. After the men had conducted their business, he sent for his mother. Then there was that time when Uncle Guido married his Aunt Paula, and they spent their honeymoon night on that sofa. Joey wondered how many more stories it could reveal if it could talk. Hearing Frankie's knock on the door brought his attention back to the present.

"**Entrare, chiuudere la porta**."

Frankie entered and closed the door, following Joey's command.

"Joey, I brought you the books to go over. It looks like it's going to be a good weekend. I just got a reservation for the banquet room, so we will be booked up the entire weekend."

Yes, business was booming. Joey was smart to have opened the pizza palace when he did as the summer season was just commencing and the busiest time of the year on the Island. The town would be brimming over with tourists and all the summertime events would bring in even more people every day.

"Yeah, yeah, Frankie, that's good. You handle it. You're doing a great job."

Joey didn't want to be bothered, right now. He had his mind on other business, women business. He'd been on the Island for several months without a woman and was getting restless. He noticed that it didn't seem to bother Frankie.

"Hey, Frankie. What's with you, huh? How come you never talk about the women here? What's the matter with you?"

Frankie shrugged off Joey's questions. He wasn't interested in women because he was too shy, and it was too painful for him to talk to them. Joey should have understood, as he was the same when he was at home in Venice. Besides, he was content in running the pizza palace and being Joey's right-hand man. This satisfied him and when Joey complimented him, as he just did, well, this was enough for him. He didn't need anything more.

Joey knew he was lucky to have Frankie with him. He was his perfect ally because he got along with the Islanders. Frankie was the diplomat. He was the one the merchants did business with. They liked and respected him and were comfortable with this quiet soft-spoken man. He was accepted by them, and Joey was not. They thought him cocky and obnoxious. These qualities were viewed as charismatic and charming in Venice but not so here. They feared anyone that was different and, therefore, were intimidated by him. This was the climatic attitude of the island.

This was exactly what Regina feared would happen. She knew these people and she knew her Joey. She knew they would never accept him. So, Frankie became Joey's buffer. Yes, they made a perfect combination. They both benefitted from this partnership.

"**La dolce**, vita. What a sweet life." Joey locked his fingers and stretched them, contentedly, behind his head as he smiled at Frankie. *So, he isn't like me, chasing the women. So what? He's a good guy, my cousin.* Joey felt so good, so happy with his life that he got up from his chair, walked around his desk and gave Frankie a warm tight embrace.

"Frankie, you're all right, you know that. I'm glad you're here with me. I would be lost without you."

That did it. That was all Frankie needed to hear, that Joey needed him. He was now content. Where Joey needed women for satisfaction, Frankie only needed Joey's approval.

"Frankie, I have to go do something, tonight. Are you going to be okay with the banquet by yourself?"

"Oh, sure, Joey, sure. I'll be fine. You go and have some fun; I know you need it." Frankie knew just what it was Joey needed to do.

Ever since they arrived, Joey had his eye on a pretty, young salesclerk. One day, while shopping in the town plaza, Joey caught a glimpse of a tall, slender young girl with long blonde hair and the deepest blue eyes he had ever seen, working in one of the shops.

The sound of the bell over the shop door cause Cnythia to look up and meet the hypnotic stare of his large deep brown eyes. She was immediately mesmerized by his sensual eyes as he lowered his long, curly eyelashes, seductively while studying her.

"May—may—I—I—help you?"

Cnythia tried to control her trembling, stuttering voice as his continuous silent stare completely unnerved her.

What a beautiful, sweet girl. I simply must have her, Joey decided.

"Yes, I want to see that black lace head scarf, in the window. And while you're at it, give me the white one, also."

Joey remained near the front store window, leaving very little room for Cnythia to reach in the window. As she bent down and leaned into the window, she felt his hot breath on the back of her back-less sundress. Joey made no attempt to give her room as she accidentally brushed by him. He grinned when her small breasts brushed against his arm.

"Oh, by the way, I'm Joseph Visconti but you can call me Joey and you are …?"

Cnythia watched him leave carrying his purchases. *Hmm, I wonder if those scarves are for his girlfriend, or perhaps, girlfriends?* Cnythia mused to herself. She would have been surprised to learn that the scarves were for his mother and his godmother.

Cnythia felt a tug at her heart thinking about him and hoped he would come into the shop again, soon. She was definitely attracted to him and wondered how old he was.

Hmm, I wonder how old she is. Well, she's the right age for me, whatever she is. I like them young and virginal, and this one is definitely a virgin. I'm positive! Joey affirmed to himself.

Joey knew just how to woo Cnythia. He visited her store often, when she was alone. First, he checked inside, before entering. If he saw an older woman with long straight, gray-streaked blonde hair and deep blue eyes, he knew this was her mother as she looked just like Cnythia. Joey figured out Cynthia's work schedule. He found out she was still in high school and worked in the boutique after school and on weekends. Sometimes

268

with her mother and other times, alone.

"Frankie, I tell you this girl is something special. I've just got to have her. I'm taking my time with her, though. I'm working her slowly, keeping her guessing, and wondering when or if I'll return to the shop. I can tell that each time she sees me, she looks relieved, like she was afraid I wasn't coming back. Now see, that's where you want them. You know what I mean? You have to keep them on edge, so when you attack', they're ready and willing and even grateful you want them. You see, Frankie, you have to make them think it's 'their idea, capise? You understand?"

Frankie loved listening to Joey talk about women. He learned so much from him. He admired the way Joey knew how to handle women. Not that Frankie would ever do anything with the advice. He remembered the time Joey thought he was ready to become a man. On Frankie's 18th birthday, Joey brought him to a house of ill-repute and introduced him to his puttana, his whore. He gave her a lot of money and told her to take "good care" of his cousin. Afterwards, when Joey asked him how it went, he answered, "Great."

How could Frankie tell him he was still a virgin? He was too embarrassed to tell Joey what happened. As soon as she unzipped his pants and brought her mouth down to meet his pulsating penis, he "came" all over her. She didn't even get a chance to place her lips around him. Frankie was so humiliated when she laughed at him that he hadn't been with a woman, since.

CHAPTER 46

"Yeah, Pop. Everything is just fine here. Hey, you would be proud of me, we're making a

real good profit and the place is always filled. What did I tell you, Pop? I told you I could do good business here."

Dominic wasn't interested if Joey made a profit or not, he was more concerned in knowing if Joey fit in and how the Islanders related to him. He also wondered if they ever mentioned him.

"Well, you know how it is here, Pop. It takes time to fit in. You and Mom told me that.

Yeah, the people do remember you and ask about you."

Joey didn't add that he knew they would rather have his father here instead of him. He was getting sick and tired of his parents always asking the same thing. Every conversation started the same.

Joey had been on the island for about a year and things still hadn't changed with him and the Islanders. They did not like him and they crossed the street when they saw him coming their way.

"Hey, no skin off my nose. Who the hell cares if they like me or not. I'm the one with all the money, not them," he told Frankie.

But Frankie knew that it did bother Joey and that it hurt

him. However, Joey didn't let it affect him or his business. Like he told Frankie, he was the one with the money.

The atmosphere of the pizza parlor was a lot different now than when his father owned it. In those days, the Islanders dropped in and socialized with Dominic, and he always took the time to sit and chat over a cold pitcher of beer and pizza which was usually on the house. Ever since Joey became the proprietor, no one dropped in to chat because Joey never had time for them, and they knew he would never pick up their tab. The Islanders were a stingy lot and endeared themselves to anyone that offered them a free meal. If Joey caught Frankie treating any of them, he chastised him.

"Frankie, what the hell did you pick up the sheriff's check for? What do you think we're running here, a charity? This is business and I don't ever want to see you do that again, capise?"

"Yeah, Joey, I understand, but you really ought to bend a little now and then. This deputy remembers your father and has great respect for him, and it wouldn't be a bad idea if you tried to build a good rapport with him, also."

Joey should have heeded his cousin's advice and he would have saved himself a lot of trouble with Deputy Sheriff Ernest Frye.

Thirty years ago, Sheriff Ernest Frye arrived on San Lucci Island and worked under Deputy Sheriff Dan Dawson. Ernest had a hard time fitting in, at first. Dan made his life hell, always harassing him and delegating menial chores to him, such as sending him to pick up his lunch each day from Al's Coffee Shop and berating him when he forgot his extra onions.

Dan was never liked among the Islanders because of his pugnacious personality. They found him to be uncouth, obnoxious, mean and unscrupulous. He was very vindictive to anyone who crossed him.

When Ernest was finally accepted among the Islanders and inundated with dinner invitations, Dan bristled with anger as he was never invited. The only one nice to him was Dominic. Whenever he paid a visit to the pizza parlor, Dominic took the time to sit and chat with him and pick up his tab. In return, whenever there was some illegal business going on and it was suspected that Dominic had an involvement in it, Dan turned the other way. Ernest saw this and resented it. Like the time they found a young woman's body in the mountains, and he knew Dominic had something to do with it but Dan never did anything about it. Dan called it an accident and marked Sylvia Lawson's file, closed.

When Ernest took over as Deputy Chief, he vowed he would never be like his predecessor. He would run his department with integrity. However, as he became more entrenched into the island's way of life, he underwent a complete metamorphosis. Little by little, before he even realized it himself, Deputy Ernest was slowly turning into everything he once despised. Another "Dan Dawson."

This is what happens when you stay too long on San Lucci Island. You change, and don't even know it. You become "one" with the island and the people and you don't have tolerance for anyone coming in and wanting to change the "flow."

Newcomers to the island found the deputy reluctant to investigate their complaints against the Islanders. Ernest found it more convenient and advantageous to look the other way. The Islanders were grateful and repaid him, generously. So, when Joey snapped his check out of Frankie's hand and slapped it back down on the table, in front of him, he boiled over with indignation.

What is this? Doesn't he know who I am? He should have more respect for my position, and not go making an enemy of me. If his father was here, he would know how to treat me.

He remembered how respectfully Dominic treated Dan, his predecessor, and in return, never had any trouble with the local authorities. At that time, this infuriated the honest deputy.

Now, he wished Dominic was here, instead of his son.

...

Joey was working late in his office when he heard a ruckus coming from the pizza parlor. He looked at his watch, 10 minutes to midnight, almost closing time.

"What the hell is going on out here, Frankie?"

Joey stormed out of his office and confronted a drunken brawl, in progress. Frankie, trying to break it up, got knocked down.

"Hmm, you boys look pretty young to be here drinking all this beer. Let's see some ID."

Joey spun around when he recognized Deputy Ernest Frye's voice and was stunned to see him. *Now, how in the hell did he happen to be passing by here at this precise time of night?* Joey looked at him suspiciously.

Ernest surveyed the empty pitchers of beer and the inebriated state of the two young men that were now sitting on the floor with their hands locked behind their backs, in handcuffs.

"Well, well, what have we here? Well, what do you know? It says here that you boys are only 20 years old." Ernest gave Joey a sarcastic look.

"Yeah, just 20 years old and we know that the legal drinking age in San Lucci is 21." I got you now, you bastard, the deputy mentally verbalized as he gave a malevolent smile to Joey.

Meanwhile, Frankie was up on his feet, rubbing his jaw which was beginning to swell.

"Sheriff, I can assure you, the ID they showed me was not this one. The ones I saw had their age at 21. I am positive."

Frankie was becoming increasingly upset to think he could have made such a stupid mistake. Could he have been so tired that he "thought" he saw the number 21? Perhaps, it was 20, instead. No, Frankie knew he was always very careful who he served and never allowed anyone to be served who remotely looked underage. These two guys, with their beards, certainly looked of age.

"Better call a lawyer for your cousin, Frankie, cause he's sure gonna need one!"

When Frankie got Joey out of jail on bail a few hours later, they returned to the Pizza Palace.

"Frankie, it was a setup. That son-of-a-bitch set me up! You know that don't you, Frankie? And how come that damn deputy showed up at that exact time, huh? Shit! That bastard never did like me and now he's threatening to pull my license. Can you beat that?"

Livid with anger, Joey paced back and forth in his office, like a caged animal.

Frankie didn't want to tell Joey "I told you so," but he knew it was true. It was a setup. He was always afraid something like this would happen, the way that deputy hated Joey. He only wished Joey did not make a point of making enemies on this small island.

"Okay, okay. I know what I have to do. Don't you worry, Frankie. It's going to be all right." Joey nervously tried to convince himself.

When Matthew received Joey's phone call, he was surprised with the nature of the call. He knew it had to be important for Joey to ask for his help. Joey was always too proud to ask any favors from his cousin.

Joey was now asking him to come to San Lucci Island as soon as possible as he needed some legal advice. Matthew was not a lawyer, yet. He was still in his last year of law school, but he didn't hesitate to tell Joey he would come even though it was an inconvenience as he had to rearrange his school schedule. However, Joey was his cousin and when a member of the family needed help, you didn't refuse. He told his father about Joey's trouble and Vincent immediately called Dominic, knowing Joey didn't tell him.

"Thank you, Vinnie. No, I didn't know. You did right to call me. Grazie. Tutto mio amore tu familia. Thank you. Give all my love to your family."

Vincent knew that Dominic would take care of the problem and by the time his son arrived on the island, it would be over. However, he did not tell Matthew. Since Matthew went straight to college from high school and never had a break, Vincent thought he could use one now and it would also be good for him to be with his cousins, again.

Dominic did not tell Regina Joey was in trouble. He knew she would get upset and prove to him, once again, she was right with her intuitive feelings against Joey going to San Lucci Island. No, she didn't need to have this worry. He would take care of it, as he always did whenever Joey got into trouble.

The cousins embraced, warmly. Being together like this, enjoying the closeness, brought tears to Frankie's eyes. Frankie was always the sensitive one among his cousins. He was the first one to cry when they were little, for any reason, but especially when Joey yelled at him. In contrast, Matthew held his head high with dry eyes and never let Joey see how much he hurt him. Joey was very mean to Matthew when they were young, out of jealousy. Joey's father always bragged about how polite Matthew was, how he had such good manners, and how intelligent he was. However, all of that was now forgotten in the close camaraderie they felt for each other when they met again.

...

Chief Deputy Ernest Frye ordered his young deputy, Lonnie, to go to Al's Coffee Shop and pick up his lunch.

"And don't forget the extra onions!" The deputy yelled after him just as Matthew walked through the door.

Ernest took his feet off his desk, pushed back his chair,

and scrutinized the newcomer. He noted his expensive three-piece gray flannel suit, white silk shirt and red and gray silk tie. He got up from his chair, walked around his desk, to check out his shoes. They were of a black leather "banker" style with a high-gloss shine. His only jewelry was a gold tie tack with the initials MC. That did it for Ernest, he immediately made up his mind he didn't like the stranger. Matthew was too self-assured, too classy. Ernest was intimidated.

Matthew's confident presence would unnerve the jealous, unintelligent person as he had an aristocratic air about him due to his upbringing and intellectual environment and not due to any egotistical trait. He was rather a sensitive, gracious, humble, sweet young man.

"I beg your pardon. I am here to see Chief Deputy Ernest Frye."

Hmm, he even talks fancy, this city boy. Ernest confirmed, mentally, he had made the right assessment by not liking him.

"So, what do you want him for?" Ernest was going to "play" around with him while waiting for his lunch.

"I am here on official business and if you don't mind, I would like to speak to Chief Deputy Ernest Frye." Matthew attempted to sound firm, raising his voice slightly.

"Yeah, yeah, okay, it's me. I'm him. So, what do you want with me?"

"I represent Mr. Joseph Visconti and I would like to hear the full details of the charges brought against my client." He was not prepared for what happened next.

"Oh, that! Yeah, well, that's been taken care of. Yeah, those charges are dropped."

Matthew stood there, befuddled, waiting for some kind of explanation from the deputy and when he saw none was forthcoming, he started to speak but just then, the door opened, and the young deputy walked in with a bag.

"Well, it's about time. What took you so long? I'm starved. Okay, put it down right here. Now, I better have my extra onions this time." Ernest cleared off his desk, rapidly. He looked up at Matthew, impatiently.

"Are you still here? I told you, it's over. You can go now," he told him, dismissing him.

When Matthew returned to the Pizza Palace, he was met by an anxious Frankie.

"What happened, Matt? How does it look? Can you straighten it out? Gee, Joey is really upset."

Joey was sitting in his office waiting for Matthew's return.

"It's okay, Joey. It's over with. He won't be bothering you anymore. All charges have been dropped."

Joey jumped up, ran around his desk and pulled Matthew toward him in a big bear hug.

"Gosh, Matt, how did you do it? What the hell did you say to that asshole?"

Matthew gave Joey a big, helpless smile. He didn't know what he said or even what happened, for that matter. Perhaps his presence scared the deputy off. Not knowing that Matthew was not a lawyer officially, the deputy might have thought Matthew had a lot of influence high up in the judicial arena and was afraid of him. Matthew speculated to himself.

"Ah, hell. What do I care what you said or did. The main thing is you DID it, Matt. However, you did it, I'm eternally grateful. I owe you one, cousin. Now, let's celebrate. Frankie, go get that bottle of vintage brandy I've been saving for a special occasion. Now, we will enjoy Matt's visit. Matt, tomorrow, I'm going to show you something very, very special."

Deputy Ernest Frye scanned through the letters on his desk until he found the one, he was looking for. He smiled as he re-read the words of praise about what a fine job he was doing as chief deputy and that he was always respected and liked by the recipient of the letter. Then he unfolded the high four figure check made out to him and pressed it to his lips. *Ah, that diego always was very generous.*

"Lonnie, put this folder in the dead bin." Ernest took a black marker and put "closed" on the front and filed it under the last initial, "V".

CHAPTER 47

The shop door opened, and Ingrid walked out just as Joey and Matthew arrived.

Ingrid hesitated outside the shop and pressed her face against the window squinting her eyes to focus in on Joey. She thought she recognized him. He looked so familiar. She knew she hadn't seen him around town or in church. *Could he be someone from my past, when I first lived here on the island? No, no, of course not. How could it be? This man is too young.* Confused, Ingrid mulled all this over in her mind.

Ingrid was a young woman of 23 when Aaron Holtz brought her over from Sweden to be his housekeeper. Aaron was much older than Ingrid and from the way he treated her, the Islanders suspected she was much more than just his housekeeper. Aaron hovered over her everywhere they went and if he caught any of the young men talking to her, he swiftly took her by the hand and walked, rather pulled her home. Ingrid was only five feet tall, and Aaron was a lanky six foot, so Ingrid had to run to keep up with him.

Ingrid was a beautiful, svelte, blond-haired blue-eyed woman and all the men in town were smitten with her. Aaron never let her out of his sight and weeks went by without catching a glimpse of her. Aaron did all the shopping and left Ingrid at home. Ingrid's only outing, without Aaron, was her daily attendance at church. Aaron felt it safe for her to be with Father Albert, and Ingrid welcomed her chance to break out of her "prison."

St. Mary's by the Sea Catholic Church became Ingrid's refuge. She became involved in the church and was very useful to Father Albert. She took care of the altar providing it with fresh flowers daily. She oversaw the yearly bazaars, festivals and also ran the church's thrift shop. Father Albert was thrilled to have such a dedicated worker in his parish.

One night, Aaron returned home earlier than usual from his weekly card game. When Ingrid heard his key in the front door, she panicked. Aaron walked in to find Ingrid, nude, in bed with the sheet pulled up under her trembling chin and a frightened look on her face. Just then, he heard the slamming of the back door. It was dark when he ran after the shadow limping down the street with just his underwear on.

At the top of his voice for all to hear, Aaron swore after the shadow.

"When I find out who you are, I will cut off your balls!"

By the next day, the whole town heard about Ingrid's secret lover. They were happy for her and wondered just who it could be. They knew she never went anywhere, alone. The only place they could think of was the church.

As soon as Aaron found out Ingrid was pregnant, he threw her out of his house and not having anywhere to go, she left the island. Seven months later, Ingrid gave birth to a baby boy which she immediately gave up for adoption. Many years later, when she learned Aaron had passed away, she returned to San Lucci. She was happy here before, despite Aaron's dominance, and now that she was older, decided to retire here.

Ingrid found work as a housekeeper and rented a small apartment. She became active in the Catholic Church and offered to help the new young priest. She finally established a new life for herself and was content. Twice a year, Ingrid paid visits to the local shops to pick up their donations of off-season clothes to sell at the church's thrift shop. That's what she was doing the morning she ran into Joey at Heather's boutique shop.

Father Michael was very happy to have Ingrid assist him. He found her to be a very religious, hard-working woman. However, he often wondered about her life, her past and just what was troubling her. Day after day, he watched her from his study window, sitting in the courtyard praying to the patron saint of the church, Virgin Mother Mary. Ingrid sat there, for hours speaking audibly to her. Sometimes her conversations became very animated, and she became quite agitated as tears flowed freely down her aged-lined face. Father Michael wondered what ghosts she carried with her. What was this thing that weighed her down and made her stoop over, in despair.

One day, as Ingrid took up her post in the courtyard to begin her barrage with St. Mary, Father Michael sat down next to her and took her hands in his.

"Ingrid, what is troubling you? I watch you here, day after day and you seem so lonely, so lost and I want to know why. If you have remorse, guilt, about anything, you can tell me. In fact, if you like to make your confession to me now, here, please do so. You know, in all the years you have assisted me in the church, I have never heard your confession. It can't be so bad that you stayed away from confession for so long. You are such a good woman, I'm sure your sins are not that bad. Besides, I was named after St. Michael, and you know he forgives all sins."

Father Michael paused when he saw Ingrid's eyes overflow with tears which fell onto the back of his hands.

"Fa—th—er," Ingrid found it difficult to speak through her choked up tears. "Fa—ther, oh, I have sinned. It's been so long, too long since my last confession. I have sinned, father by—by—I—have—sinned—by, oh, I can't—I … "

Father Michael put his arm around her and held her firmly, lovingly, giving her the strength she needed to continue.

"Father, I—had—a—baby—out of wedlock." There, she finally got it out. Never had Ingrid told anyone this. As if relieved to have confided in the Father, she allowed herself the freedom to put her head on his shoulders, in complete exhaustion. She rested a moment, before continuing. When she spoke, she regained her composure.

"Father, I had the baby and then—well-then, I gave it up for adoption.'

So that's why she felt so guilty. Of course. Father Michael now understood her cross.

"I blame myself, Father. How could a mother give up her baby, her old flesh and blood? Oh, it's so unforgiveable. But you see, Father, I was so young. The father was gone, and I had no job, no money, no family and no one to turn to, nowhere to go. I could never go back to Sweden. My parents would not understand. You see, they thought Aaron was going to marry me when he brought me here to San Lucci Island, but he never did."

They sat, quietly, not saying a word. Each consumed in their own thoughts.

Finally, Ingrid broke their silence. "You know, what the worst part is, Father. I never even saw my baby. They wrapped him up and took him away the moment he was born. One night, I crept down the halls to the nursery in hopes of seeing him, but I didn't know which one he was. It was as if I never gave birth. Ever since that day, not one single day goes by that I don't think about him and wonder where he is and if he is happy. I wonder what kind of a life he has and if he is loved. Oh, Father, I pray every day that he is."

Father Michael felt her passion as she squeezed his hands, in desperation. "My dear, Mother."

Ingrid jumped when she heard this salutation coming from Father Michael's lips.

"Oh, forgive me, Ingrid for startling you. I know how sensitive that word must be for you. It slipped out in my desire to console you and in my love for you. Not that I wouldn't be very thrilled to have you for my mother. You are a very saintly woman. And you know, Ingrid, I can emphasize with you as we all have our crosses to bear. Shall I tell you mine?"

Ingrid nodded, numbly, still not quite recovered from hearing herself being referred to as "mother." How she longed to be greeted by that name, but she knew she threw away that gift long ago.

"You see, Ingrid, I am an orphan. I never knew my parents. I was to be adopted, shortly after my birth. It was all pre-arranged and the adoption papers were to be signed on the day my new parents were to pick me up. However, when they took one look at me asleep in the hospital nursery, they walked right out of the hospital. I was then placed in a Catholic orphanage for boys."

Ingrid's mouth dropped open, in surprise. "Oh, no. You poor, poor baby. But why? Why would anyone walk out on you?"

Father Michael drew in a big sigh, letting it out slowly, "You mean to tell me you never noticed, Ingrid?"

Ingrid looked at the father as if seeing him for the first time. He had a big, dark cleft on one side of his mouth and a left club foot which added to his ominous appearance and gave him a sinister look.

Ingrid never saw these imperfections when she looked at him. She only saw a "saint." She loved the Father, like a son. He was always so kind to her.

Father Michael continued. "Those years in the orphanage were lonely for me, especially when I saw each one of the boys leave for their new homes. I was never chosen. The caretaker at the orphanage felt sorry for me and befriended me. He observed the way the prospective parents turned away when they saw me and gave their smiles and attention to the other boys. The caretaker was a very religious man and read the bible to me every day. That's when I decided to become a priest, when I grew up."

Ingrid now understood why Father Michael had at a young age and just out of the seminary been given his very own parish. She recalled the Islanders discussing the church's dilemma in placing him. Every church he was assigned to had a drop in attendance. The children made fun of him and called him names and the babies screamed whenever he came in contact with them. So, San Lucci Island was the perfect place to "hide" the Father. The Islanders were happy to have any priest as they were presently without one.

St. Mary's by the Sea Catholic Church had the exclusive reputation of being the only church to have revolving door priests. Every few years a new priest appeared and brought their infamous past with them. Being assigned to the parish of St. Mary's was considered a form of ex-communication for the priests. They were sent here because the church needed to remove them from the mainland. The various priests that came here had their particular problems. Father Ed was so mentally disturbed; he appeared at Mass with just his underwear on and not know where he was. Father Riley loved his drink and finished all the communion wine before Mass began and was inebriated while giving the Mass. Father Calhoun was very fond of his altar server boys and later died of aids. Father Albert had lots of company staying with him. He told his congregation his relatives were visiting when they witnessed him riding around the island with his 5'8" buxom blonde "cousin."

When Father Michael arrived at St. Mary's, the Islanders were, understandably, suspicious and wondered what his "problem" was. They watched and waited for his "slip." As time went by and Father Michael didn't "slip," they began to trust him and eventually accept him.

Father Michael embraced his new parish, lovingly and with humility. He knew why he was sent here and was not offended. He understood. He had endured so much humiliation and rejection that to be accepted by a community, was a blessing, a gift from God. He explained it this way to Ingrid.

"You seem my dear Ingrid. God loves me. You see where he brought me? Nothing happens by chance, dear Ingrid. There is a reason for everything that happens to us in this life, and I believe the reason I was sent here was to meet you, my dear sweet lady."

Father leaned over and kissed Ingrid on the forehead and a deep heartfelt sigh escaped from Ingrid's lips.

CHAPTER 48

As soon as Ingrid walked out of the shop, Cnythia turned her attention toward the two young men.

"Cindy, I want you to meet my cousin, Matthew. Matt, this is my girl, Cindy. Matt came all the way from England just to meet you, Cindy," Joey added, with a grin.

Cnythia blushed hearing herself referred to as "my girl." This was the first time Joey showed he thought of her in this way.

"It's nice to meet you, Matthew."

"The pleasure is all mine, Cnythia." Matthew was immediately attracted to her and hesitated in releasing her hand.

"Okay, Matt. You can let go of her hand, now. She's mine, remember?"

Matthew slowly withdrew his hand, embarrassed Joey noticed his attraction toward Cnythia.

"So, listen, Cindy. When you get off work, come to the Pizza Palace and we'll show Matt around the town and take him to Pelican's Beak for dinner."

Cnythia knew her parents would want to meet Joey before she was allowed to go with him. Up to this time, they had their "dates" in the shop when her mother wasn't around. Now that Joey wanted to take her "out", she would have to introduce him to her parents first. She had already made plans to invite him to her Junior/Senior school prom. Cnythia was not prepared for the reception she received from her mother when she mentioned his name.

"Joseph Visconti? Hmm, that last name sounds very familiar. Now, where have I heard that name before?"

Heather mentally retraced her past life, prior to marrying Mark. She was raised by her grandparents when her parents were killed in an automobile accident. After her graduation from San Lucci High School, she attended the prestigious fashion designing school, "Casa de Alta Moda," in Italy. When her grandfather died, she returned to the island to settle the estate. She intended to return to school but with the passing of her grandmother shortly after, she never did. Heather opened up a boutique shop and made a life for herself on the island. When she attended her tenth high school reunion, she re-connected with her classmate, Mark Riley, fell in love and married. Mark sold his successful pediatrician business on the Mainland and opened up a practice on San Lucci Island.

Cnythia was their miracle baby when Heather got pregnant with her at age 45.

"Oh, but of course. I remember that name now."

Heather's face darkened as she recalled Joey's father, Dominic Visconti. She remembered all the times standing at her living room window peeking out from behind the drapes as the succession of weddings in their decorated limousines made their way to St. Mary's.

This was before Heather was married. How she envied the brides and wished she could see the bride in her wedding gown, but Heather was never invited as Dominic didn't know of her existence, but Heather knew him and of his unsavory reputation. She knew he owned a lot of property on the island and was very wealthy. She heard his pizza palace was a front for his more lucrative business, drugs. Heather was the one who stumbled upon that dead woman's' body, Sylvia Lawson, while on her daily run in the back hills of the island. However, there was never an investigation, and rumors circulated there was a cover-up involving Dominic Visconti. This was never proven but the island gossiped about it for years, afterwards.

Then one day, Dominic's yacht, The Regina, was gone from the harbor. Dominic left, very mysteriously, one morning before sunrise and since then became a legend among the Islanders. They made him their hero and missed his good-natured ways and the money he spread around the island. Dominic donated money to every cause, anytime he was asked. The Islanders also missed not being able to drop in the Pizza Palace for conversation and a free beer. Heather had to admit that Dominic's presence did liven things up. She missed the grandiose lifestyle she watched parade by her windows.

"Well, mother. What are you thinking? Will you please come back to us?"

Cnythia smiled as she watched her mother deep in thought, not realizing they were not favorable ones towards Joey.

"I absolutely forbid it, Cnythia. You are not to see this boy, or date him, or even speak to him." Heather commanded her vehemently.

Mark stared at his wife. He wondered why she was so upset over this young man. Mark left the island after high school and never returned until his tenth high school reunion. He never met or even heard the name Dominic Visconti, until this evening. *What was it about this young man that was so upsetting to Heather?* he asked himself.

"Sweetheart, what's wrong? Why are you so upset?"

"It's just that this boy's father was a notorious gangster ..." Heather stopped talking when Mark and Cnythia started laughing.

"Oh, you two don't know anything about this. This was way before you came back here, Mark. I know you think I'm just being a hysterical, possessive mother. Well, I assure you, that's not the case, at all. Just let me tell you about Mr. Dominic Visconti!"

Heather shared Dominic's infamous past with them, satisfied that once Mark knew, he would support her on this matter.

"Oh, honey, really now. I think you're overreacting. You're making this Dominic guy to be another Al Capone. Ha! Ha! Oh, I'm sorry but I just can't help it." Mark wiped his eyes while apologizing after Heather gave him an irate look.

"You know, Heather. These were all rumors. You said that yourself. And as far as his son goes, well, he sounds pretty nice to me from what Cnythia tells us and why hold his father's bad reputation against him? What does that have anything to do with his son?"

He gave Cnythia a smile as if to say, "It's okay, I'm on your side." Cnythia sat down next to her father and took his hand into hers.

"Mother, he really is so sweet. I know you will like him if you meet him. Can't I please bring him home so you can meet him? Just talk to him, that's all."

Cnythia knew her mother could be very stubborn and if pushed too hard, her Irish temper would erupt and that would be the end of the discussion. Cnythia decided to give it a rest, for now. She would wait until her mother brought up the subject.

Meanwhile, Cnythia lied to her parents, in order to keep seeing Joey. He asked her best friend, Liza, to back her up. Her parents gave their consent to go out with Liza and did not expect her back before midnight. Cnythia did not like keeping secrets, but she could not give Joey up as she was falling in love with him.

Pelican's Beak was a very expensive, sophisticated restaurant 2500 feet above San Lucci Island Harbor. It was 15 miles of winding mountainous roads but well worth the ride, as the view from the top was breathtakingly magnificent.

Cnythia regretted not being dressed elegantly for the occasion but since she was supposed to be roller skating with Liza, she couldn't possibly be in dressy clothes.

Joey took the liberty of ordering dinner for her. Cnythia liked it when Joey took charge. An experienced woman would have resisted his domineering ways but not Cnythia.

She was young, inexperienced, and unknowledgeable about the ways of the world, especially men. Cnythia felt safe with Joey and loved the security he provided. Of course, Joey loved being in control of women. He knew he could with Cnythia, and this satisfied his manhood. Thus, they both derived a value from this relationship.

Cnythia was not much of a conversationalist as she was shy. She was content to sit back and listen to the men talk.

"So, Cnythia. How do you like living in San Lucci and working in your mother's shop?" Matthew thought her shyness was charming and tried to make small talk to include her in the conversation. He found her unpretentious, and rather humble. He thought it touching the way she blushed whenever a well-deserving compliment was given to her about her looks. She was beautiful and so ethereal looking with her long blond hair and deep blue eyes and her lovely fragile figure, just beginning to blossom. Matthew was attracted to her the first moment he met her.

Matthew spent one month with Joey and saw Cnythia often. Whenever he had the opportunity to be alone with her, which wasn't often, and only when Joey was tied up in his office, he got to know more about her and developed a growing respect for her. She was the kind of sweet, innocent girl he would love to bring home to meet his parents. Knowing Joey's aloof attention toward women after he got what he wanted, he was concerned for her. *How lucky Joey is to find such a girl. I hope he appreciates her and treats her with respect,* he mentally prayed.

It was time for Matthew to leave. Joey and Cnythia walked him to the ferry dock.

"Matt, thanks again for all your help. I'll never forget it," Joey hugged him and gave him a pat on the back.

"Take care of yourself, Joey, and stay out of trouble!" Matthew warned him.

"It was a real pleasure getting to know you, Cnythia. I sincerely hope we will meet again."

"Thank you, Matthew, for all your kindness with Joey. I know how much he appreciates you coming here."

Matthew took both her hands in his and firmly squeezed them, not wanting to let go.

Cnythia blushed and her hands trembled as she slowly removed them for his tight grasp.

CHAPTER 49

It was prom night at San Lucci High School and held at the Venus Ballroom. This was an old historic Mansion once owned by the late sugar millionaire, Nathan Chandler. It was now a theater, museum, art gallery and a gym located on the lower floors and a spacious ballroom on the tenth floor.

Joey asked Cnythia to stay out all night with him. He told her that after the prom, they would have a picnic on the beach and watch the sun come up. It sounded so romantic to Cnythia. She worked out a plan with Liza. Liza's brother, Billie, would be her date and pick her up at her house. He would drop her off at the school where Joey would be waiting. She told her parents she was spending the night with Liza. This time, when she lied, she had a sinking feeling in the pit of her stomach. It scared her that she would be with Joey all night for the very first time. However, she trusted him. *He said a picnic on the beach, it will be all right.* Cnythia tried to reassure herself.

"Here, let's put these on you. You know, Cnythia, you are the fourth lady in our family to wear these. Let's take a look at you." Heather stepped back and with a sweeping look at her daughter and nodded her approval. Her eyes came to rest on the pair of pearl stud earrings similar to what her grandmother wore on the night of her reunion.

Cnythia chose the most lascivious dress in the store. It

was a black halter dress with a sweetheart neck and short enough to show off Cynthia's long, slender legs.

When Heather saw Cnythia in the mirror, she gasped. She thought she was looking at a reflection of herself, 33 years ago, as she was preparing to attend her tenth high school reunion at The Venus Ballroom. How uncanny that Cnythia picked out a dress almost identical to the one she wore that night. As Heather thought back to that night, the color rose to her cheeks. She brought Mark home that night and they made love.

...

It seemed like yesterday when Heather received her invitation. She wasn't sure she would attend."Oh, why bother? They will probably all be married or at least have a lover and here I am still single and no lover in sight!" She rationalized her decision out loud.

But the more she thought about it, the more she leaned toward going, especially when the dresses arrived at the shop, and she spotted one that was perfect. *If I don't go, then where would I wear it?* she mentally asked herself. That settled it. Heather's mind was made up.

Heather admired herself in the mirror. She picked out the most sensual dress in the shop. It was a short black halter dress with a plunging neckline. It showed off Heather's trim muscle-bound back and long, lean legs. She beamed at the image staring back at her. *Hmm, all those workouts at the gym sure paid off!* She complimented herself on her strict discipline. To complete the outfit, she put on the pearl earrings her grandmother handed down to her that was originally her mother's.

When Heather entered The Venus Ballroom, she was greeted by one of her classmates as he placed a lei around her neck. She wished she recognized him when she thanked him.

The ballroom was majestically adorned with streamers of the high school colors, gold and blue. Masses of balloons hung from the tall ceiling. She was soon surrounded by her classmates.

"Heather is it really you? Oh, my goodness. You look great. Have you been working out?"

"Hi, you look great too. How have you been?" Heather couldn't remember her name but managed to bluff her way through all the exchanges.

Heather looked around the room and studied her classmates. Some she recognized, others she didn't or wasn't sure. She spotted the ones that were snobbish, cruel, the click groups in high school. She thought it interesting to see how they now bonded with one another, and the past forgotten. Everyone seemed relieved to see each other-perhaps because it allowed them to recapture their youth of those carefree high school years. It was as if they all sensed their immortality and needed to hold on to their past, at least for one night, and feel a sense of safety as if the trials of the past ten years never happened. Heather was so engrossed with her philosophical thoughts; she didn't see him approach her.

"Hello, Heather. I'm so glad you came tonight. I was hoping to see you here."

Heather turned and met the face behind the sweet soft voice that greeted her. She stared into his deep blue eyes. *Who is this?* she wondered. *I don't remember him at all.*

What seemed like an eternity went by as she scrunched up her face forcing her memory to save her, but he came to her rescue.

"I can see you don't remember me, do you?" He let out a small laugh. "I'm Mark Riley. You know, the one that always stared at you every time we passed in the hall. I sat behind you in social studies. Well, I guess you don't remember me because you were always so popular with the other guys and never paid attention to me. I have to tell you; I had the biggest crush on you!"

"Oh, my goodness. Of course, Mark. Yes, yes, now, I do remember you but—you looked different then—I mean—you look different now." *Oh, my gosh, I am rambling*, she scolded herself. Heather did remember a small, pudgy boy with blemishes, protruding teeth and big ears. This man standing here was tall—at least 6'2, slender with a beautiful clear glowing complexion. His teeth were straight, and his face filled in his ears.

Mark let out a roaring laugh.

"Yes, you're absolutely right. I most certainly look different now. Thank God! But you—you haven't changed at all, except perhaps just prettier. You were always the prettiest girl in high school. But look at you now!" Mark took a step back to take in a full view.

"Wow! Your body! What definition! I can see you work out. You are very sexy, Heather."

Heather giggled girlishly and the color rose from her neck to her face. She was indeed charmed by Mark. The rest of the evening was a blur for Heather as she spent the entire time engrossed in conversation with Mark. She had so many questions to ask him. She was content to spend the rest of the evening with just him.

"I am a pediatrician on the Mainland and no, I never married. Guess I'm just too picky. I just haven't found the right woman to spend the rest of my life with." He gave her an intense look.

Heather heart skipped a beat when she heard this. She was becoming more excited by the minute as the evening wore on. She loved listening to him speak. He had such a fascinating, hypnotic voice. She liked the way he looked at her when he spoke. His eyes were riveted on her so intently as if he was the only one in the room that evening. She was enchanted with him.

"Let's go out on the balcony, Heather, and get some fresh air."

Heather took his arm and followed him as if in a trance.

It was a pleasant, warm summer evening. The night sky resembled a black canopy filled with millions of blinking diamonds. Mark pointed out the Milky Way. A sudden breeze passing over Heather's skimpy dress made her shiver. Mark put his arm around her, and his hand accidentally slipped under her halter dress and on her cold erect nipple. Mark face reddened as he rapidly withdrew his hand.

"Oh, Heather, I am so sorry. I didn't mean to do that. It was an accident."

Heather smiled and put her hand over his.

"It's okay, Mark." And it was! It had been a long time since she had the pleasure of a man's touch.

It was now one in the morning and the party was over.

"It's such a lovely evening; I believe I will walk home instead of taking a cab. Would you care to walk me home, Mark?"

They walked slowly, holding hands and speaking softly to each other. They both knew how the evening would end. Their desire for each other shone brightly in their eyes.

The moment they walked into Heather's house, they tore at each other's clothes, desperate to satisfy their immense hunger. When Mark entered Heather, a searing hot flame ripped through her body from her long celibate years and she cried out.

"Oh, did I hurt you, Heather? I'm so sorry." Mark lifted his body off of Heather and began to move out of her when Heather immediately wrapped her legs tightly around him preventing him from moving.

"No, no don't stop. It's okay. I'm fine, now, Mark."

...

The sun streamed through the thin chiffon bedroom curtains and Heather turned over and traced her hand on the other side of the bed. She smiled when her hand came to rest on Mark's back. She studied him.

296

"What a beautiful body. And such smooth skin. How nice it is to wake up next to a living, warm body," Heather said softly to herself.

"What did you say, Heather?" Mark turned over, rubbed his eyes, punched his pillow and sat up.

"Oh, nothing. It was nothing. I was just thinking what a glorious day it is."

They decided to spend more time together, so Mark called his office and had his secretary cancelled all his appointments for the coming week. Heather called the boutique where she worked and told her boss, Roxanne, she needed the week off. She was happy Heather finally had a man.

Heather spent the week showing Mark "her island." They went jet skiing, snorkeling, Parasailing and picking on an isolated beach on the other side of the island. On their last night together, Heather prepared a picnic basket of wine, cheese and fruit and took him up to *High Mountain* where they overlooked the harbor with all the lights shining from the village below. It was the perfect setting for what Mark had in mind.

"Heather, I have really enjoyed our time together this past week. I'm so happy to have found you again and single. I guess what I am trying to say is that I realize I could never go back to the way I was living before. I never realized how lonely my life has been. This past week with you made me realize that. My life will never be the same now without you. I can't say that I have grown to love you ... because I fell in love with you the first day I saw you in high school. What I need to know is—if you feel the same way—because I would like you to come back with me to Meadowbrook as my wife."

"Oh, Mark. Yes, yes, I do love you and I do want to be your wife—but—but ..." She hung her head sadly.

"But, what, Heather? I don't understand. What's wrong? Why are you looking so sad, so troubled?"

"Well, you see, it's like this ..." Heather hesitated in an

attempt to find just the right words that would make sense.

"Well, you see. I really do want to marry you—but—I don't think I can move to Meadowbrook. I mean, I don't think I can live anywhere but here on San Lucci Island. I have been here so long now, it's my home. I feel safe here and I don't think I can leave. Do you understand what I am trying to say, Mark?"

"No, Heather, I'm afraid I don't understand. I mean, this is just a place, and as long as we love each other what difference does it make where you live. I have a thriving practice in Meadowbrook and always expected to make my home there with my wife."

"Oh, Mark. You just don't understand. You left San Lucci right out of high school. You just don't know how it is here with me. It is such a different way of life here and you have never experienced it the way I have. You were so young when you left. You never got involved, never became a part of the island the way I have. It—it just grows on you, and—oh, I don't know—it's like it captures you, gets a hold on you and you can't break away. Sounds crazy, I know, but that's the way she is!"

The next day, they walked slowly and quietly to the boat dock, not speaking.

"Heather, I left my business card on the nightstand. Please call me if you change your mind."

Heather stared out to sea as the boat drew further and further away from the island. She remained there in a trance, until Mark's boat was just a speck in the ocean. She walked back to her home, haltingly, tears streaming down her cheeks. Her heart was heavy as she realized what she had done. He told her he would keep in touch, but for how long? Soon his calls would become fewer and less frequent until one day they would stop. That would be the day he found someone else—someone who would be happy to make a life with him in Meadowbrook.

"Oh, what have I done? What is wrong with me? How could I send him away? After all these years, I prayed for someone like Mark to come along, and I just set him away. Have I been on this island so long that I'm afraid to leave? Is this what San Lucci Island does to one? Oh, how did this happen?" In anguish, Heather berated herself loudly to the walls of her home.

Sleep did not come easily that night. She was restless, exhausted, she finally fell asleep, only to be awoken, in what seemed like a short time, by a loud incessant banging at her front door. She glanced over at the clock. It was 10 A.M. She couldn't believe she slept so late. The knocking got louder and determined.

Now, who could it be? she thought as she threw on her robe and rushed to the door. She barely got the door opened when the visitor pushed his way into her kitchen and forced Heather back against the wall. He roughly pulled her towards him.

"Okay, Heather, you win. I got all the way home-thought about the situation all night—couldn't sleep a wink and hopped on the first ferry back here. You are so damn obstinate, but I still love you even though I don't understand this at all. So, if you won't move to Meadowbrook, I guess I will just have to move my practice here. The way I figure it, these poor kids deserve a good pediatrician in town!"

Heather started to speak but Mark silenced her with his mouth as he opened her robe, let it fall, and carried her into the bedroom.

CHAPTER 50

"Thanks, Billie." Cnythia gave Liza's brother a kiss on the cheek when he dropped her off in
front of The Venus Ballroom where Joey was waiting.

"You look great, Cindy and all grown up." Joey took her arm and escorted her inside.

At midnight, they walked out on the balcony. They were met with a full moon and thousands of stars winked at them from the pitch-black sky. Far beneath them, the harbor was filled with boats, swaying in the gently swells of the water. The cool, damp ocean breeze sent a chill down Cynthia's body, and she shivered, uncontrollably. Joey put his arm around her and deliberately slip his hand under Cnythia's back-less dress and onto the smooth bare skin of her breasts, sans bra. His touch caused Cnythia's body to become taunt and her small nipples become erect as she let out a surprise gasp.

"Oh, excuse me, Cindy. That was just an accident." Joey quickly removed his hand when he saw how nervous she became. *I must not scare her. I'll take my time. After all, I do have her for the whole evening.* As Joey thought of the evening he had planned, an electric thrill traveled up his groin and his lower body became rigid.

It was 12:30 A.M. when they left The Venus Ballroom.

They strolled, arm in arm, down the street to the Pizza Palace.

"Just a quick stop to pick something up for our beach picnic." He told her. However, when he brought her into his office where he had a bottle of champagne chilling on ice, he filled a glass and gave it to her.

Cnythia giggled as the bubbles tickled her nose. As the champagne began to relax her, she kicked off her shoes and tucked her feet under her on the buffalo leather sofa and relaxed her body, completely. She emptied her glass just as fast as Joey filled it. Not being accustomed to alcohol, she soon felt the full effects of the champagne.

"Oh, Joey. I feel so—so good. Ha! Ha! Oh, what are you doing, Joey?"

Cynthia's arms went up in complete compliance as Joey untied her dress and slipped it over her head. He straightened her legs and removed her black lace panties. He lowered himself on top of her and took her left nipple in his mouth and hungrily sucked it while his fingers massaged her right nipple. When Joey inserted his erect penis into Cnythia's small, tight vagina, she began pounding him with her fists. She then felt a stretching pain followed by a burning sensation and she let out a piercing cry. This should have been enough to stop Joey, but it didn't. He became a daimon, consuming his victim.

Joey's arousal was so intense; it was all over in a matter of moments. He relaxed his body, allowing his full weight to fall heavily on Cynthia's light frame and he smiled, in complete satisfaction.

Disgusted, in tears, Cnythia wasted no time pushing him off her. She hurriedly put on her dress and rushed out. She slammed the door behind her so quickly that it cut off Joey's shouting declaration to her.

"Cindy, I love you."

...

The sound of the bell tower chimes woke her. She was surprised to discover she had slept at all. It was now 8 A.M. and her mother would be coming to open the shop at 9 A.M. She straightened the blankets on the cot and removed her dress from the night before and replaced it with a simple cotton dress from the store rack.

Heather was surprised to see the store opened, with Cnythia behind the counter.

"Cnythia, what are you doing here? I thought you were spending the day with Liza. I told you didn't have to come to work today."

"Oh, well, I decided you could probably use me today. I know how busy the shop gets on Sundays with all day tourists."

"So, how was the prom? Did you have a nice time?"

Cnythia mumbled a "yes" while avoiding looking at her mother.

Her mother, sensing something wrong, took Cnythia by the shoulders and whirled her around to face her.

"Why, Cnythia. You look awful. Your eyes have black circles under them. Have you been crying? What happened last night?"

Cnythia swallowed hard as she attempted a feeble smile while fighting back the tears.

"Na—nothing, Mother. Liza and I were up all night talking and playing games. I just didn't get much sleep, that's all. I guess I'm really tired, after all."

"Well, young lady, I certainly can see that. Now, you get right out of here and go straight home and rest. If I get busy this afternoon, I will call you."

Cnythia was glad to get out of the shop. She couldn't wait to get home and scrub away the ugliness of the past evening. As she relaxed in the tub and watched the bubbles swirl around her, she thought back on the events of the previous evening.

After she left Joey, she didn't know where to go. She couldn't go home because her mother thought she was spending the night at Liza's, and she couldn't go to Liza's because it was too late and she couldn't tell her what happened. She decided to go to the shop when she discovered the shop keys in her purse. Cnythia curled up on the cot in the back storeroom, hugging herself for comfort. She cried when she thought how stupid and naïve, she was to believe Joey when he told her they would have a picnic on the beach, talk and watch the sun come up.

...

The bright sun streaming through the windows of his office caused Joey to flinch from the glare. He aroused himself, slowly, stretching out thoroughly before placing his feet on the floor. He wondered why he felt so wet, then remembered as he looked down at the "remains" of the night before. On the black buffalo sofa was a semi-dry combination of semen and blood.

An overwhelming acknowledgement of guilt swept over him as he relived the events of the previous evening. "Damn! What have I done? I wanted Cindy so much, for so long, I was out of control. How could I have 'taken' her like that? I plied her with champagne all the while knowing she never drank and then—I ... Damn me, I'm so ashamed of myself." Joey yelled out to the empty room and buried his face in his hands in remorse. "Hell, I'd better get this all cleaned up before Frankie walks in. I have to go see Cindy and make sure she's all right. Oh, damn it all!"

Days passed but Joey didn't go to her. He couldn't get up enough courage to face her. He was so ashamed, so guilty for taking advantage of her. He was now afraid she wouldn't want to see him or have anything more to do with him. He decided to stay away.

Three weeks went by since that horrific assault she

suffered and Cnythia tried to put it all behind her when she awoke one morning, sick to her stomach. She thought she had the flu. When the following month went by and Cnythia missed her period, she began to worry. She never missed her periods and she continued to be sick. She hid her sick days from her parents until one day, while waiting on a customer, she fainted.

Heather immediately brought her into Mark's office. Mark took one look at his daughter and suspected what was wrong. He ran the usual tests. It was now confirmed. Cnythia was pregnant.

Heather and Mark were indeed shocked and upset. "But who is the father?" They asked each other.

"Oh, of course! It is that Visconti kid! He's the only one Cnythia talks about and the one she was adamant I meet. It has to be him! I just know it!" Heather clenched her teeth, in anger.

...

Joey was on the phone, with his sister, when there was a sharp rap on his office door, and it simultaneously opened.

"Hold on a minute, Connie. Frankie is at the door."

As Frankie opened the door wider, Joey was startled to see an older couple with him.

"Ah—Sis, I gotta go. Yeah, I love you to. Ciao." Joey recognized Heather from the shop but never met the man with her. He figured it was Mark Ryan, Cindy's father.

They got right to the point. They did not mince words but told Joey just what they thought of him and how appalled they were at what he had done to their daughter. They had considered filing charges against him for statutory rape as Cnythia was a minor, however, upon Cnythia's insistence, they relented. Cnythia told them that it was by mutual consent and in fact was her idea and that Joey was not the aggressive one. Her parents did not believe her.

The Ryan's were now demanding to know what

responsibility Joey would be taking towards Cnythia and their baby. Since Cnythia loved him, they wanted to know how he felt. What were his intentions? Did he love her or was she just a conquest? The only reason, they were giving him some options was because of Cnythia, because she told them, he wasn't to blame.

When they left, Joey sat numb, in disbelief. He couldn't believe Cindy was pregnant so quickly, after only one night! Nothing like this had ever happened to him before. But then, he never went after young, innocent, underage virgins, before. He always dated older, experienced women who took responsibility for "protection." If word ever got out about this among the Islanders, they would surely lynch Joey, with Deputy Sheriff Ernest Frye gladly tying the knot. This incident would give them one more reason to hate Joey!

"I can't believe this Joey. How could you be so low, so despicable, so stupid? And why Cnythia? Why not one of the cheap whores in town? They have a few here, you know. Good God, Joey!"

In all the years growing up with Joey, Frankie never felt such disgust with him as he did at this moment. For the first time, he had no respect for him. He really liked Cnythia and knew Joey took advantage of her, despite what she told her parents. He knew she did that to spare him. Frankie always respected Cnythia but her self-sacrificing actions in the face of such humiliation, made him realize what a special person she was. He knew, as did her parents, that she did not give in to Joey. She was the kind of girl that would remain a virgin until she married. He was certain of this.

Frankie did not hesitate in calling his Uncle Dominic. He knew Joey would not tell his father about this, but something had to be done right away. The Ryan's left Joey with an ultimatum. He either marry their daughter or go to jail.

"Uncle Dominic, this is Frankie. There's something very

important I have to tell you."

CHAPTER 51

Guido watched Dominic's face turn ashen as he sadly hung up the phone.

Dominic decided not to relate the information he just received from Frankie to his wife. He would spare himself from hearing her words she spoke long ago.

"I fear something bad happening to Joey if he goes to San Lucci Island."

"No, it is better this way. Of course, Joey will marry her and let Regina believe this wedding to be natural, just two people in love who can't wait to be together," he reasoned this out with Guido.

However, Dominic did share this with Sammy, Johnnie and Vincent but not their women. The women would be too emotional, too judgmental. They would not understand that Joey was a hot-blooded Italian and got carried away. Not that Dominic was condoning Joey's actions. No, not at all, on the contrary, Joey would certainly be admonished for his stupidity when Dominic saw him.

When Matthew found out, from his father, that Cnythia was pregnant, he was depressed, and disappointed. He never imagined Cnythia would give in to Joey. She didn't strike him as being so easily swayed by Joey's charms. He was certain she had some strong values concerning sex and this came as quite a surprise to him. Ever since he met her, he could never stop thinking of her. He didn't have much social life because of his school commitments, but after meeting her, he stopped dating altogether. It was as though there was a silent agreement between them that they were meant for each other and would one day be together. This was something he kept to himself, in his heart. The news only made Matthew concerned about Joey's true feelings towards her. He knew his cousins' reputation for chasing woman and once he conquered them, he got tired and moved on. He was ashamed to hope this would happen and then he could step in. I must keep myself available for her, just in case, he mused silently.

If Matthew only knew the real story behind Cynthia's pregnancy, he would have been outraged. But, as it was, no one ever found out what really happened that night. Since none of the family knew Cnythia—what she was really like—what kind of family she was from, they weren't sure it was all Joey's fault.

Father Albert was to accompany the family. At first, he hesitated, unsure about leaving The Palazzo since he hadn't left it in over 25 years. But after Dominic told him that since he had married all of the couples, it was only fitting he preside over Joey's wedding. Besides, most of the Islanders that were around at that time, either left the island or were no longer alive. Since Aaron, the man who chased Father Albert out of town was now deceased, he had nothing to fear. Anyway, wasn't he at all interested in seeing Ingrid again? Yes, he had to admit, he was very curious about Ingrid, about what her life had been after Aaron kicked her out of the house. He knew she left San Lucci Island and only returned when she learned Aaron passed away. Dominic's rationale won him over and he agreed to go. What Father Albert didn't know was that Ingrid was carrying his child when she left the island. This information was passed on to Dominic, by his broker, Bernie Goldstein. Of course, no one knew for sure it was his baby but since Ingrid was never seen with any other man, they swore it had to be his. Dominic didn't see any reason to tell him as he thought that chapter of his life was forever closed. Who would have thought that Joey would be the catalyst for reopening that chapter.

Dominic chartered a plane to fly them to the island. They landed at the island's private airport. Vincent and his family were also coming by plane and would be arriving after them.

Frankie was waiting in a limousine when Dominic's plane landed.

Vincent's plane arrived shortly after. Hugs and kisses abounded. Dominic pulled himself back from Frankie and glanced around.

"So, where's my son? Why didn't Joey come to meet me, eh?" Dominic's rough tone conveyed his hurt by this lack of respect from his son.

"Oh, he wanted to come, Uncle Dominic. But he got busy at the restaurant. He was sure you would understand."

Dominic's dark look told him that he didn't understand but Frankie couldn't tell him the real reason—that Joey was afraid to face him.

It was a long 15-minute drive down the winding mountain road, past the exclusive restaurant, Pelican's Beak.

Meanwhile, back at the pizza palace, Joey was pacing in his office and downing shots of Jack Daniels to fortify himself for the barrage of questions he knew would be forthcoming as soon as his father walked into the pizza palace.

Constance was the first one to run through the front door and into his office.

"Joey, Joey. Oh, how happy I am to see you." Constance ran into his arms, planting kisses all over his face.

Joey was glad to see his sister and have her loyalty. He knew she would stand by him, no matter what. *Well, at least this is one member of my family that won't ostracize me*, he thought. Then, he saw his mother.

"Joey, sweetheart. How are you? Why did you lose weight? You are too skinny. What is this? You're not eating? And why this rush wedding? We haven't even met this girl. Why didn't you tell us about her? What kind of a girl is she, what is the family like? I don't understand any of this at all! I ..."

Joey knew his mother would not stop talking unless he stopped her with his hugs and kisses.

"Mom, I'm fine. Really, I am. I never mentioned Cnythia to you, because, well, because I wasn't sure myself how serious this was for me. Then, before we both realized it, we fell in love. Now, we just want to be married as soon as possible. And that's it, nothing more to it."

Dominic stood, motionless, surveying his office. It seemed surreal to him to be back on San Lucci Island after sailing out of the harbor on The Regina, over 25 years ago. He never dreamed he'd be standing in his office once again. He looked around, slowly, taking it all in. He had plenty of time to deal with Joey, but right now, he was more interested in his surroundings. He smiled, wistfully, as he saw it was just like he left it. His eyes rested on the eight-foot buffalo leather sofa. He noticed the leather on the arms had thinned out and was cracked; still it looked and smelled delightful to him as he lowered his face and took in a deep breath, inhaling the smell and enjoying the moment. Guido nudged him when he saw the far-a-way look in Dominic's eyes. Their eyes locked and they laughed, remembering how they both made love to their women right on this sofa. Dominic was the first, right before he married Regina. Then, on Guido's wedding night, Guido locked himself and his bride, Paula, in this office where they spent their wedding night on this sofa. The men would be surprised to learn that a second generation now made the claim of leaving his "mark" on this sofa.

Dominic closed the office door after the last family member left. He regained his former power by seating himself behind the desk in the black leather desk chair. He poured himself a glass of brandy from the tray on the desk and lit his Havana cigar. He took a leisurely, long puff and gave Joey a nod.

"Okay, Guiseppe, let's talk."

Joey knew he was in real trouble when his father resorted to the Italian pronunciation of his name which he did whenever there was a serious matter at hand. His hands trembled as he helped himself to a double shot of Jack Daniels from the half-emptied bottle. He knew he was drinking too much, which was unusual for him as he was not an excessive drinker, but this was a very unusual situation he now found himself in.

"What do you mean, Pop? What is there to talk about? I'm getting married, that's all." Dominic's penetrating stare at Joey caused him to look away, guilty. "Don'tcha get cute with me. What, you think I don't know all about it? You didn't have the balls to call me yourself. No, I had to hear it from Frankie! Lei avere testa duro. **Dovrebble vergognarso**." Dominic was becoming increasingly incensed as he scolded Joey for having a hard head and should have known better and used some protection.

"**Le dovrebble avera usato questo testa; invece di questo testa**." "You should have used this head," (Dominic points to the top of Joey's head) "Instead of this head," (Points to his groin.)

"So, you love this **venditrice**, this shop-girl, eh?"

Joey hesitated before answering.

Dominic shook his head, in disappointment when he didn't get answered right away.

"Yeah, sure, of course, I do, Pop. It's just that ..." Joey let out a long sigh.

"But what, Joey?"

"Well, I do love her, and I want to marry her—but I just never planned on marrying, just yet. I mean, I'm still young and I wanted to wait awhile before I got married, you know, like you did, Pop. I mean, you had lots of women, before Mom. You had

311

lots of fun before you settled down and that's what I want to do."

Dominic looked at his son, sadly.

Che peccato. *What a shame. I raised such an irresponsible boy.* ***Mamma Mia***. *How did this happen?* Dominic shook his head.

"Joey, Joey. I never got any of my women pregnant. Now you—you don't have any options. You should have thought of what you were doing before you let the 'stallion out of the corral.'"

Despite the seriousness of the situation, Dominic couldn't help displaying his witty side. He let out a small chuckle in self-appreciation. Then he resumed his sternness with Joey.

"Well, I'm gonna tell you right now, Joey. You will marry her, and you will make a good husband and a good father. You will get married as soon as we can arrange a nice wedding. We Visconti's do not run away from our responsibly. No! we do the honorable, the right thing!"

Dominic's loud bang on the desk sent the liquor tray flying across the office floor. It was heard throughout the pizza parlor. Not an eyebrow was raised among the family as they continued to eat their lunch.

CHAPTER 52

When Dominic told Father Albert that Ingrid was working at the church, he went straight there. He found her sitting in the church courtyard, in front of the statue of St. Mary. She didn't hear him approach as she was deep in prayer and her eyes were closed. She did not become startled when he put his hand gently on her shoulder. She was familiar with Father Michael's habit of coming to her as she sat in the courtyard and placing his hand on her shoulder. With eyes closed, she smiled as she reached up to pat his hand. Her body stiffened and her eyes flew opened and she leaned forward, rigidly, when she realized this was not Father Michael's young, smooth hand. No, this hand was old and coarse. Ingrid slowly turned her head and looked up into the age-worn face of her past lover. She squinted at him with her now near-sighted eyes as her body leaned in closer to him. She studied him, then recognition slowly set in.

"Oh, my dear! Can it be? No, I can't believe it! Is it really you, Albert?"

Albert sat down next to her and took her hands in his.

"Yes, my dear Ingrid. It is me."

Albert would have recognized Ingrid anywhere. True, she was now older, stooped over and not as svelte as she once was. Her blond hair was now all white, but her eyes were still a deep blue and as clear as pools of blue water. She was still very beautiful to him.

Thereafter, every day, Albert appeared in the courtyard and sat with Ingrid, holding hands, without saying much. They didn't need to speak. It was enough to have each other's company after all those years apart. They both lived such very lonely, uneventful lives these past 25 years.

Father Michael was introduced to Albert, as her dear old friend whom she had not seen in over 25 years. He was happy Albert was here when he saw Ingrid smile more and how her face lit up each time Albert paid her a visit.

One day, as Father Michael sat in the rectory reading the birthday card he received from his old caretaker friend at the orphanage, he glanced out the window which overlooked the courtyard and was surprised to see Ingrid crying and Albert trying to console her. He never interfered with them when they spent time together, but this time he did.

"What is the matter, Ingrid? Why are you crying? Why are you so upset?"

"Oh, Father, I told him. I told Albert all about the baby and that I gave him up." Ingrid put her head down in her lap and wept, uncontrollably.

It took just a moment for Father Michael to understand why she was upset. *Of course, Albert was the father. So, this was the man she laid with, out of wedlock.* Father Michael realized.

Albert's mouth dropped open, and his hands shook. It was hard for him to accept the fact he was a father, at his age, and never knew about it all these years. The realization unnerved him so much; he got up and began pacing in the courtyard.

Father Michael could not believe his eyes. Albert was limping. He had never seen Albert walk in or out of the courtyard. He only observed him as he sat with Ingrid. Now, he was amazed to see the reason for his limp. Albert had a LEFT CLUB FOOT.

"I just couldn't help myself, Father. Albert noticed how upset I was today and asked me why. It just came out. I could no longer keep this secret locked up in my heart any longer. I had to share this very special day with him."

Ingrid looked at Albert, with eyes filled with tears.

"You see, Father. Today is a very special day for me. Today is my baby's birthday. My son turned 26 today."

Upon hearing this, Father Michael's face turned pale with the realization of what this meant. All the blood drained from his face and his body went limp as he slowly sat down alongside Ingrid.

Ingrid was surprised at Father's acute consternation.

"Oh, Father. You are taking this much too hard. I am so sorry. I should not have burden you with my sorrow."

Father Michael looked first at Albert and then turned his attention to Ingrid. He very gently and lovingly took her hands into his and brought them up to his lips and kissed them fondly, as the tears fell silently down on them.

Ingrid was astonished at such an overt display of affection from him. In the past, he took her hands, occasionally, to comfort her, but never with such deep devotion, such passion.

"Do you know what day this is, my dear one?" Father asked, with a choked-up voice.

"Yes, of course, Father. I just told you. It is my son's birthday."

"Yes, yes, that's right. It is your son's birthday, and your son is here right now celebrating with his mother and father."

Ingrid stared, in numbness, at the Father and then her hands flew to her mouth in a mixture of astonishment and disbelief. She mentally sized him up. *Oh, but of course! How could I have missed it? How could I have not seen the resemblance all these years? His deep blue eyes, like mine, and the club foot like Albert's. Why, I had forgotten that Albert had one and—and—he even inherited the love of the priesthood from his father!*

"Oh, my son. My dear, dear boy. My own baby."

Ingrid pulled her son to her in a deep, heart-filled

embrace. She held him so tight, not wanting to let him go. Then she saw Albert looking sadly at them. She reached out to him, and he entered into their embrace.

...

The limousines drove up in front of the Hotel Capri. A tall, svelte blue-eyed, blonde-haired woman stepped into the first one, along with her parents. The family occupied the second one.

Cnythia looked regal with her long blonde hair pulled high on her head with cascading curls framing her face. A row of little white rose buds was threaded throughout her fancy hairdo. Her dress was not as elaborate. It was a simple A-line white satin gown with plain trim, but Cnythia's beautiful, smooth translucent skin made up for the missing ostentatiousness of her dress.

When the limousines passed Heather's house on the way to St. Mary's, Heather laughed when she saw the drapes part and the face of her Akita, Heidi, staring back at her. *What irony*, she thought. *I was the one who parted those same drapes in hopes of getting a glimpse of the wedding parties, 25 years ago. Now, here I am sitting in this limousine with the bride-to-be. My! Life is so strange.*

Father Michael stood at the foot of the altar as the couples made their way down the aisle. Cnythia and Joey made their vows first. Then Father Michael turned to the other couple.

"Do you, Albert, take Ingrid here to be your lawful wedded wife to …?

Not a single sound was heard throughout the small church and not an eye was dry, including his own, when Father Michael married his parents.

The town came alive as residents and merchants lined the streets and store fronts watching the limousines drive through the town, honking their horns, on their way to the pizza palace.

The musicians, Charley and Eddy, along with Eddy's

nephew, Winston Chandler, were just setting up and as soon as the couples walked in, The Anniversary Waltz was heard playing. Dominic was happy to find his favorite musicians still alive and well, especially his favorite one, Eddy, who was well in his 80's now. Although Eddy's stride was slower, and his hands shook with age, and his hair was now all silver, he still had the same debonair persona. Behind his thick glasses were the familiar twinkling brown eyes. When Eddy took his guitar in his arms and caressed it close to his body, he became transformed into a young lustful lover making passionate love to his mistress as his fingers flew adroitly over her neck.

Eddy was happy to have this occasion to take his guitar out of retirement. When Dominic was on the island, he hired him for all his functions. He had a regular gig playing at Dominic's nightclub, The Lei. After Dominic left the island, his professional gigs came to an end.

How he missed those times and reminiscent about them to his nephew, Winston.

"You weren't born then, Winston. But if only you could have seen San Lucci back then. Dominic brought this little island to life, in every way, especially economically. He was so generous, and he created many jobs for the people here. Those were certainly the good times."

Winston was curious about this so-called "benefactor" of the island. When his uncle asked him to accompany him to help with his equipment, he readily accepted. He had to see for himself this "Italian do-gooder." This man that his uncle held in such high esteem.

It was just like the old days when Dominic, Regina, Guido, and Paula got married, even down to the decorations. The glass lanterns were on all the outside patio tables. The myriad of balloons and fresh flowers abounded throughout the restaurant. Plastic replicas of the bride and groom were placed strategically in the center of each table. The baskets of carefully wrapped white net confetti sat on the bridal table. The expensive champagne bottles were in their silver ice buckets at each table. Large platters of rack of lamb, roast beef and duck-under-glass were served. A corner table housed a buffet of sandwiches and pizzas for the less discriminating guests.

Dominic invited all his old friends that were still living on the island. Mario and Louis, the brothers of the local barber shop, Remo, the town's shyster and his boyfriend, Reginald. Heather invited Roxanne, Charley's girlfriend. Heather once worked for Roxanne in her boutique shop, and they became close friends. When Roxanne retired, Heather bought the shop.

"Everyone, listen up. Now, we have a toast to the brides and grooms. Okay, everyone fill your glass." Dominic waited, making sure everyone was ready for the special toast he prepared.

"Lungo vitale. Long life, Joey and Cnythia. Ingrid and Albert and their very special figlio naturale, their love child, Father Michael. It is good we are all together again here in this beautiful place. The family has a lot of memories of San Lucci Island, eh?" Dominic looked at Guido and his "boys" for confirmation. They nodded, let out a small laugh, and mumbled to each other, in agreement.

"Yes, that's right. And we have this boy right here to thank for this happy reunion," Dominic pinched Joey's cheek.

"Yeah, because of you, Joey, because you wouldn't take no for an answer," Dominic looked at Regina when he said this.

"You see, Gina, everything turned out all right, after all, just like I told you it would. It was a good thing Joey came here. Just look at all the good that came from it. Ingrid found her lost son and Father Albert found her and now they are married, and their son married them. How could it have been any better? This is truly a blessing-a gift from God, no?"

All the tense events of the day, coupled with many glasses of wine, left the emotional Dominic flushed and drained. He could not continue.

"Okay, fermata, enough. Now, we eat!"

Regina squeezed Dominic's hand, endearingly, when she saw her husband wipe his eyes.

Matthew approached Cnythia when he saw she was alone.

"Cnythia, I want to welcome you into our family, and I wish you all the happiness in the world, with my cousin. You deserve it."

"Why, thank you, Matthew. You are so sweet, and since I'm now in the family, I guess it's okay if I kiss you."

Cnythia leaned over and kissed Matthew on the cheek. This made Matthew's heartbeat quicken.

"Yes, we are a very emotional family, and we do a lot of kissing in the family. You must come to The Palazzo, in Venice, with Joey. Then you will witness it for yourself, how close we all are."

Winston Chandler couldn't take his eyes off Constance the whole evening. He watched her every move as she fluttered, like a butterfly, from table to table playing the perfect little hostess making sure everyone had everything they needed. When Constance saw Winston watching her, she coolly nodded at him and went about her business, completely ignoring him. This made him more interested in her and at the same time insulted she didn't pay any attention to him. He was not used to this as he was considered the biggest catch in all of San Lucci with his charming, good looks and his grandfather's immense fortune. His grandfather was the late sugar millionaire, Nathan Chandler.

Winston mistook Constance's indifference for snobbishness. On the contrary, Constance was used to being stared at and admired from all the young men in her town and took it all in her stride. He would have been surprised to learn she thought him cute and was sneaking looks at him when his back was turned.

"Do you remember the first time we met, Paula?" Guido asked her as they walked out onto the patio with their champagne.

"Yes, Guido, I do." Paula smiled, as she recalled how shy she was when he first approached her the night of Dominic's wedding.

"It was love at first sight for me, Paula. In fact, when I invited you into Dominic's office and we sat on his leather sofa, I told myself that the next time we were on this sofa, it would be our wedding night."

Paula laughed and felt her body temperature rise in recalling their honeymoon night. She was now aroused and whispered in Guido's ear.

He smiled at her in delightful surprise and his eyes lit up.

Dominic couldn't restrain himself and the room filled with his loud, jovial laughter, on hearing of Guido's request. As the last of the guests left, Dominic turned to Guido and with a grin, told him.

"Buno divertimento," His parting words to him were "have fun," as he ushered the bridal party out of the pizza parlor.

The Pizza Palace was now empty and silent. Guido locked the front door and entered the office. Paula had removed her dress and was sitting on the leather sofa in her pale apricot lace chemise. Guido locked the office door and went to her.

...

The limousines deposited the bridal party at the Hotel Capri, once owned by Dominic. Joey and Cnythia spent their wedding night in Joey's place, the penthouse suite. This was Joey's home ever since he moved to the island. At one time, Dominic's home and where he brought Regina on their wedding night. Frankie was staying in a similar, but less opulent suite, below them. He gladly turned his room over to Ingrid and Albert for their wedding night. The rest of the family occupied the smaller rooms.

Joey and Cnythia used the private elevator leading to the penthouse. When Dominic acquired the hotel, he made some new additions starting with the elevator and had it completely redone in plush red velvet brocade and added a large jacuzzi in the dressing room area.

The elevator door opened to a large circular glass room with a skylight. Joey pressed the button behind the bar and closed out the ocean view of blinking lights from the boats in the harbor.

The present owner left everything exactly the way it was when he purchased the hotel. All the furnishings remained. This included Dominic's favorite black and white leather sofa and chairs. The once white rug, now somewhat discolored with age, laid in front of the fireplace. Earlier in the day, Dominic requested the hotel staff furnish the suite with a basket of fruit, nuts, cheeses and champagne. He personally brought up a bottle of Christian Brothers Brandy so he could take a nostalgic look around. He sat down on the 12-foot circular bed and ran his hands over the soft, black mink coverlet and silky black satin bed sheets. It was amazing to him that everything remained the same, even down to the original sheets, after all these years. He questioned the new owner.

"Mr. Visconti, the penthouse suite is not used much. You see you had such impeccable, rich tastes that we didn't want to change a thing, Unfortunately, it proved too expensive for most of the tourists that come here. In fact, it was reserved only twice in the past 25 years. Then your son arrived. I can't tell you how happy we are to have it occupied by a Visconti, once again."

Hmm, I bet you are, Dominic mused to himself. I receive the astronomical bills from you each month. Dominic agreed to pay Joey's expenses until he got his business off the ground. Now that he was married, he expected him to take care of his own affairs.

Cynthia's eyes opened wide as she slowly walked around the suite. She was enthralled. She had never been in a hotel room

321

before. In fact, she never expected to be here at all, let alone as Joey's wife. She never wanted to see him again, after that horrible night, but once she found out she was pregnant, everything changed. She had no idea her parents paid Joey a visit but shortly after that, Joey came to her house and asked her out. She didn't want to go but her parents insisted. This attitude towards him surprised her. *Why is he here and why are my parents encouraging me to go out with him. This doesn't make any sense*, she wondered.

Her parents knew some impropriety had occurred, as they never believed Cynthia's story about what happened that night. They knew their daughter well enough to know she would never give herself to any man before marriage. Heather liked seeing Joey's contrite, humble attitude when he came to their house. Joey was, by no means, their first choice for their daughter, but under the circumstances, they believed marriage was the best solution. Despite everything, they knew Cnythia loved Joey. It was the right thing—that they straighten everything out, between them, before the wedding.

On the way up the mountains, Cnythia did not speak or look at Joey. She kept her distance by sitting on the far side of the passenger's seat and stared out the window.

When Cnythia returned home, several hours later, she was happy and smiling broadly. Heather breathed a deep sigh of relief.

...

Joey filled two glasses of champagne and brought them into the jacuzzi. Cnythia let her body slide down, luxuriously, into the warm bubbling water as she sipped her champagne. This time, she wasn't afraid of drinking too much and soon they were both relaxed and comfortable.

Cnythia wiped herself off and stepped into the darken

room where Joey was waiting. The moon shining down on her from the above glass skylight cast a glow on the top of her head.

"Cindy, you look like an angel with a halo around your head."

As they lay in their massive bed and looked upwards, it appeared as if the whole celestial heavens were heading straight down on them. It was a glorious sight as the stars glimmered like a beautiful diamond necklace against a black velvet gown backdrop.

Cynthia's lover was a very different man, tonight. A man she never met before. Joey was the quintessential lover, in every way. His only thought was in pleasing his bride.

He took his time, starting with the top of her head, caressing and kissing each strand of her hair. Then he moved slowly down her face, dropping feather-like kisses all over her face. He licked her neck and nibbled on her ear lobe. As he moved teasingly brushing past her nipples, Cnythia's body became taunt, with excitement and anticipation. Joey swirled his tongue around her small nipple enlarging it with each vacuum suction. Cnythia felt a tingling sensation in her breasts. Joey moved methodically downward, returning upwards from time to time, making sure he didn't miss any area of her body. Cynthia's body became rigid as she felt him lifting her upwards to meet his lips. Her pelvic area was now throbbing and pulsating. These were all new sensations for Cnythia, but she was completely relaxed with Joey because he was so gentle. She allowed herself the enjoyment of the moment.

Joey separated her loins and wrapped her long legs around his head as he buried his face in her soft, silky blonde pubic hair. Her combustion was imminent and intense. Cynthia's screams were carried high up through the open skylight to the black silent heavens above where it fused with a shooting star, in celebration of her climax.

...

323

Dominic announced to the family that it was now time to go home. They spent one month on the island and Dominic satisfied his desire to relive his past. He was looking forward to returning to The Palazzo. His soul was now content, and he didn't feel a need to return to San Lucci Island, ever again. However, Dominic would return, in the not so far future, and this time, it would not be for such a joyous occasion.

Cnythia was sad to see them leave. She was becoming fond of the family. It would be so quiet now without their gaiety and their boisterous personalities. She was beginning to get used to all the noise and their excitable natures. Cnythia being an only child. was raised in a quiet, reserved home. She was now opening up and losing some of her shyness and was looking forward to visiting The Palazzo, after the baby was born. It was decided, by Dominic, that the baptism would take place in Venice, at St. Mark's Basilica, just like all the other baptisms.

After the weddings, everyone resumed their lives. Ingrid and Albert rented a small house near the church and visited their son every day. Cnythia continued working at the boutique. Joey was now a changed person. Gone was the young, immature, selfish man. In its place was a very devoted loving man committed to making a good husband to Cnythia. He bonded with the Islanders and chatted and picked up their tabs when they stopped by. All was well on San Lucci Island.

Life at The Palazzo also continued and soon Constance would be graduating from high school. Constance was at the very vulnerable ripe age of 16 ½ and felt an irresistible desire to experience life away from the Palazzo. Metaphorically speaking, she was a precious oyster that had been slowly irritated over time from her father's neglect and was now ready to burst out into a beautiful luminous virgin pearl.

Dominic called her into his office the week of her graduation and asked her what she wanted for her graduation present. Constance did not hesitate to tell him.

"Greece! I want to go to Greece and stay on the Island of Crete," Constance jutted out her jaw, determined not to take no for an answer.

Dominic was taken aback by Constance's request and her determination. He expected her to say—a new wardrobe—a car-jewelry, but a trip to Greece?! Why, he never heard her mention Greece before, and besides, they didn't have any family there, so why Greece?

If Dominic had communicated with his daughter over the years, he would have discovered her interest in that country. Ever since studying the language and culture of Greece, in school, she fell in love with it. It was so familiar to her, the people, the foods, and music. It reminded her so much of her own culture, her homeland, Venice. She just had to experience it for herself.

The women knew of Constance's long-time dream, and they decided if Dominic gave his consent, Angela, her Godmother would chaperone her.

"But why Greece, Constance, I don't understand. I mean, if you want to go to a Mediterranean place, why not go where your heritage is, Sicily! Why don't you go to Sicily? Ah, Sicily is such a beautiful place. It is the best place in all of Italy. That reminds me of something I once read, 'To have seen Italy without seeing Sicily is not to have seen Italy at all, for Sicily is the clue to everything!' There, you see, Constance. Now, this would not have been in a book by some famous writer if it was not true, eh?"

When Dominic saw the way his daughter looked at him with surprised respect, he was glad he told her he read it somewhere. The truth was that this quotation by Goethe was passed on to him by Vincent.

Dominic recognized that Constance was determined by the way she jutted out her chin in the same way he did when he would not accept "no" for an answer. Yes, Constance was more like him than he ever realized. She could be quite stubborn and headstrong and very independent when she wanted something and would allow nothing or no one to stop her. However, she still managed to remain sweet and charming, especially with her father. This was what made it so difficult for Dominic to refuse her anything. She knew just how to manipulate him with her girlish ways to get whatever she wanted. Constance was more adept at this than her own mother. Regina was a very innocent young lady growing up. She never learned how to play these games. She was taught by her mother and the church to be an obedient and totally submissive wife to her husband. It was fortunate for her, that Dominic was such a good man and never took advantage of her naivety.

CHAPTER 53

The early summer night's balmy breeze rustled the thin white chiffon drapes as it blew in off the ocean. Constance reached for her blanket and huddled under it. Her room overlooked the harbor, which was filled with big, expensive yachts. They were staying at Elounda, near Ayios Nikolaos, Crete's most luxurious resort. Her godmother had an adjacent room with an adjoining balcony. Constance felt so peaceful when, with a minimum effort, she made it from her bed to the hot tub on the balcony where she had an expansive view of the gorgeous harbor. Whiffs of scented jasmine floated up to her room from the gardens of jasmine that flourished in Crete. Her wake-up call each morning was a silver pot of coffee, a tall glass of freshly squeezed orange juice and some croissants delivered to her room. In her school studies of the island of Crete, she recognized it had a similarity to her hometown, Venice. Now that she had seen San Lucci Island, she noticed how much the island of Crete reminded her of that island. Just like San Lucci, Crete was dominated by a mild Mediterranean climate with hot, dry summers and rainy winters. It even had ferries similar to San Lucci that traveled to neighboring points and the mainland of Greece. Again, like San Lucci, it was a mountainous country with many gorges and wind-haunted valleys. This was where all similarity ended. Crete claimed fertile valleys where agriculture prospered; the main production consisted of potatoes, olives, vegetables, grains, and wine.

"Oh, look, Godmother. It's just like the Rialto Market back home."

They were walking through the village, taking in the sights when they came upon the markets where the mounds of herbs; rosemary, thyme, oregano and basil filled the air.

Constance was a walking schoolbook quoting facts to Angela about Crete.

"Back in 1211 for the next 450 years, Crete became part of the Venetian Republic. That's why the Venetian influence is so strong here, as evidenced by the architecture and art."

Constance smiled, smugly, when she saw how impressed her Godmother was by her knowledge of Greece. After sightseeing all day—they visited the archaeological museum and the ruins—they were exhausted and famished. They stopped at a little café and that's where she first saw him.

When the waiter asked if they wanted to order in Greek, Constance decided she would try out her school learned Greek and answered him in his language.

"**Malista**." "Yes."

"**Theloume ghevme**." The waiter smiled, with approval, and handed her a lunch menu.

Constance hid her face behind the menu and nonchalantly peeked around it, to get a better look at the handsome stranger seated at a nearby table.

Nikolaos Pappas, who was named after St. Nikolaos, as well as his birthplace, Ayios

Nikolaos. He was a stocky man about 5 ft 9 inches. He had very thick, wavy, black hair and a black well-kept mustache which made him look much older than his 25 years. He had large jet-black eyes with bushy thick eyebrows, which matched his mustache.

Why, he looks like he has two mustaches! This thought

made Constance laugh, out loud, which caught Nikolaos's attention, as well as her Godmother's.

"What are you laughing about, Constance?"

Constance blushed, embarrassed, when she saw Nikolaos frown at her.

Oh, dear, he thinks I'm laughing at him. When Constance realized she really was, she laughed again.

Angela turned in the direction of Constance's merriment and saw Nikolaos staring at Constance.

"Okay, now, young lady, that's quite enough. Shame on you! Flirting with that man over there. Now, what would your parents say?"

The waiter returned to take their order.

"Parakalo ferte mou ena filitzani kafe."

When the waiter brought them the coffee Constance ordered, Angela was indeed impressed with her goddaughter's command of the Greek language.

"Well done, Constance. Now, do you think you can order some sugar for my coffee?"

"Parakalo ferte mou ksidhi."

Constance beamed with pride and didn't notice the waiter give her a strange look. She looked up when she heard Nikolaos, who had been listening, laugh.

The waiter returned, shaking his head, and put down the "vinegar" Constance ordered.

As Constance stared down at the vinegar, she felt the heat rising from her neck all the way to the top of her head. Her face was now beet red, and she was on the verge of tears, when she heard a deep, velvety voice coupled with a slight English accent, address her.

"Excuse me, ladies, but I couldn't help overhear your order." Turning to Constance with a very sincere sounding voice, he complimented her.

"You speak my language very well."

Constance kept her eyes fastened to the ground, too ashamed to look up at him. She shook her head, in disagreement.

"No, no, I mean it. The Greek language is one of the hardest languages to learn. Believe me, I know." With a laugh, Nikolas added, "I still make mistakes!"

At his confession, Constance looked up and smiled, instantly liking him for trying to make her feel better.

"Allow me to introduce myself. My name is Nikolaos Pappas and if it pleases you, I would be most happy to order for you or ..." Nikolaos let out a small chuckle, "I'm afraid you may go hungry."

They laughed, and nodded, in agreement.

Nikolaos was a gregarious, candid man. He was born in Greece, an only child. His mother died in childbirth when he was four. He has lived in Ayios Nikolaos, in Eastern Crete, all his life, except for the time he attended school in England. Nikolaos was the son of a very prosperous olive grower. His father's estate consisted of several hundred acres of huge and ancient olive trees which grew in the Plains of Mesara.

The rest of the ladies' stay was spent in Nikolaos' company after he offered himself as their personal guide. He took them on a tour of Ayios Nikolaos that only a native Greekman could show them. They attended a Cretan wedding. Constance was surprised to see that it was traditionally similar to the Italian wedding. The dowry consisted of, among other items, a mattress. The guests threw walnuts, almonds and placed a little boy on it. This reminded Angela of what Dominic told the family during dinner at The Palazzo, just before Joey was born.

"The first born must be a boy. Italians must always have sons, at least for the first one. This is very important."

Immediately after the ceremony, a pomegranate, the symbol of fertility, was thrown down and as it broke into many small pieces, the family and friends all wished the couple a large family. The sugar covered almonds arranged in small packages of white netting were handed out to each guest.

The main instrument, the Cretan lyre, was played and the dancing began. Constance was amused when the men got up, formed a circle and placed their hands on each other's shoulders as they commenced to do the hasapiko, the fast Greek dance performed in Crete.

Nikolaos noticed the amused look on Constance's face and whispered in her ear.

"Constance, I know this may look strange to you to see the men dancing together, while the women sit and watch, but dancing is not considered effeminate in Crete. On the contrary, being a good dancer is a prerequisite for being a real man."

Nikolaos smiled seductively at Constance when he leaned on the words "real man." He then added,

"I will have you know, Constance that I am considered a 'very good dancer!'" Nikolaos winked at her.

Constance blushed, as Nikolaos' sexual overtones did not go unnoticed.

Nikolaos brought them to his home, or rather, his mini palace, high in the hills overlooking the harbor. Its opulence was similar to The Palazzo. It was now apparent to Constance that they had much in common. They were brought up in wealthy environments and their cultures were very similar. The Cretans, like the Italians, love liberty and refuse to accept enslavement. They are proud, stubborn people with a great sense of honor. They enjoyed the same kinds of Mediterranean foods and wines. The Cretan cooking was a blend of Greek, Roman and Byzantine traditions. Nikolaos and Constance both possessed the same, excitable, vibrant personalities, even to their constant expressive motion of their hands, when speaking. They enjoyed each other's company immensely.

Nikolaos was a gracious host. He treated the ladies extravagantly by taking them to the finest restaurants and discos on Crete. He brought them to the finest boutiques where

Constance purchased a handmade, cream-colored off the shoulder gauze handkerchief-style dress with matching scarf. The short, puffed sleeves and the white satin ribbon tied at the waist added a charming, peasantry look to the dress. The style was most becoming on Constance emphasizing her slim body and small waist. It was cool and comfortable, a perfect dress for the hot, dry August weather in Crete. A pair of tan Roman-style sandals completed her new outfit. It was the ideal dress to wear when Nikolaos invited them to spend the weekend on his father's yacht.

The yacht, The Nikolaos, was as big as The Regina. A marked difference, however, was in its furniture. No leather was to be found anywhere. The cabins were decorated with richly, brightly colored fabric furniture and thick plus Persian rugs.

Constance stood on the deck watching the sun go down. The hot day had now turned to a breezy, cool evening. The ocean breezes sent a chill throughout her body, as it whipped her long brown hair wildly about. Nikolaos removed her scarf from around her neck and wrapped it, gently, around her head. They were finally alone. This was the first time since they met, that they manage to escape Angela's strict supervision. Nikolaos was very attentive in keeping Angela's wine glass filled and by the time they had finished dinner, she was "finished" also and retired early to her cabin.

"So, you are leaving tomorrow. I sincerely wish you did not have to go back home, Constance. It has been such a deep pleasure meeting you and I will miss you, terribly."

Constance looked deeply into his eyes. She, too, was sorry to be leaving. She was beginning to fall in love with Nikolaos and she believed he felt the same way. She loved everything about him. She especially loved his quick mind, his intelligence and his eloquent, articulate way of speaking. Such as now. He could be so formal, yet so charming. She did not overlook the fact that he was nine years older than her. The fact that he was older, the same age as her brother Joey, gave her a sense of security. Perhaps this was another reason for her attraction to him. Constance felt comfortable with older men, having been around them all her life. She never cared for boys her own age. She found them too immature and socially insipid.

"Oh, Nikolaos, I am so sorry to leave this beautiful island. I just can't explain it, but it has somehow touched my soul. Right now, I am experiencing a range of emotions raging through me which I find so difficult to express."

"I know exactly how you feel and perhaps this quote by Nikos Kazantzakis, as reported to Greco, can best sum up your feelings: 'There is a kind of flame in Crete-let us call it soul-something more powerful than either life or death. There is pride, obstinacy, valor and together with these, something also inexpressible and imponderable, something which makes you rejoice that you are a human being, and at the same time tremble.'"

Nikolaos' voice, coupled with the poetic words, mesmerized Constance. She was transfixed, hypnotized. She could not, nor did she wish to speak. To do so would have been sacrilegious, to break the mystical spell she was under from hearing Nikolaos' deep, rich, full, sensual voice resounding in her ears.

Nikolaos broke the silence.

"Constance, I want you to know that these past weeks have been the happiest of my life. I know we have just met, and you are still so young, but I must confess … I have fallen in love with you. Perhaps in another year and a half, when you turn 18, I can come to Venice and ask your parents for your hand in marriage. I have already asked my father for his blessing, and he has happily given it as he loves you also. So, it is all settled, that is, if you feel the same for me?"

Just like that, he proposed. Constance could not believe her ears. A moment ago, he was so formal and now this! *Why, he has never even touched me or tried to kiss me,* she mentally pondered.

Nikolaos was so respectful of Constance, and she felt completely safe with him. She knew he would never try to violate her.

Nikolaos did not wait for her answer.

"I would like you to have this, Constance. It belonged to my mother. My father gave it to me after she passed away. He told me my mother would have wanted me to give it to the woman I marry, so now I present it to you."

Nikolaos leaned over and fastened the pin to her dress. It was a very old, antique solid silver pin with an encrustation of diamonds in the center, in the shape of a rose. It was the most beautiful piece of jewelry Constance had ever seen, even more beautiful than any in her mother's jewelry box.

Constance was so touched by Nikolaos's words and gift and to show her acceptance, she leaned over and kissed him, innocently. It was a long kiss, and they slowly and reluctantly pulled apart, but not before Constance felt Nikolaos's well-endowed manhood digging into her body. She had never felt this marvelous part of a man's anatomy against her before and she experienced several delicious sensations of short, quick throbs in her pelvic area. That moment cemented their engagement, as she whispered in his ear.

"I love you, too, Nikolaos."

CHAPTER 54

Constance shared her "secret engagement" with her Godmother. She knew it would be safe with her and that she would not tell her parents. Her godmother always understood her and was never judgmental. Constance felt closer to her Godmother than to her own mother, for this reason. Her mother seemed to even encourage this, which struck Constance as strange. She wondered why her mother was not jealous or hurt when Constance turned to her Godmother more and more over the years, while growing up. She never knew about the bond they formed before her birth.

After she showed her Godmother the engagement pin, she pinned it to her bra, right next to her heart. It would remain there, hidden, until such a time she was ready to tell her parents about Nikolaos. She knew her parents would never allow her to have a steady boyfriend, at her age, especially one they knew nothing about. They were very protective and old-fashioned. They would have to meet his father before allowing a courtship to take place. If they found out he wasn't Italian and much older than her, they would put an end to the relationship. Constance wasn't taking any chances.

Constance gave Nikolaos Joey's address and phone number. She knew she could depend on her brother for his support and could hardly wait to tell him all about Nikolaos and was on her way to San Lucci Island to do so, Angela returned to The Palazzo as she knew Constance no longer needed her.

Joseph Dominic Visconti was born two weeks before Constance's arrival. The whole family, especially Dominic, was satisfied it was a boy. The baby's baptism would be held at St. Mark's Basilica in Venice when he turned one month old. The women began the arrangements for the big celebration that would follow.

Constance looked down at the sleeping face of her nephew and smiled.

"Oh, Joey, he looks just like you. He has the Visconti's dark features."

Wait till Daddy sees the resemblance.

"Well, he does have Cnythia's blue eyes." Joey's thoughtfulness in not allowing Constance's prejudiced appraisal offend Cnythia, made her smile.

"Yes, but mother said that all newborn babies have blue eyes, so his eyes could change to dark brown," Cynthia chimed in.

A big change came over Joey when he married Cnythia. They were very much in love and their marriage was a happy one. Joey was a perfect husband and father, and Cnythia forgave him for raping her.

Constance was happy to see the blissful union as evidenced by Cnythia's bubbling excitement.

"Oh, Constance, I must show you the blueprints of the new home Joey is building for us. The builders are starting tomorrow. It will be built on *High Mountain* and it will have the best view of all of San Lucci and just miles and miles of ocean view!"

Constance was pleased to see the marked change in her brother. She knew the Islanders didn't like him because of his attitude. But this had all changed. Gone was Joey's cocky attitude and rudeness. He was now nice to everybody. The Islanders frequently dropped in at the Pizza Palace to chat and enjoy a free glass of beer. Joey was finally accepted into the community.

Joey was happy his sister found someone very special in Greece. From the way she described him, he was sure he would make an ideal husband; however, he would reserve his opinion until he met him. He would have to approve of him, officially, before he would be accepted into the family. That was the way things were done in the Visconti family.

"Of course. I will wait for your approval, Joey."

"So, is this the way it's gonna to be, sis? You're going to keep this guy of yours a secret from Mom and Pop? It's gonna stay between you and me?"

Constance nodded her head.

"Yeah, yeah, it's okay, I understand. You're afraid to tell Pop, because he still sees you as his little girl, well, actually, you still are, you know. But don't worry, I won't say anything."

...

Constance was working in the restaurant when Winston Chandler and his friends walked in.

"Well, well. If it isn't Joey's little sister," Winston sarcastically said as she handed them their menus. "I never did get your name that night of your brother's wedding."

Winston remembered how she slighted him that night and he gave her a frigid stare as he looked her over.

Constance felt chills go up her spine seeing him undress her with his cold steel eyes."Are you ready to order?" She asked, trying not to look at him.

Constance's deliberate lack of acknowledgement infuriated him. He was embarrassed in front of his buddies. He gave Constance a contemptuous stare as she walked away.

"Wow, did she give you the cold shoulder, Winston. Well, I'll be darn. I believe this is the first time any women ever did this to our Casanova, here," They laughed, teasingly.

"No girl treats a Chandler like that. Who the hell does she think she is, anyway? That diego slut is not gonna get away with this. I'll get her, just you wait and see!" Winston mentally formed a plan.

"Hey, Winston, take it easy, buddy. What are you getting so worked up about? So, maybe she didn't remember you from the wedding. What's the big deal?"

His friends weren't too surprised to see Winston get incensed over nothing. He wasn't used to being snubbed by women. Still, they felt his overreaction was extreme.

"Connie, phone call for you. It's someone with an English accent," Joey winked at his sister knowing it was Nikolaos on the phone.

Joey walked into the restaurant from his office just as Constance was bringing a pitcher of beer to Winston's table.

Winston looked up when he heard Joey call out to his sister.

Okay, gottcha name now, you little bitch! Winston smiled to himself as his scheme to get even with her formulated in his mind. Just then, he caught Joey's eye and Joey acknowledged him with a smile.

Stupid diego, he thinks I'm smiling at him. If he only knew what I was thinking and plotting in my head, he'd kill me on the spot.

"Hey, you guys don't know much about women, do you? She remembers me alright; she's just pretending she doesn't. She's just playing hard to get. You should have seen how she looked at me at the wedding. Yeah, I tell you guys, she's got the hots for me and she's just begging for it. And guess what? I'm not going to disappoint her. Yes, sir, I'm going to give it to her real nice and hard!" Winston had to save face in front of his friends.

His friends shook their heads.

"What are you, crazy or something, Winston, to go after a Visconti? Everyone knows about that Visconti kid. He's got a real

338

hot temper. He will kill you if you lay a hand on his sister. You sure don't know anything about these Italians, do you? You don't want to mess with any one of the family. Shit! They will get the whole damn mafia after you!"

"Yeah, well, you don't know anything about us Chandler's. When we want something, we get it. Now listen up, because I have a plan."

The men had known each other all their lives. They were born and raised on the island. The Chandler's were a powerful, wealthy family. Winston's great, great grandfather, Nathan Chandler, discovered the little island in the 1800's. When he passed on, his fortune was divided with his grandchildren and the island for the conservation of the historical monuments he erected during his lifetime.

Winston's friends knew better than to get on his wrong side. Their fathers owed their livelihood to Winston's father as he owned much of the businesses on the island; they knew his power and also his vindictiveness. He would make trouble for all of them if they didn't cooperate. Besides, the Visconti family meant nothing to them, so they decided to help Winston with his plan.

It was 11 P.M., an hour before closing when Winston and his friends walked into the Pizza Palace. Constance was serving the outside patio and didn't see them enter. While waiting for their pizza, they huddled over their beer, talking in a low voice.

"Okay, you guys. We're all set now, right? I don't want any foul-ups. It's got to go just like I planned."

They glanced at each other, with doubt-ridden faces. They did not look Winston in the eye, instead looked away, with their heads down.

Winston read their faces. He saw their reluctance. He clenched his fists and his face reddened.

"Hey, you guys better not back out on me, now. It wouldn't be too good for anyone, if you know what I mean."

Winston glanced at his watch and looked around the

restaurant. There were only two waitresses serving the tables. He made sure they were short of help by paying the girls for not showing up for work. It was time. He instructed them:

"It's time to go. It's now 11:25 P.M. and they will be closing in half an hour. Here, give this to the help on your way out." He handed them a roll of bills.

Frankie stepped out onto the balcony for some fresh air. He had been helping out in the kitchen, all night, because they were short of help. Two of his kitchen help and three of his waitresses called in sick. This seemed strange to him, so many sick in one night. He turned to go back inside when something caught his eye. He saw a large glow of light coming from the harbor. He squinted his eyes, to focus on the direction of the light. He grabbed his head in shock when he realized where it was coming from.

"It's the Regina. The Regina is on fire!'

Frankie ran through the restaurant and tore open the office door.

"Joey, Joey. It's the Regina. The Regina is on fire!"

Joey jumped up from his desk, stared out the window and saw the now large flames shooting sparks into the dark skies, flying all over the harbor, like hundreds of fireflies.

Constance was busy, at the register tallying the nights' receipts, when Frankie and Joey ran frantically past her.

"Connie, the Regina is on fire. Will you be alright? Can you lock up?

In the hysteria of the moment, Joey did not notice that all his help had gone, and Constance was now alone in the restaurant.

Winston watched the pandemonium break out from a back booth in the darkest corner of the restaurant. He smiled, smugly, as he looked around and saw all the help gone and the last couple getting up to leave. Soon they would be alone. Everything was going exactly as planned.

At 12 A.M., as Constance was closing up, she realized that she was alone. She wondered out loud.

"Hmm, that's strange. I wonder what happened to the staff. They left before we closed. They have never done this before. They didn't even finish clearing the tables. I must tell Joey. He will not like this."

Constance locked the front door after the last couple, and turned off the lights, when she heard a noise coming from the back corner of the restaurant.

"Jessie, is that you? Becky? Ellen?" She called out to the three waitresses but there was no response. Just then, a tall, lean form came towards her. The only light streaming in from the office cast an eerie glow on Winston's face. Constance gasped when she recognized him. Realizing she was alone, her heart pounded, and she trembled.

"What—what—are—you doing here?"

"Don't look so surprised, Connie. You know what we both want!"

Winston lunged for her as Constance ran into the office and tried to lock the door. Winston was too fast for her and put his foot in the doorway pushing it so forcefully against her, it caused her to fall backwards, and she landed on the black leather sofa.

"Ah, yes, that's just perfect, Connie. That's exactly where I wanted you. So nice of you to accommodate me."

Winston wasted no time jumping on top of her and tearing off her clothes. Constance thrashed out at him, kicking, biting and hitting him, yelling at the top of her lungs for her brother.

"Go ahead; scream all you want, Connie. It's not going to do you any good. He can't hear you. He's too busy putting out the fire on his boat."

The more Constance fought him off, the more aroused he became. He rested, just moments, in between orgasms, his whole-

341

body weight heavily on top of Constance's small frame. It seemed an eternity for her when he finally finished and removed himself from atop her body.

Winston grinned at her, as he zipped up his fly.

"Nice, Connie. That was a real nice surprise. I didn't think you were still a virgin. I thought all you hot-blooded Italian girls had your cherries busted by the time you turned 16. That was real sweet of you to have saved yourself for me."

Winston started out the door, then turned back, as if he just remembered something.

"Oh, by the way, there is just one more thing."

Constance's head reeled backwards from the force of Winston's hard fist striking her face.

"That, my dear, was for embarrassing me in front of my buddies."

Winston's sinister laugh followed him out the front door.

When Joey and Frankie returned, they found Constance huddled under the desk, clutching her ripped bra to her breasts. She was sadly fingering her now broken engagement pin that dangled from her bra. She was in tears and mumbling inaudibly. She was shaking uncontrollably and unable to speak.

"My dear, Connie. Who did this to you?!"

Joey took her in his arms and rocked her gently, kissing the top of her head and smoothing back her wild and tangled hair from her eyes. He spoke softly in her ear.

"It's okay, Connie. It's going to be all right. My sweet little sister."

Tears welled up in Joey's eyes when he saw the red hand impressions on her neck, stomach and inner thigh and the big bruise now forming on her face.

Frankie got a blanket from the closet and put it around her partially nude body. The first thought that came to him was that they had been robbed and when they discovered Constance, raped her. But when he checked the cash drawer and found all the money still there, he abandoned that theory. *Then, who could have committed such a despicable act and why?* All these questions kept turning over in his mind. Almost instantaneously, a bright light flashed in his head. He spoke his thoughts to Joey.

"Joey, I remember seeing Winston Chandler and his friends sitting in the far corner booth when I walked out on the patio. I wonder if ..."

Joey looked at him and their eyes locked, in agreement. Joey knew that Winston never liked him, however, he never understood why as he never had any encounters with him. Perhaps he just didn't like Italians, Joey concluded. However, he did recall that night he was away from the restaurant, Frankie related an incident that had occurred between him and Winston. One evening, Winston was causing a ruckus in the restaurant and Frankie asked him to leave. He remembered Frankie telling him about the threatening look Winston gave him. *Could that have triggered off such a horrific attack on my little sister?* he wondered.

These thoughts raced through their minds and, as if they reached the same conclusion at the same time, they both started out the door. Joey put his hand out and blocked the doorway.

"No, Frankie. This is my fight. This is something I must do alone. You have to stay here and take care of Connie. She must not be left here alone."

My, life is so strange. How our past offenses always catch up to us. I literally raped Cnythia on that same sofa when she was just Constance's age, Joey reminisced.

"Can it be that? Can it be my poor sister had to be the sacrificial lamb for my past sins? For my atonement?" Joey shouted out in anguish to God.

CHAPTER 55

"Well done. You guys did a great job on that yacht. Hell, that fire is gonna smolder for days. I can still see the sparks flying from here. She's a goner, all right."

Winston steered his boat out of its mooring just as the fire patrol boats arrived, trying, in vain, to save The Regina but the fire was roaring out of control. The strong gusts of wind blowing in off the ocean enticed the blaze even more. The top deck was almost gone. They managed to control the fire enough before it hit the lower cabins.

"So, what now, Winston? What's gonna happen when he finds out who caused this and comes after us?" His friend, Billie asked.

"What do you mean, what's gonna happen? Nothing is gonna happen. Because I'm gonna beat the shit out of him, that's what's gonna happen. Anyway, he asked for it by coming here. We Chandlers own this island. What right did that diego have coming here, anyway and acting like he owns it. I'm sick and tired of my Uncle Eddie paying homage to the Visconti's name, just because he gets him gigs. That Visconti kid got what he deserved."

...

Constance was slowly healing from her ordeal mentally,

although her bruises were still very prominent on her body. She was expected home to start college, but could not, under these conditions. Joey called his parents and requested she stay on for a few more weeks. His parents protested, at first, not wanting Constance to miss her first semester but relented when Joey insisted he needed her in the Pizza Palace. It was agreed they would all travel home together, for Joseph's baptism. Joey did not want Connie in the Pizza Palace, anymore. She was to remain either in her room, at the hotel or with Cnythia's parents. Cnythia emphasized with the traumatic experience Constance had endured, having experienced a similar one, herself. Fortunately for Cnythia, it was not brutal, and it was with someone she knew and loved. To this day, no one ever knew what really happened that night, except Frankie.

Joey was in his cabin on board The Regina trying to salvage what was left of the yacht, just as Winston was piloting his boat into his mooring. He stayed away for two weeks to let things cool down but now as his buddies looked over at The Regina and saw all the damage they caused; they were ashamed. When they moved out in the middle of the night, they saw just the flames and now they saw the total aftermath. They were happy to get off Winston's boat and distance themselves from him. They wanted to get as far away from him as possible. They knew that no matter how long Winston tried to hide, Joey would find him.

When Joey came top-deck and saw Winston's yacht in its mooring, he clenched his fists and the veins in his neck and face enlarged and pulsated as his face turned livid, with anger. After the incident, Joey searched all over the island for him. Night after night, he parked outside his home and waited. He went to all the night spots Winston frequented. When he saw his mooring empty, he spent his days and nights aboard The Regina. Joey's long vigil was now over. This time, he would not escape.

Frankie was in the office when Joey ran into the room, opened the closet and took down his fishing tackle box from the

345

shelf.

"I found the bastard, Frankie. He's back. I'm going for him, now."

"Joey, what do you think you are doing with that?"

Joey was clutching a 6-inch serrated knife. Frankie jumped up in alarm and blocked the doorway stopping Joey from leaving.

"Get out of my way, Frankie. **Io quasi tu insegnare quello scoria lezione diritto qui**."

Joey pointed to his groin area with the tip of his knife when he told Frankie he was going to teach the scum a lesson right in his groin area.

"I'm gonna cut off his balls!"

"Joey, Joey. **Piacere lei controllo**. Please control yourself. Non fare qualunque costa le vuol pentimento. Please don't do anything you will regret. Joey, I realize we were just two hot-tempered Italians when we stormed out of here the night of Connie's attack. We weren't thinking, Joey. I thank God that we didn't find Winston, or we might have killed him. I know you need your revenge. I love Connie too, Joey, like my own sister, you know that, and I want to see him suffer as much as you do but we can't run off half-cocked. No, what we need is a plan. Let's think like your father. What would he do in this situation, huh? His contrivance would be planned very carefully, and his tracks would be covered, and no one would ever find out what happened, right? His revenge would be ever so sweet. Now, that's the way we will handle this, okay, Joey?"

Frankie's calm rational impressed Joey and he slowly put down the knife and sat down, deep in thought.

My cousin makes good sense. Yes, I must think like my father. How would he handle this if he were here? Joey rubbed his forehead in deep thought. It took him just a few moments before he jumped up, excitedly.

"That's it, Frankie. I got it! We will get Pop's errand boy,

346

Pipe, to assist us. This way, nothing would get back to us. Brilliant! Do you remember me telling you about the time my Pop and Uncle Guido were talking in the library about hiring this Indian to do jobs for them?"

He waited for an acknowledgement from Frankie before continuing.

Frankie didn't remember because Joey eavesdropped on them so many times over the years that he forgot most of the stories. Anyway, he was never interested in his uncle's past life on the island the way Joey was. Joey had such an insatiable appetite for anything his father related to him about the island.

Frankie nodded his head, so Joey would continue. "Okay, now, I just have to find him. It shouldn't be too hard. I remember my father mentioning he lived in a trailer in Rocky Beach. Now, here's the plan."

...

Pipe recognized him as soon as he walked up the steps of his run-down trailer home. He was sitting in his rocking chair, contentedly smoking his corn-cob pipe. The potent sweet smell emulating from his pipe engulfed Joey and caused him to cough.

"Hey—there, Dom-Dom-inic, how you've been? Where you been?"

Pipe's once smooth olive skin was now lined and weather-beaten. His hearing and eyesight had diminished. His long ponytail was now all white. His long years of substance abuse left him with lapses of memory.

Joey introduced himself as Dominic's son, but Pipe kept insisting he was Dominic.

"You su—sre—are—are looking good, Dominic. How come you looks so—young—how come you—look—look younger, instead of—of—older like me? By gosh, it—it—is sure good to see ya again. How—long—long—how—long you been away, huh? One-

347

two months? I—I-don't know—but I lose track of time, these days."

Joey explained why he was there and what he needed him to do. Would he help?

"Sure, Dom—Dom-inic. Any—thing for you. Since when have I ever refused any job for you, huh? You—you—have always treated me real good, too."

Pipe got his nickname because he was never without his corn-cob pipe, which Dominic kept filled along with his bottles of whiskey. Whenever Pipe ran low on either, Dominic promptly replenished it. He knew how to keep Pipe ready to do his bidding.

"Ah—ah—one more thing, Dom ..." Pipe paused to take a big swig from his whiskey bottle.

"I—I—gotta have the car for this job, okay, Dom?"

Pipe was referring to Dominic's old black Cadillac with the red leather seats that Dominic let him use whenever he did a job for him. Pipe loved driving that car. It made him feel like a "big man."

Joey knew what car Pipe was referring to because he heard his father tell his uncle that his biggest regret, when he left the island, was leaving behind that car. Well, he would have to find a close replacement and if Pipe was high, as he usually was, he wouldn't notice the difference. He was just hoping he wouldn't be so out of his head that he would screw up his plans.

Pipe understood what he was to do and no matter how drunk he was, he always had the capacity to function and never failed to complete a job. He forgot how he blotched the last job he did for Dominic and how upset Dominic was.

...

Joey was parked around the curve of the mountain, with his lights off. The night was pitch black and there was a dead silence which ricochets off the mountainside. It was a desolate, isolated area that Pipe chose for this job. It was his favorite place

348

and the very same spot he did another job for Dominic a very long time ago.

Frankie wanted to accompany Joey, but Joey insisted he stay at the Pizza Palace and conduct business, as usual. It would raise suspicion if both owners were absent from the restaurant. Joey assured Frankie he would be all right. They were both pleased with their concurrence on the plan.

"My father would have approved on how I am going to handle this, Frankie."

Since they knew that Pipe was Winston's supplier for his pot, they devised a plan whereas when Winston paid his visit to Pipe, he would tell him that he knew an old guy in the mountains that had a real fine pure quality of pot, and he would take him there.

Joey promised Frankie he was not going to kill Winston, although he wanted to. No, he was just going to beat the hell out of him. By the time he got through with him, he would be alive, but barely. Nothing short of that would satisfy Joey. He thought himself very benevolent to let Winston live, at all. He wondered if his father would have been so magnanimous. He doubted it—he knew his father would probably finish the low-life off! Contrariwise, he could do it, but not Joey! He never would want Joey to do such a thing. At one time, before marrying Cnythia, Joey wouldn't have hesitated. However, Joey was now a changed man. He was a responsible husband and father, who alter his outlook on a lot of things and killing could never be part of his new life now.

Winston never suspected a thing when Pipe invited him to come along with him to pick up the "stuff." In fact, he had forgotten all about the incident with Constance and thought Joey had to. He was confident that all this was behind him when he told his buddies.

"What did I tell you, guys? It's been two weeks now and that diego hasn't come after me. I told you he was just full of hot air. He's a coward-always knew it."

It was very late when Pipe made his way up that dark mountain road with Winston.

Pipe pulled the car over to the side of the road about 75 feet from where Joey was parked and got out of the car.

"Hey, what are you stopping here for? There's nothing out here," Winston asked, annoyed.

"Gotta take a leak." Pipe mumbled as he disappeared into the dense brush.

Winston got tired of waiting and got out of the car. He looked over the steep embankment to a 20-foot straight drop and shuddered. He kicked a rock and waited to hear the resounding sound of it hitting the bottom. He called out to Pipe and, getting no response, turned back towards the car, just as a dark figure came towards him.

"Who's there?' Winston strained his eyes, and then recognized the stranger, dressed in black, approaching him.

"Is that what my sister asked you as you lurked in the restaurant, waiting to pounce on her?"

Pipe watched, from behind the bushes, as the two shadows fought each other. First one, then the other had the upper hand, pinning each other to the ground. He couldn't make out who was who but then he heard a piercing scream from the first one and shortly after from the other. The screams got fainter and fainter until they finally stopped.

Pipe looked over the embankment, but it was too dark and too far down to make out anything. There was no sound or movement from below. He decided to get out of there as fast as possible. After all, he did what he was hired to do—deliver Winston to Dominic.

Pipe drove down the mountain fast and erratic, eager to get back to his trailer and relax with his pipe and the case of whiskey Joey dropped off, earlier.

"Nice guy, that Dominic. I sure hope he has another job

for me real soon."

CHAPTER 56

A loud racket made by a family of pigeons landing on the roof of the pizza parlor woke Frankie. He jumped up, in alarm as he remembered his dream of the night before—that something terrible happened during the night to Joey. He glanced at the clock on the desk. 6 A.M. He waited up for Joey's return all night until finally falling asleep on the sofa. Joey told him he was coming back to the office, afterwards. He wondered if perhaps he had changed his mind and went home. He dialed the penthouse suite at the hotel and woke Cnythia.

"Cindy, it's Frankie. Sorry to wake you so early, but I was wondering if Joey was there."

Cnythia felt his side of the bed and it was cold. "No, Frankie. Joey is not here. He never came home last night. I thought he was spending the night at the restaurant."

Cnythia was not overly concerned when she woke in the middle of the night and Joey was not beside her. Occasionally when he worked late, he spent the night on the sofa so he wouldn't wake her up.

Frankie didn't want to alarm her since she wasn't aware of the previous nights' occurrence.

"Don't worry about it, Cindy. He probably spent the night on The Regina. It's okay, go back to sleep. I'll call you when I find him."

However, Frankie became worried after he went aboard The Regina and Joey wasn't there. This was not like Joey not showing up at the restaurant. He was always here early. And as far as the plan went, he never told him where in the mountain he planned to attack Winston. He didn't know where to look for him. He mentally retraced Joey's steps from the night before. *Joey told me that Pipe lived in Rocky Beach. I must find him and maybe he can tell me where Joey is.*

"He lives in that trailer at the end of the trailer park,"

Frankie walked in the direction the little boy pointed to. He knocked several times on the torn screen door until a groggy voice was finally heard from within.

"Who is it? What do you want?"

"Pipe, I'm looking for Joey. Can you tell me where he is?"

When Pipe appeared in the doorway, his body odor from his urine-stained pants and mouth caused Frankie to recoil. It was apparent; he passed out in the night.

"Who are you?"

Pipe squinted at Frankie through the screen door.

"I'm Joey's cousin, Frankie. I am looking for Joey. He didn't come home last night, and I know he was meeting you last night."

"Hey, I don't know nothin' about no Joey. All I know is, Dominic hired me to do a job. I brought Winston to him and then I left. That's all I did."

Frankie realized Pipe's mental state and decided to go along with it.

"Pipe, please try to remember where you met Dominic. I need to know. Will you show me?"

Pipe refused to take him but told him the location. Frankie saw the car that Joey rented for Pipe, parked at the side of the trailer and made a mental note to return for it later.

After 10 miles of narrow, winding mountain road, Frankie

spotted Joey's car. Frankie examined the ground and saw where the rock and dirt had been disturbed. Frankie's heart skipped a beat and he had a lump in his throat when he saw two sets of footprints in the dirt near the edge of the embankment. He hesitated, not wanting to look, then forced himself to look over the sharp precipice. He stared, motionless, at the two lifeless bodies lying on top of the rocks side-by-side. He gingerly made his way down the mountainside.

Frankie's loud wailing cries echoed throughout the canyon floor and carried up the mountain as he cradled Joey's lifeless body in his arms and rocked him tenderly while kissing his bold stained head.

"Please, please," he cried out to God. "Not Joey. Not my cousin, my best friend, not my Joey. Oh, dear God!"

Both men were hoisted up the side of the mountain and rushed to San Lucci Hospital. Mark was on duty when Joey was brought in. He immediately notified Heather who called Cnythia and Constance at the hotel. By now, everyone was aware of the previous nights' events.

Winston was pronounced dead on arrival. Joey was barely alive with a faint pulse. Both men suffered head traumas.

"It's all my fault. I should never have let him go alone. I knew that, but Joey insisted I stay in the restaurant. Testa duro. He has a hard head."

Realizing the irony of his words, he put his face in his hands and cried.

"No, Frankie. You mustn't blame yourself. It's all my fault. If I hadn't been here, working in the restaurant—then—I wouldn't have met Winston—and—and—then he wouldn't have come after me—and—and—then Joey … Oh, Frankie. That's my brother in there, that's my Joey!"

Constance fell into Frankie's arms as their piercing cries filled the hospital waiting room.

Heather was comforting Cnythia who sat motionless,

numb with grief, when Mark entered the room. All eyes turned toward him, apprehensively.

"I'm so sorry. We tried to save him, but it was too late. Perhaps if he had been found sooner ..."

"You see, I told you so. I told you I should have been with him. What did I tell you? I could have saved him—I ..." Frankie looked up pleadingly at Mark as if hoping he could bring Joey back.

Mark put his hand on Frankie's' shoulder. "Frankie, even if you were there and brought him in right away, he wouldn't have recovered, fully. Joey suffered a massive head hemorrhage when he landed on the rocks. Even if he survived, he would have ended up a vegetable. Knowing Joey, as briefly as I did, makes me believe he never would have wanted to live like that. No, Frankie, you mustn't blame yourself," Mark hoped explaining the diagnosis of Joey's condition might alleviate Frankie's guilty feelings.

They sat, in shock, motionless, not saying a word. The disbelief that Joey was gone shone on their faces. Mark and Heather put their arms around their daughter as she continued to stare into space, incapable of displaying any emotion. Mark gave her and Constance a sedative to help them sleep. They went home with Heather and Mark that day, not wanting to return to the hotel.

...

An irresistible cry of loneliness swept over Frankie as he sat in Joey's chair and stared out the window at The Regina. The sad, worn-out condition of the once beautiful yacht, with its tattered green and red Italian flag flopping, lamely in the wind, echoed Frankie's feelings. He felt incredibility dead inside, as he surveyed Joey's office. He looked, expectantly, at the door hoping to see Joey sailing in, in his familiar jubilant style, smiling and yelling out orders to Frankie.

"How can Joey be gone? It is impossible. He was such a charismatic, powerful figure, a man of epic proportions. How could he die? How dare he leave me behind," he angrily anguished, out loud. Frankie would have gladly fallen down that mountain with him, he loved him that much!

Frankie's feelings of loss were only matched by Dominic's. After receiving Frankie's call, he sat with the phone hanging from his hand, hearing Regina's voice ringing in his ears. Those words of hers which seemed to have been uttered a century ago.

"Please, Dominic, tell him he can't go. He mustn't go to San Lucci Island. I keep having this same dream that something horrible happens to him there."

No one spoke throughout the long, lonely drive down the mountain from the San Lucci Airport. Each member of the family was lost in their own thoughts and memories of Joey. Dominic finally spoke in an agonizing soft and slow voice. His voice was unrecognizable.

"Frankie, I want you to take me to the place where Joey fell."

After dropping the rest of the family off at the hotel, Frankie drove Dominic to the isolated mountain road, and parked in the same spot Joey had parked on that fatal night.

Dominic stood looking over the embankment for a brief moment, and then they carefully made their way down the steep mountainside. Frankie pointed out the location of where Joey's body was found.

In a grieving anger, Dominic kicked the rock that had Joey's dried-up-blood still on it, so hard, it rolled over and down the mountain. Half-hidden, in the dirt and now very rusted with age was a wallet. Dominic bent down and opened it. Staring back at him was a picture of a young pretty woman and below that her name. Sylvia Lawson.

He gasped and grabbed his throat; a frightened look of

realization crossed his face and the significance of this moment hit him by what Vincent once shared with him.

"There's a just law in the Universe that keeps a list of checks and balances. Ralph Waldo Emerson said it best in his essay on 'Compensation': 'Every act rewards itself. It is inseparable from the thing, but it is often spread over a long time, may follow late but they follow because they accompany it; crime and punishment grown out of one stem; means and ends; cause and effect; seed and fruit; cannot be severed, for the effect already blooms in the cause, the end pre-exists in the means, the fruit in the seed."

The crime committed on Sylvia Lawson decades ago had now come full circle back to its perpetrator. The debt was now fully paid.

CHAPTER 57

The family walked up the steps at St. Mark's Basilica and through the massive ornate lattice-wood doors where Monsignor Mazzarino was waiting at the foot of the altar.

"**Requiem aeternam donna ei Domine. Et luc perpetua luceat ei. Requiescat in pace. Amen. Fidelium defunctorum per misericodiam Dei requiescant in pace. Amen**." "Eternal rest give unto him, O Lord. And let perpetual light shine upon him. May he rest in peace. Amen. May his soul and the souls of all the faithful departed through the mercy of God rest in peace. Amen."

This was to be Joseph's baptism day. It was now combined with Joey's funeral Mass. It was decided, by Dominic, that Joey's body lie next to the baptism font where his son was to be baptized. Dominic knew this would please his son.

Dominic's eyes filled with tears when he looked down upon the face of his only grandson.

"Oh, look, Regina. He looks just like Joey on his baptism day. Do you remember? Look at his lips. They are curling into a smile, just like Joey's when he tasted the salt. And those big brown eyes and long eyelashes, just like yours Regina. Ah! He has all the Visconti's features. **Bella bambino**! Beautiful boy!"

Cnythia smiled and put her arm through Dominic's, lovingly. She was happy Joseph's eyes did turn dark brown, just like Joey's.

The Monsignor accompanied them back to The Palazzo for the celebration that Cosmo and Celeste had prepared.

"Nome Padre Figlio Spirito Santo."

After the Monsignor gave the blessing, Dominic raised his hand for everyone's attention.

"I wish to say something here, before we eat."

Dominic paused as he surveyed the room, as if to make sure everyone was present. His eyes rested, for a moment, on each member of the family. First on Regina and Constance sitting on the right side of him. Then, across from him, Guido and Paula, and alongside of them, Vincent, Annette and Matthew, then Sammy, Kay and Frankie, and Johnnie and Angela. His eyes came to rest on the seat on his left, Joey's seat, now occupied by Cnythia and gave her a warm smile.

"This was to be a very happy occasion when Joey brought his wife and newborn son home to The Palazzo for the very first time. Instead, we come together here, without him."

Dominic's voice caught and he reached for his handkerchief and blew his nose, before continuing. "I just want to say that Joey would want all of us to be happy on such a festive day as this. He would want us to rejoice in his son's baptism. So, we will do so. Now, I want to welcome you, my dear daughter, to The Palazzo and to the Visconti family. Ah, you noticed I did not say daughter-in-law, eh? That is because we love you like our own flesh and blood. You have made this family very happy, my dear, Cnythia, by giving us our first grandchild and a boy, at that!" Dominic leaned over and kissed Cnythia warmly on the forehead.

"Okay, now, we eat!"

After dinner, everyone scattered, feeling the need to separate and be alone with their thoughts. There was still much healing to be done and each family member needed to grieve in their own way.

Constance was filled with remorse. She thought if she

359

hadn't stopped off in San Lucci but continued on home, none of this would have happened. She wouldn't have met Winston and there would be no rape, and her brother would be alive today.

Angela was full of guilt for not accompanying Constance to San Lucci. She never should have let her go on alone.

Frankie felt he was to blame because of his run-in with Winston. He believed this occurrence incited the whole situation.

Dominic and Regina felt guilty for having spoiled Joey and allowing him to grow up so irresponsibly. They should have taught him to have patience and tolerance for other people and control his hot-Italian temper. If they had only known the reason for his anger, they would not have blamed him.

Matthew was ashamed of his thoughts now that Joey was gone—the thought that, perhaps now, he might have a chance with Cnythia.

None of the family ever found out the real reason behind Joey's fight with Winston. Instead, Frankie told them that Winston made some lewd remarks to Constance and Joey flew off the handle. Dominic believed this, knowing how hot-tempered his son could react to small things. Yes, Dominic agreed that Joey had every right to defend his sister's honor but not in this way. If Frankie had only told Dominic that Constance had been raped by Winston, he would have taken matters in his own hands and Joey would not have been involved. In time, Frankie regretted his decision not telling Dominic and Regina the truth. By the time he realized it wasn't fair to Joey's memory, it was too late, they both passed away. It was a shame that they never knew how much their son had changed since his marriage. They would have understood that what happened that night was an accident, and that Joey had no intentions of killing Winston.

At nightfall, Matthew walked into the courtyard for some fresh air and saw a lone figure sitting in the dark in front of the Statue of St. Jude. He approached her quietly, so as not to frighten her. Cnythia looked up as Matthew sat down next to her. He respected her silence by not breaking it. They sat together, not moving, for a long time, looking pensively out into space.

Cnythia adjusted herself, stretched her legs and turned to Matthew, with sad eyes and voice.

"The Palazzo is certainly a beautiful place. It is exactly as Joey described it to me. Now, I know why Joey loved it so. He told me he was very happy growing up here. Now, I can see why."

In empathy, Matthew reached out and put his arm around her and in so doing experienced a voltaic charge which caused an involuntary jerk in his arm. He was glad that his apparent excitement touching her went unnoticed by her. Matthew's feelings for Cnythia that had been buried for so long were now beginning to surface.

The family spent one month together healing. It was time for the grieving to end and for all of them to return to their lives.

Guido and Paula returned to Switzerland, Vincent and Annette to England. Matthew accompanied Cnythia, Joseph and Frankie back to San Lucci Island. He convinced himself that Joey would be pleased if he stayed with Cnythia and comforted her.

Frankie sat at his desk, staring at all the mail that had accumulated while he was away. The Pizza Palace was closed in his absence and even now, the closed sign hung on the front door. Frankie couldn't bring himself to open the restaurant. He contemplated selling it and returning to Venice. He didn't see any reason to stay on. After all, this was Joey's dream, not his.

Frankie had his own special dream, a dream kept hidden in his heart all these years. A dream he never shared with anyone, not even Joey. He shared everything with him, except this. He was afraid Joey would laugh at him.

Ever since Frankie was in grade school, he was fascinated by the books he read on farming and tilling the soil. Oh, how he longed to put his hand down into the rich fertile earth and feel the cool dirt sift through his fingers. Frankie's dream was to own a big ranch with all kinds of animals and a wine vineyard. He versioned over-seeing acres of land and being the biggest wine maker in the land. Now, how could he tell any family member this dream? No one in the family ever had any interest in wine vineyards. The only interest his Uncle Dominic had in wines was in consuming them! How could he expect them to understand when all they knew was "clean business," never getting their hands dirty. How he suffocated all those years working in the bank. No one knew how miserable he was, so when Joey told him he was going to San Lucci Island, he jumped at the chance to escape. At least, it was better than the bank and he would be with Joey.

"Ah, just like Don Quixote, my dream is 'The Impossible Dream'", Frankie mused, out loud.

Frankie put his head in his hands. He felt so tired, so old, suddenly. He wasn't sure just what to do. He turned his attention to the business at hand. He listened to his phone messages. Most of the calls were for Constance from Nikolaos. He finally tackled his mail and among the usual bills, were at least 15 letters, all in the same handwriting, all postmarked Greece and all addressed to Constance. Nikolaos wrote to her every single day since she left. As Frankie was putting the letters in a large manila envelope to mail to Constance, the phone rang.

"Hello, this is Nikolaos Pappas. Am I speaking to Joey, her brother? Constance told me all about you."

Before Frankie had a chance to respond, he continued.

"I have been trying to contact Constance for weeks. Is she there? I would very much like to speak with her, please."

Frankie introduced himself and explained that Constance was no longer in San Lucci—that she returned home to Venice. He went on to tell him there had been an accident and her brother was killed.

"Yes, that's right, Nikolaos. It was a boating accident."

Since Nikolaos thought it was a boating accident, Frankie merely confirmed it. It was not his place to elaborate on what really happened. This was something Constance needed to tell him.

"Connie, Nikolaos just called again. Yeah, this time I picked it up. I have all his phone messages, one a day, every day. I've also got a desk full of his letters that I'm mailing to you. Listen, Connie, this guy is not going to go away, so why don't you give him a break and write him, for heaven's sake."

Constance knew she owed Nikolaos an explanation and mentally agonized over it.

Oh, my dear. What can I tell him? How can I tell him what really happened? If he knew I was now soiled, used, and no longer a virgin, he wouldn't want me anymore. I am too ashamed to face him.

With this resolution, Constance threw away her first love. She burned all his letters and never returned his phone calls.

A few days went by, and Nikolaos called again.

"Hello, Frankie. This is Nikolaos, again. Listen, Frankie. I am really concerned about Constance. I am so sorry for her loss and understand how hard it must be for her as I know how close she was to her brother, but I would like to be there for her, to comfort her, if she would let me. But she never answers my letters or phone calls. Is there something else going on here that I am missing? Is there someone else, Frankie? Is that it? If so, I will accept that and I promise, I will not bother her again. I just need to know, that's all. You know Frankie, I really care for Constance, and I thought she felt the same for me."

Frankie was very moved by his pleading and sincerity. Why didn't Constance answer him? When he spoke to her last, she promised she was going to write to him.

I must do something about this. This is not right. She should not be ignoring him in this way with no explanation, at all. Perhaps Connie will be angry with me for interfering, but Nikolaos deserves an answer. Besides, I believe she is underestimating him. I believe he really does care for her and nothing he finds out will change that. Frankie decided to take matters in his own hands.

CHAPTER 58

It was a cool, brisk October afternoon when Constance and Angela sat in the courtyard in front of the Statue of St. Jude. They sat, in complete silence and watched the autumn leaves from the nearly sparse trees fall to the ground and listened to the wind as it rustled the leaves across the courtyard and deposited them at their feet. They were so engrossed in the beauty of the changing season; they didn't hear the clanking of the wrought iron gate as it hastened to close after the intruder.

Constance looked up at the ominous dark clouds and thought how much it resounded with the dead ache in her heart as she wrapped her shawl tightly around her shivering shoulders. The book she had on her lap fell to the ground making a loud noise on the concrete floor of the courtyard. As she leaned over to pick it up, another pair of hands met hers.

It was a very sweet reunion when Nikolaos and Constance fell into each other's arms, with not a word passing between them.

Angela smiled through her tears as she quietly left the couple.

Constance knocked softly, at first, then when no answer was forthcoming, louder until she heard her father's soft, weak voice giving her permission to enter.

"**Entrare**."

A cold gust of wind coming in from the open balcony slapped against them as they entered the library.

Dominic was sitting in his favorite leather side chair, by the fireplace, seemly oblivious to the cold draft.

"Pappa, why are you sitting here in the cold, with the doors wide open? And where is your wrap?"

Constance took a wool plaid throw cover out of the closet and wrapped it around her father while Nikolaos closed the French glass doors.

Dominic eyed Nikolaos, suspiciously, squinting at him over his glasses as Nikolaos helped Constance pick up the clutter of papers that had blown off the desk and were now scattered all over the oriental rug.

"**Si comodo. Chi e questo uono?**"

Dominic, always the gracious host, told Nikolaos to make himself at home, meanwhile, asking Constance who he was.

"Pappa, this is Nikolaos Pappas. I met him when I went to Greece with my Godmother. You remember that trip you gave me for my graduation present, don't you, Pappa?"

Constance waited for her father to show some acknowledgement. Her father stared at her, glassy-eyed. He didn't remember.

"He came all the way from Greece just to meet you and Mamma."

"**Piacere. Come si chiama? Questo uomo Italiano? Posso offrire qualcosa da bere da manigiare?**"

Despite his loss of memory in asking Nikolaos's name again, he did not lose his caring hospitality as he welcomed him into his home and at the same time, offered him some food and drink.

"No, Pappa. Nikolaos is not Italian. He is Greek," in answer to his question. "We had something to eat earlier. We have to go now. You rest, okay?" Constance kissed her father on the forehead.

Now that her parents had met Nikolaos and her mother gave her blessing, Constance felt secure enough to go ahead with their wedding plans. Her father, although seeming to like Nikolaos, was not told of the intended wedding. Since he was not well, they decided not to tell him as he probably would forget it, anyway. The couple were to be married in Venice at Regina's favorite little church, St. Josefina. It was to be a small wedding with just the family present. After the wedding, the couple would leave for Greece where they would make their home.

While the family busied themselves in preparation for the wedding, Nikolaos left for Greece to take care of business and to bring his father back with him.

In the excitement of the upcoming wedding, everyone forgot about Dominic, except Regina. In all those years with Dominic, Regina never felt so alone, rejected and unloved as she did now. She felt her husband died the day Joey died. Dominic was never the same after Joey's death. His health and memory deteriorated. He lost all track of time. He asked, repeatedly, for the day, the time. Sometimes, he didn't recognize his family. It was quite a pathetic sight watching the decline of this once powerful, vibrant figure with an alert, quick-witted mind. He was completely heartbroken, a finished man. He spent his nights sitting in the library talking to himself and crying. Gone were those festive family dinners that Dominic presided over with such enthusiasm. No one could reach him now, not even Regina. She lost both her son and her husband. It was heartbreaking for her to see this man she fell in love with live out the rest of his days in the confines of the prison he made for himself. If Regina only knew what was going through her husband's mind, she would have understood why he could no longer face her, look her in the eyes or make love to her anymore. Dominic felt such guilt, such remorse for not taking her seriously, for laughing at her premonitions when she told him of her recurring dreams about Joey. He knew he was to blame for granting Joey's request. He was convinced that Joey would be alive today if he had only listened to her.

Regina stirred when she felt the tug of the blanket being lifted off of her. She turned, just in time, to see Dominic escape through the walk-in closet on his way down to his refuge. She knew she would not see him again until the following morning. She brushed back the tears from her eyes as she turned over and went back to sleep.

Cosmo was the last one to hear Dominic, the night before he died.

"Joey, Joey, I'm coming. I'm coming. Oh, it's so good to see you, again. I miss you so much, my son!"

The eerie cry of a desperate father's voice sent chills down Cosmo's spine. He had heard Dominic mumbling to himself, on many nights before, but never like this. This time, it startled him—it sounded so real, like Joey was actually in the library with him. In the background, he heard Dominic's beloved music, the Bacarolle playing. Even this familiar music that Cosmo heard playing many times before sounded different tonight, as if it knew this would be its finale, its last performance.

The next morning when Celeste brought in Dominic's breakfast tray, she found him stretched out on his leather sofa, clutching a picture of Joey taken on his Confirmation Day. She tried to wake him and was met with a cold, unresponsive body. Dominic had passed away during the night. The scratching sounds of the phonograph needle as the record whirled around and around filled the dead silence of the room.

Regina took his passing very hard, ever harder than when Joey died. Dominic was her first and only love; he was everything to her, and now he was gone. She didn't have the heart to go on living and passed away, quietly and peacefully, in her sleep six months later. She was laid to rest next to her beloved husband

and son in their family plot, in Venice.

Now, The Palazzo was lonelier and quieter than ever, with just the few remaining family members still residing in it.

...

Meanwhile, life continued on San Lucci Island. The Islanders had ceased discussing the deaths of the two young men. Frankie re-opened the Pizza Parlor and was doing a robust business, once again. Matthew made frequent trips from England to the island. Joseph was getting bigger every day and now calling Matthew "daddy" which pleased him. Matthew finally expressed his love for Cnythia.

"Cnythia, I love you and I have always loved you. From the first moment Joey brought me into your store, I never stopped thinking about you. I want to marry you and raise Joseph, like my own son."

Cnythia hesitated, before answering. Yes, she believed she loved him, only not in the same way, with the same passion she had loved Joey. Perhaps it was because Joey was her first love. Could that be? She wondered. She knew Matthew would make a devoted husband and an excellent father to Joseph, so why did she hesitate now? Was it guilt? Nonsense! Joey would have approved; she was sure of it and who better to raise his son than his own dear cousin?

"Yes, Matthew. I will marry you."

The summer that Matthew proposed to Cnythia was an extremely hot, humid one with suffocating days and breezeless nights. This was very unusual. San Lucci was now an inferno.

Matthew was in England when he heard the news announcement.

"A 4.0 earthquake has hit the little island of San

Cassiano—just 10 miles east of the larger sister island, San Lucci Island."

Matthew immediately called Cnythia. "Cnythia, I just heard the news. Are all of you all right there?"

"Yes, Matthew, we are fine. Although we felt it here, there wasn't any damage. The house shook and little Joey became frightened, but other than that, everything is fine."

"Well, just the same, I'm flying out there first thing tomorrow. I don't want you and Joseph there without me in case there are aftershocks that may hit closer to home."

Cnythia smiled as she hung up the phone. *He is so caring, and he is so good with Joseph. I do believe, in time, I could love him as much as I loved Joey.* Cnythia spoke all this to her heart.

Matthew arrived on the island the following day. Cnythia was so happy to see him that it surprised her. She never realized how much she missed him and how attached she and Joseph were becoming to him. Matthew always brought him a toy and played with him on the living room floor.

Matthew was back only a few days when the big 7.9 aftershock hit the neighboring Island of San Cassiano which eventually reached San Lucci Island. It happened in the early morning, after he and Cnythia spent an evening out.

It was a Saturday night and Matthew was taking Cnythia to the exclusive Pelican's Beak Restaurant for dinner. Cnythia hadn't been back there since she went there with Joey and Matthew. This was Cynthia's first evening out since Joey's death, almost one year ago. She was quite excited about dressing up and having the whole night alone, with Matthew.

She dressed, with care, in a sophisticated long-sleeved blue dress. She accessorized it with a long strand of pearls. She looked elegant and royal. Matthew presented her with a rose corsage. When she examined herself in the mirror, the image of that 16-year-old innocent girl going out on her first date, stared back at her.

They kissed Joseph goodnight, and her parents wished them a good time. Little did they all know that this would be their last night on San Lucci Island.

Matthew ordered a bottle of Cabernet Sauvignon, and when Matthew slipped the head waiter a sizable bill to serve the under-age Cnythia, the waiter smiled and nodded. They dined on pheasant-under-glass. They savored their two-hour candlelight dinner. Afterwards, they stepped out on the balcony where they enjoyed an expansive view of the harbor with its small dots of lights coming from the boats far beneath them. Since they were 2500 feet above the town, the night air was cool and damp which sent a shiver throughout Cynthia's body. Matthew lovingly and protectively placed her wrap snugly around her shoulders. He turned her toward him, cupped her face in his hands, leaned down and kissed her gently. A short, brief, sweet kiss and they momentarily pulled apart. Then, in the next instance, as if they were attached together by an elastic cord, they snapped back into each other's arms. This time, passionately, hungrily, pressing their lips and bodies hard against each other, devouring each other's lips. Just then, a loud rumbling was heard in the dark sky. It was coming from Mt. Stella, the island's 1000-year-old volcano. This impressive stratum volcano with lava domes, whose two-kilometer wide rim was a horse shaped crater and which reached an elevation of 2549 meters, was not to be taken lightly. The crater bottom was more than 1200 meters below the summit elevation. A huge eruption cloud shot upward from the volcano. The last time this active volcano erupted was five years ago but not with such force as that night's eruption. The Islanders should have recognized the early signs when the familiar rotten-egg smell of the hydrogen gases swept through the town several days ago, prior to this eruption. Ever since the earthquake, days ago in San Cassino, the volcano had become louder and more ferocious, like an angry lion's roar ready to strike.

Matthew didn't like the sounds of the volcano, so he immediately ended the evening. Just as they started down the mountain, a loud burst, reminiscent of Fourth of July fireworks followed them down the mountain. They didn't know that the hot lava, from the erupted volcano, was on a straight path heading towards the town. Matthew was uneasy and decided not to go back to his hotel.

"Cnythia, I will spend the night on the sofa. You try to get some rest. I need to see just what Mt. Stella is going to do. Now, don't worry. I'm sure everything will be fine." Matthew reassured her when he saw the frightened look on her face.

"It will probably quiet down as it has in the past. I just want to be sure, that's all." However, Matthew wasn't so confident. Despite his efforts to stay awake, he dozed off only to wake abruptly when he heard loud voices coming in from the open window. He glanced at the clock. It was 4 A.M. He rushed outdoors to find chaos in the streets as the Islanders raced down the streets towards the ocean in an attempt to outrun the hot lava before it reached the town. Some of them left their homes with only their clothes on their back, while others tried to save as many of their possessions as possible by dragging their luggage after them. They all rushed to the ferry dock—their only way off the island. Climactic eruptions now swept the island with hot pyroclastic. The insidious, colorless, odorless carbon dioxide came with no warning, suffocating the animals and the people.

They took roll call in the dark night. "Is that you, Doug? "Have you seen my sister?" "Oh, I can't find Mary anywhere," "Have you seen Clara?" "Is Nancy with you?" The calls went on and on in the night.

There was only one ferry docked for the night and not enough room for everyone. Those lucky enough to get on watched in despair as their neighbors jumped in the water in a desperate attempt to escape the lava which was rapidly descending upon them.

As the lava poured into the sea, the glow of red-hot rock illuminated the steam cloud and the orange tongues of lava glowed as they plunged beneath the waves. Lifeboats tried to rescue the tired people trying to stay afloat in the dark, cold water. Some of the elderly did not have the strength to stay afloat and they slipped away, quietly, unnoticed, under the deep velvet sea to their ocean floor graves.

Matthew came upon Ingrid and Albert as they headed towards the church. "Albert, Ingrid, come quick, follow me. I have a chartered plane waiting for us at the airport."

"No, we can't come right now, Matthew. We must go to the church and get our son, Michael."

"Okay, but you must hurry. We can't stay here much longer as San Lucci Island is about to go under the sea!"

Matthew returned to the house to find Cnythia and her parents huddled together.

"Get dressed. We must leave as soon as possible. I must go get my cousin, Frankie. I'll be right back, and you need to be ready to leave."

Frankie was at his desk when he heard the rumblings coming from Mt. Stella. He immediately stuffed his attaché case with papers and money, meanwhile wondering how he was going to get off the island. *I guess I could take The Regina out and hopefully she can make it a few miles out to sea, just far enough from the inferno, and then get picked up by one of the yachts moored out there.* He mentally considered. But when he glanced out the window and saw The Regina leaning lamely over on one side ready to sink at any moment, he knew that wasn't going to work.

"Frankie, Frankie," Matthew yelled out for his cousin to open the door.

"Matthew, what the hell are you doing here? Get Cnythia and Joseph and save yourselves, now."

"No, Frankie, not without you. Come with me. I have a

373

plane."

Everyone was dressed and waiting for Matthew. "We must wait for Albert and Ingrid," he told them. They went for Michael. We will give them a little while longer, then we must leave."

Albert and Ingrid ran into the rectory, calling after their son. "Michael, Michael. Are you here, my son?"

They saw the light in the church and when they entered, they found Michael kneeling at the foot of the cross, deep in prayer. "Oh, Michael, my son. Please come with us now. Matthew is waiting and he has a plane for us."

His parents waited, by the door, as Michael made the sign of the cross, turned and started walking towards them. Just then, the church shook as another aftershock rumbled through it. They watched, in horror, as the large wooden cross of Jesus, that hung over the altar, dislodged and fell on top of Michael, pining his body to the floor. He lay there motionless.

"Oh, my God, help my son!" His parents ran to him and tried to lift the 10-foot-50-pound cross, to no avail. It would not budge. It was too heavy for these two old people.

"No—no—It's okay—please leave me—and—and—save yourselves. Don't you see? This—this—is a message—from God. I am—to remain here—in the place—I was conceived. Thi—is—a sign—this is to be my final resting place. This—is meant to be. I—I-am not afraid." The weight of the cross pressing down on his chest made it hard for him to speak.

The very soft, weak, halting voice was barely audible as Michael tried to give his parents a parting smile. His last words were a whisper.

"I—love you both. Thank—thank you—for giving me life." They embraced their son as the roof came crumbling down burying all of them.

As Matthew hurried everyone out of the house, his heart sank as he turned in the direction of the church and saw the destruction.

There was only one road left for them that the lava was not traveling down. It was a back road to the airport. It was a rough, narrow, dangerous road and one very seldom traveled. It took them much longer than usual to reach the airport, but they finally made it. There was no time to spare as the ground beneath them began to shake. Their ascent was smooth and quick and soon they were flying over the town which was now rapidly disappearing before their eyes as building after building collapsed. Gone were the Hotel Capri, Joey's Pizza Palace, The Lei, The Venus Ballroom, Angie's Fish Market, Chris's Rent-a-boat, Rodran's Restaurant, all gone! They watched, helplessly, as the Islanders were swallowed up in the inferno. The dark sky lit up from the bombs of red and orange glows and the ash cloud reached a height of 14 kilometers. It would have been quite a beautiful sight if it wasn't so destructive.

The boats in the harbor were now all ablaze and they watched, sadly, as the last remaining view of The Regina's flagpole nodded its final farewell to them before going to rest in the deep sea, below. In a matter of minutes, they witnessed the entire island of San Lucci disappear under the deep dark cold water of the ocean. The night was now so still, so quiet. All gone—just as if it had never been!

One, by one, each of them forced themselves to turn their eyes away from their past and look straight ahead to their future. The skies grew lighter, and they were greeted by a large orange ball in the sky coming to meet them. It was the start of a glorious new day as their plane headed for England.

THE END